T0299533

TALES
OF A
MONSTROUS
HEART

TALES OF A MONSTROUS HEART

JENNIFER DELANEY

First published in Great Britain in 2024 by Gollancz
an imprint of The Orion Publishing Group Ltd
Carmelite House, 50 Victoria Embankment
London EC4Y 0DZ

An Hachette UK Company

The authorised representative in the EEA is Hachette Ireland,
8 Castlecourt Centre, Dublin 15, D15 XTP3, Ireland (email: info@hbgi.ie)

5 7 9 10 8 6 4

A CIP catalogue record for this book is
available from the British Library.

ISBN (Hardback) 978 1 399 61597 6
ISBN (Export Trade Paperback) 978 1 399 61598 3
ISBN (eBook) 978 1 399 61600 3

Typeset by Born Group
Printed in Great Britain by Clays Ltd, Elcograph S.p.A

MIX
Paper | Supporting
responsible forestry
FSC® C104740

www.gollancz.co.uk

To the girls who get lost in their daydreams,
with stories in their heads and romance in their hearts.

Chapter One

Mortals came from the South Seas, seeking a magic of their own, to make deals with the darkness that slept beneath the earth, seduced by its lies and promises of power. Such greed unleashed that darkness onto the earth and curses came to life in monstrous forms. Still, those mortals were gluttonous for more, so they sold their souls for power. The world burned as punishment, and the cursed earth devoured them, becoming as gluttonous as those mortals longed to be.
— Compendium of the Lost, 1536

An ancient tale about the consequences of greed, and the beginning of the world's end. A story made to scare children and keep them from the path of dark magic. I was too old to be entertained so easily, yet I turned another charred page of the story, seeing illustrations of the dark fiends in question, demons made of smoke and curses. Twisted into serpent-like shapes as they rose from the earth.

Verr. Creatures of the deep. Monsters that were nothing but fables now, but all stories start in truth, even if fragments of that truth are lost to time, carried away on harsh winds before campfires or slipping too easily from ailing memory.

There was truth buried in these ancient words. Another mortal king *had* longed to possess a magic of his own, sold his soul to conquer and devour the world. His forbidden spells and occult worship of those Verr had awakened that darkness beneath, had almost destroyed us all.

A story that had been repeated too many times by too many mortal kings, cursed with greed and a hunger for magic.

Despite how well I knew the history, my hand still traced over the dulling ink, thin paper rough beneath my fingertips. The words lit by a hovering ball of soft white light from my illumination spell, casting shadows across the charred stone walls of the ruins surrounding me.

The Grand Fifth Library. An abandoned quarter deep beneath the Institute of Magic made up of old corridors held together with roots, decrepit vaulted ceilings, crumbling statues and rot-devoured spell books.

My spell flickered weakly, casting long shadows across the stone, threatening to plunge me into darkness at any moment for relying on the spell too long. Forgetting my limits.

I withdrew my hand from the text, the enchantment I'd created to reanimate the destroyed pages dispersed, returning the book to nothing but charred, smoke-stained remains.

Nothing but a memory once more, a relic of the past. Just like the towering, dilapidated maze of bookcases surrounding me that held the fragmented remnants of scrolls from the Third Kingdom of Elysior centuries before, when these very halls had been alive with magic and study. A place dedicated to the exploration of the fey and all the powers they possessed, to understand what magic could do before mortals finally understood they could never possess magic as fey did. Not unless they defiled their blood and mixed with beings they saw so far beneath them. Fey they deemed feral and regressive with their strange, godless ways.

2

Then knowledge of magic wasn't treasure, but chains to bind us to a mortal king's will. To control. To take.

So, the mortals centuries ago began to gather magical texts, like old dragons collecting gold. To keep them from the fey who wanted to know their history, to connect with their ancestors. Those mortal kings brought down lesser fey civilisations, desecrated sacred grounds and built their new mortal Kingdoms on top of the remains. Then as their kingdoms failed, they rebuilt them. Pressing the ruins of their mistakes deeper beneath the earth with each new mortal king, until the next war claimed them too.

The endless cycle. The curse that the lands of Elysior were fated to endure.

I turned to the old tapestries, sagging with mould against the brick. Depictions of fey in the wildlands centuries before. The fight they'd put up trying to keep their magic, trying to stop a tyrant king who summoned dark power from beneath the earth with his madness. Who allowed the Verr and their old, cursed gods to corrupt this land.

That was how it began, this curse mortals had brought upon themselves by selling their souls.

Maybe they deserved it. Maybe we all did.

As if in answer to that dark thought, the orb of my spell flickered out, abandoning me to the dark. Weak slivers of moonlight pierced through the gloom from small cracks high above, where these ruins had managed to crawl back through the earth.

Remaining hidden in the dark had its benefits, but even the ghosts that lingered here couldn't offer me comfort in this strange grave so far beneath the earth.

All that awaited me above were rejected applications. Either from the Mages I tried to partner with, healing placements or teaching positions in the north. All too afraid to annoy the Council by agreeing to take a fey like me on.

A partnership . . . the last requirement to graduate from the institute. To grant me the freedom to wield my own magic under the protected title of Mage. Something no fey had survived long enough to do. Something I was currently failing at. Dreadfully.

The familiar pain of a headache clawed at my temples. How had I lost control of my own future so easily?

You never had control. The voice of doubt hissed in the back of my mind. A voice I'd given too much credence to recently.

A dull clicking echoed across the room, coming from one of the ruined desks in the shadowed, damp corner. A glimmer of silver from the fluttering of a tiny set of iridescent wings caught my attention.

A dust sprite perched precariously on a pile of damp-riddled books that I moved foolishly towards, its small rotund body too heavy for its thin, spindly legs. Its wings only ceasing their clicking to consider me. Large, interested eyes like pieces of coal, dominating its tiny, furry head and minuscule sharp teeth bared in a strange, slightly demented smile.

'You shouldn't be here,' I warned, glad no one was around to witness the questionable interaction.

Dust sprites were rare. Most forms of such ancient magic had died in the wars, but that was the power of the pest: to form out of nothing but forgotten spells. Touching one would return it to its unanimated form, such was the fragility of their existence, and I was tempted to do just that.

A heavy, irritated sigh slipped between my lips. 'I don't need the kind of trouble talking to you will bring.'

The sprite didn't appear to be in the mood for negotiation as it skittered across the desk. Sharp legs clicked loudly against the peeling leather of the desk's top. A warning it couldn't give with words.

'Stop,' I hissed, worried it would set off one of the wards.

The beast's tiny body trembled in annoyance as it bared its sharp teeth again. Dark eyes glanced down to see the torn scribbled mess of papers I'd left on that desk – my notes on transfiguration and healing that had taken me all day to write. Things I needed for my latest application.

My last hope.

An icy sense of dread washed over me, just as the dust sprite glanced up at me again, something smug about the slight tilt of its head.

'*No.*' The pleading whisper left my lips too late.

The menace snatched up my notes in its grimy, sharp mouth and scrambled away.

'Stop!' I shouted, rounding the desk and stumbling after it into the sinister remains of the library.

I needed those notes. *Alma* needed those notes.

The clicking of the sprite's wings guided me around corners and between drunken, leaning shelves, every turn guiding me to a more dangerous section of the ruins, my boots skidding on the remains of burnt, ashy books. I stumbled over twisted roots growing out of the wooden floor or jutting dangerously from the crumbling brick.

Dust stung my nose as I rounded another dim corner, only to hear a clamour of motion as I came to a skidding halt behind a derelict bookcase.

Nobody should be down here, especially not me.

Then came a hissed curse, making me duck into the shadows and move the abandoned scrolls aside on the shelf, fingers tangling with thick cobwebs, to see what remained of the entrance to the restricted section beyond. Through the rusted, filigreed gates stood a lone, cloaked figure, lit by the sickly-green light of an eternal lantern.

There was an irritable clicking as the sprite tumbled onto the shelf next to me and dropped my notes. I eyed it accusingly, considering swatting the winged pest out of existence, but another hissed curse turned my attention back to the restricted section. The figure stepped into the stream of light as the hood of their cloak fell back onto their hunched shoulders, revealing Finneaus Ainsworth. Bright blond hair uncharacteristically unkempt and still wearing his evening robes beneath his cloak.

Master Hale had said Finneaus was failing his classes, and not even his father's heavy purse could save him from the humiliation of being an idiot.

I watched as he hunched over what remained of a reading table, the lantern sitting precariously on the edge. Head bowed as he grasped at the latched cover of an ancient metal-bound book and pulled, as if he could tear it open by sheer force despite the rusted lock. The familiar ancient family crest of the stag catching that horrid green light.

The air grew thick in my lungs, the pinching irritation of a headache almost overwhelming. My magic flared in response, heating my blood.

I knew that book.

Commander Ainsworth's compendium, a forsaken text the Council should have destroyed long ago. A book encased in forsaken iron – a cursed metal that ensured no fey could touch it.

The book had been missing since the old Institute had fallen centuries ago, buried beneath the new Institute where the Mage Council now sat, hiding behind the pretence that they'd reformed. That they'd turned their backs on their dark king's rule for the mortals and fey of this world to exist in peace. Yet, here was a compendium that should have been destroyed long ago.

Finneaus continued to struggle with his great-great-grand-father's book, not noticing the silver inscription on the spine, the warning. How a creature in service to the compendium's owner was bound inside – one that would be over two centuries old, probably close to starvation and so rabid from its containment no simple spellcasting could contain such volatile hunger.

I should have retreated, made my way up into the Institute halls, returned to my room and changed before Alma caught me. I should have let the stupid fool open the book, let the creature steal his soul and then pretend to politely mourn at his funeral. I *should* have . . .

'Bugger it!' Finneaus hissed, the book clattering onto the table as he held his hand to his chest, blood running down his fingers from the sharp spine and dripping dangerously close to the cursed book.

Blood-sealed books require a sacrifice. That warning echoed in my mind as fear overrode my senses. Dark magic had a way of calling to us, even when we wished not to hear it.

'What are you doing?' I shouted, emerging from my shadowed hiding place. Finneaus let out a cry of alarm, spinning on his heel and almost knocking over his lantern.

His distress was quickly replaced by a sneer of pure disgust.

'None of your business, *troll*!' He shoved his injured hand into the pocket of his dark robes.

I ignored the slur, a vulgar summary of my bloodline. As a fey, I was used to prejudice. Being Kysillian only made it worse, everything from my pointed ears, gold-tinged skin, lavender eyes, and imposing height was met with disdain from mortals.

'You shouldn't be touching that book,' I cautioned as softly as I could, hoping reason would get through to the spoiled halfwit.

'You dare to tell me what to do?' His thin lips curled. 'If you're looking for a reason to get expelled, *Woodrow*, I don't mind providing one.'

'I think *you're* in graver danger of that than me, Finneaus.' My voice held a calmness I wished I felt. No matter how much he hated me, once he dabbled in the dark magic that text contained, there would be no coming back.

'We'll see,' he challenged tartly, but I could see the slight tremble in his fingers, the distant panic in his eyes. He'd already let it tempt him.

He wasn't going to listen to me. Couldn't. Not anymore. He was too far gone. The pull of the dark was always strongest to those with weak minds and desperate hearts. His bloody hand moved back to that book and – by the panic in his eyes – he wasn't controlling his fingers as they reached out for it.

'Don't!' I threw out a quick enchantment that was meant to send the book flying off the table, but my spell simply simmered on contact, like water on a hot stove, the lavender aura of the spellcasting scattering uselessly.

Thankfully it shocked Finneaus enough to stumble back from the book.

'You almost hit me!' he spat.

'That book is cursed.' I sneered my warning, struggling to rein in my temper.

'This is my family's text,' he jeered, tipping his chin in defiance, despite the bright pink flush on his cheeks.

'A lineage just as idiotic as you to curse their own books,' I replied sharply.

Outraged, he charged towards me, despite the fact I was at least a foot taller. 'You impudent *troll*.'

'Listen you little—' I began, resisting the urge to throttle him, only for the words to catch in my throat. A strange rattling came from the table, stopping Finneaus mid-stride. Bookcases began to tremble around us, the uneven floor shifted beneath my feet as the rusted gates gave a weary groan.

It was too late.

The buzzing of a hundred sets of tiny wings echoed through the chamber as a dusty wind ripped past us. Finneaus curled into himself with a shriek.

The dust sprites were fleeing, deep into the cracks of the stone arches high above, some diminishing into plumes of dirt in their haste as they brushed past my skin. Becoming unmade. There wasn't a moment to mourn them. Not when my rage kept my gaze fixed on that table.

That cursed book started coming alive as it bounced and shook, trying blindly to open itself. It knocked the eternal lamp off the desk, glass shattered, and the flames spilled across the floor; devouring abandoned papers that littered the ground. Illuminating the horror of what was about to happen in that sickly-green hue.

'What did your heathen spell do!?' Finneaus squeaked, stumbling away from the mess.

'This was you!' I hissed.

The book thrashed desperately, moving nearer and nearer to the small pool of blood from Finneaus's hand. It was then I understood.

Before I could act, the book finally landed on the droplets it sought, stopping its savage dance as black smoke seeped from its pages. Wisps of darkness twisted together to form a clawed hand that slipped from between the yellowed pages. It crawled upwards towards the cover and broke the lock with a careless flick.

9

A horrid, shrill screech tore through the room, reverberating off the arched ceiling as the book snapped open. Smoke burst forth from its pages in an almighty powerful storm that sent dust and ash swirling around the room, pulling my braid free and stinging my eyes.

I felt it on my skin: a pinching and twisting coldness. Lungs full of the sulphuric stench of dark magic.

The book gave another bone-chilling screech that left a ringing in my ears, and in response, magic burned molten in my veins, willing me to set it free, to fight whatever was trying to tear its way out of those pages. The tips of my fingers glowed with their own soft lavender light.

I curled my hands into fists to resist it. Sweat beaded on my temples. I couldn't lose control again, not here and *not* in front of the dean's son.

There was a cracking of ancient bones, as a shadowed hand reached out of the book and dug its nails into the tabletop. A dark, gelatinous substance spilled from the pages, dripping onto the wooden floor as the creature unfurled, dragging itself out of the text.

'Bloody saints,' Finneaus whispered, his voice breaking with fear, as if the useless words could help. The stench of the coward's urine quickly followed, which helped greatly in catching the fiend's attention.

It was eyeless, with rows of sharp, yellow and uneven teeth that clicked together as it crouched on the desk. Long spider-like limbs stuck out from a dark, humanoid body, only slightly bigger than Finneaus's narrow frame. Its slitted nostrils flared as it scented us, large sharply pointed ears twitching with every sound. One flap of its dark sinuous wings sent a gust of wind so powerful that it knocked the dilapidated bookcases to the ground and sent papers flying through the air. Its long leathery tail snapped out behind it like a lethal, barbed whip.

Finneaus tried to run, but stumbled over his own feet, landing on the floor. The creature snapped its head towards the sound, launching itself at him within the space of a panicked heartbeat.

'Woodrow!' he cried as the creature tore across the floor.

My magic flared viciously in my palms with no spell or incantation leaving my lips. This was blood magic, forbidden and relentless.

Kysillian fire, bright blue and purple flames roared from my hands to form a blockade between Finneaus and the beast, twining effortlessly with the flames of the eternal lantern, turning them deep blue, commanding them to do my bidding.

The creature recoiled from the heat, screeching and clawing at the floor as it was denied its feast. Lethal claws making deep gouges in the damp wood.

It roared, wings slapping sharply behind it, fanning the ravenous flames as they began to climb up the only tapestry still pinned to damp stone. The remaining woodworm-eaten bookcases crashed down in the force of the demonic wind, covering Finneaus in a cloud of dust and ash as heavy volumes hit the damaged floor beside him. There was a terrible splintering as the unstable floor broke apart to form a deep hole. He squealed, clawing at the slanted floorboards, but slid into the dusty abyss with a scream.

'Finneaus!' I rushed for him but the creature emerged from the cloud of centuries-old grime and lunged.

I blindly sent out a blast of magic, but as with all dark creatures, the longer they existed, the more they learned, and the dark fiend was learning too quickly about its prey.

About me.

I only managed to catch it on its shoulder, the bone cracking out of place as it darted past my panicked, sloppy spell. It crashed into the old fireplace, bricks crumbling down around it. The room shook with the impact, almost sending me to my knees.

'Finneaus!' I coughed the dust from my lungs, leaning over the edge of the opening to find his prone form below, moaning as planks of wood and old plaster covered him. He'd landed on a settee in what looked to be a common room one floor beneath the library.

Clearly, bigoted fools had all the bloody luck in the world.

'Bastard,' I hissed under my breath, allowing myself the mere moment of relief that I hadn't accidently been involved in the demonic murder of a councilman's son.

The rest of the fireplace crumbled with a worrying crash. I turned, just as the creature's scaled tail whipped for my head. I ducked out of its path, hearing the impact as it cut through the wall behind me and showered me in sharp brick shards.

I darted beyond its reach, rolling the wild flames of my magic between my palms, as the thing scuttled towards me, belly low to the ground.

I summoned more fire against my palms, illuminating the room in a fierce lavender glow, making the other fire in the room roar in unity. The sharp features of the demon grew all the more horrifying in my magic's light, before I threw the fireball outwards, hitting the creature's sinuous wing, searing a hole through the dark flesh. The fiend screamed, mangled wing sagging as it turned sharply in defence.

The potency of the spell left me breathless, too distracted to notice the long serpent-like tail strike. It caught my side, throwing me across the room. I crashed into the table, shattering it into large splinters. The impact winded me as I rolled across the rubble-covered floor. The creature was on top of me in seconds. Its jaw opened with a screech, flashing razorlike teeth as the back of its throat began to glow with demonic black fire.

I wedged my forearm beneath its leathery chin, deadly teeth gleaming in the light of my magic. I grunted and kicked to keep it at bay as I reached blindly into my enchanted bag at my hip, digging past books and papers, feeling the warm hilt of my father's sword. I wrenched it free, the blade materialising upon recognition of its true heir. The gold gleaming, long and lethal.

I drove the blade up, plunging it into the creature's throat. Its flesh sizzled and melted around the steel, dark gunk running down my hand, pungent and rotten.

The fiend tore itself back, retching black smoke and glutinous dark blood. It howled, wings beating wildly, as it rose clumsily, high into the darkness of the vaulted stone ceiling, claws catching on the remains of a rusted chandelier above.

It perched there as that sulphuric stench of its blood made bile burn the back of my throat. It shook its head, jaw snapping open wider than before, revealing where I'd maimed it as black sour blood rained down. There was a deafening shriek, followed by a cracking and twisting of limbs as its head began to split into two.

The chaos of duality. The words of Insidious Theory came to my mind, a warning lost in time.

I turned to see where the cursed compendium had fallen and spotted it beneath a collapsed side table. I rolled, got my trembling knees beneath me and ran, skidding to a halt to stand over the book, ignoring the horrid burning sensation that came over my skin from being anywhere near the forsaken metal that covered it.

The pages were yellow with age, the symbols inverted and twisted. Ancient scripture with dark intent for only the darkest creatures to feast upon. An Insidious beast.

Unable to be killed, only contained.

The demon roared; the ominous cracking continuing as the chandelier groaned under its weight. I cast my father's sword aside, allowing the more potent gift he'd given me to flow through my veins and materialise in my hands.

Fluid flames of indigo, sapphire and lavender twisted between my fingers as ancient words echoed through my mind. That's all magic was, a turbulent dance between knowledge and imagination. A song in the blood awaiting command.

Nothing is stronger than your will. My father's words whispered in my memory.

No, it wasn't.

I let my chaos free, aiming the fire skyward with a scream of exertion, heating the chandelier from beneath. It glowed molten red, the creature shrieked, trying to pull away, but it was instantly trapped within the liquid metal that stuck to its flesh.

Kysillian fire. Pure and beyond the corruption of dark magic.

The fiend tried to pull away, wings flapping harshly, but the harder it fought, the more the metal fused to it. Two heads screaming as black smoke curled around it, as it tried to change. Tried to shrink to escape.

My arms trembled from the weight of my spell until another backdraught from the fiend's fight sent me tumbling backwards, almost extinguishing my flames.

The ceiling groaned, plaster beginning to rain down before the chain of the chandelier snapped, crashing down in a tangled burning mess. I covered my head as sharp debris struck my back and shoulders, curling into a ball, panting as dirt and debris coated my tongue.

Only when the trembling of the weakened floor stopped did I look up, squinting through the dust to see the creature thrashing inside a newly formed metal cage of the chandelier's remains, still glowing red, the beast now no bigger than a small bird to try and avoid the molten bars.

Fragments of pages fluttered down, dust swirling in the air, as small embers shifted in the darkness like fireflies.

I hung my head, dragging myself to my knees, winded as I wiped sweat from my brow. The fiery magic in my blood was almost unbearable as it simmered, waiting for another command. There was little relief in the ache of my muscles as my magic sank slowly back into my bones but, still, I held out my burning palms, let the sweat slide down my temples and back. Pulling in a dust- and decay-coated breath, silently commanding my magic to silence the flames around me. I pressed them into nothingness, the stench of charred wood and forgotten things my only reward.

Then the distant echo of the Institute warning bells obliterated the silence.

Bollocks. I'd set off the wards with my chaos.

I knew what came next. My heart sank with the thought of the Council's punishment as I rested my burning palms on the damp wooden floor. Hunched over, arms trembling from the effort, watching through the curtain of my matted hair as the two-headed demon hissed and screeched as it still fought to escape, gnawing hopelessly at the still molten bars.

Perhaps I had made a mistake. I should have let the dark fiend finish me off. It would have been a more peaceful fate than the one I was about to meet at the hands of the Council.

Or worse . . . Alma.

Chapter Two

Only fear can bind your hands.

My father's warning echoed in my memory, too late to be of any use. I wasn't afraid; it was everyone else's fear that held me back. Their fear of my Kysillian blood, and the madness I must have inherited from my mortal mother, who had chosen to lie with a monstrous fey.

To ruin herself.

Thankfully, on this occasion, my inferior, chaotic blood wasn't my crime. No, that was my reckless pursuit of a dust sprite and trying to help a fool from getting soul-snatched.

The fool in question was safe in the healing wing with a rag over his bloody nose, a hideous black eye forming and one arm in a sling. I shouldn't have taken satisfaction in his discomfort, but I indulged myself as I sat alone in the east wing hallway, the old wooden bench creaking beneath me. It was supposed to be for nothing more than decoration, carved with hideous depictions of mortal saints, but I was too tired to stand. Too drained to even think of the waiting rage from Finneaus's father and the rest of the Council. Not allowing myself to begin to wonder how they'd twist my most recent indiscretion against me.

My magic surged in annoyance, flushing my cheeks. The cool night air from the open arched windows down the long dim hallway doing little to calm the heat of it. The lanterns high above flickered with sharp crackles of bright orange light. Each reminding me what I'd done.

Dejected, I dropped my focus back to my filthy hands – smeared with dirt and the blood of the creature – as they lay in my lap. No evidence of the chaotic magic I possessed in my aching fingers, only the slight weak tremble as they gripped my torn and ash-smeared notes that I'd recovered from the ruined shelves. Useless now. What healing house would take in an apprentice as destructive as me?

'That *thing* should be on trial for an assassination attempt,' Master Grima's voice hissed down the empty stone corridor from one of the Council Mage's offices just beyond. The door left ajar, so I could hear every word and be humiliated some more. Their shadows moving across the slash of warm light that spilled across the floor.

'Unjustified claims fuelled by nothing more than prejudice,' Master Hale snapped, voice brittle with age. Guilt pierced my chest. How quickly he'd come back to the Institute from his visit to the South Courts so late at night. He'd gone there to fight for more fey liberation, and I was here, causing nothing but trouble in his rare absence. Forcing him to return. To clean up after me once again.

'This is ridiculous! She should have been cast out a year ago!' Madame Bernard interrupted, shrill and vicious as always. 'The volatile creature should be cleansed. Immediately.'

I flinched at that. *Cleansed.* What happened to reckless fey like me with no control of their magic: spellbound to never use magic again. To be stifled and slowly driven mad by the loss of it, just like those forced to work the farms off the southern shores or indentured to the workhouses.

'Unless you're trying to convince the records department she's *eighteen* for the third year in a row?' Master Grima mocked. I could almost picture the thin-lipped sneer on the Head Librarian's face.

Shame burned through me. The lies Master Hale spun, the desperation to keep my ward status, so the Council didn't have full control.

'It is possible. Fey don't keep birth records,' Master Hale half spluttered with indignation.

True. However, I knew I was twenty-three and so did Master Hale.

'She still has applications for partnerships pending with—'

'They've all refused her!' Madame Bernard chortled darkly. I couldn't hide my wince at her joy, the certainty that the game was over.

They knew.

All my worst fears confirmed, my time really was up. No Master Mage wanted to partner with a fey, especially not a woman, and *certainly* not a Kysillian like me.

After all their attempts to ruin my chances of independence, the Council had finally won. In my defeat I let their shrill hateful voices become nothing more than a distant hum in my ears, unable to bear the desperate weak defence from Master Hale.

I looked down again at the unusable notes in my hands, blinking back the threat of useless, stupid tears.

Demure. Quiet. Still. Master Hale's voice commanded in my head. One of the first commands he'd given me. My only defence against the Council's hypocrisy when I'd arrived at barely twelve years old.

Despite spending over ten years here, nothing had changed. Not their hatred, or the fragile Peace Agreement my presence here had promised. All I could do was pull in another calming breath, knowing my temper wouldn't gain me any ground. That was what they wished to see. A Kysillian out of control. Wild and undisciplined. A female to be restricted and controlled.

Trapped.

I stuffed the ruined notes in my bag before rolling my stiff shoulders, feeling a strange cool prod at the exposed nape of my neck. A brush of frigid air, far sharper than the night breeze, like some strange presence trying to get my attention.

I looked down the shadowed corridor, the bench squeaking in protest, but there was nothing but the open window and the endless night. Thick shadows lingered in the corners of the hallway. The gold stitched tapestry of Elysior pinned to the wall rippled in the night air. The lanterns flickering more dimly than they had before.

Here. Something whispered in my mind, sending me slowly to my aching legs. To wander cautiously into that darkness, letting my palms run down the worn fabric of my stolen breeches, torn and ruined by my most recent misadventure.

Cautiously my magic flared, making my fingers glow slightly, but I curled them into fists, refusing its help. I wasn't afraid, not as those shadows seemed to weaken, slipping carefully away, brushing over the stones in retreat to let the moonlight back in through the window. In a blink it was as if they had never been there at all.

'Katherine.' Master Hale's voice sent me lurching around, hand to my chest to see him standing behind me, curiosity marking his weathered features.

The once-great war hero was still an imposing figure despite his old age and ailing health. His greying brown hair was in disarray as he limped down the hall to me, leaning heavily on his cane. Those deep navy Council robes dragging across the ground, the silver pin of the scroll and sword showing him to be a Master Mage.

Guilt and shame rushed through me. 'I didn't—'

'I know.' He sighed, shaking his head almost incredulously. 'The ruins?'

'I'm sorry.' I let my shoulders drop with defeat. He didn't ask much of me, but I still managed to break the few promises I'd made.

'Poor Alma will be scandalised.' He huffed, leaning more heavily on his cane.

I'd forgotten about Alma. She'd lose her mind the minute she found out. I only hoped gossip didn't travel faster than I could get back to my room. Silently scolding myself for not trying to slip away sooner. To find her and explain.

'This hunger for knowledge isn't going to end well, Katherine.' Hale spoke softly as he stepped closer, cautious of anyone else hearing the warning. 'No matter how much I know you enjoy the older texts these fools have forgotten about deep beneath these floors, it will never end well.'

He wasn't wrong, but stubbornness was unfortunately another flaw I possessed.

'When did that ever stop you?' I challenged.

'You should take this old fool as a warning.' A small laugh left his lips, which turned too easily into a retching cough that stopped him in his tracks as he fumbled with trembling fingers for his handkerchief.

'Master Hale?' I took a firmer hold of his arm, trying to make him sit on that horrid bench to rest, but he shook his head as he pressed a handkerchief to his lips, only for it to come away bloody.

The sharp sting of fear consumed my heart. This man, who used to be the greatest warrior in Elysior, who once served the Mage King before joining the Lord's rebellion to free Elysior, was reduced to nothing but a weakening husk. This strange illness that no healer could cure was like a curse put on him for helping me.

'Go on, it's best you get out of sight for a while. I'm certain Alma will want to sort you out.' He cleared his throat, avoiding my concern as he tucked the bloody fabric back into his robes, revealing the cuff to be speckled with more blood from a previous bout. 'We'll talk in the morning.'

He was getting worse.

'The Council . . .' I began, letting my gaze wander down the hall to closed doors of the Council Chamber, where the disciplinary hearings usually took place.

'It's late.' There was a sharp dismissiveness to his voice. 'They'll take a day or so to gather if they wish to raise a complaint. Let us hope they lose interest in their pettiness before then.'

Hope. What a fickle and cruel thing. Crueller for how long ago it had abandoned me.

My lips parted in protest only for a distant ringing to begin, halting the very breath in my lungs. A sound I knew all too well.

Warning bells. Loud and thunderous from deep beneath the stone floor, making it rumble with the sound. Something from the ruins beneath had awoken, something big enough to set off the wards.

The lanterns flickered violently, almost plunging us into darkness as the guards down the hall jumped to attention, rushing off in the direction of the old entrances to the ruins beneath.

'Go to your room, Katherine.' Hale patted my arm, something in his expression guarded before he left me standing there in the draughty hallway as he hobbled away. That feeling of unease remaining inside me, nibbling insistently, telling me that something wasn't right.

I ignored it, knowing nothing was ever right here.

'Idiot,' I hissed to myself, as I finally took my chance to flee. Moving through the stone hallways, the echoing taunt of those warning bells made the dread sink deeper. Ignoring the old leering statues of previous Mages holding scrolls of wisdom, feeling their judging stone glares as I passed each one.

I moved up the narrow spiralling staircase, past the students' floor, higher and higher until I reached the cramped fey quarters. A dark corridor greeted me, considering I was the only remaining resident and had to light my own lanterns.

Too tired and troubled to bother, I pulled the key from my bag and retreated into my room, not allowing myself to be relieved until I was pressed back against the closed worn, wooden door. Thanking the ancestors for the small mercy of Alma's absence as I took in the confined space, a magical lamp still burning in the corner as the moth-nibbled curtains let moonlight spill into the room.

Home, I lied bitterly to myself, ducking under the low wooden beams to my small, dilapidated desk, untying my bag from my belt and dumping it on top. I leaned over the desk to push the small murky window open, letting the night air try and cool my flushed skin.

I needed to change, hide my clothes, put my nightgown on and pretend it all wasn't as bad as it seemed. I pushed my papers into a neat pile as the wind disturbed them, hiding the ones from the ruins deep beneath all the others. I was almost done covering my tracks when a sharp smack to my arm and the distant slamming of the chamber door startled me.

'Ouch!' I snapped, turning to see the annoyed face of my assailant.

Alma stood there, brow creased, dark curls in disarray beneath her maid's cap. The imprint of scales beginning to show on her left cheek with her wrath. Her vibrant green eyes alight with fury.

'I can't believe you have the *audacity* to be reading!' she hissed, hands resting on her small, apron-covered hips. Her maid cap flopping onto her brow before she pushed it back with irritation. 'Look at the bloody state of you!'

'Alma, I wasn't—' I grimaced, not prepared to duel with her.

'Don't *Alma* me!' she seethed, her cat-like pupils thinning into reptilian slits as she smacked my arm again for good measure. 'I bloody told you not to go down there. You could have brought a ghoul back with you like last time!'

I winced at the memory of the flesh-eating ghoul still locked in a tin box beneath the floorboards under my bed. How thunderstorms made it rattle and try to escape. Reminding me I'd forgotten to put it back once again.

'That wasn't completely my—' I began, but the sharp glare she sent my way made me swallow down the lie. 'I'm sorry.'

'If I have to listen to one of those fucking saint-loving maids say another horrid thing about you in the kitchens, I'll lose my mind.' She tore the maid's cap from her dark head and tossed it onto a stack of my papers with disdain.

'I needed a book on Vercarus theory to finish my paper. The last copy was in the Fifth Library before it fell. I really think it's going to work this time.' Or at least I did, before Finneaus Ainsworth and a demented dust sprite had ruined everything.

'I don't care about bloody papers, you menace. I care about you.' Her words were followed with a heavy sigh, defeat clear in the fall of her narrow shoulders. A softness darkened her feline gaze. 'The last fey student to go wandering off anywhere near the ruins got themselves killed, Kat.'

I flinched at the memory. The white sheet-covered lump at the bottom of the restricted stairs. An unlucky tumble while practising with an unpredictable spell. Out after curfew. Enough to deserve a death sentence for the likes of us in the Council's eyes.

Lie. The word hissed mockingly through my mind, bringing the sharp pinch of a headache that threatened to return with all my worries.

'We both know I'm not that lucky,' I smiled, only her serious expression didn't falter. Worry burning fiercely in her eyes.

'I'm serious, Kat.' Those words were softer, weighted with everything that had come before.

'I'm not going anywhere.' I ignored the weight of that truth as it sank like a stone in my gut. Clearly, my fate was to be locked in these dusty walls until the Council came up with some use for me, or worse, dispatched me the same way they had all the others.

Alma's petite form flopped down onto the stool with a heavy irritated grumble that was close to a growl.

Quiet. Demure and still. Master Hales' command coming back to me. The same simple rules Alma was forced to follow. To pretend. To lie.

Alma didn't have magic. This was the falsehood we had dedicated ourselves to for the last ten years. She possessed something beyond simple magic and the Council's control. As I watched, those scales slipped back beneath her smooth, tan skin.

Wild magic. Too feral and easily spread to be taught reason. To be leashed.

It was why she'd ended up at Daunton, the lost children's home with me all those years ago. Another unwanted creature for the horrid Lord's entertainment, in a place for beings nobody was looking for.

The last place she should be was here with me. Right under the Council's watch. But greed had always blinded mortal men, and a Kysillian in their control was enough to distract them. Enough of a danger to keep them occupied and keep their gaze off Alma, the poor serving fey Master Hale had taken pity on.

I didn't allow myself to wonder why Master Hale had brought Alma with me. Whether it was his guilt for the wars, for the fey that had died in these very halls that he didn't save, or to show a little lost girl he meant no harm . . . but the older I got, the more the truth burned through those lies, leaving me with a sour taste in my mouth. Alma had been something to keep me in line.

She was the only thing of value to me that they could take away. The reason why I'd shackled myself to the Institute's peace treaty until I could graduate, why I'd become their toy to keep the rebellion quiet, to keep a revolution against mortal power at bay.

The games they played and my place as a pawn at their centre left me exhausted and burdened with guilt for the things I pretended I didn't see, didn't hear.

A guilt I couldn't escape, even as I worked at getting out of here, travelling beyond the Council bounds. Maybe finding a healing house to practise in, or even a small teaching position in a fey village. Anything. There was a whole world beyond these walls.

Thoughts of my past might have kept me from sleep, but that small glimmer of a future pulled me back to the present, to consider the profile of Alma's dark, annoyed face. Her gaze distant, looking at the tiny window, how it sagged sadly, dark mould staining the wood. Her brow furrowed with too many thoughts.

'You seem irritated,' I mused, regretting the words as her sharp murderous gaze came back to me, 'by something other than me for once.'

She shrugged, reaching back to rub her shoulder as if it were stiff. I saw the darkness at her nailbeds, the threat of the claws that could emerge at any moment. How weakly those fingers trembled. 'I'm fine.'

'Alma, I—' I leant forward, trying to reach for her but a sharp knock at the door sent her surging to her feet, grabbing her cap off the table and forcing it back on top of her raven curls. Back into her role.

'If these are disciplinary summons, I swear on the ancestors . . .' she seethed, unable to finish before something slid beneath the door and she stormed over to claim it.

I waited for her to whirl on me with rage but she went deathly still, back tense and I wondered if she was even breathing.

'Alma?' I asked.

I'd gone through quite a few trials. Most done when Master Hale was in better health and had more support within the Council. Now, with fey rebel attacks growing in the north and the Council's contempt for magical beings stronger than ever, I doubted I'd get much sympathy.

'They're not trial summons.' Her voice was nothing but a trembling breath, turning to me as that paper shook in her grasp, green eyes wide as they shifted from owl to feline pupils and back again. 'They're partnership papers.'

I didn't remember leaving the desk or crossing the room. All I remembered was the weight of that paper in my grasp, the fire at my back and the short, panicked breaths of Alma at my shoulder.

Papers in presentation of a Mage Partnership Agreement between:

Lord Emrys Silverous Blackthorn and Miss Katherine Woodrow.

The words were embossed in gold, and the strange dark wax seal of the Blackthorn crest covered in thorns. The paper was thick, luxurious and sealed in an envelope with singed corners telling me it had been delivered by fire-post.

Lord Emrys Blackthorn.

The Blackthorns specialised in occult studies and were one of the Mage King's most trusted before the war. The last experts in dark magic and its effects on the earth. There were many stories about Lord Emrys Blackthorn, the only surviving member of the family. That he served in the Great War. How he'd commanded the Lord's rebellion to bring that Mage King down and quelled the dark entities who had consumed the south fields of Elysior.

Ever since the monarchy had been overthrown, the rebellion settled and the High Council of Elysior formed, Emrys Blackthorn had become something of myth. Some records claimed he was dead, others that he'd gone mad.

He was little more than a rumour that plagued Mages' meetings, whose name was spoken in whispered tones like one mention would summon him.

Dark magic had a habit of consuming those who paid it too much attention, which was the reason most rumours stated he was dead. Yet the papers in my hand were very real.

I supposed this new dangerous twist of fate was my own fault for wondering just how much worse this could all get.

Chapter Three

The clamouring chaos of the morning after was unbearable. The hissed gossip of my demonic worship, constant irritated scowls from passing tutors and the silence from Master Hale.

Worse were the muttered rumours about a potential sighting of the mysterious Lord Blackthorn in the Institute last night, which only sharpened my fear.

I'd already checked the partnership papers three times as Alma and I moved through the arched hallways and high-walled Mages' Garden on our way to the portal office. Still real. Still there despite the impossibility of them.

I reached up to make sure the sharp points of my Kysillian ears were tucked neatly beneath my braided crown. A foolish habit considering my strange, luminous skin was impossible to hide, along with my bright lavender eyes.

The papers in my hands were nothing more than a crumpled cylinder that I rolled tighter with every panicked thought as my anxious eyes dragged over every detail of the portal office, drenched in the low winter sunlight.

It was a vast space, with a decorative, tiled floor of reds and golds polished to a high gleam so the chandeliers' light could bounce around the room. The curving staircases to the higher levels were set back against the ceiling-high record shelves, depictions of phoenixes sitting on each banister with torches in their grasp.

The stench of dust from the old books was pungent, as the smell of bitter coffee and men's cologne sat thick in the air. The portal clerks scratched away at their desks, writing incantations for the Council Mages' travel plans that week.

I'd hoped Master Hale would be here to greet us, but the waiting benches were all vacant. I glanced down at the pages in my hand that had sent Alma into a frenzy of nervous energy last night, only to get worse when a message arrived from Master Hale, a hurried note asking me to leave at my earliest convenience this morning. More things he wasn't telling me.

I couldn't decide what worried me more – that a supposedly dead Lord was offering me a partnership, or how unbothered Master Hale was about the whole affair.

Run. That voice mocked in the back of my mind just as a sharp pinch came at my forearm, jolting me to look down at the annoyed face of Alma.

'Ow!' I shoved her hand away, rubbing the underside of my arm.

'This whole bloody mess is your fault. The least you could do is pay attention,' she scolded. Her pupils taking on the horizontal slits of a prey animal, needing them to better sense the threats lingering here.

'I thought you weren't talking to me,' I noted dryly. She'd slipped into silence despite her frenzied activity after the papers arrived, which only deepened when Master Hale's orders came next.

'I'm taking a reprieve to make certain you're not getting any more reckless ideas.' She straightened the sleeves of her dull maid's dress, as her eyes darted accusingly around every inch of the office she didn't want to be in.

29

'What trouble could I get into in a portal office?' I tried to smile in reassurance, but her glare only intensified, dark, bumpy scales of slate-grey becoming more prominent beneath the collar of her dress.

'It wouldn't surprise me.' She slapped a crease out of her simple black cloak, my art folder and our meagre bags at her feet. 'You should have let the bastard get soul-snatched.'

'Alma!' I hissed, glancing around to see if any of the clerks had heard her.

'It's what he deserves.' She shrugged. I couldn't argue with her there. I wasn't in the business of wishing foul fates on people, but the spoiled brat deserved more than he'd got.

Alma quickly resumed her hawk-like watch of the room. Ignoring the messenger boys who hurried by and the glances they gave, almost stumbling over their own feet at the fierce, dark beauty of Alma that no drab maid's uniform could dent.

'The maids spread terrible rumours about Lord Blackthorn,' she said quietly, oblivious to the commotion her mere presence had caused. 'They say he killed his sister and that he was born of a witch's curse.'

'They say many things,' I hedged, being slightly relieved they hadn't said he was a lecher at least.

'Apparently he doesn't make appearances because he's riddled with a rotting disease after the war,' she continued, straightening the cuff of her dress. 'He probably only has one tooth left in his head.'

'Really, Alma. The rubbish you listen to.' I sighed in an effort to resist asking just exactly what rotting disease they thought it was and just what dark entity had caused it. In Blackthorn's line of work, the possibilities were endless.

'Katherine Woodrow.' My name echoed around the chamber. The scratching of quills stopped.

Clerk Roberts strode towards us, considering me over his small oval glasses, a stack of portal papers in his grasp.

'Clerk Roberts, I hope you're well.' I bowed in greeting.

'Well enough,' he replied curtly, reaching up to straighten the collar of his maroon tunic. 'Weren't you causing chaos in the ruins last night? I'm certain that's a removable offence.'

Of course he'd know about that. The whole Institute probably knew.

I ignored the remark, my smile sharp as I held out the papers. 'I have my partnership papers.'

The old bastard reluctantly took them, his beady eyes growing wide as they drifted over the papers, once and then again. From his suddenly grey pallor, the papers were real.

Roberts' eyes darted from the papers to my face, the edges of his glasses beginning to fog.

'Is there a problem?' I asked politely, ignoring his hateful gaze. 'If you wish to summon Lord Blackthorn, I don't mind waiting.'

He continued to glare, something working behind his eyes, building up to a familiar cutting insult. Master Hale's whore . . . or maybe his bastard.

'Does she need to repeat herself?' The deep voice of Master Hale came from behind me, making the clerk nearly drop his papers in shock.

'No, sir,' Roberts grumbled as he bowed deeply, turning on his heel and snapping commands at the gate assistant perched on a low stool, awaiting instructions.

Hale hobbled closer, his breath laboured as his navy robes were buttoned up wrong and his cloak was in need of a good pressing.

'Good morning, Alma,' he greeted, laying a reassuring hand on Alma's shoulder, which slumped in relief, colour filling her pale cheeks.

'Good morning, Sir.' She smiled.

His tired gaze came to me, a redness to his eyes. There was something distant about his expression, which worried me that his ailing mind was catching up to him.

'Master Hale?' I frowned in concern, wondering if he'd taken any of the healing draughts I'd made for him.

He shook his head as if to dismiss a dark thought with the weakest of smiles, and instead extended the large volume he had tucked under his arm, holding it out to me, a thick red ribbon tied around it like a gift. The roughness of the leather was familiar to me, as were the delicate spine and yellowed pages.

The Myths of Shadow by Bartholomew Browbeak. The most revered text in the ancient study of magic. Few volumes remained, and none in such good condition as Hale's. It contained the most powerful spells, even those of forbidden dark magic that lingered beneath the earth. A complete collection of magical histories without the Council's sterilisation. Hale had allowed me access to his copy a few times, but it was closely guarded in his study.

'This is your first edition.' I took it from him reluctantly. It was his most prized possession.

'Now it's yours. To commemorate your achievement.' He smiled.

My being under his care put him at risk, almost as much as it protected me, so perhaps this was for the best. A dying man deserved some peace after all.

'Thank you.' Yet, I couldn't stop myself from asking, 'Is this Lord Blackthorn the same one the Council have recorded as deceased?'

I'd made it my mission to know all my enemies within the Institute, and being dead meant Blackthorn hadn't been added to my list.

'The Council have recorded numerous things incorrectly,' was his dry response as his gaze drifted absently around the portal office and the gawping portal clerks pretending they were working.

'Besides, occult studies has been one of your interests for as long as you've been here. It could help with your dark healing papers and Lord Blackthorn is an expert in that field. There is much you can learn from him.' His smile didn't falter despite the lie I sensed pressed between his words.

'I'm sure Alma will be glad to see the back of this place and experience the countryside too,' he continued, sensing my suspicion.

I couldn't argue with that. Alma hated the Institute more than me, and the further I could get her away from prying eyes the better. Her magic was just as deadly as my own and less inclined to behave.

'Trust me, Katherine. Blackthorn is . . .' He hesitated, seeming unsure of his next words before he reluctantly pushed on. An intensity crept into his gaze that unnerved me more than my current situation. 'See this as a blessing. You need all the help you can get.'

'I do trust you.' I hated the bitterness that lie left on my tongue. He had done nothing but protect me thus far and he didn't deserve my doubt.

'I have other clients who need the portal,' the dry tone of Clerk Roberts interrupted us.

The gate loomed behind him, a large doorway made of metal dials and cogs that contained magic from the earth, meaning it responded to incantations and opened with the right level of skill. The clattering of the wheel grew louder with the potency of the spell.

33

'Go on.' Hale nudged me forward. 'I'm sure I'll see you when you're settled in your new role.'

Of course, having a partner Mage finally got me a Grand Library key, but even such an elusive gift couldn't distract me from the horrid feeling in the pit of my stomach that I might not see him again despite his words.

There was too much to say and I knew my hesitation was only causing Alma further discomfort.

'Come on, Alma.' I smiled weakly.

Thankfully she gathered our belongings and followed without argument.

'I expect you'll be back for another disciplinary shortly.' Roberts smirked, pushing his glasses up his greasy nose, as he returned the papers to me.

'I look forward to your disappointment,' I retorted as the clacking of the portal grew louder, telling me it was safe to cross. The waft of heat from the spell drenched my exposed skin like a flaring hearth. The doorway glowed, the marble dissolving with magic as bright white light filled the space.

'Kat,' Alma whispered cautiously, her hand finding my own as I pulled her through the doorway, unwilling to linger a moment longer.

There was a brightness, the familiar sting of enchantment, before we were greeted with the bustle and noise of the busy, crowded streets of the carriage station, with the unnerving screeching of steam engines in the distance.

I should have been joyous at the bitter fresh air on my cheeks, but all that consumed me was dread. Dirty smoke filled my lungs as the bustle of the crowd bumped into us, knocking the bags from Alma's grip. I bent to retrieve them, tucking my art folder under my arm, straightening only to catch sight of the continuous trembling of Alma's hands, sweat on her brow catching the lamp light.

This was more than nerves.

'Have you taken your tonic?' I asked, a new fear creeping into my chest.

'There wasn't time,' she admitted weakly, the unusual paleness to her darker skin more obvious beneath the harsh station lights. No, I hadn't given her time.

I moved us out of the crushing swell of passengers, through the station and out towards the carriage stops. Beggars rattled their cups under my nose, thin boys sold hot pies wrapped in newspaper and women gossipped while waiting for their trains. But there was nothing that the loud bustle could do to distract me from the large sign hanging on the back of a waiting-room door.

No beggars.
No fey.

'Miss Woodrow!' came a voice from across the packed platform, almost swallowed by the shrill whistle of a departing train. The gangly form of a young man hurried towards us, skilfully navigating the busy crowd. He had fiery red hair, a handsome young face covered in freckles, warm brown eyes and dimpled cheeks emphasised by his beaming smile. He came to a stop, pulled off his cap and bowed in greeting, revealing two short dark horns that protruded from his curls.

'William Roydon,' he announced in a thick Devrick accent. He couldn't have been older than sixteen, and if he was put off by the imposing nature of my Kysillian height, he didn't show it. 'I've come from Blackthorn House to fetch you.'

'Mr Roydon.' I bowed, trying not to seem too flustered by how strangely this day was unfolding. I was startled as to how he had recognised me. Then again, Kysillians weren't a familiar sight in the south.

'William,' he corrected, looking past me in confusion. 'I thought you had a maid?'

I turned, expecting to see Alma standing safely behind me. But in her place, sitting on the dirty platform, peeking out from the pile of Alma's dress and underthings, was a small tabby cat.

'Alma.' I reached for her, just as another swarming crowd surged forward, kicking one of her shoes across the platform and trampling all over her dress. My hand was almost crushed as I yanked it from beneath the passengers' filthy boots. Alma let out a hiss of annoyance as her small body leapt onto the safety of my shoulders.

Frustrated tears burned in my eyes as I stuffed her dress into my enchanted bag. Feeling her small paws kneed my shoulder.

I should have noticed, should have known she was close to changing. I mentally cursed myself turning for her shoes and underthings, only to find William kneeling next to me on the grimy platform, stopping the crowd trampling over us. The rest of her things were neatly folded, along with her shoes, piled in his hands.

'Thank you.' I smiled with a relieved breath, pushing them into the bag as I got back to my feet. William picking up the rest of the luggage effortlessly, like he dealt with stray clothes and vanishing maids all the time.

'This is Alma Darcy. She's working on her transformations,' I explained, as I clutched my art folder to my front, waiting for his harsh comment or disbelieving glance as his warm eyes fell to the cat on my shoulder. Alma meowed in greeting from her perch, her tail brushing my other cheek, clearly more sociable in her feline form than her human one.

'Pleasure to meet you, Alma.' William bowed again with that same welcoming smile as he put his cap back on. 'I have the carriage waiting for us.'

His polite businesslike manner returned as he struggled with the bags through the packed crowd, leading the way. I gathered up my skirts and tucked my art folder more securely under my arm and followed, knowing there was no turning back, and that might have been the most terrifying thing of all.

Chapter Four

Alma let out a disconcerted meow from where she sat curled up in my lap. It was late, but darkness hadn't completely enveloped our surroundings. A fine grey mist fell upon us the minute we left the city outskirts and travelled quickly through the workers' towns that surrounded it. We only stopped once at a small travelling post for a pot of tea and hard travellers' cake before we went west across vast moorland, heading for a border of dark forest in the distance that soon swallowed us.

The road was craggy and forgotten between the towering ancient trees. The everlasting lamp at the front of the open carriage guided the horse easily across the uneven terrain.

I couldn't speak feline, but I shared Alma's meowed concerns as we finally came upon a gravel path almost overrun with weeds.

Before us was what once may have been a cottage but was now nothing more than a hulk of crumbling stone. Plaster peeled from walls to show uneven bricks beneath, the thatched roof sitting drunkenly and the window supports sagging with rot. If it wasn't for the small flickering of light behind the filthy glass of the windows, I would have given up hope completely.

The suspicion I'd been duped was almost overwhelming as I waited for the Council Mages to come running out of the surrounding dark wood laughing as William brought the carriage to a stop and jumped down, humming cheerily to himself.

From what rushed research I'd been able to do before leaving the Institute, Blackthorn resided in a grand manor house in the western fields, surrounded by an ancient wood. The family had owned an excess of land before the wars, land that had mostly survived, but the rundown cottage building before me didn't speak of wealth or the power of a family that possessed such old, magical blood.

Alma let out a growl of unease at my silence. I shook my head and petted her in reassurance.

'Miss Woodrow?' William called, holding his hand out as he waited on the path.

Could such a kind and curious creature be involved in such a horrid ploy? Then again, I'd seen everything beings were capable of, so nothing should surprise me.

I took his offered hand. Whatever trap I was in the centre of was bound to reveal itself shortly. There would be no benefit in delaying it for my pride.

'Transfiguration is fascinating. McDale's research into it is my favourite,' he continued effortlessly with our earlier conversation regarding Alma, oblivious to my suspicion. 'Lord Blackthorn has the original texts on the theory. I'm sure Miss Darcy will find them useful when she returns.'

'You're studying?' I asked as I pushed my art folder neatly beneath my arm. I'd never seen him at the Institute, and I knew I'd recognise another fey, especially in a place like that. Although our conversation on the journey about earth magic, root curses and perilous forsaken weeds should have told me as much.

'When Lord Blackthorn has time. I've passed the majority of my summoning tests. It's the research element that lets me down.' He retrieved our bags quickly and turned sharply on his heel in the direction of the decrepit cottage. I rushed to follow, Alma growling cautiously from where she remained on my shoulder.

Blackthorn was teaching William, a fey who hadn't attended the Institute. The thought stunned me.

'Come along. I'm sorry about the house, it's how it's chosen to look today,' he called over his shoulder as he made his way down the path at an alarming pace. 'It's wary of visitors.'

He juggled our bags awkwardly as he reached the door and produced a key from his pocket. Surely an irrelevant item considering the door was so warped, and oddly hung. I doubted it offered much in the way of defence.

Nevertheless, he unlocked it and stepped inside, giving me no choice but to follow. Alma leapt down from my shoulder to go first, and I tried not to trip over her as we were greeted with the pungent scent of herbs and the tartness of old spells.

I ducked inside with caution, expecting to bump my head on a low-hanging beam, but instead, I straightened easily.

A grand entrance hall opened before us, boasting a sweeping double staircase with chequered black and white flooring. Thick burgundy carpet covered the stairs, held in place with gleaming golden rods that reflected light onto the dark wood-panelled hallway. The passage into the rest of the house was lined with varying doors, painted or stained different colours, differing in size and age. Brass knobs glinting in the light, where others possessed rusted latches or exquisitely carved golden handles.

It had a strange, majestic warmth. Nothing like the Institute or the formal mage buildings I'd been permitted to visit. An opulent chandelier hung above, surrounded by a beautifully carved and arched ceiling. Wooden depictions of wrywings and griffins resting on the beams, peering down with interest at their new guests. Smears of painted figures and flowers marred the walls at a child's height, flaking with age. Small wooden fairy doors were nailed into the skirting boards – despite the fact fairies hadn't been seen for centuries.

The house creaked and groaned in greeting, the lights flaring brighter in recognition of our presence. Alma meowed in response and I put my art folder precariously on the side table to pick her up before she went wandering.

'Impressive, isn't it?' William smiled as if the magic had been his personal accomplishment as he shut the now grand door behind me. 'The first Lord Blackthorn made a bargain with a powerful witch who owed him a debt. Her magic has kept this house hidden for centuries.'

I hadn't seen anything like it, nor the mess of clutter that covered sideboards and entrance tables. There was also dust, and a lot of it.

'Is there not a . . . housekeeper?' I queried lightly, not wishing to offend William.

'Lord Blackthorn doesn't employ many people. He's rarely ever home.' William smiled again, swinging his arms with a relaxed ease I found charming. 'Let's get you settled into your rooms. I'm sure you're worn out from the journey. That wind over the west moorlands is vicious.'

He retrieved my bag with a badly concealed groan at the weight and strode down the entryway towards the stairs. I was hesitant to follow, unable to stop looking at the peculiarities that surrounded me, the scent of fire spice to keep unwanted pests away, a sweetness of old incantations, the pungency of dried flowers and the bitterness of book dust.

'Is Lord Blackthorn home?' I asked, cautious he might materialise out of thin air as Alma squirmed for a better view in my arms.

'He's occupied today,' William replied apologetically. I couldn't say I was surprised. It was quite apparent from the cobwebs that Lord Blackthorn didn't have regular guests.

William led us up the carpeted stairs. On the first landing was a grand portrait of a woman, her bright blonde hair scandalously unbound, the fashion she wore luxurious as she sat before a great hearth. Her smile was playful, and her eyes a silvery blue, with a knowing glint that made me feel watched.

Alma's mutterings of Blackthorn being born of a witch came back to me with disturbing clarity.

'You're welcome to wander about the house. Lord Blackthorn mostly keeps to his study.' William continued to throw comments over his shoulder, and I had to focus on trying to remember the path and not to stop and look at every item en route, whether it was a discarded spell book, a ward against dark magic or a bunch of dried flowers intended for healing – all items fey used for their spells, tools to assist with old magic before the Council took ownership of it.

I'd seen mortals collect trophies before, items of curiosity used to brag about conquests. They made a habit of displaying taxidermy of ancient beasts, turning their flesh into masks or trinkets. The Mage King was famous for holding grand balls where guests wore fey-fleshed masks and danced in celebration of his victories. The Council had a collection in their archives. A room I avoided for the horrid feeling of the unfortunate creatures, how they still suffered now, calling out endlessly just as they had been when they'd been killed. How those cries sometimes followed me into my dreams.

However, these items remained peacefully silent, quite content to exist in this old house.

Blackthorn's specialty was the occult and crimes of dark magic, caused by monstrous creatures who lingered in the world after the great war, feasting off the chaos of misery. He'd somehow given himself the role after the war and had written numerous laws, which had been placed in the peace treaty of Elysior under Accord Seventy-Four. What he was doing offering me a partnership and helping me graduate from the Institute was beyond me.

Many disregarded the need to study dark magic despite dark anomalies still littering the countryside and villages, blaming the nearest fey for causing trouble and instead just getting on with their lives. Breaches of dark magic were on the rise – if the papers and gossip sheets were to be believed – but so was fey persecution.

I'd studied the occult in depth, mostly because the history of the Verr was linked so closely with the history of the Kysillians. My history. Through a bloody rivalry that had spanned centuries. Two sides of a very tumultuous coin. Of darkness and chaos – ending when the Verr were finally trapped beneath the earth. Nothing but myth now, but with most Kysillian histories destroyed and not having any other connection to my people, the sodden, cursed books from the ruins were the best I could get.

'This will be your room,' William announced, pulling me from my confused thoughts to see he was holding open a set of mahogany doors polished to a high shine.

The space was vast, bookcases heavily stacked beside a large fire and writing desk. Ornate windows consumed most of the north wall. The Blackthorn Forest loomed beyond, like a dark shadow in the distance.

In my surprise Alma slipped out of my arms and trotted into the room.

'I'm sure you'll need time to get settled.' William huffed as he placed my bag down by the bed. A stunning monstrosity with thick curtains embroidered with foliage and wildlife to conceal the bed itself, which was covered in an ostentatious counterpane of velvet depicting a woodland scene in vibrant colours.

'It's beautiful,' I replied, a little breathless.

I had worried about being stuffed in the maids' quarters, knowing the bed would be too short, but at least I'd be with Alma. Besides, any maids' quarters in a Lord's residence would be better than my Institute dorm.

'This is the best room I could freshen up at such short notice.' William smiled, running a hand over the curtains as if they weren't straight enough. 'Blackthorn had me deliver some books to read. He said these are all the papers you'll be needing. I argued you should have time to settle but he was adamant.'

Argued? The word startled me. I'd never heard of anyone arguing with a lord – well, apart from myself, and I had the lash marks and the sour disposition to prove it.

'I took the liberty of starting the bath. The incantation should have kept it warm enough,' William continued as he strode to another door by the desk, revealing a tiled room with bright copper pipes. Lavender-scented steam was released.

The grandeur stunned me, my lips parting, but William was moving again.

'Miss Darcy's room is attached.' He opened a small door between two bookcases that led into another, smaller room that looked no less comfortable. 'I'll deliver dinner to you later.'

With that, he bowed and vanished as quickly as he had appeared, leaving me stunned in the centre of the room.

It couldn't be real.

Alma meowed from where she sat perched on the bed, tail swishing from side to side irritably, probably equally suspicious.

I pulled off my heavily repaired gloves, touching the desk and feeling nothing but the solid wood beneath my fingertips. Enchantments on objects left a residue, one too subtle for mortal touch, but it sang to the magic in my blood. Almost taunting it. However, no such enchantment existed in the room. No trap or illusion made to cause me any embarrassment. It was just a room. Alma mewed sorrowfully once more to catch my attention. Of course, she'd abandoned me to her feline form.

'It's not your fault.' I smiled, bending to kiss the top of her furry head. The magic of transfiguration was so lost to us that I couldn't help her through it, and I hated that helplessness.

Unwilling to allow myself to dwell on the strangeness of my situation any further, I was left no choice but to begin the laborious job of unpacking.

'We'll figure this out,' I whispered to myself, wishing it didn't sound so much like a lie as I unbuckled my travelling bag. Somehow . . . I'd figure this out.

Chapter Five

Be careful, my love.
If you show them how bright you burn, they will only seek to smother the flame.

The ghost of those words haunted my dreams as I struggled to sleep. The way my mother had whispered them, skin chilled and damp with fever. Her grip weak, fingers thin in my grasp where she'd laid her hand over my heart.

I touched the flushed skin of my throat as I lay in bed, feeling the rapid nature of my pulse as my magic rose in recognition of the painful memory. The peace in her features as she basked in the warm feeling of my magic. My father's magic. Wanting to feel him one last time.

I wiped the tears from my sleepy eyes and exited the bed, refusing to be consumed by things I couldn't change.

My new and unfamiliar bedroom was faintly illuminated by a small everlasting lamp I'd left burning on the desk, knowing Alma's fear of the dark. Thankfully, she remained curled up in a tight feline ball on the pillow next to mine.

Sketching usually helped settle my restlessness but as I rooted quietly through my things, I wasn't able to see my art folder.

No, I'd left it downstairs. Too distracted by Blackthorn's manor and the impossible nature of my day. A frustrated sigh left me as I put on my badly knitted slippers and my robe, stuffing my enchanted bag into the pocket just in case.

Then I looked to the stack of books Blackthorn had left me and gathered them up, hoping the library was easy enough to find to return them considering I'd already studied them all a few months prior.

Despite how archaic the house was, the floorboards didn't creak as I closed the bedroom door softly behind me. In the darkness of the hallway, I let the small glow of a summoning spell claim the tips of my fingers. Imagining a guiding orb, letting the magic appear against my free palm.

I nudged it softly, directing it silently to lead the way. It bobbed before me, leading me down the long wood-panelled hallway, past trinkets and the peculiar objects that lined the walls and cast strange shadows. Against my better judgement, I let my fingertips trail across them, expecting to feel the sorrow that usually accompanied the history of such stolen things.

There wasn't any sadness here. Just magic slumbering peacefully. Confused, I withdrew my hand and hurried to catch up with my own orb as it made its way down the stairs.

Only to freeze a few steps from the bottom.

The layout of the main hallway downstairs had changed, not a play of the dark, or my tired eyes. Where the front door had been now sat bookcases, various archways leading off down other dark hallways. The black and white chequered floor continued as far as the eye could see. Unfamiliar to me, and for a moment, I was worried I wasn't in Blackthorn's house anymore. However, the banister beneath my hand was the same, and the portrait that had caught my attention earlier was seemingly amused by my sudden panic.

A set of large oak doors, just beyond the foot of the staircase, stood open. They hadn't been there before.

Be wary of old spells, they grow thoughts of their own over time.
One of Master Hale's warnings came to mind as I took the
final step off the stairs, still holding onto the banister just in
case the floor decided to change its formation too. I didn't
know magic this old, but if this was where it wanted me to
go, I wasn't about to fight with it.

Moonlight poured in through a vast glass ceiling, more
fitting of a greenhouse than a library from what I could make
out in the dark. A maze of bookshelves, with tall ladders leant
against the intricately carved shelves; depictions of a forest
and the woodland beasts that dwelled there. The rest was too
shadowed in darkness to explore.

Every piece of furniture in the room was piled with texts,
except two chairs sat before the cold hearth.

My orb bobbed impatiently at my shoulder. I reached up
to extinguish it, knowing how strangely magic concealed in
books could respond to new energy, like feral cats fighting
for territory.

In the centre of the room was a large ornate table, legs
carved to look like those of a griffin. Books rested against its
clawed feet. The surface was overfilled, scattered with papers.
Maps, mad scrawls of simple incantations and summoning
charms. Crystals were strewn haphazardly with the skill of a
madman trying to call on the dead for favours. Small carved
bones related to ancient fey worship and dried flowers were
amongst the mess.

My curiosity urged me to turn over the maps, cautious
of how the pages crackled with their fragility. The sharp,
smoky scent of beasam bark lingering in the air – an ancient
summoning element that witches preferred. Moving the maps

gently aside to reveal the volumes beneath, all coated in dust, which was pressed firmly into their peeling leather covers, pages curling inward like claws with age.

The gold embossing had faded, forcing me to tip them towards the light to see the titles. *The Book of Mort*. A book of ancient occult spells, most of which were now disallowed by the Council, including necromancy. A book that spoke of the Verr and the darkness beneath the earth.

Disturbed, I moved it aside, as a different tome caught my eye. It had a heavier leather binding than the rest, cracked and clawed by time. Thick straps with tarnished brass buckles encircled the text, as if stopping something from falling out.

I slid the clasps free, slipping my fingers beneath the heavy cover. My magic almost stinging as it flooded to my fingertips, curious and demanding.

'I wouldn't open that one,' came a dark voice over my shoulder.

A cry of alarm left my lips. I turned, only to find my fingers trapped between the book cover and a gloved hand, cold leather against my burning flesh.

The fireplace roared to life behind me. A soundless panicked command I'd subconsciously given it. Illuminating the tall, imposing figure stood before me.

There was a stillness in his expression, oddly dark eyes set in a handsome, angular, but somewhat cruel face. A face that reminded me vividly of the portraits of the saints that mortals worshipped.

His raven hair was wet, as if he'd been caught in a storm. Longer than fashionable as it curled slightly against the collar of his grey suit jacket. A pale slash of scars ran through his eyebrow and down to his jaw, one into his lip, silvery in the firelight. The skin on his neck was nothing but a mess of damaged flesh. Like some monstrous creature had gone for his jugular . . . once it had finished raking its claws down the side of his face.

'What are you doing hiding in the dark?' I demanded, snatching my hand from under his touch, heart pounding wildly. William hadn't said anything about another guest.

'In my own library?' His dark brow lifted arrogantly.

His library. My heart dropped to my slipper-covered feet.

Lord Blackthorn was standing before me, considering me with barely contained annoyance, and he couldn't be a day over thirty.

I stepped back, flushed with embarrassment. This was *his* house; he could sneak about like a spectre all he wanted.

'Did your snooping prove rewarding?' he enquired, unmercifully. Undoing the buttons of his jacket with relaxed ease he moved past me to the chair before the now-blazing fire, spots of rain clinging to his shoulder, but as I looked to the glass ceiling above, there was no rain. Hadn't been all evening.

'I wasn't *snooping*,' I insisted with annoyance, rubbing my hands together to ease the lingering sting of magic. Anything to hide my unease of how he was nothing like how I imagined him. Younger, colder and clearly disfigured by a horrific war that the world pretended hadn't happened.

'That's what all snoopers say.' He dropped unceremoniously into one of the chairs with so little decorum I wouldn't be surprised if he threw his feet up onto the small table before him.

He didn't.

'William said I was free to wander the house,' I said, aware I did need to impress this man on some level if I had any chance of staying here.

'Of course he did.' He pulled a pile of papers off the table next to him and into his lap, almost causing an avalanche of clutter.

With a careless wave of his hand, he indicated the chair opposite him. 'Sit.'

The dominating nature of the word made me stand straighter.

'I don't follow commands.' I informed him coldly.

His head turned lazily in my direction, his irises suddenly a pale grey that took on the warm hue from the fire. Maybe it was a trick of the light that they'd appeared so dark.

'Please,' he nodded respectfully, but something about it still held an aloof quality. As if the last thing in the world he'd want was company, despite asking for it.

Choosing to ignore the fact that proper ladies didn't sit in dark rooms with men they didn't know in nothing but their robe, I took the seat.

I surveyed him more closely now he was distracted with the papers in his lap. Too young and rugged, unpreened by the standards of the elite class. But I wasn't foolish enough to be distracted by the sharpness of his jawline.

'You were quick to accept the partnership. I see none of the other old fools were interested?' He tugged off his gloves, revealing more scars on his hands, oddly shaped like thin vines wrapping around his long pale fingers.

'I'm Kysillian. Unless you're unfamiliar with the vulgar lies spread about my kind . . .' Being fey was enough for prejudice; being Kysillian was another danger all together, one he should understand in his line of work.

'I fought in the wars, Miss Woodrow,' he replied, those otherworldly eyes taking me in. 'I'm well aware of the lies spread to expand the King's rule.'

'A king your family once served,' I countered. If he could be rude then so could I. My temper was getting the better of me. The Mage King had persecuted the fey.

Despite the bastard being overthrown, nothing had improved. I wondered how much of Blackthorn's involvement he regretted. Those burdened with such guilt usually chose drink, denial or decided the world was better at war or in the grasp of a mad king.

'As I'm the only one left, I see the price of their mistakes as duly paid.' There was a genuine regret in his voice that eased me slightly.

I found myself too interested as to why Blackthorn had mud on his boots despite the lack of rain, and how he had appeared from the shadows without even a hint of magic to give him away.

'Did you paint these?' he asked quietly and I was horrified to see the papers in his lap weren't papers at all. He was looking through my paintings.

Blurry watercolour memories of my mother, soft features filled with a sharp wit, her unruly dark hair and freckled skin. Next, the kind eyes of my father, the same colour as my own. The beauty of the village I'd grown up in, the endless magical wood around our small cottage.

Then came the dark ink drawings of the Institute, the city smoke and the sharp angled faces of the horrid creatures who lived there. The only softness in that section coming from small drawings of Alma as she worked, always pensive and staring off into the distance, wishing perhaps to be somewhere else.

'Yes.' I cleared my throat, watching helplessly as he continued to flick through my illustrations, turning and adjusting them to better see the detail in each one. Like peeling back layers of my very soul, seeing things I knew I shouldn't have left unguarded.

I didn't reach for the file, didn't dare expose another weakness.

'Master Hale said you came to the Institute at twelve years old?' he continued in a tone no more intimate than if he were discussing the weather, and not my tragic childhood.

'I came from a children's home. Daunton Hall.' I tried to keep my voice neutral, knotting my fingers together in my lap so they didn't tremble.

'Daunton,' he pondered absently. 'The records were always unclear as to whether anyone survived the fire.'

My magic simmered in my blood at the unease that rushed through me. The flames in the hearth next to us flaring before I could stop it.

I didn't discuss Daunton. Not with anyone. It was nothing but a reminder of my grief. The bitter and all-consuming nature of it.

Daunton Hall. Where fey children were left to be forgotten, orphans from a war they'd rather not remember. There was no relief in knowing Master Daunton had been exposed and they'd found the unmarked graves of the children he made suffer. They were just bones now, with nobody left to remember they had ever existed.

'I did.' It was the only truth I offered. The only one I could stomach. 'I was discovered not long after, my ease with spellcasting and summoning declared a marvel despite my lack of training.'

An entertainment for the Institute, after all, a free Kysillian was something the Council needed to keep an eye on. My control over magic was something they didn't like, even if they'd been convinced I didn't possess a spark of my ancestors' magic, that any ancient flames in my blood had long been smothered and the Kysillian power was dead, just as their many mortal kings had wished.

'The Council suspected the fire was an act of rebellion, but they shut down the investigation when they saw just how guilty Master Daunton was.' His innocently curious words pierced my chest with uncontrollable fear. The taste of smoke on my lips. Dark things I refused to remember.

Murderer. A voice hissed through my mind before I could shake the thought away.

'That's how Master Hale found you?' He raised a brow, the facade of aloofness lifting slightly for me to see that sharp interest in his eye. As if the details mattered.

'The Council needed fey children to fill their quota for the peace treaty. That's all that Master Hale said.'

There had been seven of us at the start. Fey children with perfect control of their magic, each submissive and willing to learn. Willing to be moulded by Council rule, to prove it was possible for peace. All in the hope of being set free – back into the world we'd been stolen from.

Now there was only me.

A cold dread licked down my spine at the thought as I pushed my loose hair behind my ears, eager to get off the subject. 'I was moved to the Institute for mere amusement.'

That truth I hated most of all.

'Are they still amused?' he asked, his gaze brushing over the sharp point of the ear I'd revealed without thinking.

'No.'

His soft, curious gaze assessed every inch of my face, as if I were a riddle he was trying to solve.

'The first act of a partnership isn't usually to defend the applicant against corruption charges or dark summoning.'

I bristled at that, straightening the sleeves of my robe. 'I'm certain Master Hale made you aware of my . . . *situation*.'

'Cleaning up your mess in the ruins left me little time to converse with the old bastard.' His smile was small with secret amusement. 'If I was more vainglorious, I'd assume the whole production was simply to get my attention.'

My cheeks heated at the insinuation, mostly because that was exactly what it looked like.

'I doubt there would have been much point in that, my lord, considering the Council records have you listed as deceased,' I pointed out wryly.

'The Council have a habit of trying to manifest their desires. Some would say it's the only thing they're honest about.' He picked at a piece of lint on his sleeve, dark hair falling onto his brow as he glanced up with a small, almost teasing smile. 'Any other nasty rumours I should be aware of?'

'Something about a rotting disease,' I added, cautious of his amusement.

'If only my misfortunes were that simple.' His smile remained as his focus moved back to that table across from us, littered with his cursed books and the ones I'd returned. 'You didn't agree with my reading list?'

Did this man miss anything?

'I've already read and noted those texts.'

Those curious eyes came back to me. 'Most senior mages haven't even read those tomes.'

'I have . . . peculiar interests when it comes to personal study.' I cleared my throat again, not knowing any other way to explain my morbid curiosity. 'I can produce my files tomorrow if you wish.'

'I doubt I'll have the time. That was quite a mess in the ruins you left behind. Most of the wards didn't survive.'

'The dust sprite—' I began, watching a dark brow rise, the barest lift of his lips. I quickly changed topics. 'I didn't anticipate Ainsworth being foolish enough to let a demon out of a compendium. I also hadn't anticipated how vicious they can be.'

'Which compendium?' He sat up with interest.

I couldn't help the shudder that rolled through me at the memory of the book. Of that forsaken iron so close to my skin. 'They have more than one?'

'If the rumours are to be believed, there were seven in total that Commander Ainsworth possessed. Some more deadly than others,' Blackthorn mused thoughtfully, a sudden distance in his tone. 'Five I've managed to hunt down. The Ainsworth house sold them off two centuries ago to pay off family debts.'

How carelessly mortals handled such deadly things. 'Well, they didn't sell them all. One was in the ruins. It's covered in forsaken iron and Finneaus's blood opened it.'

'Interesting.' He pressed his knuckles against his lips in thought. 'It appears we have our *own* questions for the Council tomorrow.'

'Tomorrow?' I frowned, a horrid unease slipping into my gut.

Blackthorn motioned his hand absently and then something small and white was suddenly fluttering on to the arm of my chair. I jumped, looking down at the creature, only to see it was a tiny bird made of paper. An enchanted message.

'That was supposed to be delivered to you in the morning,' he added, making me wish the overstuffed chair would swallow me whole with embarrassment at my reaction.

I held out my hand, letting the little message hop into my palm and unfold itself, trying my best to contain my childish wonder. I'd never seen an ink spell before, only read about them.

The Council request our presence in the grand hall at ten o'clock.
William will meet you in the entrance hall.
Blackthorn

Curt and to the point. Each word made my heart sink a little further as the small note folded itself up into a neat square without command.

'I wouldn't worry about it,' Blackthorn commented sardonically. 'The Council like to perform when they make mistakes.'

Easy enough for him to say in his grand house, with his title, and his ability to throw together partnership papers whenever he pleased.

'I think they'd argue the mistake was including me in the treaty in the first place,' I muttered darkly, watching his gaze move over the paintings again. 'You have an interest in painting?'

'My father used to paint,' he said softly, the words appearing to have slid free against his will. I was reminded of the portrait on the stairs.

He closed my art folder with a sharp snap, pushing it unceremoniously onto the already overfilled side table – a move I took as a dismissal, so I got to my feet.

'I'll let you continue with . . .' I paused, finding myself troubled by his words about the compendium and just what Ainsworth could have been up to. 'The compendium had a warning on the spine in Salvor tongue.'

'Not many take the time to learn the old summoning language,' he observed quietly. 'Are you certain you weren't up to anything *nefarious* in those ruins?'

'As I said, peculiar interests,' was all I offered. If he asked Alma, she'd probably tell him nefarious was my middle name for all the hassle I caused her.

A clatter from the bookshelves made me turn sharply to consider the dark beyond us, wondering if William would emerge, or Alma. But there was nothing there.

'The house doesn't like to sit still,' Blackthorn said, a reluctance in the reassurance he offered.

Mad Lords, manic houses and clutter. Alma was going to kill me when she returned to human form.

'Those other compendiums, they're here?' I asked carefully, looking back to him. Surely he couldn't trust the Council to keep them contained, but I didn't know what to think of a man who kept such close quarters with evil things.

'The house wards keep them contained, as well as a multitude of other spells.' His words weren't much, but I forced myself to remember that Master Hale trusted this man. That this was part of some plan.

I sighed, holding out my hand for my artwork he'd stolen, eager to excuse myself. 'Well Lord Blackthorn. I'll let you continue with—'

Unexpectedly, he rose. The sheer size of him blocking out the weak fire, casting us in shadow as he held out my art folder to me.

'Emrys,' he corrected. His eyes seeming pitch-black in the darkness.

'That's improper.' I was startled by the request. Especially after having such small rebellions beaten out of me.

'Partner mages call each other by their first or last name. I thought you were here to be one?' he challenged and I hated that he was right, but I swallowed down my unease.

'Emrys.' I nodded.

It felt strange on my lips, too intimate, but something about it made him withdraw, turning his attention back to the fire in dismissal.

I clutched the art folder to my chest like a shield, deciding it was best to make a quick exit. However, I'd only made it a few steps to the doorway before he spoke again. As if curiosity had got the better of him.

'Why did you use an Insidious spell?' The question startled me, but then again, so did everything about him.

'How did you . . .' I flushed, stumbling over my words. 'They're the strongest.'

'And the most difficult.' His eyes narrowed ever so slightly. 'They don't teach Insidious Theory at the institute.'

'No, but they have books on it, if you know where to look.'

'In forbidden places I assume?' His lips twitched. I was unsure if he was amused or mocking me.

'Curiosity isn't a crime.' If the Council cared that much, they should put better concealment spells on the ruins, or fill it up once and for all.

'You taught yourself how to cast a centuries-old spell on a gobrite from reading a book?' Blackthorn seemed to take in every inch of me as he considered the weight of his own words.

Gobrite, an Insidious creature of blood bargains. That was what Commander Ainsworth had locked in that book. I was annoyed I hadn't figured it out myself.

'I explained the method in a paper . . .'

'. . . the Myth of Insidious Curses.' He finished my sentence effortlessly.

My lips parted with shock.

'You've read it?' It had been one of many papers I assumed the Council had burned upon submission, left to rot in a drawer or, worse, allowed to be plagiarised by an idiot.

'Why did you save him?' His voice was soft, as if we were sharing a secret.

There was no threat or menace in his strange crystalline eyes. Just genuine curiosity. I didn't know what to do with that.

'Letting him get soul-snatched is a harsh punishment for stupidity,' I replied easily. For once not ashamed of my weak heart.

'It would have taken yours.' He frowned

'I had a spell ready for that.' Perhaps my confidence could be mistaken for arrogance. Those dark eyes moved from my slippers right to the top of my head, dipping to focus on the sharp tip of my ear for the longest moment before coming to meet my gaze once more.

'I see,' was all he said, a tension in his jaw, something else he wished to say lingering in his eyes before he turned back to that fire.

With that final dismissal, I left the room. Hoping I could think of something to calm the uneasy pounding of my heart before I got back into bed.

I see. Those two simple words chased me up the stairs and back to my room. Along with the fear that he did. That he saw too much. If that had been the first lesson in our mage partnership, I wondered how peculiar the others were going to be.

Chapter Six

There was a yowling in my dreams. Like banshees howling through the night, hunting for souls. Shadowy robes swirling like storm winds, long, sharp, bony fingers glistening in the moonlight with the blood of a fresh kill. Then came the stab of something biting into my chest. A pressing weight that pulled me slowly back to consciousness.

I opened my eyes, not to the milky eyes of a banshee, but those of a cat. The yowling didn't stop.

Alma screeched into my face, her tiny white paws a dead weight, claws cutting through the thick duvet to poke into my skin.

'Ow!' I half groaned, trying to roll her off, but those sharp canines nipped at my swatting hands.

'Alma!' I snapped, but her urgency didn't stop and it took one look at the clock to realise why.

I was late.

'Bollocks!' I kicked off the covers, sending Alma flying with the cushions as I darted out of bed, my feet sliding on my loose sketches from where my art folder had dropped to the floor. A reminder of the mysterious Lord Blackthorn who gave me no answers, just more questions.

I *never* overslept. It was an impossibility considering the saint bells went off every morning at dawn in the Institute for prayers. Normally, I'd be thankful for Lord Blackthorn's apparent heathen ways, but I could have used the cursed bells today of all days.

I hurried to the wardrobe, finding my only remaining good dress. Slate grey with a severe black lace collar and cuffs. I stuffed myself into it, messing up my charm three times to lace the thing. It ended up far too tight, but I'd rather suffocate slowly than make myself any later. I twisted my braid up onto the crown of my head and pinned it in place, ignoring the hair that my restless sleep had allowed to slip free.

Alma's tail thrashed with annoyance as she pawed at the creased hem of the skirts, but I shooed her out the way, grabbed my bag and rushed for the door. I doubted the Council cared much about a creased hem considering they probably wanted to try me for attempted murder.

After almost tripping over the breakfast tray that had been left outside my door, I rushed down the stairs, almost falling off the last step as I caught sight of the stern form of Lord Blackthorn waiting in the entryway, head bowed in contemplation as William was listing off different types of soil with enthusiasm.

William was in a simple white shirt rolled up to the elbows, dirt clinging to his freckled forearms and smeared all over the stained, brown work apron he wore.

Emrys was an imposing figure in the warm morning light, wearing a sharply tailored black coat and trousers, cut perfectly to his commanding form. The only colour coming from his deep navy waistcoat and the gleam of a silver chain from his pocket watch.

It appeared I hadn't imagined the unnerving handsomeness of him, then.

Without warning, and clearly impatient with my tarrying, the step beneath my feet tipped forward, sending me stumbling across the entryway. The clatter of my arrival caught their attention.

I straightened quickly, looking back at the step, only to see it was straight once more.

Bloody mysterious lords and cursed houses.

'Good morning, Kat.' William's greeting grin was big enough to show his dimples as he tried to dust some of the dirt off his apron.

'Morning, William.' I smiled back, making sure my Kysillian ears were obscured by my hair as I met the lord's assessing gaze.

'Emrys.' I nodded in greeting or in challenge, I hadn't quite decided yet.

Those strange grey eyes were focused not on me, but on that bottom step behind me, considering something before they drifted to me almost reluctantly.

A tension in the harsh line of his jaw made me bristle for a reprimand, but he simply turned back to William.

'I'll take a look when we return, William.' Emrys nodded to the boy.

'Of course.' William rocked back on his heels, digging his hands into his apron pocket. 'I hope it goes well.'

I didn't think William realised just how much hope I needed. Whatever charitable deed Blackthorn was trying to accomplish by having me here was about to bite us both sharply on the backside. The Council didn't like a challenge, especially where it concerned me.

I wasn't given the chance to dwell on that too long as Blackthorn made his way down the corridor, leaving me no choice but to follow. I struggled to keep pace as he moved through the arched hallways. Trinkets and paintings catching my eye and tiny stone gargoyles looming down from their small pedestals high above. Their curiosity wicked as we turned another corner and through a grand dark, wooden archway into another room.

'I'm sorry I'm—' I began, fumbling for some reason for my tardiness, only to almost slam into Blackthorn's broad back as he came to a sudden stop.

We were now standing in a small chamber with an intricate dark floral wallpaper design of birds eating berries. A very ordinary nondescript door with a large brass knob and a slot ready for the incantation paper was waiting before us. Blackthorn effortlessly pulled something from his breast pocket and slipped a rune covered piece of paper into the slot as the whirring and clatter of the mechanisms began.

'Is that a Council portal door?' I asked, a bit breathless, trying not to be impressed that he wrote his own portal papers.

'Yes.' He considered me over his shoulder, brow furrowed, troubled by something. 'Didn't William bring you this way?'

I shook my head.

His fingers ran though the dark mess of his hair as a small phantom smile graced his lips. 'He has a fondness for the scenic route. I hope he didn't bore you too much with talk of ground goblins and the benefits of Dulmor weed.'

'Of course not.' I flushed, running my hands over my skirts to try and straighten them. 'Dulmor use is fascinating, and the abandoned studies of Mage Septimus Barton about wild root magic have been an interest of mine for . . .'

My words ran out as I glanced up, expecting his polite disinterest, but he was closer than I anticipated. That aloofness had left his expression once again. That small smile still touching his lips, dark hair falling onto his brow, head tipped to better hear every rambling thought I had.

Under the force of his attention, I suddenly couldn't remember another word and my only salvation was the door clicking open as the incantation worked.

Emrys stepped through first and all my wonder was lost as the horrid, draughty Council passages greeted us. The reek of saint smoke was thick in the air from their morning prayers. I swallowed down my cough at the sourness it left on my tongue. I barely had a moment to gather myself before Blackthorn was off again, striding down the corridor like some dark, threatening shadow.

Considering he was a man I'd never seen in the Council chambers, he certainly knew the way. Whispers followed us around each corner as maids and the few students who were not in class scrambled from our path. At least their unease distracted me from my own as we arrived at the stained-glass doors that led into the Council's grand chamber.

A shudder ran through me, hearing the horrid creak of the old wooden doors as Blackthorn opened them and moved inside. I reached to catch the door before it swung back, only for my hand to meet air – to see Blackthorn holding it open for me. Those dark, unreadable eyes waiting for something.

I snatched my hand back, muttering my thanks as I entered the room, ignoring the dark rich scent of that troublesome beasam bark as Emrys's powerful steps put him back in front to lead.

I gratefully followed, trying to calm myself, but as I watched the broad expanse of his shoulders move before me in the confines of his dark jacket, I didn't feel any calmer, so I settled on the boring white tiled floor between us.

The chamber doors were open, two Institute wardens standing guard. Their bright blue tunics looked as stiff and

uncomfortable as ever as they shifted slightly with unease at
Emrys's presence as he walked through the grand arches and
into the Mages' Hall.

The room was vast, many desks abandoned by Master Mages
who weren't in residence or couldn't be bothered to attend.
The walls were lined with garish tapestries of their achieve-
ments, battles fought against fey in the name of their dethroned
Mage King. They seemed to forget that they allowed him to
bring darkness back into this world, remnants of that royal
dictatorship covering every inch of the new Institute.

The King's crest depicted in the domed ceiling of stained-
glass above showered the waiting Council's disapproving faces
in a wash of colour. The main desks faced us in a semi-circle,
the dour wrinkled face of Master Ainsworth sitting at the
centre. I wasn't surprised Ainsworth was here, despite his
son being the guilty party. Council hypocrisies had stopped
shocking me long ago.

Master Grima and Master Stone sat on either side of
Ainsworth, their desks littered with papers and teapots.
Madame Bernard, the Institute matron, lingered behind them
like a thin, hungry crow.

Master Hale had situated himself at the end, hand resting
on his cane as if he could rise to my defence at any moment.
The skin beneath his eyes appearing bruised with his failing
health. His presence did little to unpick the tight knot of
anxiety in my chest, my mouth suddenly too dry.

They'd moved one lone chair of dark mahogany into the
centre of the room, just to one side – probably for Blackthorn
to witness my humiliation from.

'Lord Blackthorn,' Master Ainsworth grumbled, those cold,
hateful eyes finding me too swiftly. His powdered white wig
sat off-centre on his head. 'You're late.'

'You should be counting your blessings I could find the time to entertain you at all, Master Ainsworth,' Emrys drawled, turning to me to indicate the chair between us with the barest motion of his gloved fingers.

An offer to sit.

My heart pounded wildly against my ribs. The chair was clearly intended for him. Not me. I always had to stand.

He sent me a slightly irritated glance and I dropped into the seat.

I'd made him late, the least I could do was not cause a scene. So, I folded my hands neatly in my lap and kept my chin high, refusing to be cowed by the hateful glare of Ainsworth and his bench.

I knew the plain dress I wore was useless. They still saw the wildness of every other indiscretion I'd made. Saw how the dark slate grey of the fabric made the golden tones in my skin glow, made my ethereal eyes sharper in my face.

Master Hale's wrinkles deepened with worry despite the reassuring smile he gave me.

'Miss Woodrow is accused of a severe violation of section nineteen of the Peace Agreements,' Master Ainsworth proclaimed, his puffy red face pulled into its usual frown. 'I'm certain such *disregard* for the safety of Institute students is more than worthy of your time, *Blackthorn*.'

'Do you contest the claims against you, Miss Woodrow?' Master Grima asked impatiently, pushing his glasses up his bulbous nose.

I clenched my fists tightly in my lap as magic continued to flush my skin.

'We're waiting to hear them,' was Blackthorn's dark response from my side, arms folded, forearms testing the limits of the stitching of his coat.

67

'I'm certain Miss Woodrow can speak for herself, Lord Blackthorn,' Master Stone's nasally voice added with disdain.

'If you asked her a question worth her time, I'm certain she would.' Blackthorn's tone had gone even colder. I noted the slight drop in Master Hale's shoulders, evidence of his relief at Blackthorn's defence. I, on the other hand, felt like a rabbit in a snare, my magic moving uncomfortably through my limbs.

'I thought the charges were clear, considering the injuries to the Ainsworth boy and the state of the ruins,' Master Grima pressed through his thin lips as they curled to show his yellowed teeth. 'It clearly lost control of its wild magic, partaking in vengeful dark creature summoning.'

'She was probably trying to call on the Old Gods while she was at it,' Madame Bernard added scornfully.

Old Gods. The ancient Verr of the deep. The creators of dark magic, if the myths were to be believed.

'Miss Woodrow has been extensively tested,' Master Hale objected sharply.

Brutally was a better word, trying to see if I was a deadly threat. Fortunately for me, the Council hadn't realised Kysillian fire couldn't be enticed from its wielder. No matter the cruelty of their examinations.

'I'd also remind the *Council* that dark magic is no friend of the fey,' Master Hale finished, breath rattling in his throat as he contained another coughing fit.

'*It* was in the restricted section, which as you know, Hale, is strictly forbidden,' Ainsworth huffed out with an unamused sour laugh. 'Have you abandoned all sense of reason along with your responsibilities to this council?'

'The Ainsworth compendium was left—' I began, knowing I needed to say something.

'A book that hasn't been seen in two centuries,' Master Grima interrupted me, a viciousness to his tone.

'Finneaus opened it,' I challenged, confused as to why I needed to state such a fact. Surely the Wardens had found it?

'Be careful, Miss Woodrow, or we may be forced to summon the Truth Seeker,' Ainsworth threatened coldly.

The Truth Seeker, a being who devoted themselves to their saints' cause, mutilating their bodies with the words of ancient spells in order to be able to pull truth from your very soul.

'Perhaps you should,' I countered, some dark hateful part of me wishing they would. No matter how horrid someone rummaging through my soul would be.

'Insolent—' Madame Bernard began to crow from her perch, but my anger didn't give her a chance to finish as I took hold of the armrest, needing something to anchor myself.

'Finneaus released a demonic entity into the lower chambers from that compendium.' Silence struck like a lightning bolt. A blood seal was dark magic made to keep all, apart from the direct bloodline, from opening it. 'A blood-sealed compendium that I can't touch.'

I turned my hands over for them to see. No red welts or burns from the forsaken iron that coated the text.

Dark, silent fury crept over Master Ainsworth's pale face. Blood-sealed texts were outlawed for their lethal unpredictability, and it was a crime to own one, yet this one had sat in the Council's very own library for years, and he knew that. Knew because it belonged to him.

'The book was—' I tried to continue.

'No such book was discovered, you *vicious* thing. If anything could be found in the destruction to those sacred ruins at all,' Madame Bernard half wailed, as if she'd ever given a second thought to the dusty chambers beneath her feet until I'd stepped foot in them.

'Your charge won't stand, Master Ainsworth. Under clause five, blood-sealed texts aren't included,' Emrys pointed out with bored observation, ignoring every word they'd said as his hands slipped easily into his pockets.

'Have you not been listening?' Ainsworth spat.

There was no anger, no harsh words or sneers in response from Blackthorn at the vulgarity in Ainsworth's tone. Instead, a slow, almost cruel smile came to his lips.

Then I felt it, a strange tension rolling through the room like the beginning of a storm – cold, lethal magic. The morning sun dimmed as if great storm clouds passed overhead.

Clearly oblivious to Blackthorn's mood, Ainsworth unwisely continued his tirade. 'If you wish to believe it's—'

Out of thin air, the small, mangled cage I'd made to hold the gobrite in question crashed down onto Master Ainsworth's desk, sending papers skyward. Chairs scraped against the wooden floor as the Master Mages jumped to their feet, stumbling backwards with cries of alarm.

My own hands gripped the arms of the chair in disbelief, my magic hot in my veins at the resurgence of a familiar foe. The cage rattled as the creature turned its head to me, hissing and thrashing. Clearly in an unforgiving mood.

'Blackthorn!' Madame Bernard shrieked, holding tightly to Master Ainsworth's arm, who shrugged her off in annoyance.

Blackthorn simply ran a gloved knuckle beneath his chin in thought as he approached the Council's desks and the creature.

He was mad. Completely mad.

Then, in the blink of an eye, in his grasp was the blood-sealed text, its forsaken iron cover gleaming even in the dim light.

I cringed away from it, hating the painful sensation that rushed over my skin.

If Blackthorn noticed, he didn't show it as he dropped the book onto Ainsworth's desk, sliding it closer to the Insidious beast. The creature calmed, almost whimpering to return to its home.

'You seem to have misplaced this.' Blackthorn's voice was quiet, the words clipped with an ominous warning as he met Ainsworth's stare.

A fury burned behind the old mage's eyes, one that I'd been on the receiving end of too many times, yet now he remained silent. As Blackthorn pressed his palms to the table, leaning closer to challenge him, the gobrite cowered ever so slightly with a low growl.

'That . . .' Ainsworth began to splutter. To try and twist a lie, but at the mere sound of his voice the book swivelled and pushed itself across the table towards him, making all the mages lean back from it, chairs creaking.

'Cursed things always return to their master in the end.' Blackthorn's calm tone almost verged on boredom. 'You shouldn't need a spell to work that out, *Councilman*.'

I was stunned, both that Blackthorn could summon a cursed text, as well as how flawlessly he challenged the Council. How he hadn't challenged me the same to prove I was telling the truth. He'd just taken each fact from me. Effortlessly.

'With your infrequent visits, *Lord Blackthorn*, you won't be aware of just how much of a menace Miss Woodrow has been,' Grima replied tartly. 'She is a danger to this Institute, the treaty and her fellow students.'

'Unjustified claims fuelled by nothing more than preju-dice,' Master Hale snapped. His grip on his cane was white-knuckled, making me worry he'd bludgeon Master Grima to death with it.

'The burning of the east workroom, assaulting students, stealing four ancient texts, having poison on her person and now trying to unleash *monsters!*' Madame Bernard threw in for good measure.

My gaze shifted awkwardly to see if Blackthorn had paid any attention to the accusations. Unfortunately, all were true.

His attention had indeed turned towards me. I expected annoyance, or disgust perhaps, but he was simply looking over his shoulder at me with a raised brow, as if I'd impressed him.

'I would remind the Council that, when trialling someone under laws written by myself, I hold complete authority.' Blackthorn continued to consider me with unexpected curiosity before his dark focus slipped back to the old men. 'The verdict therefore falls to me.'

He straightened to his full height and pulled a long envelope from his inside pocket, dropping it with little decorum onto the desk.

'My findings. I think you'll agree Miss Woodrow is the only reason the Insidious beast didn't breach my wards.' Blackthorn's smile was tight, seeming more like a sneer under the constraints of his pale scars. 'Her spell crafting is flawless where dark matter is concerned. Therefore, she's passed her Dark Defence theory, making her a partner mage without papers under the old laws.'

Dark Defence theory – an antiquated test where they'd lock fledgling mages in a room with all manner of dark creations or creature traps. Most didn't survive the ordeal and the council had shelved the test a decade ago, largely because lords weren't about to risk their heirs. Yet some desperate fey students still attempted the test . . . their deaths a gruesome warning to the rest of us.

'However, we'll go along with the pretence of a partnership agreement. Just to make certain there are no more *oversights* where Miss Woodrow's study is considered. One year of mentorship, under the old laws,' Blackthorn added as an afterthought.

'Dark summoning is forbidden, Blackthorn,' Master Grima stated warily. Desperation clinging to his words.

'I saw no evidence of dark summoning on her part.'

'You are the expert after all, Lord Blackthorn,' Master Hale added, his smile filled with relief. My magic wasn't soothed. It all felt too easy, that sense of a trap not leaving me. Too used to things going horribly wrong.

'I strongly advise you let this one go, Ainsworth,' Blackthorn finished, a lethal quiet to his voice that confused me. 'If you wish to antagonise the rebellion by removing the last fey from the Institute for nothing more than *spitefulness*, I am certain that's a greater breach of the Peace Accords.'

'The rebellion died a long time ago,' Master Stone argued.

Ainsworth didn't react; couldn't, because he knew it was a lie. The fey rebellion had never been more vicious in their fight for freedom, in their hunger to bring a mortal council down. They wished to govern themselves from the northlands, which they still held. A group so ruthless that even my father had warned me against them – how they coerced fey to do their bidding, forcing them to take inescapable blood vows as evidence of their loyalty.

'Is that why Montagor has asked for more troops in the north?' Blackthorn's head tipped in dark contemplation, straightening the cuff of his jacket. 'Why your attempts to summon him here didn't work?'

I couldn't be hearing these things.

Lord Montagor, the bastard son of the Mage King, was currently seeking the same power his father had possessed, just as tyrannical and ruthless. He'd worked his way into the

Council through corruption and the sudden unexpected deaths of other, more peaceful members.

Another topic Master Hale told me to keep away from. Montagor had made himself the expert on fey attacks and wild magic. Giving himself jurisdiction to persecute fey without just cause. His radical followers were devout to his dogma, calling him a saint in mortal form.

'With the unrest in the north, the rebellion appears to be knocking at our door, Councilman. I for one am not seeking to open it for them just yet,' Master Hale added. Another uprising was coming. A truth they couldn't deny much longer.

'As Miss Woodrow has accepted her partnership, I'd like her key to access the mage facilities.' Blackthorn held out his hand expectantly and I watched as Master Grima's face went almost purple with rage.

'No fey has ever been allowed in the Grand Library!' Ainsworth half-spewed the words.

'It seems you'll need to contact the records department,' Blackthorn mused. 'I'm certain they'll be thrilled to update their files.'

'They're a risk to the texts!' Madame Bernard hissed, taking a cautious step back from all the hideous evidence now covering the desks.

'You can charge me for the damage,' Blackthorn replied quickly, undeterred, and still holding out that dark gloved hand. 'Her key, if you'd be so kind.'

Master Ainsworth let out a cursing breath before he reluctantly began to rummage in the desk drawer. One of the most prized items, and it just sat in his drawer. It felt like a slap in the face.

'You cannot be serious, Blackthorn,' Master Stone bristled. 'That *thing* has been running rampant for too long.' He threw his yellowed finger in my direction, leering over his desk so suddenly I flinched. Forgetting the company we were in, the years that had passed. Somehow, the one slap I'd been given by the hateful councilman had remained with me, just like the ones from Daunton. Every strike still fresh, still burning upon my flesh with the shame of it.

'It—' Master Stone's next slight didn't escape his thin lips. No, his face had gone quite pale, hand grasping at his neck as he slumped back into his chair, trying to drag in air that rattled worryingly in his chest.

'You don't seem yourself, Master Stone,' Emrys offered conversationally, leaning into his palms that he braced on the table, as if he had all day to stand in the odious man's presence.

Master Stone coughed suddenly, greedily dragging in a breath. His hateful eyes remained on the lord before him despite how his fingers trembled, disregarding Madame Bernard, who scrambled to give him water. She was looking quite pale herself.

'I'm fine,' Stone half-croaked.

'I'm certain Miss Woodrow has many things to be getting on with and entertaining this council isn't on that list,' Blackthorn finished with menacing authority.

Having no choice but to sit there gawping at Blackthorn's boldness, I tried to pretend such disregard for the Council was natural to me, despite the sweat gathering at my palms and the nauseating swirl of my magic deep in my gut.

Sensing my unease, Blackthorn turned his attention to me.

'I have some remaining questions for Master Ainsworth and his questionable collection of compendiums, Miss Woodrow.' He nodded, those eyes so dark I wondered if it was a trick of the light as they suddenly shifted to a more mortal grey in the blink of an eye. 'You're free to continue with your day.'

I didn't wait to be told twice. Standing and giving him and the Council a respectful bow, I left the chaos behind me, trying my best to keep my steps measured.

I knew without a doubt Alma was going to murder me. Not only had I riled up the Council, but I'd also got myself partnered up with a lord who was clearly insane and took enjoyment from humiliating the Council on my behalf. Something I knew they wouldn't be in a hurry to forget.

Chapter Seven

You don't belong here, Katherine, but if you let me, I can help you find somewhere you can.

Master Hale's first words echoed in my mind frequently, but never more so than when I'd made a mistake.

A simple offer as he crouched before me on the worst day of my life. The strange, tall man who should have scared me, but something about his size, the calmness in his voice and the honesty in his eyes that reminded me vividly of my father.

On that day, I'd needed my father more than ever and he wasn't there. He never would be again, so I clung to Master Hale, foolishly hoping he wasn't like all the others.

He had never disappointed me. It turned out *I* was the one who had become the disappointment.

I couldn't rid myself of the guilt. Not even as I stood beyond those Council chambers to wait in the hall. I would have returned to the portal and Blackthorn Manor, but I didn't know the way, not from the mages' entrance and I didn't fancy trying to talk to Clerk Roberts again.

So, I wandered the small reading area just beyond the Council Chamber.

Finding little interest in the modest collection of poetry on the back shelves, I occupied myself by studying the painting framed above the grand fireplace. The violence depicted in vivid oil paints on the large canvas. The night King Balin III was beheaded by his wife, a suspected sorceress and fey sympathiser.

Stories said the King had built temples to the Old Gods beneath his castle, paved with fey bones, and drank ancient creatures' blood in sacrifice to the darkness. How he'd met his end, driven mad by the dark he worshipped and by the tip of his wife's sword.

The world was supposed to heal under a Queen's rule, fey set free from the mines and liberated, only for her to be drowned in the west river as a Verr witch, and for her son to take the throne, leading us to the mess we were in now. To that Mage King that had ruined my life. Taken everything so easily. Who had carried on his father's vile practices. Only to be overthrown by the Council, whom I finally understood were no better.

I wondered if it was the murder of his father that had fuelled him, or simply the madness of the darkness beneath. Had it fuelled all the others? The bloodshed and tyrannical reign of all the Mortal Kings before, who desired magic enough to forfeit their souls?

Something strange moved across my shoulder blades, sharp eyes digging into my spine.

I turned, only to see a passing of shadow at the end of the hall as the morning sun seeped back through the clouds.

'Katherine,' came the breathless greeting from Master Hale, as he hobbled through the chamber doors, his smile bright, shoulders pushed back with pride.

'You did excellently.' He grinned, placing a reassuring hand on my arm. 'How has Alma settled?'

'She changed again,' I sighed, finding some relief in admitting that worry.

'Bird?' He frowned.

'Cat,' I half-winced, knowing I should be grateful. Alma as a bird left a mess everywhere; at least as a cat she had more control.

'I'm sure her nerves will settle.' He rummaged in his pocket before pulling out a small tin of chocolates, Alma's favourite from the southern markets. 'I picked these up on my travels. I'm sure they can entice her back.'

'Thank you.' I smiled, turning them over. If anything could convince Alma to come back, it was chocolate. I ran my thumb across the metal tin, thinking of how Alma secretly kept each one, like they were precious treasures, never having received a gift until she'd met Master Hale.

'Blackthorn is delayed.' He rummaged in his robe pocket again, pulling out that key and handing it over to me. I took it gingerly, and felt that it was warm from his touch. The silver was intricately carved with the swoop of knowledge runes.

How long I'd wished for such a thing, and how easily Blackthorn had handed it over. It was something even Master Hale couldn't grant me.

'Thank you,' I whispered, despite knowing I was speaking those words to the wrong person as I curled both hands around the key. Unease lingered at just how quickly Blackthorn had accomplished such impossible things. Especially here.

'I have so much I wish to tell you.' Hale took my arm to guide me further down the hallway and away from the chamber. 'However, you have important studies to be getting on with.'

In his usual guiding manner, Master Hale showed me the way to the mages' doors, pointing out Blackthorn's – the one we'd come through.

79

He was talking about the records halls, the libraries, the sections that might best interest me, but all I could taste was the bitterness of failure as Blackthorn's words about the rebellion came back to haunt me.

The churning unease in my gut after seeing the Council's hateful stares stayed with me. No matter the weight of that key in my grasp, all I could see was the empty fey quarters above, the sheet-covered body in that stairwell and how everything had fallen apart so easily.

'I'm sorry it didn't work,' I whispered, trying to release some of the guilt gnawing at my bones. 'That I wasn't enough.'

Hale turned abruptly to face me, a solemn expression on his old face, his frail hand coming to rest on my shoulder. 'We cannot see a decade of peace as failure, my dear.'

Peace for whom? I wanted to argue, but bit my tongue. Master Hale was trying. He was trying and that had to count for something. No matter how small his own rebellion was.

'I have more meetings this week that I'm confident about. Peace Agreement amendments that should have happened sooner.' His tone was soft but I could see the depth of his frown, the shadows beneath his eyes and how his old shoulders bowed under the weight of it all.

'Was Blackthorn right about the rebellion?' I asked, unnerved at just how unruly the world beyond these walls continued to be.

'He would know better than me. The Blackthorns had a closer connection with the rebellion during the wars.'

That answer only troubled me further. Most who worked with the rebellion were taken care of as radicals after the wars, exiled in the name of peace to the far islands in the west. Others went underground to build up the fey rebellion again. One that was supposed to be dead.

'If the rebels attack, Montagor and the Council won't hold back,' I whispered that truth, knowing I shouldn't speak it at all. Not here.

'If they attack, it's because they seek a war as ardently as he does.' Hale sighed with defeat.

'Innocents will pay the price,' I noted darkly. That's all that would come from another war, the fey in the far lands suffering, being further oppressed and punished for crimes they hadn't committed. Seen as rebels for merely possessing magic.

'That hasn't bothered either side before.' Hale's tone was clipped with irritation. I understood why, as he leaned heavily on that cane, breath rattling weakly in his chest. All the time he'd put into saving this world and it still wished only to tear itself apart. 'Now you can help them in your own way with your partnership.'

'You trust him.' It wasn't a question.

'I do.' He nodded without hesitation. 'I would have called on him sooner but he's a hard man to track down. A ghost, some would say.'

I thought Blackthorn was more mysterious than a ghost, but I was better keeping those fears to myself as we came to the grand doors that led to the libraries reserved for mages.

Master Hale patted my arm, only the mirth in his smile didn't distract from the regret burdening his gaze. 'Make the bastards pay, Katherine.'

Then he left me there. I should have been excited or filled with wonder, but as I turned that key over in my hand and looked up at the grand curved arches of the library, a strange sadness consumed me.

I'd imagined myself here a hundred times. Lured by the smell of the old records, the harsh bitter scent of spelled pages. Only it wasn't exactly as I imagined it. No, because I'd never imagined myself standing here alone.

Despite it being that way for so long, I always thought things would be different. Maybe the mages would see my potential. Maybe a paper would pique their interest, make them change their minds. Maybe allow them to see past my blood, to see all the potential I possessed.

Hopeless stupid wishes that had got me nowhere.

I turned that key over once more before pushing it deep into my pocket. A gift I needed time to process. I had other things to work on, was the lie I told myself as I made my way back to the portal doors, not quite able to breathe until I was back in Blackthorn's entrance hall – until I locked eyes with the annoyed feline perched on the stairs. A relieved breath huffed between my lips, suddenly exhausted.

'I'm alive.' I held my hands out at my sides in a show of surrender.

Alma gave me a bored blink, jumping from the third stair, tail high as she led me down the hall to a stone staircase that headed down into what smelled like the kitchens.

The clattering of someone at work and a cheery hum greeted me, as well as the delicious smell of fresh bread. William stood before a large stove, stirring something before Alma's meow announced our presence.

'You're back.' He straightened to dry his hands on his apron, flour clinging to his red curls. 'Take a seat, I've just finished with lunch.'

He didn't give me a chance to answer before he pulled a cloth away that covered a still-steaming pie, a bowl of roasted vegetables waiting next to it as he started to plate up some food at the wooden table that dominated the centre of the small brick kitchen. 'Did you enjoy the halls?'

I slid onto the bench at the table, grooved from all the people who had sat there before. One of the planks rose so a glass of water slid until it was before me and the board returned to nail itself back down.

I noticed Alma's saucer of water and a small fish on the table, she too a guest.

'I hadn't expected it to be as lonely as it was.' I sighed, letting my finger trace the small gouges in the wood, worn so smooth with time it practically gleamed.

Alma leapt onto the bench next to me, distracting me as she pawed insistently at my bag.

I laughed softly. 'Master Hale sent you a gift but you can't have it until you're back.'

Her tale swished in irritation but I petted her head and returned my attention to William.

'Did Lord Blackthorn return?' I asked, suddenly ravenous, remembering I'd missed breakfast as William slid a plate towards me.

'He's been called away on business again. You'll find it happens a lot.' His smile dampened as he sat on the opposite bench with his own plate.

'I'm sorry if you got into trouble for my wandering last night.' I sighed, hoping Blackthorn wasn't too harsh with him.

'Trouble?' William laughed, shaking his head. 'I haven't had a telling-off from Emrys since I was ten and let a lost goat into the study. It ate his Pervanthus herb collection.'

'He had Pervanthus herbs?' I choked on my water. They were mythical herbs, some scrolls claiming they had immortal properties. Although, it was how young William must have been then that surprised me most. Mages didn't take on apprentices or assistants until they were twelve.

Which made me wonder as to William's story and just how he'd ended up here, but I shook away the thought. Those things weren't mine to wonder about as I let my gaze drop back to the table, where I saw the stack of books to his side and papers piled next to them.

'You're reading about the Bracken theories?' I asked with excitement, seeing the title of the top tome.

'I'm trying to create a more powerful variation of the Abatrox nettle.' He nervously rubbed the back of his neck.

'Can I see?' I asked, watching excitement light his eyes as he quickly picked though his notes to hand me his most recent work.

'If you could help me understand his footnotes in section nine, I'd be eternally grateful,' he half-pleaded, and I couldn't help but laugh.

'Of course.' I turned the papers around, reading over his first lines, seeing where he'd lost his way. Able to forget the horrid morning with the warm cosy air of the kitchen and William's honest enthusiasm as he scribbled down my interpretation of the pages. Knowing I was glad to be here. Mad lord or not.

Chapter Eight

After spending the rest of the day helping William, I returned to my own studies, occupying my evening by skulking about my huge room, unable to think of anything other than a mysterious, occult-worshipping lord as I tossed and turned in my massive bed that night.

Alma bit me twice for disturbing her sleep, so I was relieved when dawn arrived. Hoping a walk around the grounds of Blackthorn Manor in the fresh air would return my senses.

With Alma slumbering in cat form, I dressed quietly in my shirt, tightening my walking-skirt belt, my bag hanging from it with everything I needed concealed inside: a healing pack, sample containers, fresh ink and my notebook. Ready for whatever could greet me in the wilderness, I shrugged on my walking jacket before slipping from the room.

The entrance hall and front doors had returned to where they had been when I'd first arrived, and luckily were unlocked. Sharp morning air struck my cheeks as I slipped outside, gravel crunching under my boots in greeting.

Moving quickly off the path to begin my wandering, the cold dew from the long grass soaked quickly into my worn boots. The woods in the distance were like something from one of the wild-folk storybooks. Twisting ancient trees wrapped in moss and ivy, the muted morning light almost blue with the winter fog. So old I wondered if they'd been here when the ancient fey kings had ruled, when banshees hunted the night and dragons guarded mountain passes in the west. If these lands had seen all the things I could only read about now. Truths turned to myth too easily.

It had been so long since I'd wandered free amongst the wilderness. The Institute only had the small Mages' Garden, not big enough to get lost in, and too well-maintained for anything exciting to grow.

The wilder lands were where all the big advancements in magic could be found.

Here I was greeted by fresh cold air. No city smoke. The sweet tang of magic from the earth. Real. I closed my eyes and for the barest moment, I could imagine I was home. Back in the northern lands, hearing the sea crash against the rocks. Back before everything fell apart so easily.

Shaking off the dark thought, I trudged through the grass until I came to the overgrowth that marked the border to the woods, dark and tangled before me. The mist refused to lift as I ducked beneath the low branches.

The rich scent of damp earth filled my lungs as I climbed over large rocks and thick, knotted roots. Strange bird calls grew louder as the sun rose, my palms running over the thick moss that wrapped around the tree trunks as I avoided the bright mushrooms and small flowers that littered the patches of earth the sun touched.

My hair slipped free of its braid with all the exertion, falling heavy down my back, though not enough to distract me as I stumbled upon the remains of a small wyverns' nest deep between ancient tree roots. It looked recently abandoned, egg shards left and the feathers of the mother's prey tangled beneath the intricate webbing of branches and animal bones, sitting deep in the damp soil.

I set myself down, opened my bag and pulled my papers free. I sketched the nest, the smoothness of the egg shards and the sharpness of the beaks of the creatures that would have once lived inside them. Stealing feathers, egg shards and branches, to push between the pages of my book, making a quick note of all the wyverns' territorial markings on the trees close by.

Small eyes glinted like tiny fireflies from the darkness inside hollowed-out tree stumps. Tiny wildwood creatures called folk, made of remnant earth magic, they were the distant relatives of dust sprites. Creatures that willed themselves into being, existing long before fey, and perhaps long after.

I laid down quietly on my stomach, hidden by the weeds as my chin rested on my folded arms, waiting patiently, just as I had as a child, when my mother had lain down with me, waiting for the creatures to emerge, as they did now. Cautious of any shadow or noise. Their tiny, soundless moss feet and toadstool heads with beetle wings glistening with dew before they scuttled off back into the long grass.

I watched them scurry across the earth and into their hiding places, thick cracks in an ancient oak's trunk. Quietly, I dragged my notebook closer to draw them. Every detail from their root-made bodies, acorn heads and thin twig arms.

I watched them until they vanished with the morning mist, the weak winter sun making me sit up as long shadows stretched across the forest floor. The vastness of the knotted wood before me lured me deeper into the ancient Blackthorn Forest until I spotted a valek nest high above, hidden between great ancient tree branches. I debated climbing up to it, but then thought better of it as I considered the worn sole of my boot. Alma had done her best to repair it and I couldn't go back with it any more damaged.

A glint in the long grass sent me forward to a perfect collection of smooth shed scales. Lying there like a small offering. I dropped to my knees, amazed I'd beaten the folk to finding such a treasure. I rummaged in my bag for a sample jar.

Valek were rare, a creature of enormous size, both scaled and possessing feathers like a strange reptilian bird. They had a sharp jaw with lethal fanged teeth that had the ability to feast on dark magic, and were covered in both silver scales and white feathers. They'd been hunted by the King's followers to near extinction, lies peddled in papers that the creatures were attacking beings. The only beings they attacked were those who summoned the dark.

I settled down against a fallen tree trunk, marvelling at my find before tucking it safely into my bag. Then I shrugged off my jacket, rolled up my sleeves and focused on my research to pass the time, soon reaching my fifth page of notes, as I rolled the remaining shell fragments between my fingertips.

Such vast nature called to me in a way I couldn't fully explain. It wasn't a battered book or a torn page I had to decipher. It was real, undeniable in its potency and all the lessons it had to teach. Yet, I knew it wouldn't be a good idea to get lost in it, despite my urgency to learn more during whatever short period Blackthorn could stomach my being here for.

The bird calls grew louder, fog dispersing as the sun rose high, making me realise just how much time had passed.

My neck ached from my stooped position, fingers muddy and ink-stained, pages of notes littered around my feet in the long grass.

I'd lost track of time again.

Quickly, I tidied up my things, tucked my jacket into the crook of my arm despite the cold wind and headed back the way I'd come, following the disturbed path through the thicket. The icy wind persisted, forcing me to circle back to the house over the uneven, thick grass as my legs began to ache, unfamiliar with the freedom to wander over such unforgiving terrain.

The remains of the cottage came closer, a slight blur around it that I should have noticed the first time. It seemed sad and forgotten in the vastness of the landscape. Exactly what the ancient glamour around it wanted me to see.

The clouds parted, rays of sunlight drenching the grass before me. The brightness catching on a patch of white flowers. A sharp jab of grief between my ribs stopped me in my tracks.

I knew they weren't uncommon so far west, but it had been so long since I'd seen them. Azenia, the small white flowers mistaken for weeds by most. I crouched, twisting one of the thin stems so it came away from its patch easily. The petals as soft as I remembered with a vibrant purple middle.

The everlasting bloom. Kysillian Kings had worn it woven around their crowns during coronations, and warriors kept them close to their hearts before battle. Burial shrouds were covered with lengths of them.

I remembered braiding the stems with my mother, knotting them tightly before we hung it around my father's neck as he left. The bittersweet smell as the stems stained our fingers green.

Amartis. My mother had whispered into his ear, as she held him close with her pregnant belly between them. A phrase she thought I wouldn't hear as I clutched her skirts.

'Call me back to you,' I whispered now, knowing why she'd spoken the promise in Kysillian. The words of devotion I didn't understand then. Of a love so strong that no matter where he went, she would follow him. All he had to do was call her name.

Then I remembered braiding the stems again. Alone. Cold, trembling fingers as I pushed the flowers into her hair, between her fingers, where I'd laced them over her swollen stomach, still whispering for her to come back even as I prepared her for burial.

The sharp smell of smoke filled my lungs, the screams of a younger version of myself echoing in my mind and the heat of a fire I should never have started. Pain radiated through my chest as I stumbled back from the memory, letting the wind snatch the flower from my palm as I hurried back to the house, reminding myself there was nothing in the past for me. Just ghosts and grief.

Arriving in the entrance hall, I expected a wailing Alma ready to pounce on me for my foolish roaming, but there was nothing but the persistent ticking of the grandfather clock as I caught sight of myself in the hallway mirror. My hair half unbound, leaves stuck to my skirts and a streak of mud down my cheek.

Wonderful.

I wiped my face with the back of my hand and made a half-hearted attempt to fix my hair, but it was clumsy and unladylike. The table I rested my things on rattled suddenly, sending one of my overused bent pins clattering to the ground before it bounced under the sideboard. Annoyed, I dropped to my knees to retrieve it. Finding myself having to reach deep beneath the sideboard.

'Bloody bastard,' I cursed, reaching desperately for the pin.

'Anyone I'm familiar with?' a voice asked, startling me into smacking my head on the underside of the sideboard before I stumbled to my feet.

Blackthorn stood in the middle of the hallway, a book tucked neatly under his arm. His face impassive, dark hair pushed back from his brow, dressed sharply in a dark suit and matching cravat, making the pale scarred flesh of his face more prominent. His riding boots polished to a startling high shine.

'How do you do that?' I grimaced, rubbing the sore spot at the back of my head. 'Just appear out of nowhere like that?'

'I think you've brought half the forest back with you.' His attention dropped to the hem of my skirt, ignoring the question.

'My maid remains in her feline form,' I said with a sigh. 'I'm afraid I'll be unpresentable until she returns.'

'William did mention your maid had an affliction,' he mused as he came a step closer. 'I need your eyes.'

He took the book from under his arm, flicking the pages and turning it for me to see. I forced my attention on the page, and not the strange feeling his proximity brought, or the imposing nature of him as he towered over me – a feat not many gentlemen had managed thus far.

I took the book as he leaned closer to tap a specific page. A small crescent-moon scar sat above the knuckle of his index finger that somehow seemed purposeful compared to the others that marred him. The crescent moon was a bad omen. A story from too long ago. Of a prince cursed by death.

Fey still remembered, deeming a child born under the crescent moon to need a special blessing. To make certain nothing came from beneath the earth to steal their soul.

I shook the thought away, focusing on the task at hand, and tried to ignore the sweet earthy scent of beasam bark coming off his clothes. Trying not to think about what he was doing brewing such an unpredictable substance or what ancient dark incantations he'd been meddling with.

He was pointing to an incantation to deal with a Lazur entity. A creature that dwelled in towns and used a reanimated corpse to do its bidding.

The book was old, and his notes were scrawled all around the page, pressed into the smallest margins.

'This is a complex incantation.' I ran my fingertip over the mess of his script. He'd written it in Mican. I tried not to be startled that he knew a fey language. The Council didn't see any benefit in learning an earth language, even if it did strengthen spells.

'You've written similar spells in your notes.' He shrugged, a familiarity in his gaze that felt inappropriate as I quickly returned my eyes to the safety of the book.

'You've barely given the ink time to dry,' I commented. The complex mixture of words and languages would have melted the brain of a lesser mage. It appeared Lord Blackthorn's spellcasting mirrored his mannerisms: difficult to determine. No matter how long I looked at his words, there was always a new angle to discover, a new way the spell could be imagined, a new power to be mastered.

'Master Hale said you had an affinity for such incantations,' he pressed gently.

'As usual, he has too much faith in my abilities,' I observed.

The solution came to me on my second reading. 'You need to move this.' I pointed to one of his squiggles I interpreted as a power mark, too deep in the spell for it to work correctly. 'The verse isn't strong enough, and a few of the words in the second row disrupt the balance.'

I tapped the page just as he had, pleased with myself as I looked up to check he was paying attention, but he wasn't looking at the book. He was watching me.

'Not many choose the path of the occult, even fewer make it. I advised Master Hale about the dangers of this partnership, but he reassured me of your . . . capabilities.'

'I've survived this long.'

'Spoken like a woman who wanders the Wilder Lands unescorted.' The ghost of a smile barely touched the corners of his uneven mouth. 'Some would suspect you of being a Croinn.'

Croinn. I was familiar with the ancient term for a witch. It wasn't the worst thing I'd been called.

'Is that all you needed?' I sighed, folding my hands politely before me.

'I wanted to show you the study.' He indicated down the hallway, before leading the way.

'What were you doing in the woods?' he asked.

'I had need of some fresh samples for my research. The door was unlocked, otherwise I would have asked William.'

'The house must like you.' He sounded troubled by the thought as he led us deeper into the house.

Chapter Nine

In *The Mages' Codex of Behaviour* I'd outlined two of the most important rules: order and perfection – the two things that I found severely lacking as I entered Blackthorn's study. Despite whatever favour he owed Master Hale, I hadn't anticipated he'd actually want to teach me anything, that his mentorship would be a distant and hollow thing just to keep the Council at bay.

However, the lord was very much present as he strode the vast comely halls of his manor, leading the way. The arched green doors of the study were hidden at the end of a maze of endless shadowy corridors, almost willing you to get lost. A similar room to the library, the space was a mess of unfinished papers, potion bottles, wonky shelves and imposing bookcases that seemed to open passageways that led deeper into the room.

Enormous, latticed windows covered the far wall overlooking Blackthorn Forest, and an impressive fireplace dominated the space between bookshelves. Large ornate lamps hung from the walls, held by golden talons that formed hooks. The air was filled with the scent of burnt candles and the remnants of wax stuck to the wooden surfaces.

'Your desk.' He indicated to the only clear surface in the room – a large dark wooden desk with legs carved so that each looked like a phoenix taking flight. Mages used to take great pride in their desks, the place they created their spells, selecting a creature from the earth to symbolise their character and bless their work.

At least that's what they used to do. Now, most of the mages at the Institute had a plain, gilded desk. No trace of the earth that they had stolen their magic from now that it was sterile from centuries of mortal conquest.

'I've gathered some more papers and cases for your consideration,' Emrys continued effortlessly, as if he hadn't given me an incredible gift. Moving to another desk, the floor around it stacked high with so many books I couldn't see what creature was carved onto its legs. There appeared to be another in the far corner of the room that was in worse condition than his.

'It's beautiful.' I ran my fingertips over the smooth wood, the dark red leather top, worn with time and use.

'It was my sister's,' he replied quietly, beginning to root through the drawers of his desk. 'Her name was Emmaline.'

The mysterious dead sister. I wouldn't lower myself to listen to gossip; anything I trusted about this man would have to come from my own observations. So, as I looked at him, all I could see was the dark sadness of grief lingering in his gaze before he pulled off his jacket to drape it over the back of the chair.

'I'm sorry.'

'It was a long time ago.' He busied himself by rolling up the sleeves of his white shirt to reveal toned forearms. Streaks of pale scars marring the surface, but clearly not affecting the strength of the muscle beneath.

Then I realised I was staring.

'I'll have to try and memorise the way,' I observed stupidly as an excuse to look back at the large green doors, whose paint had begun to crack with age.

95

'There wouldn't be much point. This is where the study has chosen to be today. It must have thought I needed the exercise.' He turned to lean back against his desk, arms folded to consider me.

Then I remembered the table moving of its own accord to lose my hairpin, how the hallway had shifted that first night. The house clearly had a mind of its own.

My mother had told me stories of magical houses, of rooms being charmed so they were harder to discover, bank vaults and even the King's bedchamber, but never a study. Which only made me wonder what the Blackthorns of the past had been up to.

'What theories have you been working on?' he asked abruptly, startling me back into the present.

'A cure for saltorvarious pox.' A complex and deadly disease, foolish perhaps, but it was a small debt I owed my mother's memory.

He frowned, clearly surprised by the impossibility of my self-imposed study.

'It took my mother's life,' I added quietly. The moment mortals carried fey children their blood was affected, enough to leave them vulnerable. Her illness was deemed her own fault for debasing herself with my father, so no help came.

He seemed to contemplate that for a moment, his expression giving nothing away, but I could have sworn his eyes darkened ever so slightly. 'I'd be interested to see them.'

Hesitantly, I crossed the space between our desks and reached into my small bag, finding the notes tucked at the bottom next to my father's sword hilt, holding the file out to him, watching the flare of something cross his features – surprise, perhaps – before he hid it again behind his cool indifference.

'Are you always so prepared?' He plucked the file from my hands and opened it effortlessly.

'Yes.'

'Do you have any other unsavoury pastimes I should be informed of? Or are they limited to snooping? Or summoning demons in the Fifth Library?'

'Such as the study of necromancy?' I raised a brow, catching his attention once more. 'I believe interest in such things to be frowned upon?'

'How could you tell?' That ghost of a smile came to his lips again.

'Beasam bark. It has a distinct smell,' was all I offered, knowing it probably wasn't wise to disclose just how much I knew about forbidden texts. Another crime the Council would be only too happy to accuse me of.

'It can be used in other spells.' The hint of a challenge crept into his tone, making me stand a little straighter.

'Not on this occasion. *The Book of Mort* gave you away.' I smiled, remembering the tattered compendium that lay on the cluttered table in the library.

There was the slightest twitch at the corner of his mouth before it vanished as something shifting in his expression. Focus caught on a page of my notes.

'You've been studying Lux Theory.' His attention shot to my face, eyes bright once more, crystalline almost.

'It helps when working through the poisons, and in finding which incantations can be used to balance dark matter,' I replied calmly, confused by his interest. 'They have the same rhythm encased in the spell. I've been using it on dark herbs to extract their energy. The saltorvarious strain began as a curse after all.'

I moved closer to point out the section of my notes where I'd documented the change. 'I found the strongest part of the incantation and inverted it instead, so the poison becomes the opposite of what it was intended to be. It's an old theory from one of Amrock's . . .'

I glanced up to see if he was following but he wasn't looking at the notes or my finger as it dragged across the page.

No, he was looking right at me.

Those strange, stormy eyes filled with sharp intensity, as if seeing me for the first time. That harshness in his features faded. Those scars seemed less brutal, his expression softer as that dark hair fell across his brow.

Being what I was, I had been on the receiving end of all kinds of looks in my life, but nobody had ever looked at me the way he did at that moment. As if he couldn't fathom if I was real. Yet in a moment, it was gone.

As if remembering himself, he straightened, looking back at the page between us. 'You're using poison in your healing?'

'Well, it's . . .' I struggled to find the words, unsettled by his attention as I retreated back to my own desk, quickly taking a few items from my bag: *The Myths of Shadow*, and notebooks I still needed to make sense of. 'It's based on Sorcerer Amrock's studies.'

'The bastard son of a witch?' Sharp amusement coated his words, making my pen box slip from my fingers, clattering loudly against the leather-top.

The gossip Alma had told me began to echo around my head. It would make sense if he *was* the son of a witch, the way his eyes appeared to change colour with his mood and the intensity of his stare, like he could hear every word in my head.

I really bloody hoped he couldn't.

'His magic was powerful, most of his theories were destroyed, apart from the few notes that survived. I copied his method with great success.' I shrugged, turning back to him and trying to seem impervious, which only appeared to amuse him more.

'Amrock wrote his tales in earth languages, but all his theories were coded,' he countered as he flicked through my notebook with ease.

This was normal – partner mages were supposed to share information on their studies – but I'd never done it before, and my skin felt tight with both embarrassment and shame. I'd have an easier time standing here in my undergarments than have this man examining my private research.

'You've translated it.' There was a sharpness to his eyes as they came back to my face, settling on my lips in anticipation of a lie in my explanation.

'Exilian might be a difficult language, but it's close enough to Kysillian,' I countered. It wasn't that much of a marvel; anyone with a brain could see the similarity.

'It's a dead language,' he pressed. 'A dead language where the only remaining record was written phonetically by a madman.'

'Nothing is truly dead when it comes to fey magic,' I challenged, unwilling to accept his praise.

'I've been trying for five years.' There was a glint in his dark eyes that looked oddly like admiration, before he thankfully looked to the papers again, so my heart had a chance to settle.

A shy tapping on the door made me turn to find William standing there, oddly straight backed, as if he'd decided to start wearing a corset.

'Yes, William?' Emrys asked without glancing in the boy's direction.

'A letter's arrived in the fireplace.' The boy shifted uncomfortably as he crossed the room and handed the letter over.

'Again? Has everyone forgotten I'm a recluse?' Emrys rubbed his brow as he took it. The envelope was deep burgundy, which I found strange, the wax seal a golden hue.

'I see,' he muttered.

'Good afternoon, Kat,' William greeted, his smile a little too tight as his eyes kept returning to Emrys, studying him to gauge his reaction.

Emrys cleared his throat, folding his hands behind his back to hide the letter. His eyes darkening, lips tightly pressed together with displeasure. 'William, gather my most recent files for Kat to study.'

'One minute.' The boy spun on his heel and began to rummage through the nearest shelves.

'I'm certain you're anxious to catch up on the most recent breaches,' Emrys continued speaking to me, something strange about his voice. Distant and cold, remembering what part he was supposed to play.

Breaches. What they called surges in dark magic that came from the earth, caused by the misuse of magic, or so the Council claimed. I found things not to be as simple as that when it came to dark magic, especially the kind that could break the earth's natural seal and disturb what ancient Kysillian Kings had buried.

'I've been summoned to Merton Valley,' Emrys announced, his face an unreadable mask.

'In the north? It must be a mistake.' William frowned, continuing to grab papers and files from the mess of the study shelves, knowing instinctively what was valuable, and stacking them on the side.

'It will be. That's why I'll leave Miss Woodrow in your care, William.' He nodded, making the boy flush as he ran his hands over his apron and darted between the

TALES OF A MONSTROUS HEART

bookshelves, continuing his search for the papers Emrys had requested.

The lord turned to excuse himself but those dark eyes drifted to see the items littered across my desk. Stopping him.

'That's Hale's copy.' He reached out cautiously to turn *The Myth of Shadow* around, as if moving it could cause damage. He turned to the first page in curiosity. 'I never thought the old fool would let anyone touch it.'

'I think he probably wanted me to strengthen my studies.' I pushed my hair back from my face as it slowly slipped free from my poor excuse of a braid. 'I was hassling him about it before—'

Before I ruined everything. Only as I looked back to Emrys, he was considering me thoughtfully. Those pale grey eyes with that same curiosity made a foolish thought enter my head. That perhaps I hadn't ruined anything at all.

Maybe fate had just finally played into my hands.

'I've been hassling him about it for a decade.' His head inclined to one side in consideration, revealing the strong line of his throat.

A strange nervousness moved through me at the ease of talking to him. Then I decided to be a little braver.

'Perhaps if I can see your notes on Ren Cardia Theory, you can borrow it,' I challenged, sliding the large book carefully out of his reach, never breaking his gaze.

His dark eyes shifted to where William was swearing at a tome that seemed determined to fall apart as he tried to move it from its dusty shelf. Then his focus came solely back to me, as intense as a caress, a small uneven smile on his lips.

'How did you work that one out, Croinn?' he asked quietly.

'William said something about Pervanthus herb. Ren Cardia was the only one who connected it to dark summonings and Insidious sickness.' I shrugged.

'I'm beginning to worry I'll have nothing left to teach you, Miss Woodrow,' he cautioned wryly, the ghost of a smile still there as he rubbed the back of his neck.

'I'm certain a man of your expertise will find something.' A challenge lay in my words I hadn't anticipated as I returned his smile, feeling the intensity of his focus brush against my skin, as if I stood too close to a fire.

'I was . . .' I began, raising my hand again to brush the loose hair from my face, only for a different tension to ripple in the air between us. The mirth in his eyes replaced with a darker grey like a storm blowing in.

His attention was fixed on my forearm and his jaw tightened with displeasure. Then I saw it. The nasty fading bruise from where I'd fallen in the ruins. His annoyance was a clear reminder of just how much of a liability I was.

'The consequences of dabbling with a gobrite.' I flushed, quickly rolling down my sleeves.

'The healer wasn't summoned?' The words were cold and flat.

I blinked in surprise at his tone. 'Nobody asked.'

Frowning at the ridiculous notion that the Council would care about anything that happened to me or waste coin on a healer. 'I have a balm for bruising. I just need to remember to put it on.'

'Got them!' William exclaimed, making me jump and turn to see him stumbling between the books and boxes littering the study, arms full of ledgers. 'I left them in one of the storage boxes on the back shelves.'

'Thank you, William.' Emrys's voice was gruffer than before as he strode purposefully towards the door, hand flexing at his side as if with discomfort, leaving me with nothing but confusion at the sudden change in his mood.

Thankfully, William offered a distraction as he struggled with the large stack of ledgers.

'Here.' I rushed over, taking the leaning top half of the pile as we both distributed the work on my desk.

'These are the most recent.' He sighed, palms flat on top of the mess before he blew an errant red curl off his forehead. 'Tea?'

'Yes, please, William.' With how much reading there was to do, I knew I'd be needing it. Even if my time here would be spent reading and drinking tea, I suppose there were worse fates to endure.

'At least you'll have company.' He grinned, confusing me until I heard a caterwauling of complaints. The feline form of Alma made her way across the room to jump up on the desk and consider it with suspicion, pawing at the mess of dry wax stuck to the priceless mahogany top.

'Well rested?' I asked, watching her ears flatten and a low purr leave her as she stretched out her one ginger leg. 'I should have left you some notes and pages to read.' If Alma hated anything more than my foolishness, it was my relentless tutoring.

'You're teaching her?' William asked, genuinely curious.

'I want her to have the same education as me before we leave the Institute.'

'Most wouldn't,' he reasoned softly, troubled by the fact.

No, they wouldn't. Fey in service weren't provided with education. Most had no option but to enter into an indenture or try and survive on the streets.

'Well, as you know, I'm not like most beings.' I smiled.

'No. I don't think I've ever met anyone willing to wander the Blackthorn alone.' William practically shuddered.

'How did you know?'

He gave me an apologetic glance. 'You look like you tumbled through it backwards.'

I couldn't help but laugh at my own stupidity and clear dishevelment.

'I was collecting samples and updating my notes. It's been a long time since I could wander in a wood like that.' I made an attempt to smooth my hair only to find an errant leaf tangled in it. 'Then I came across a valek nest that took up most of my attention.'

'Valek?' He asked.

'Yes, fascinating creatures, they hold so many secrets about healing.' They had immense healing properties, but many people had hunted them for sport, lowering the numbers and limiting their power.

'They're hideous and greedy.' He frowned, rubbing the back of his neck. 'They've ruined two of my cabbage patches.'

'Perhaps, but they're one of our last links to the ancient time and the magic we once used.' When it was in abundance. Before mortals saw fit to take charge of it and regulate the beings who should possess it freely.

'Here.' I pulled my collection jar from my small pouch and held it out to him. The reflectiveness of the scales catching the afternoon light perfectly to show rainbow hues when twisted in a certain direction. 'Their scales continue to glow even days after they shed. Theorists believe that all the cures for the ailments that plague us were gifted from the earth the same time magic was. We just have to find them.'

'You make it sound exciting.'

'Does Lord Blackthorn not?' I asked cautiously, placing the sample on the desk and stroking Alma as she fussed with my papers.

'I fear Emrys finds little excitement in anything these days,' he explained carefully. 'However, he is glad of your arrival.

He was telling me all about your Insidious charm. He said he hasn't seen one so potent since the wars.'

I wondered if we were talking about the same Lord Blackthorn.

'My own studies have got away from me since we've ventured into the older texts.' He let out a deep sigh of frustration. 'I don't know quite how to read them.'

'If you need any help, let me know,' I offered. The old texts were my favourite, despite their dense and unforgiving tone.

'Really?'

'I assume if you're Blackthorn's assistant, that means you can assist me too,' I reasoned with a smile. 'Unless of course he comes to his senses.'

He let out a small laugh and shook his head. 'Thank you, Kat. I'll bring you a few problems to keep things interesting, don't you worry.'

With that he gave another grin and rushed off, leaving me to consider the mess on the table before me.

'I hope he does; it will be a welcome change to dealing with my own.' I sighed, Alma's tale swishing in annoyance the only sign of her agreement.

Chapter Ten

The chaos of duality. Sacred fire of the heavens and demonic fire of the depths. Burning eternal. Unwavering and pure. Unable to be smothered or unmade by the other. Both occupying sides of fate's twisted coin. A summoning beyond magic itself. Too ancient to be given creed or command.

– Insidious Theory. Myths of the Deep, *1145*

The rumours of Emrys Blackthorn being a madman might have been justified. I'd never seen anyone work with such intensity, which was evident in his notes. Half of them didn't even make sense, comprising mostly symbols and fey shorthand he hadn't bothered to translate.

No wonder the man hadn't been seen much in the Council chambers. I doubted he'd had time. He'd travelled Elysior numerous times this year alone, to each corner and back again. I was exhausted just considering the different locations mentioned in his notes.

His passion was easy to understand on paper; numerous evidence bundles showed his attempts to defend fey accused of wild magic breaches or dark summonings in the midlands. He'd stopped seven fey cleansings this year alone. His facts and writings were just as unforgiving as his temperament.

It was no wonder William ran everywhere; being close to Blackthorn was like how I imagined the eye of a storm would be – one wrong step and he could easily drag you off course.

How a brilliant being such as Blackthorn had ended up in service to the Council worried me, as well as the fact he'd been a king's mage, just as his father had been. Servants to a madman. Then again, Master Hale had also been in service to the same king.

I'd forgiven Hale without thought, perhaps childishly, the moment he'd promised to keep Alma safe. However, one good act didn't eradicate a lifetime of wrongs.

My gaze drifted to where Alma lay curled up on top of a small stack of books I hadn't got to yet. The ones I had managed to study were a mixture of dark-magic-caused illnesses that had gone untreated, violent malevolent spirit attacks or simple demonic torment caused by lesser fiends. The number, frequency and recentness of them worried me, considering the Council's current denial that Verr and dark magic were even a threat. No, in the Council's eyes, it was the fey who hungered for power and wished to undermine authority.

The darkness of the crimes reminded me of stories my father had told, tales of the Old Gods and the Alder Kings, rulers of the endless dark. Ancient demons with no form. Nightmarish tales I should give little credence to, but again I was pulled back to my own history. When Kysillian Kings had ruled Elysior and the fey here, their greatest enemy were Verr, dark beings that wielded the darkest of magic and fed off the earth, giving fey no choice but to go to war and force such creatures deep beneath the earth. Over time Verr lost mortal form, becoming the dark magic they once wielded. Dark, demonic beasts made of smoke and curses that seeped from the earth.

The Kysillian Kings used their fire to heal the earth, molten-enchanted metal burning seals into the ground, making it impossible for such darkness to ever escape again.

But if a being indulged too fervently in dark magic, if they summoned too strongly, it could cause a weakness in the earth and such forsaken power could surge forth. Creatures created from such a summoning would corrupt the land, causing sickness and disease. Other dark beasts grew from the lack of earth magic left to defend the world and went hunting for flesh to eat.

The victims in Emrys's files were all fey, the descriptions of their deaths brutal and relentless. It seemed the Verr beneath the earth still sought revenge, despite the Kysillian Kings who trapped them being nothing more than myth now.

A loud crash of glass breaking and a wail of alarm from beyond the study doors sent me to my feet. Alma jumped awake, skittering off the desk and scattering papers across the floor.

I rushed in the direction of the noise and into the hallway, seeing it had shifted once more, light spilling across the tiled floor as a maze of halls lay before me. In the mouth of one archway carved with dragons doing battle, trying to juggle books and jars under his arms with glass shattered at his feet, was William.

'William?' I asked, his bright hair in disarray, half of it tangled around his horns as he glanced up with flushed cheeks.

'I'm sorry, I wasn't looking where I was going.' He shook his head, gathering up the mess of glass with a simple enchantment, reforming the jar easily and adding it carefully to the stack in his arms.

'Here. Let me help.' I crossed the hall and took the most precariously stacked jars from him with an easy smile.

'Is that a mouse?' he asked, at the same moment I felt a small pressure on my shoulder.

I turned my head and there, perched on my shoulder, rubbing its ear with a small paw, was indeed a mouse, one with familiar green eyes.

'Alma.' I sighed, knowing I should be relieved she was changing once more, even if it wasn't into the right being.

'Can she transfigure any smaller?' asked William, watching her with the same fascinated concern I was.

'Don't tempt her. I think she's beyond the usual rules of transfiguration,' I admitted, worried by the concept. Another reason why it was so hard to find tonics that repressed her changes. When I found one that worked, her magic found a way around it.

I just hoped she didn't change into something so small I couldn't find her.

'I just need them in the workshop.' He nodded in the direction of the open doorway, where sunlight poured in. I followed, Alma perched on my shoulder and clearly sharing in my curiosity as we entered a large space. The warmth of the air was the first thing that hit me. Then came the pungent scent of soil, the sweetness of enchanted flowers and the fragrance of so many plants. It was overwhelming.

The ceiling was stained glass, geometric shapes that drenched the room in multicoloured light. Rows and rows of plant boxes, some housing small forests that almost reached the glass ceiling, others barely shoots emerging from the dirt. A rusty watering can levitated over the boxes, showering whatever plant it deemed in need.

This wasn't an ordinary greenhouse. The energy in the air was too potent, and my own magic flared with curiosity, heating the tips of my fingers as I ran them over the soil, feeling it practically vibrate with magic.

Taeformery. The art of earth magic, a far more refined form than the earth spells written about in Council books. Most earth-born fey possessed some power over that element, but I'd never seen something like this.

'Earth manipulation.' The words fell from my lips in a mixture of amazement and confusion.

'Not the most impressive of talents.' William shrugged, running a hand through his hair to try and smooth it.

'It depends how you use it,' I corrected, never having seen a spellcasting chamber like this. Every plant in here created by a summoning, grown with spells and given life by his patience.

'Emrys said these study chambers belonged to his mother. Nothing was alive when I arrived.' William grinned, stuffing his hands into his muddy apron pocket.

'She studied Taeformery?' I asked. Witches didn't usually waste their time on earth magic – the earth could do us little damage after all. They were more interested in tempting the dark to increase their own hold on magic than growing items to assist in spells and healing.

'No. She mostly studied the poisons from rare plants,' he admitted with a worried smile, clearly not knowing all the facts about Emrys's mother either.

I returned my attention to the boxes, considering the wealth of greenery each contained. Magic that would have been punished outside these walls, fey secrets Emrys had protected.

I rubbed the leaves of a longmore plant, lifting it to my nose to smell the bitter scent. Unable to stop my mind from wandering back to William's words. Earth manipulation wasn't revered as much as it should be.

Emrys had seen worth in William's gift, one others would have dismissed. There were plants here that some would argue should be extinct and, amongst the oddities, the ash-coloured leaves of a plant I had only seen once.

'Is that thaddeus root?' I asked. 'It's supposed to be extinct.'

'Yes,' William said with a grin. 'Emrys asked me to grow it.' William grinned.

I'd seen it around Master Hale's office. One seed was able to detect poison in any liquid by turning it black. Master Hale was always secretive about where he acquired it – just on one of his travels, he'd said. It was a plant I'd tried to find myself and failed, because it had died out long ago. And yet here it was.

Had Emrys had William grow it for him?

'Why?' I pressed gently.

'Like most things involving Emrys, it's a mystery. I was just happy to be able to study it,' he carried on, clearly not sensing my suspicion. More worries I didn't need.

I sighed, realising I should get back to my own studies. If only the pile of papers he'd given me were as easy to understand as the plant.

Seeming to sense my exhaustion, William pushed himself up to perch on the edge of the workbench. 'What cases are bothering you the most?'

'The recent killings in the village of Fremby,' I told him. Not the most pleasant of reading material, but I needed to accept the cruelty of this world if I was to stand any chance of understanding it.

He nodded. 'It was awful. Most were all killed in the same manner.'

The sketches of each victim had been highly detailed. A dark fiend had terrorised most of the village. The villagers had believed it was a thief slitting throats and robbing what little coin they could find.

All the victims had a laceration to the throat, no defensive wounds and were all found to have been robbed. A dark fiend that fed on blood and liked to collect shiny objects. Dismissed by the Council as mortal evil.

'What caused the surge in dark activity?' I asked. The cause hadn't been mentioned in the paper. Just the suffering of those who didn't make it.

'A businessman was trying to mine close by, digging too deeply into cursed earth. The rock in that part of Elysior contains various gems. His greed was easy enough for what-ever dark energy remained to feed off.'

Women and children. Innocent beings murdered for nothing but greed – one of the callings of the dark. Its magic was easy to learn . . . even easier to lose control of.

'My mother use to tell me about the danger of the occult and stories of the Verr. I never truly believed such things were possible.' William spoke softly as he ran his fingers through the soil, breaking up the clumps.

'Where is she now?' My curiosity was probably rude, but I wanted to know more about him. How he ended up here under Blackthorn's care.

'Dead . . .'

'I'm sorry.' It seemed all our stories were too familiar, especially after the wars. I didn't want that grief for William, or for any of us, and yet it always found us in the end.

He shrugged, rubbing his hands together as crumbs of dirt dropped to the tiled floor. 'It was a long time ago.'

'How did you meet Emrys?' Perhaps I should have kept my questions to myself, but I felt an ease speaking to another fey, finally unwatched.

'My father tried to sell me on the east roads to one of the pleasure markets, deeming me queer enough to get a profit,' he continued in a horrifyingly conversational tone. 'I was six then.'

My magic surged at the mere mention of those roads, my hands clutching the stool beneath me, wood creaking in my grip. Alma rushed down my arm to slip into my dress pocket.

The east roads were a prolific slave route, where most menageries' victims were recruited, and lords got cheap servants. The same roads I assumed Alma had been sold on, and where I would have been too if Master Hale hadn't taken me in.

'Emrys happened to be working a case in town when I escaped,' he continued, unaware of my internal struggle, or just how closely linked we could all be. 'He was about to leave. I still don't know what made him stop.' There was a sad amusement in his smile, a distance in his gaze as I watched him relive it.

'I'm sorry, William.' I was – sorrier than he could ever know, that any of it had happened at all.

'I've never given much credence to the notion of fate or ancestral guidance, but I can't deny someone was looking out for me that day.' He smiled weakly, pulling in a deep breath before pushing away from the table. 'I should go and start on dinner.'

There was a loneliness about this boy. One that made me instantly annoyed with Emrys for leaving him behind, but also grateful to him for taking him in and protecting him from the cruelty of the world.

'I can help.' I reached into my bag, rummaging until I was elbow deep in my things before pulling out a small notepad filled with a few pages of recipes my father had taught me. 'We can work on one of these together.' I held out the offering to him, suddenly anxious he wouldn't want such a troublesome friend as me.

'Are you sure?' He frowned but didn't hide the excitement in his eyes. 'I thought you'd want to get to the Institute to check over the records?'

The key Master Hale had given me felt like a dead weight where it still rested in my pocket. That strange unease from I'd felt the last time I'd been in the hallway slipped over my skin before I shook it away.

'I need some time away from occult papers, and it's been a very long time since I was in a kitchen,' I said by way of explanation. 'Maybe tomorrow is the day for the Institute.'

Coward. The word came hissed into the back of my mind and for once I couldn't shake it away.

'If the house wants to let you go,' William warned playfully. 'It has a habit of messing up plans.'

I had noticed, hearing the constant creaking groans of the wood, almost passing comment.

'Let's get Alma some cheese,' he offered cheerily, making her appear from my pocket with a squeak and scurry up my arm.

'Emrys taught me how to make bread, but everything else is a mystery to me,' William continued with a grin, extending his arm to guide me to the kitchen.

114

Chapter Eleven

Madman, elusive lord or the cursed offspring of a witch? I told myself I didn't care as I sank lower into the hot bath, relishing the feeling of stretching my legs and dipping beneath the water into the peaceful silence beneath. The small metal tub in my room at the Institute was by now a distant memory. The discomfort for myself and Alma as we had to share the shallow water. Too tired by the end of the tedious days to lug more up the narrow stairs.

The memory of the confining cruelty of the place made me linger beneath the surface of the water. Hoping to drown away the shame and anger of it all.

However, no matter how much I wished it, I couldn't dwell in the bath all morning. If I hadn't worked that out myself, Alma's squeaking from the chair in the corner told me as much.

Begrudgingly, I pulled myself from the warm water and set about the gruelling task of getting dressed without help once again.

Despite William's endless conversation and reassurances in the kitchen as he made dinner, I couldn't shake the feeling of unease that had followed me like a dark shadow into the next few days. My inability to study my own papers, the dark events still taking place in this world and the fey that seemed to suffer the most from it.

Alma was still a mouse, more unable to communicate with me than before. Emrys hadn't returned, and I began to worry he never would. I should have been relishing the calm, but it appeared I wasn't made for the quiet as I found myself dressed, damp hair tied back into a sensible bun as I approached the west wing portal, which William had shown me during a house tour when we both grew bored after dinner.

However, on my journey to find it, the rug beneath me suddenly curled up of its own volition, making me skid into the sideboard.

I waited to hear the rattle of drawers or creak of the wood panelling echoing with the house's dark amusement, but nothing followed. I put the incident down to my own foolishness, despite my unease that *maybe* the house was trying to stop me. With accusations of my madness already rampant, the last thing I needed was to be talking to houses.

I found the door I needed. Reluctantly and with an unsteady hand, I slid the instruction paper I'd written into the slot, listening to the creaking groan of the cogs turning. A soft glow emitted from the edges of the door as I opened it and stepped through into one of the Institute's opulent greeting halls.

Apprehension rolled through me as I saw the stone archways inscribed with ancient runes leading in various directions and depictions of ancient beasts carved around their bases. The eternal lanterns omitting sharp white light, making the gold they were cast in glow.

It had been mere days and yet the place suddenly seemed foreign, too big as every tiny sound echoed back to me.

Fighting the childish urge to go to Master Hale's office, I accepted the bitter realisation that he couldn't help me anymore. I was on my own.

I took the endless west corridor that led to the Grand Library, ignoring the childish thrill that shot through me as I saw the ornate door.

I pulled the key from my pocket, slipping it into the lock. It turned of its own accord, a cracking of the mechanism as the door flung itself open, leaving the key in my palm.

Before me stood the grandeur of the library. White marble floors polished to a high gleam so the early morning light that poured down from the stained-glass ceilings bounced around the room, making multicoloured flecks of light dance. Rich, dark wood bookcases and tables filled the space. The golden inscriptions on each book glistened as if freshly labelled.

A large greeting desk sat in the centre that I approached cautiously. The echo of my footsteps too loud.

'Can I help you?' came the brittle voice from behind the desk, and the librarian looked up over her spectacles. She had a thin, disapproving face and her mousy hair harshly pulled back into a bun.

'Can you point me in the direction of magical ailments and earth diseases?' I asked politely.

'Southern section, two floors down. Keep right.' She scowled at me – at my ears specifically – before ducking back behind the desk.

'Thank you,' I murmured to no further response, moving cautiously deeper into the cavernous library.

I wished Alma was here to see it with me, despite knowing they'd never let her. The loneliness inside of me returned, eating ravenously at my heart.

I found the section just as spacious and empty as all the others. Where I'd anticipated the endless chatter of mages working and the excitement of new spells being formed, there was nothing. Just silence and a dreadful draught.

It wasn't what I imagined it to be. Everything too clean, nothing but the strong citrus scent of polish to greet me. No chaos trapped in compendium pages, no dust sprites or wayward spells. They had killed it all.

The key in my grasp became a dead weight.

I didn't belong here. Not in their sterilised version of the world.

I longed for the damp of the ruins and the dust of the Fifth Library. Worst of all, I wanted the comfortable disorder of the Blackthorn study – William's cheery interruptions and Alma's presence.

Annoyed, I began to rummage through what little books they held on fey illness, seeing barely any records of use to me.

I needed to extract the magic from the valek scales I'd collected before it dried out. Only there were no books on the art of extraction for healing here.

I pulled a few new and recently printed volumes from the shelves, the pages sliding easily past one another as I flicked through the depictions. A bland and sterilised take, written more as a cautionary tale than with the purpose of giving any advice on how to help. It put most fey illness down to poverty, lack of intelligence and heathen practices.

I pushed the book aside, going for another, but finding little change. Not even a simple remedy to cure a rushing cough or goblin rash. Nothing. Like they didn't exist at all. I found only charms to help with mortal ailments, or cures for common diseases from which most healing houses in the south made great profit.

I turned my attention to the volumes on curses instead, looking for any with ground sickness that could be quoted. Quickly copying down the sections of any use, I found myself uncomfortable in the silence. No crackling hearth or murmur of voices. Not the creak of old wood or the whispering of wind through an open window. Just the endless silence, and how it seemed to swallow me whole. My thoughts too loud in my head in the hollow space.

I grabbed my notes, shoving them into my bag, and made my way back to the portal, annoyed I'd allowed myself to be fooled into thinking that an Institute library would solve any of my problems, or that it would be so vastly different to the men who ran it.

Early-morning light streamed through the Blackthorn library, dust dancing in the beams as I weaved my way through the shelves to the back section where William had indicated the books I'd find most interesting were kept. Finding myself in a small open space, wooden beams high above, curving up to a turret of a ceiling. Gargoyles made of black stone leering down as cobwebs hung from their claws.

A worn green velvet chair sat beneath a grand window, cushions welcomingly sunken with years of use. Remains of candles burned down to stubs were scattered across the window ledge, and water rings stained the wood from various cups over the years – evidence that this was once someone's favourite retreat.

I pulled off my jacket and tossed it onto the chair, taking the papers and few notes I'd managed to make and scattering them across the nearest table.

I found a few volumes on species magic on the back shelves of Emrys's collection, dumping them on the table and flicking through the pages. I knew that mages had once extracted magic from a secmor beast's scale, and I focused on journals and compendiums that mentioned the creature, looking for any sign of how they had managed it.

I had the fourth book spread open, finger running down the convoluted text before I stumbled upon another dead end. None of the tomes spoke of extracting magic from a fresh scale or a shed one. Only fossils or dried flecks.

Blowing strands of hair from my face with a frustrated breath, I turned from the table, stretching my hands over my head to relieve some of the pain at the base of my spine from stooping too long. I took the valek scale sample from my pocket, letting it rattle around the tiny glass vial. If I couldn't extract the healing potential, there was nowhere left to go with my theory.

An odd, croaked squeak came from behind me. The cupboard of the sideboard across from me rattling its drawers almost in warning.

I turned and there, gnawing at the corner of another price-less volume, was a miniature secmor beast, its bright green scales shining in the candlelight, ink smudges all over it from the book it had crawled out of.

My eyes darted to the open book in question, seeing the large gap where the illustration had been and the mess of ink now marring the page from its escape.

'Bollocks,' I whispered before lunging to try and catch the thing between my palms like a stray butterfly.

Only butterflies didn't have teeth.

It nipped my finger, drawing a curse from my lips as it slapped its tiny leathery-paper wings and took off.

'Stop!' I snapped, watching it zoom over the top of the book-case and through the library. First dust sprites and now miniature beasts from books I'd left unattended. It wove easily through the shelves with frightening speed. Clearly not its first escape.

'Bloody little bastard!' I seethed, rushing around another corner, only for an annoyed pair of crystalline eyes to be waiting for me.

Emrys. Sat at one of the library tables, clearly in the middle of working on something judging by the mess before him. His hair was in disarray as if he hadn't slept, with a dark brow raised in expectation of an explanation.

'Good afternoon to you too, Croinn,' he said dryly.

I skidded to a halt, heart jumping into my throat. His jacket and vest were missing, and his shirt sleeves were rolled up to show his forearms. His scars catching the light as they curved around the muscle. Wrapped around his right forearm was a badly tied, clean bandage.

My lips parted as I fumbled for a lie, only for a tiny growl to stop me.

There, perched on his shoulder was the secmor, almost mocking me with the swishing of its tiny spiked tail.

'I see you've found the 1664 *Compendium of Lost Beasts*,' he observed, reaching for the creature on his shoulder.

'Be careful, it—' I didn't get a chance to finish my sentence before the little beast had jumped into Emrys's palm with the familiarity of a childhood pet.

The bookcase next to the table he sat at creaked, and then spat a book out. It skidded across the table, flipping open of its own accord to the page the beast had escaped from. With a growl of disappointment, the beast slipped back into the book, becoming nothing more than a picture before Emrys closed it, sliding it aside, and contemplating me once more.

'I was looking for an extraction charm for valek scales,' I offered weakly, still eyeing the book cautiously. 'The method I used on the dried variety isn't working the same.'

He nodded absently, pushing back his chair, getting to his feet and moving to the shelves across the room, his fingers barely brushing the spines as a maroon book shot out to greet him. He caught it effortlessly, despite its weighty appearance, and held it out to me.

'Section five,' he instructed as I hurried to take the offering, still trying to catch my breath.

He slipped his hands into his pockets, waiting patiently, which only made my movements clumsier. I turned the book over to see its label, but it didn't have one. I opened it, scanning for section five, only for the title to confuse me further.

'This is for blood extraction from mythical beasts,' I pursed my lips, holding the book so he could see too, but he was still watching me, almost cautiously.

'If the magic in the scale is fresh enough, it will work the same.'

'I didn't see magical healing remedies being one of your specialties.' I frowned.

'It isn't. However, when you grow up with two healers, things rub off.' He held out his hand. 'Let me see your sample.'

I handed over the valek scale in question from the vial in my pocket.

His lips moved soundlessly, fingers radiating a sharp white light for a mere moment. The scale in the glass folded in on itself as if consumed by an invisible flame and left behind the liquid I needed.

'I assume you have another to try?' He offered me the new sample carefully. I stuffed it in my pocket and rooted for another. Following the words on the page, I repeated them in my mind.

I didn't need to move my lips, letting the words whisper through my mind, feeling my magic coil and burn as it wrapped itself around my fingers, soft blue flames devouring the glass before slipping back beneath my skin as my scale turned into the same liquid as Emrys's.

A small nod was the only evidence of his approval.

'How did you find the Grand Library?' he asked as he moved back to his table.

'They didn't have the records I needed. I was looking for extraction reports, or even pox records for the villages in the districts, but they didn't seem to have any on fey illnesses.' I still considered my new extract sample, the radiance of the liquid and all the help it could do.

'The local fey district leaders would have ledgers.'

'The Council won't accept information that hasn't been sealed by a registrar of the order. None of them are going to validate evidence for a pox study.' Especially since fey illnesses didn't impact mortals.

'I'm certain one in the west owes me a debt,' he said, surprising me. He slid a piece of paper across the table towards me. Resting on top of it was a tiny vial that looked filled with dirt. 'What do you know about an endless rotting curse?' He leant back against the table's edge and picked up a glass of amber liquid that had been discarded amongst his books and notes.

'It's a bit early for drinking, isn't it?' I observed carefully, watching how the morning light played off the liquid in the glass.

'As my brother Gideon remarked, it's always noon somewhere.' He considered me over its rim.

Gideon. The name startled me and I couldn't help but frown. Knowing from records that the previous Lord Blackthorn only had two children. One son. One daughter.

Troubled, I shut the book in my hands and focused on the new mystery he'd presented me with.

'It's formed of residual darkness,' I answered, turning the vial over and seeing it wasn't dirt but a clipping of root speckled with rot that curled against the opening of the vial, trying to find a way out. 'Corrupted earth that's seen dark activity. Or, if the stories are to be believed, where a Verr summoning has been attempted.'

But those were stories from long before the war. Long before a cruel and greedy king had condemned us all. This sample seemed too fresh, too alive, but that couldn't be.

'Is this from an archive collection?' I looked to him again, only for the bandage on his arm to catch my eye once more.

'An orteritus gremlin got the better of me.' He answered the question I was too much of a coward to ask.

I frowned, wondering how he was still coherent.

'They're poisonous.' A bite from an orteritus being could send you into madness.

He smiled sharply, but there was something dark in it that had little to do with amusement. 'It'll take something stronger than a gremlin to take the likes of me down.'

I looked down at the sample in the jar, seeing how it curled and split. The infection of the dark was so strong.

Wrong. This was wrong. Impossible, even.

'Do you think—'

The ringing of a distant bell silenced me. Less severe than the ones in the Institute but still causing a tension to come over Emrys.

A curse slipped from his lips as he downed the rest of his drink and let the glass clatter onto the table. Then he tugged his jacket from the back of the chair. 'If you'll excuse me, Croinn.'

Chapter Twelve

The bell was a summons. A Council summons, which made Emrys's irritated cursing make more sense. However, I couldn't chase away the dread of what they had to say. If it would be something else about me.

Maybe that old crone had reported my time in the library to the Council. I wouldn't put it past them to plant some ghastly deed on me. That I'd singed an ancient spell book or a misbehaving ink charm had ruined a priceless tapestry.

Unfortunately, all of the above were valid previous offences on my record. Unease coiled more tightly in my gut.

A squeak came from the table before me, snapping my attention back to the current problem at hand. Alma. Somehow sensing the thoughts that plagued me, despite still being in mouse form.

'How about another attempt at serpentine focus?' I sighed, turning over the pages of notes, flicking through to try and find the section I'd written on the process, despite it making no sense to me. But it might to Alma. It was her magic after all.

An annoyed squeak was the only response to my question, making me glance up. If her small mouse limbs were long enough, I believed she'd cross them in annoyance.

I couldn't blame her; I'd recounted a madman's notes on transfiguration to her for the past few hours. William, helpful as ever, supplying the few books Emrys held on the subject, but even he had given up hope and gone back to his own tasks.

'We have to keep trying.' I pushed stray strands of my hair behind my ears, my poor attempt at a dignified hairstyle having fallen out hours ago. Alma's small nose twitched as she rubbed her paws together, either in frustration or trying something else.

'Still nothing?' I turned towards the sound of William's cheery voice from the study entrance, where he wiped his hands on a small towel tinged green from his grass studies.

'It doesn't help most of the surviving instructions were written by a lunatic.' I sank back in my chair, rubbing my temples against the threatening headache dwelling there.

'You'll figure it out.'

'I wouldn't be so certain.' I huffed, eyes reluctantly drifting towards the shelves and my last encounter with Emrys. His helpfulness. All it did was unsettle me, so I turned my focus to the other side of the room and the mysterious third desk that resided there, the items on it dusty and untouched, waiting for its owner to return.

'William, who does that desk belong to?'

The question was met with silence, making me turn to see if he was still there. Only to find William indeed there, a deep sadness on his normally cheery face as if suddenly struck by grief. He shook his head, a small unconvincing smile slipping back onto his face.

'It was Healer Swift's.'

'Master Healer Gideon Swift?' I pressed gently through my confusion. Emrys had said the name Gideon but I hadn't put it together.

'He was raised by the Blackthorns.' William made quick work of tidying up the abandoned plates and cups that littered my desk – evidence of just how long I'd been lost in my work. 'Emrys considers him his brother.'

'What happened to him?' The Council's records on him had suddenly stopped after the war, the same way they had done when dealing with Emrys. Considering no new papers were released and the Council never spoke of their once renowned healer, I'd assumed he'd passed like all the others.

'He isn't dead,' he clarified. 'He and Emrys had a terrible fight and he left. Things weren't the same after that.'

'What did they fight about?' I shouldn't be asking these things and yet I couldn't stop myself.

'Emmaline.' William shrugged, a tiredness in the word, as if the name haunted them all. 'The only thing they ever fought about.'

Emmaline Blackthorn. Emrys's sister. The name I'd seen scrawled on the back of some tomes, as if marking her territory on the storybooks and legends.

'What happened to her?' I considered the desk I now sat at. Her desk. The ghosts that could still linger here.

'Nobody talks about that,' he replied quietly with such sadness it made the room suddenly cavernous, any warmth and comfort evaporating. The bookshelves seeming to sag with melancholy around us.

'I need to get back to my paper, but dinner is in the kitchen.' He nodded, gathering up the tray and moving to leave. 'Cheese too.'

Alma's small mouse nose twitched, looking at me and then William. She rubbed her ear with her paw and before I could even open my mouth, she scrambled off the desk to chase after William, who laughed as she darted past him.

'Traitor,' I muttered, flopping back in my chair. Not that I could blame her. I wasn't even enjoying my own company.

I set about trying to pass the time, but really I was waiting foolishly for the ominous form of Blackthorn to return. As if I had any hope of being bold enough to ask him all the things I wished.

'Fool.' I sighed to myself, picking up my pen and continuing with my notes.

The hours slipped away from me until I was practically squinting in the dark at the papers. My back ached from being hunched over my desk all day and, as I looked behind me, the fire flickered weakly. I didn't have the energy to stoke it again, my stomach rumbling with displeasure at my negligence.

The desk drawer rattled in question.

'I'm fine,' I muttered, pinching the bridge of my nose as I reached for my papers once more, ignoring the ache in my shoulder. I had only one more chapter to finish.

The papers were suddenly swept to the side in a false wind, piled and then pushed into the bottom drawer that shot open and closed before I could even blink.

'Oi!' I snapped, leaning down to pull on the small brass handle, the wood groaning but remaining closed. I tried again, even using my Kysillian strength but the drawer didn't budge. Its creaking sounded like distant laughter.

This bloody house.

'Fine.' I huffed with a frustrated sigh, knowing it was giving me no choice other than to accept defeat.

Reluctantly I went in search of the kitchen.

William was absent, but a pot of steaming stew and fresh rolls of bread sat on the table with a waiting stack of bowls.

I took a seat and dug in, wondering where indeed William had run off to as I contemplated the hearth. I should have checked his workroom before coming down here.

As if a single thought could have summoned him, someone sat on the bench opposite me. I turned, almost dropping my spoon as the dark figure of Blackthorn sat there. Not even looking at me as he reached for one of the rolls of bread, tearing it efficiently and digging in.

I almost choked on my stew. I hadn't seen him take a meal in the kitchen before.

It was only then I noticed the disarray of him. The collar of his shirt torn, his jacket creased and covered in a strange grey soot.

Somehow acutely aware of my attention on his bowed head, those dark eyes lifted, meeting my curious gaze.

'William said you'd been called away.' I frowned, wondering what on earth the Council could be up to for him to be in such a state.

'There was a ghoul running rampant in the students' quarters.' He bit into his bread with mild annoyance.

My mouth went dry.

Ancestors above.

The ghoul.

As if hearing the treacherous pounding of my heart, he paused his eating and considered me sharply. I quickly returned my attention to my stew, blinking at it like an idiot, trying to think of anything to say to detract from the subject. Internally scolding myself for being so bloody stupid.

'You don't seem surprised,' he observed, a cold calculation in those sharp eyes as he spooned stew from the pot between us into his bowl.

'I am,' I half stuttered, trying to swallow despite my dry throat. 'How terrible.'

I quickly spooned the too-hot stew into my mouth to take away any other chance of speaking.

A ghoul was a vicious foe, no wonder he was in such disarray. Apprehension made every swallow tedious but thankfully my bowl was empty soon enough and I could retreat to the sink.

Muttering something about William needing help – despite the boy's absence – I instantly busied myself with the dishes, batting away the enchanted dishcloth that tried to do the job for me, trapping it under a stack of plates and focusing intently on scrubbing a stain off an old pan to try and quell my rapid pulse.

I tried to think through any possibility the ghoul could be traced back to me. I hadn't summoned it, but, I didn't know if ghouls were protected under the Imprisoning Act. Maybe locking it beneath my bed wasn't the most humane idea, even if it was a cursed entity.

I was rummaging in the sink for another plate, pulling it out when a hand closed around my own. Scarred fingers with that soft cold bite of magic.

My head darted up, almost catching his chin with how close he was.

'What were you doing with a ghoul, Kat?' he asked softly, as if we were sharing secrets.

So close, and with him touching me so casually, I had no room for conspiring with a lie. Wondering if his fingers pressed against my wrist so carefully to test my pulse.

'It slipped into my bag from the ruins,' I half whispered conspiratorially, like it had just happened and I needed an accomplice to cover my tracks.

'When?' His brow furrowed, leaning closer until there was nothing but that bloody alluring scent of beasam bark that did little to calm me.

'A . . . a few months ago.'

He closed his eyes, seeming to struggle to pull in breath. As if he might combust. They opened again, no longer grey but black. As dark and endless as the night. 'Do I even want to know how you contained it?'

'In an old sweet tin under my bed.' I winced. 'I was going to put it back.'

His face was blank, a stony quality to it I didn't understand and I worried I'd somehow broken him.

'I forgot,' I added gently, hoping he believed me. That I didn't intend to put the Institute at risk. That it wasn't some crazed retaliation.

'You forgot,' he repeated, that dark annoyance not abating, and I wondered if he was reconsidering the whole bloody partnership.

I bit my lip and watched as his eyes followed the indentation my teeth made in the skin. Something changed in the warm air between us, that strange brush of his magic more prominent.

My heart pounded a little louder in my chest as an unknown sensation knotted in my stomach, as if travelling over a bump in a road.

'You're back.' William's cheery voice greeted from across the kitchen, making my face heat as I turned to see him grinning in the stairwell's doorway. He was carrying a box of muddy vegetables from his garden in his harms, but he halted as he took in Emrys's appearance, worry flickering in his warm gaze. 'You look like—'

'Thank you, William,' Emrys interrupted sharply. Clearly in no mood to be reminded just how he'd gotten in that state. How it was my fault.

The lord didn't break my gaze. A silence lingered between us as William huffed out a laugh and started prattling on about the stew and the mess Emrys had made of the stack of bread rolls.

An apology lay heavy on my tongue but I couldn't seem to speak or breathe quite steadily as Emrys considered me, those dark eyes following the curve of my mouth before he let go of my hand in the water and returned to the table.

William engaged with him instantly in a conversation about mud parasites. I couldn't focus on the words, drawn by how cold my hand suddenly felt despite the hot water. How long it took the chill to dissipate.

Fool. That mocking voice hissed again and I let the sharp barbs of it dig into some sensitive place inside of me. I *was* a fool. Ruining things all over again.

I went back to washing the dishes. Washing intently until I was certain Emrys was gone for the evening. Just like the coward I was.

I should have hidden in the bath. Faked a headache and gone to bed. There were many things I should have done, but instead I found myself walking into the study. Thankful at least that the house seemed to be on my side and took mercy on me by not making me hunt for it too long.

The cosy room was bathed in the warm light from the fire.

Emrys was at his desk, hair wet and brushed back as the cotton of his shirt clung to the broad planes of his shoulders. Surrounded by his usual clutter of books, clearly recovered from his ghoul encounter.

Sensing my nervousness or my mere presence, he looked up as I reached the edge of his desk. The stern expression I couldn't read made my heart beat a little faster, but I persevered.

'William wanted to learn some recipes.' I placed the small plate of biscuits I carried on the desk. My feeble offering of peace. 'My father liked to bake.'

Lavender and lemon biscuits, the tiny sugar crystals on top catching the orange light of the fire.

He looked at them for a long moment, as if he'd never seen one before. Then those eyes lifted to meet my own, a stormy grey of indecision. Probably between reprimanding me or simply kicking me out.

But I didn't care. A ghoul wasn't a nice foe to face and I should have been more careful with such dark things. Blackthorn had enough to burden him without worrying about me sending ghoul attacks his way.

'I'm sorry,' I confessed. 'I . . . I didn't know what to do.'

That admission felt like a weakness. How many times had I stumbled into danger with no way out, knowing I'd only be blamed if I sought help? My survival depended on perfection, and all I seemed capable of was making mistakes.

He sat back in his chair slowly, pen clattering onto his notes, leaving a large ink splodge on his papers.

'When you realise how brilliant you are, Croinn, I think we'll all be in trouble.' He sighed as he opened his desk drawer. Pulling something out, and placing it on the desk between us. Right next to my peace offering.

An old sweet tin that had seen better days, glinting in the firelight.

'Show me.' The command was soft and curious. His eyes suddenly crystalline, filled with challenge as he took a biscuit from the plate. A whoosh of relieved breath left me and a reluctant smile came to my lips as I reached for the sweet tin.

Show me.

So I did.

Chapter Thirteen

The dark calls all things back in the end. For to its master – all darkness must return. In those shadows deep beneath, it can be made anew. Awaiting its chance to rise, to reclaim what was taken. To sing the hymns of the Alder Kings. To awaken old gods and allow Verr to reign.

– Hymn to the Alder Kings – Unknown

All the next day thunder rolled in on dark clouds, forcing the fires to be lit early, and the day after, and the day after that. Emrys hadn't appeared again after my lesson on ghoul capture. My days had fallen into the same routine as before: study, helping William, then pestering Alma to change back, while secretly hoping a mysterious lord made an appearance.

Only, no matter how many times I sat to take my meals in the kitchen, he didn't appear again.

A crack of thunder broke above, as rain struck the study windows hard. Storms used to give me comfort, bundled up in the cottage with my parents. My mother telling stories and singing the ancient hymns of the fates, as my father refused to sit still, either returning rain soaked from training with his blade or filling the cottage with the warm scent of spices from his baking.

Now, storms only reminded me of being sat on a beach, the smell of smoke still in my nose as rain pounded my skin with icy strikes, waiting for someone to find me. Knowing the Council patrols would sense the magic I'd unleashed, the force of it.

A loneliness had sunk into my very bones with the icy rain that day. Remaining even now.

When you realise how brilliant you are, Croinn, I think we'll all be in trouble. Emrys's words tumbled through my thoughts more than I cared to admit. Fingers absently tracing my collarbone, feeling the warmth of my magic rush across my already flushed skin.

How effortlessly praise had fallen from his lips, especially considering how deadly my mistake had been. How it had soothed something inside me.

A different type of wound I hadn't noticed the Council inflict. Deeper than I'd ever admit.

A flash of lightning bathed the study in harsh white light before plunging me back into the dimness with the dying fire, reminding me of the late hour.

Frustrated, I stood from my desk and moved to stoke the hearth with my own magic.

I considered my hands in the warm light, the fading veins of lavender dissipating from my fingertips. Turning my ink-stained hands over to see the small, almost invisible scars, white in the firelight against my knuckles. Such brutality this world offered and yet I couldn't give up, because I wouldn't allow it all to be meaningless. I couldn't.

I was supposed to be here to study, but I couldn't stop focusing on dark things that weren't mine to solve: fey murders, the rise in dark summonings and fiend attacks. Impossible things that turned me back to my desk only to run into something cold and hard, sending me rocking backwards as I looked up into a familiar annoyed face.

Emrys.

His eyes were as black as midnight. Hair tousled, coat hanging open and shirt partially unbuttoned, revealing the pale webbing of scarring over the toned skin of his chest. There was a strong smell of damp earth and night air coming off him.

My magic flared in response to his appearance and the hearth surged, illuminating him more clearly. Then I saw his hands and shirt were smeared with dark red.

'Is that blood?' I asked, mildly horrified.

'I need your help.'

'Where?' I asked, instantly.

He took my arm and guided me back through the study, past his desk to the far other corner which was swamped in darkness. 'Your paper on septime weed poisoning. Remind me of its conclusion.' There was an urgency in the bluntness of the question and the unforgiving nature of his stride.

'How do you—' I began, almost stumbling over my feet. 'You've read it?'

An impatient glance was my answer as we made it past another set of bookcases.

'The plant grows after the death of most ground goblins or wood sprites. Their bones are toxic to the soil,' I clarified, shaking off my disbelief. 'When ingested by animals, they become afflicted, and the poison seeps into their milk or meat.'

'Resulting in a wasting sickness,' he simplified, still not looking back at me.

'Close to a normal fever, but there is a strange spotting formation, especially around the neck and wrists. The victim runs a wet fever, secreting a sweet smell from their skin, and the heart begins an odd rhythm.'

I wondered where he was taking me, knowing the room had to end at some point, only to see the bookshelves were staggered to hide a narrow passage that led into another room. This one was just as messy as the first, only instead of an opulent fire and large desks, an old door was the focal point.

Covered in chipped dark paint and a collection of locking mechanisms, it would have seemed inconspicuous to anyone else, but I recognised the incantations carved into the frame around it, the metal woven with spells as it connected to what appeared to be a collection of dials as well as an empty lantern that hung next to the doorknob. No, a crystal chamber, the design old and dangerous in its unpredictability.

'Is that a Portium door?' I whispered conspiratorially. Portium doors were forbidden due to their tendency to manifest anywhere, without the other side's permission. No papers needed. No Council authorization.

'An ancient model,' he replied, moving to the dials at the side of the contraption, reaching into a threadbare pouch that hung next to it, pulling out an array of small crystals, coloured differently for different distances.

'I thought they were destroyed?' I leaned forward to run my fingers over the ancient runes at the frame, unable to restrain my childish wonder. Feeling the strength of the magic bite against my fingertips.

It now made sense why the study moved itself. If it was connected to a Portium, that was best to be kept hidden . . . such doors brought unwanted guests.

'Are you going to tell on me, Kat?' he challenged softly.

I pulled back to consider his expression. The patience in it as shadows cut across his features.

I shook my head. No, I wasn't.

Satisfied with my answer, Emrys popped a small green crystal into the chamber at the side and turned the dial the rest of the way. The clatter of the incantation wheel was louder than the Institute's approved model. The outline of the door glowed green as Emrys inserted a key from his pocket and pushed it open, revealing a corridor beyond, the pungent odour of healing herbs greeting us as he stepped through, and I was left to follow.

The floor was tiled and the walls stark white. Various doors lined the hallway, bright light from lanterns hanging above to guide the way.

'What is this place?'

'Thornfield House, a healing house in the western fields,' he explained as we headed down the hallway.

We passed rooms with open doors revealing rows of beds illuminated by muted light. All empty.

The rooms all seemed the same, until we turned a corner, seeing more cluttered workspaces like Emrys's study, a communal dining hall and spacious sitting room. I tried to make out more details, only to collide with something solid, rocking back to see I'd walked right into Emrys's back. He'd stopped suddenly outside a worn door that had a notice pasted to the front of it.

Confinement.

He opened the door quickly and guided me inside. The room was small but warm, an overwhelming strange bitter stench filled the air, strong enough to cover the usual scent of beasam bark that followed Emrys.

A desk sat in the far corner, a small fire with a pot of water boiling, a chair draped in clothes and a small healing bed upon which lay a figure.

'Robert Thrombi, a farmhand from one of the villages surrounding Paxton Fields,' Emrys began as the door closed behind us.

'That smell!' I gasped, and moved to the other side of the bed, considering the man's faintly flushed face and the unsteady breaths that came panted through his lips.

His chest was bare, lying there in nothing but light cotton trousers. His feet were hooved, legs covered in thick, white hair that blended into flesh. Two tusks came from his dark chin.

He was a miroc, a creature between forms. They were a lesser fey who usually dwelled in the eastlands.

'That smell isn't septime weed.' I'd know it anywhere. I could detect that scent in my worst nightmares. How it had come off Alma's skin as she clawed at herself, mad with fever in Daunton. Just like all the other children.

'I dosed him with whelm weed before the fever took hold.' Emrys reached into his pocket for a small vial of white powder, holding it across the bed in offering. I took it, wondering if William had grown it for him.

Then I understood. Emrys suspected this man was a victim of dark sickness.

'You've seen this before?' I asked. The number of files he'd given me to study were vast, but I didn't see any notes on living subjects. Not like this.

'Three. I didn't get to them quick enough.' A coldness came over his expression quickly to hide his emotions. 'They didn't break the fever.'

He turned to the large chalkboard, already covered in his scrawl, in the corner of the room for answers.

'I can't work out the formulation for the healing draught. Not when the sickness is as combative as this one.'

I was alarmed at the chaos before me. He wasn't exaggerating when he said healing wasn't his specialty.

'Nothing is working,' he continued with the frustration of a man completely out of his depth, but trying none the less.

My attention returned to Mr Thrombi. The sickness was similar to septime weed poisoning, but something was missing. Something I couldn't place as I moved about the bed, tucking the vial Emrys offered me inside my apron.

The man was deathly pale, his skin holding a greyish hue as a sheen of sweat covered him. One side of him was a more alarming shade of grey than the other.

I summoned a small burst of my magic, rolling it into an orb of light in my hand, illuminating more details and confirming my suspicion about his right side.

I turned over his arms, revealing the rest of his side, seeing a strange injury just below his ribs. A webbing of purple and black marks, like veins, leading to the side of his thigh, where the darkness was contained. They paled in the light, something dwelling in there, reacting to being so close to fey magic.

I pressed the skin gently to see it fade and move upon contact, trying to get away from that light.

'I assumed it was bruising from labouring,' Emrys commented next to me.

Dark things hide right in front of us and use our foolish doubt against us. My father's words came back to me. How not all monsters take a monstrous form.

'It's a bite,' I whispered, trying to stop fear from tightening my chest at the brutality of the dark magic before me, impossible but real at the same time.

'What?' Emrys leant closer to see, but I was already reaching into my bag, rooting through my things anxiously as I kept an eye on the man's breathing.

I pulled out the hilt of my father's blade, letting it fit against my palm as it manipulated itself into a small knife.

'It's an anthrux bite,' I answered.

Anthrux were small spider-like creatures formed of dark magic. Only certain spells could result in their creation, and casting any of them was punishable by death – if you survived speaking the incantation. Dark magic like that hadn't been successfully wielded in centuries.

'He must have been working infected land, such a bite grows more deadly the longer the creature exists.' I hoped whatever ancestors I had watching me were paying attention now. 'Let's hope this one was in its infancy.'

With every drop of fey blood the creature consumed, it would only grow stronger until it was impossible to kill.

'Pass me those towels,' I instructed. Emrys turned without hesitation to gather them out of the small basket.

I pressed my blade carefully to the man's flesh. Sour-smelling black slime oozed from the wound instead of blood. Mr Thrombi still didn't move, no matter how large I made the wound or even when his blood finally ran red again over the towels Emrys pressed in place like any other healer's assistant would.

Mr Thrombi's reaction to pain shouldn't be this subdued, especially not with so much of the poison drawn from his blood. Even if he was dosed on whelm weed.

I turned to Emrys with that worry, realising just how closely we stood, the strange potency of his magic running over my skin, eyes dark and waiting.

'My mother swore by a mixture of black bark and a purification charm in the brewing to ease the symptoms.' I looked across the room to see a workbench in the corner.

He frowned. 'Black bark is poisonous.'

'More poisonous to dark beings than to fey,' I replied. We were of the same coin, after all – black bark would make us sick, but it wouldn't kill us outright.

'Is that your equipment?' I indicated to the desk in the same horrid disarray as the rest of Emrys's workspaces in the house.

I didn't wait for confirmation, making certain he had pressure on the wound before I crossed to the washing bowl. I put the knife down, the blade turning to nothing but a hilt the minute my palm left it. I sank my hands into the hot water and used the healers' soap to try and get the offending black gunk off my skin. I dried them on my apron, opening my bag to rummage for my vial case and the black bark I had. Hoping it hadn't dried out from disuse.

'Do you always walk around with poisons in your possession?' Emrys asked, considering me from across the room with both curiosity and caution.

'Croinn,' I replied by way of explanation, using his own ridiculousness against him.

From the work bench, I grabbed a jug of steaming water and a spare bowl that had been left discarded. I saw the container of marrow salt, which had been poorly labelled in Emrys's illegible hand, tipping it all into the bowl and adding the water. I grabbed a handful of bandages, turned, and offered them all to Emrys.

'You need to clean out the wound. The salt will stop it resealing for now.' Perhaps I shouldn't be giving a Lord such orders, but if he was offended, he didn't show it. He took the supplies from me and returned his attention to Mr Thrombi.

I pulled the pestle and mortar closer, tipping a few flakes of the bark into it, rummaging through my healing case for arcaz powder to stabilise the bark and fight the fever as well as draw the poison out. I added some herb water, mashing it into a slimy, lumpy paste that reeked of rotten fruit, muttering a purification charm. Then I carefully summoned my Kysillian flame so it engulfed my hand, heating the crucible until the stone glowed orange, the mixture shifting in the presence of my magic. Smooth and gleaming.

I dumped the mixture into another bowl to cool, grabbing more clean bandages before moving back to Emrys as he washed the wound. The area of infected skin was looking better already, but I could see the flesh trying to knit itself back together, trying to hide whatever poison was still left in there.

I pushed myself tightly into the space next to Emrys, our sides flush as I dunked the bandage in the mixture, coating my hands. Without instruction, Emrys made space as I packed the slimy fabric into the wound, pushing it in as far as it would go. Somehow reading my mind, he reached for the clean bandages and began the arduous task of wrapping them around the man's waist, timing it perfectly to seal it just as I moved my hands away.

I located my healing case for one of my tonic concoctions that should keep the other symptoms at bay.

Moving to the head of the bed, I used my forefinger and thumb to pinch Mr Thrombi's chin and open his mouth, placing three drops of the tonic onto his tongue as I tipped his head back, waiting with bated breath until he finally swallowed.

When he did, I sagged with relief, put the tonic aside and helped Emrys finish wrapping the wound. We worked as if drafted onto a battlefield, quick and efficient, unbothered by our tangling fingers until the bandage was neatly knotted and tucked.

'He's cooling down already,' Emrys commented, pulling the covers over him from the bottom of the bed as we finished.

'He needs another dose in three hours, and then half a dose six after that.' I pushed the loose strands of hair from my damp brow with the back of my hand.

'Are you certain you aren't a witch, Kat?' he asked, a softness to his features with his gentle teasing, appearing far younger than he usually did, unburdened for once.

'I've come to understand that a witch is simply a being beyond a man's control.' A being beyond their limits. Power was theirs, made of nothing but fury and chaos, woven into perfect balance. 'So perhaps I am.'

He nodded absently, the hint of a smile graced his lips as he moved to wash his hands before turning back to me.

'Let's leave him to rest,' he said, and ran a hand through his dark hair, before holding out his arm to guide me out of the room.

'We should tidy up,' I protested.

'I'll come back in a moment to finish my notes, but the portal is running unsupervised.'

I allowed him to guide me from the room, unknotting my apron, folding it and returning it to my bag as he guided us back through the mysterious hallways.

'An anthrux shouldn't be that powerful.' I frowned, looking down at the stains the slime had left on my fingers. 'I don't think there has been a recorded bite for over a century. They were impossibly rare even before the wars.' It was old magic, filled with hate from beneath the earth. One that surely couldn't have festered for this long.

Worryingly, Emrys had returned to his stoic ways.

'Where did you find him?' I pressed, suspicious I wasn't in possession of all the facts, as well as fearful he wouldn't answer. But as we came to a stop at the portal, a heavy sigh left his lips.

'He was coming to find me,' he answered reluctantly.

'You know him?' I frowned.

He shook his head, tipping it to see me. His eyes had returned to a stormy unsure grey. 'I found him outside Paxton Fields. The villagers trying to help said he'd asked for me before he went unconscious.'

He pulled a piece of paper from his pocket, thin and crinkled. A torn page that had seen better days. 'He had this with him.'

I took it gently, feeling the paper was still slightly damp, a horrid musty smell coming off it.

It was a page from a saints' holy book, one a worshipper might use for their prayers. A strange object for a fey to be in possession of, I thought, until I saw the scrawled words around the margin of the page, rushed and barely legible.

It was in Rivian, a shorthand fey used from when they were in servitude, one my mother had taught me.

'Do you speak Rivian?' I asked, curious as to why Mr Thrombi would write a message in Rivian if he was coming to see Emrys.

'No.' He frowned, watching me closely. 'What does it say?'

'How do you know I can read it?' Nobody knew that. Not even Alma. I only used it when I was writing notes I didn't want the Council to read, usually in the margins of my papers. Faint and small.

'I'm certain there's little you can't do, Croinn.' He smiled, but it didn't reach his eyes, and I wondered if he could have noticed such a small thing about me.

I moved closer to the pulsating bright light of the portal, feeling the warmth of it brush over my skin, tipping the page to see the words more clearly. One word. Over and over again until he could write it no more. Tangled with those horrid saints' prayers.

'*Reimor.*' I turned the page over but no matter how many angles I looked at it from, the message remained the same.

'Is that a place?' Emrys asked, his hand braced on the wall next to me, leaning forward to see, so close I could feel the reassuring chill of his magic. The cool pressure of it rushed over my skin like a strong winter's draught sending a pleasant shiver down my spine.

'No, it's the death of Kings. The Kysillian Kings of old.' I shook my head to focus on the paper again.

Reimor. A command that had sealed the darkness beneath the earth. Such a word made no sense now. A myth. Nothing but a child's bedtime tale.

'That was centuries ago, and there are hardly any records it even happened.' I wondered if I could have read it wrong, but Emrys's gaze had turned distant as he considered the expanse of dark hallway behind us.

'Maybe the bite drove him mad.' He sighed with little conviction, pushing back from the wall and holding out his hand for the page.

'Maybe,' I admitted, annoyed I didn't have any more information to give. 'Do you have a copy of the saints' teachings? Or a holy book?'

A dry humourless laugh slipped from his lips, startling me. 'Unfortunately, I gave up on prayer saving my soul long ago, Kat.'

The effortlessness of my name from his lips sent a strange flutter through my chest.

He pocketed the note and turned his attention back to the portal.

'That endless rot wasn't part of your archive, was it?' I tried to keep my voice steady, remembering how the darkness had curled within the glass.

TALES OF A MONSTROUS HEART

'It appears things might be worse than I first thought.' He shook his head as if dismissing darker thoughts. 'You were brought here to finish your paper in peace, not hunt dark magic. I shouldn't have disturbed you.' He gave a short, formal bow. 'Goodnight, Miss Woodrow.'

A clear dismissal. Placing a strange distance between us with the formality of my name.

'Kat,' I corrected, not allowing him to play that game.

He paused in his retreat as his lips moved to say something else before he thought better of it, then headed back through the portal, leaving me to wonder how I'd explain the blood on my sleeves to Alma.

Chapter Fourteen

Blessed are those who hold chaos in their hearts and bright molten fury in their bones. Gatekeepers of divine intention. Keeping the world as it was always meant to be. Following the glory of Kysillia, who battled the endless night and put the Old Gods to rest.

Who purged the world of the endless night.

Reimor.

— Kysillian Hymns for the Fallen — Unknown

The Death of Kings. Fragments of the story haunted what little sleep I managed to have. Wearily I pulled my exhausted limbs out of bed, only to realise my walking skirt was still being laundered by William, leaving me no option but a smart navy dress suit I'd never worn.

I laced up my walking boots, attached my belt with my bag, before twisting my hair into a smart bun and adding a ribbon, foolishly hoping it would behave.

After stumbling about the room to make sure I hadn't forgotten anything, Alma still didn't appear. Disturbed about what she could be up to or if she'd wandered into a trap, I went to the kitchen, where the large cooking pots were at work scrubbing themselves in the sink as bread continued to be kneaded by invisible hands at the table and a broom had got itself stuck in a corner bashing into the bricks as it attempted to sweep the floors.

A small plate of breakfast biscuits and milk were on the table. I took the opportunity to take my fill before freeing the broom from its stuck position and continuing my search.

'Alma?' I waited for the squeak of reply, but there wasn't one. I moved to the larder, pushing a barrel out of the way to see the large rolls of sealed cheese, expecting to see her feasting, but she wasn't there.

'Kat?' a concerned William asked, a basket full of mud-covered vegetables in his arms as he came to a stop at the bottom of the kitchen stairs.

'Morning, William. You haven't seen Alma, have you?' I put the barrel back and dusted down my skirts.

'She was down earlier,' he said, frowning, his eyes moving about the corners of the room.

'I wonder what she's found to occupy herself with.'

'She'll show up.' William smiled, placing the basket on the worn kitchen table. 'It must be hard to keep track of time as a mouse.'

Despite his sound reasoning, the feeling I was missing something remained.

'I'd better turn my efforts to locating the study instead,' I sighed, gathering up my skirts to make my way back up the stairs.

'Good luck with that,' he replied with a grin, sorting through the vegetables. Something about his cheery blissful nature seemed so strange compared to last night. The horror that anthrux bite revealed. The thought of it reminding me of that story. *Reimor.*

'William, you couldn't get me a copy of the saints' teachings, or a holy book, could you?'

'You can have mine if you want,' he said with a shrug and an easy smile. 'Little use it's done me.'

149

'I didn't know you were a believer.'

'I'm not. My father said it might save me from my own depravity, so I tried. However, I found trying to be something other than yourself is far too painful. So I'll stay strange and immoral. Too strange to be cured, perhaps'

The reminder of William's cruel past sat uneasy in my gut.

'I'll bring it to you.' He smiled, getting up and disappearing up the stairs before I could respond.

I followed, eyes on the floor for any sign of Alma, when a large worn wooden door with a beautiful gold handle creaked open – expecting me. I slipped inside, anticipating the familiarity of the study, only to stumble to a stop.

The room was large, with beautiful floral curtains, tightly closed and draped in cobwebs, the light barely able to stream through the gaps.

I could smell sage, rose oil and the bitter earthy scent of dead magic, and saw withered brown flowers still in their vases. Desks were pushed together, trunks stacked high with dresses and belongings piled on top. Healing cases and journals piled on the dusty floor. Abandoned personal objects hidden in the darkness by someone desperate to forget. Paintings leant against each other. The first was a portrait – the woman from the stairs, a man behind her with greying dark hair and an imposing nature in the silver uniform of a king's commander. On the woman's knee was a boy with black hair and crystalline eyes – Emrys. A teenage girl was stood to the side with her mother's striking blonde hair and blue eyes.

The Blackthorn family.

'Oh.' A soft sound came from behind me. I turned to find William in the doorway, hands gathered before him, sadness heavy in his usually bright eyes.

'I'm sorry, William,' I admitted shamefully, quickly making my way back to the door. 'I was looking for the study.'

'The house must have thought you'd find it interesting,' he said with a soft smile, but it faltered as he considered the sorrow in the room beyond us.

Memories of a family, a life and a world that didn't exist anymore. All crammed into one tiny space, allowing time to devour them, but I knew it didn't stop that pain. Grief was a monster all its own and there wasn't a blade sharp enough or a spell eloquent enough to kill it.

It remained. Unaffected by time. Endless in the worst way.

'The study is further down the hall; the door just nearly took me out.' He smiled, glancing once more at the painful darkness in the room before reaching into his apron and pulling out a small book. 'Here.'

The telling red cover of the Saint's holy book. I took it carefully, emotion welling painfully in my throat at the ease of his help.

'Thank you, William.'

He smiled, turning to leave me there but I reached for his arm. His warm brown surprised eyes meeting my own.

'You're not strange, William.' I smiled, hating he thought that for even a moment. 'I think you're quite wonderful.'

His smile wobbled on his lips before he nodded, sipping from my grip and leaving me in the hallway. Ashamed of my nosiness, I closed the door, allowing my palm to press against the wood as the house softly creaked in response.

The house missed them too.

I found the study in the direction William had pointed, positioning itself where I'd last seen a storeroom to be. There was no sign of Emrys, just a cup of tea abandoned on his desk, and perched next to it like a dust sprite requiring my attention was a small doll made of the rough fabric from farmers' sacks, thread and straw. At the centre of its chest was a dark smear.

Gingerly, I picked it up, trying not to disturb the delicate stitching as I examined the smear more closely. It was blood.

Be wary of spells made with blood. They are desperation given purpose, and the Verr like nothing more than desperation. Master Hale's teaching came back to me. How beings only made promises in blood if they had no other choice.

It was a Nox offering, a small doll used to protect creatures from the dark. An offering to the ancestors. A level of desperation that made me furious and sad all at once. Relying on ancient tactics because the Council were deaf to their pleas for help.

Such desperation alongside an anthrux bite made my blood run cold, too many horrible thoughts trying to crash into my mind. This was worse than even my nightmares could predict.

Reimor. An ancient tale, and an ancient charm to protect against a darker type of magic.

'*Lagnor.*' I whispered the command, an old spell that rested somewhere between a prayer and incantation. To protect.

'I didn't know persistent snooping was part of the partnership deal.' Emrys's voice came from over my shoulder.

He stood behind me, somehow effortlessly manoeuvring silently around all the clutter in the study, his hands slotted in his pockets. He was dressed in a smart long grey coat, his cravat missing, and dark trousers to match his boots. His hair was still wet and brushed back from his face.

'A saints' book? I wouldn't put that on my desk. It might combust.' He frowned down at the abandoned book.

'Where did you get this offering?' I asked.

'In Mr Thrombi's belongings,' he replied conversationally, seeming more alert and interested than usual. 'He was on his way to a reporting centre when he was struck down with the illness.'

'Or something *wanted* to strike him down,' I corrected. Anthrux were created from curses, after all. Someone had intentionally made a bad bargain and there was nothing to say one hadn't been set after Mr Thrombi on purpose.

'How is he?' I asked, shaking my head in an effort to be free from my dark thoughts.

'No change, but we'll see how he heals,' Emrys replied.

'Beings don't make Nox offerings for no reason,' I pressed.

'Nox. That's a Kysillian offering is it not?' He surprised me again by knowing Kysillian myths.

I nodded absently, looking at the slumped doll. 'The guardian of the dead. Protection against a darkness where it dwells.'

'You should keep it with you. Such things are dangerous in the hands of those who don't respect them,' Emrys offered gently, noticing my interest, but I was caught by his words.

'You're going somewhere?' I asked as he straightened the sleeve of his jacket.

'Paxton Fields. I need to see where it began if there is a chance in containing it.' He leant past me, the warmth of him brushing against my arm as he picked a battered pocket watch from his desk and stuffed it into his pocket.

I frowned. 'You really suspect it will be that severe?'

He pulled back slightly, close enough I could see the dark flecks in his light eyes. 'I'm not a fan of surprises, so I like to expect the worst.'

I couldn't help the soft laugh that left me at those words. He didn't like surprises and I seemed to be the worst kind. First the Council's wrath and then the ghoul.

'Speaking of surprises.' He reached into his interior coat pocket with a pensive expression. 'I think this belongs to you.'

There, contained gently in his fist, was a small brown familiar mouse squeaking away in annoyance at being caught.

'Alma!' I lunged for his hand, my fingers wrapping around his own as she crawled free.

'She was in my dresser,' he replied dryly, a dark brow raised. I almost dropped her with my shock, my face burning with the scandal of it.

Why on earth would she be running about his underthings?

'She . . . she gets confused sometimes in such small forms,' I lied, refusing to look at him as I dropped to my haunches, skirts spilling carelessly across the wood floor.

'Stay out of trouble, and out of other people's rooms,' I hissed under my breath, watching as she sat back on her hind legs, ears flat. 'I've left you papers on the desk to study, pages eight to thirty-five.'

She released a chorus of squeaks in protest, but I held out my hand to silence her and got back to my feet, planting my hands on my hips in my best Alma-annoyed impression.

'It's what you get for being nosey,' I warned, watching her nose twitch once before she darted off between two bookcases.

A dry laugh came from behind me, making my heart jump, but as I turned, Emrys's expression had returned to its usual impassive mask.

'Thank you for helping her.' I tucked the stray strands of hair behind my ears.

'Much like you, Kat, I don't do things for thanks,' he corrected softly.

No, maybe not, but he did it for some reason and the cavernous grief in that room came sharply to the forefront of my mind.

'Why this?' I asked. 'Of all the things to do, why this?'

Master Hale always made it seem impossible. That change or working to help the fey like this was nothing but an impossible, cursed task. I'd believed him, and maybe that was my greatest shame.

Emrys went still at my words. Something crossed his expression, making me fearful he wouldn't answer. Maybe it was his own surprise of never being asked before.

'You could say it comes naturally to me,' he said, and shrugged, only there was some heavier emotion lingering in his gaze. Guarded. 'I wasn't allowed to be a healer. Heirs are born to serve their house, even if it leads them down a wrong path. So I suppose, this is some feeble attempt to fix things. Even the unfixable.' He finished with a self-mocking smile. 'A fool's attempt to save his soul, perhaps.'

Only those words resonated too deeply with me. The regret and grief trapped in the small spaces between them.

'We find ourselves being many versions of what we once wished to be,' I countered. 'And there is no harsher critic than ourselves the further we go down a path we never wished to walk.'

I knew that better than anyone.

A silence came between us, nothing but the distant ticking of the clock as he considered me carefully for a long breathless moment before simply nodding, as if to shake a thought from his mind.

'Here.' He reached past me to pull a large file from his desk. 'They've been validated. If the contents give you any trouble, I'll send them back for a second verification.'

I opened the creased cover and there inside were the pox records from four fey villages. All authorised by the registrar. The pox evidence I needed to finish my paper.

My heart pounded with a confusing swell of emotion. Not even Master Hale had helped me like that. So effortlessly.

The retreating of his footsteps made my head shoot up, seeing him ready to leave once more. Remembering something else I shouldn't have forgotten.

Loneliness was the worst curse of all, and the last thing I ever wanted to be was alone. Yet, here I remained.

'I should come with you,' I blurted out, making him stop and turn. 'It's no good writing a paper on the pox when there are beings at risk from something far worse.'

His face remained guarded, but there was a hidden softness to his features.

Make the bastards pay, Katherine, Master Hale's words came back to me. The reminder that I had a choice in this too.

'I'd . . . I want to help. That's the point of a partnership after all.' No matter how much it scared me, or how ill-prepared I was. There was no point healing curses, only to let another destroy the lands fey needed. 'I can't very well expect my papers to help if I don't see things for myself.'

'Very well.' He cleared his throat and held out his arm for me to follow as he headed through the back shelves towards the room with the Portium door. I stuffed the papers in my bag and hurried to follow, watching the bookcases shift in response to his arrival, revealing the hidden portal chamber, the door already aglow and crystal in place.

'How familiar are you with Paxton Fields?' I asked.

'Not very, but most fey settlements have the same structure.' He fixed his jacket once more, crystalline eyes dipping to the sharp creases in my skirt and following the delicate stitching all the way up to the high collar of my jacket before meeting my eye.

'That colour suits you,' he observed, before turning sharply and stepping through the portal. Leaving me to blink in confusion, wondering if I'd heard him right, before I followed him.

Chapter Fifteen

Mortals were guided by the divine hand of their saint, who proclaimed
these green wildlands Elysior after the purity of his will. Crowning
himself with the thin sacred branches of a silver tree. Uncaring for
the names that came before, only gazing to the horizon, for all the
kings that would follow his word. Purity in the blood as the old gods
bowed to the might of his mortal's devotion.
                              — The Nameless Saint of Elysior, 1456

I found myself standing on a worn wooden floor, the bitter
smell of healing herbs greeting us, as well as damp winter air.
I should have remembered to bring a cloak, considering how
harsh the winters could be in the outlying villages so far west.

The room was barren, old floorboards stained and scratched,
the hearth unlit, leaving a dampness in the air.

A crash of breaking glass turned us towards the doorway of
the plain and vacant room, a young healer – guessing from
the white apron – frozen with shock in mid-stride at our
sudden appearance. The jars he'd been carrying lay shattered
at his feet and the herbs they'd held spilled.

His dark skin held a greenish hue, almost iridescent in the
weak sunlight, like a fish's scales or a patch of oil on water.
His bright cornflower-blue eyes taking us in with disbelief.

'Are you the assistant healer?' Emrys spoke abruptly.

'Yes,' he half stuttered, glancing down at the mess at his boots, clearly unsure if he should clean it or answer the new imposing figure before him. 'Who are you?'

'I need to speak with the head healer,' Emrys answered.

The healer straightened, glancing nervously down the hallway, but from the silence of this place he was alone.

'That might be difficult . . . he's dead, sir. We did send word a few weeks ago for assistance but heard nothing back. Then we sent another messenger a few days ago.'

So this was the healing house at Paxton Fields. From the derelict state of it, my heart ached for what kind of state the rest of the settlement was in.

'It wasn't Mr Thrombi, was it?' I asked carefully around Emrys's shoulder.

The boy frowned. 'Yes, do you know him?'

'He's currently recovering under my care,' Emrys replied, catching the boy's focus once more. I resisted the urge to dig my elbow into his ribs. He needed to be less imposing. 'He's suffering dark sickness so I need to see the most recent records you hold.'

The healer's eyes went wide.

'Of course.' He half stumbled over his own boot as he darted back into the hallway. Emrys moved to follow but I caught the sleeve of his jacket. His dark eyes met my own, and his brow furrowed with concern.

'Stop being so intimidating. You're unnerving him,' I warned under my breath.

He merely blinked, confused by the command.

'Be more . . . civil.' I released his arm, stepping around him to follow the boy. 'I'm sorry, we didn't catch your name . . .'

'I'm Devin Jacob.' He smiled over his shoulder, stopping to give a little bow in greeting.

'Pleasure to meet you, Devin.' I smiled as he continued to guide us, Emrys giving me a pointed look that I ignored. 'It doesn't seem busy.'

'There aren't enough people left here to heal. They've left for the next village over,' he continued, taking us around another corner and past the open main doors of the building. 'The crops began to fail a few months ago and the winter was too harsh for them to survive.'

I stopped at the main door, looking out at a dirt road, vacant of beings who should have been working there. Empty market stalls stood in disrepair, rotten fruit still in their baskets.

Small, wooden houses leant drunkenly against each other, their windows boarded up. A forest surrounded the remains of the village, but there was something else here, a coldness on the wind that had nothing to do with the weather, mocking in its intensity, unsettling the magic in my veins..

'Lord Fairfax has jurisdiction here, doesn't he?' Emrys called, considering the same thing I was, worry creasing his brow.

'His control has changed to his nephew, Lord Percy, with his ill health. The records are here.' Devin waved us into one of the side rooms, only it was mostly empty, the floor covered in loose scraps of paper. One lone ledger sat on a table, too thin to hold any vital records. The shelves barren.

'I want to see the logs for the past three months,' Emrys asked, unconvinced, pausing for a moment before he seemed to remember something. '. . . Please.'

I couldn't help my small victorious smile.

'Sorry, sir, the investigating inquisitors told me to keep the doors locked.' The boy practically winced, indicating a door down the hall with a large ominous magical lock in place. 'They said it needs to be burned to stop any further contamination.'

'Of course they did,' Emrys drawled, clearly unconcerned by the mention of the Council inquisitors being present. 'Mr Jacob, the village warden isn't still around, is he?'

The boy nodded. 'Yes sir, just at the outskirts.'

Emrys smiled, a sudden charm radiating from him that startled me. 'You couldn't get him for me, could you? I think it'd be best to speak to him myself.'

'Of course,' the boy stuttered, bowing before rushing from the abandoned healing house. Emrys waited for the footsteps to vanish before he moved swiftly for the locked door down the hall.

'What are you doing? That's a double charmed lock,' I hissed in worry, glancing over my shoulder down the corridor in case the boy suddenly returned or he wasn't working alone.

Emrys paid me no attention, dropping to one knee as he took from his pocket a silver tool that he inserted into the lock, turning it slowly. White light illuminated his fingers as he laid them on the handle.

The locking latches sprung free easily as he quickly stood, pocketing his tool once more.

'How did you do that?' I whispered, watching as he opened the door, turning to let me enter first like a gentleman would.

'I wouldn't get far in a war if I couldn't open a lock, Kat,' he observed wryly.

I ignored the strange, pleasant sensation that rushed through me at the softness of my name on his lips. I shook my head, refusing to be distracted by my own stupidity.

'I thought war heroes' skills were exaggerated to make Council dinners more entertaining, to make the old lords jealous and their young wives swoon?' I teased.

The room was tiny, appearing to be stuffed to the ceiling with every piece of paper the village had ever used. Crates that once held vegetables and eggs were now bursting with files and ledgers.

'Let's keep my skills off the topic of conversation or we'll soon both be in trouble,' he replied sardonically, making the file almost slip from my fingers as he moved to another box and pulled out a pile to examine.

Looking at his profile and the serious concentration on his face, I couldn't see him like that. As one of the King's performers, lethal and seductive. Crippling resistance with threats and the lies they could extract so effortlessly.

Maybe I didn't know him at all. Worried, I turned to the crates closest to the door, rooting through the papers unsure what I was looking for. I trained my eye on anything that could relate to magical sickness, or corrupted earth.

I was deep in my second box when I froze on a pile of sketches and the papers that accompanied them. Breath unsteady in my lungs.

'What is it?' Emrys asked at my side, somehow sensing my distress.

'These are missing beings.' I frowned, turning over another report. Seeing how they were all similar. 'Why would they need to burn missing being reports to stem an illness?'

'Maybe Lord Percy's lies are catching up with him.' He sighed, making me turn to see the tension in his jaw as he considered the mess before us.

A horrid realisation rushed over me. This was more than just cursed earth. Fey blood held magic. Magic that could be used to summon dark things. Rituals that meant death.

Some of them were fey girls. It wasn't uncommon for fey girls to go missing, most nobility offering a high price and promises to those who bore their bastards, children they could pass off as mortal to breed magic into their lines. Only most of those girls weren't seen again.

Emrys moved back to the other records in the far corner as I turned over the reports again, hating the bitter taste of fear that had coated my tongue.

A small cough caught my attention, taking me back to the hallway, another cough followed from just beyond the main doors. I went to the entrance, moving down a step and finding two small boys sat on a half-collapsed bench, just outside the healing house's doorway. One was trying to wrap a bandage around the other's thumb. They had a blue tinge to their skin, speckles of violet freckles and thick, dark-silver hair. Duvek, beings of the deep waters before they came to land. Creatures of great elemental powers before the purge. I didn't think there were any magic-wielding duveks left, if the Council records were to be believed.

The boys continued to quietly bicker amongst themselves.

'What seems to be the problem?' I asked, startling the pair, who stood to attention like miniature soldiers.

'Sorry, miss. I have a splinter,' the younger boy muttered, looking down at his poor excuse for shoes as he held up his thumb for my consideration. 'The mort tree got me.'

'A mort tree?' I ushered them back to sit down before I took his hand gently to examine his thumb. Just beneath the surface was the dark purple shadow of a splinter that I knew would burrow further into the flesh the minute an implement went near it.

'They have the best berries,' he offered quietly.

'They also have the nastiest bite,' I challenged, reaching into my pack and pulling out my healing kit, placing it on the ground so I could retrieve a salvor leaf. I laid it in my palm, allowing the heat of my magic to turn it to nothing but white ash. I dipped my finger in the powder and pressed it gently over the top of his thumb, watching the dark splinter beneath freeze in place. Stunned by a magic just as ancient as its own.

'Are you a mage, miss?' he whispered, leaning closer in wonder to see the points of my ears, so similar to his own.

'No.' I smiled, reaching into my pack for a sharp needle, making quick work of prying the dark object from beneath the boy's skin, trying my best not to hurt him.

'He's been told three times to stay clear of that tree.' His older companion sighed, coming closer to watch as the small thing came out.

'The berries keep vanishing,' the boy said with relief at the sight as I laid the dark worm-like splinter in my palm and reduced it to ash with a clench of my fist.

'You can only pick mort berries during a full moon,' I reasoned, getting back to my feet as I dusted the ash off my skirt. That was the tale my father had told me, cautious of my adventurous nature and the trees that grew beyond our house.

'Where is this tree?' I asked them, worried how far they had wandered to find it and on what cursed ground it was situated.

'It's over there.' The boy pointed over my shoulder in the direction of the outskirts of the wood that surrounded the village, just down a small dirt path where some people attended to horses and moved carts through the village.

'Maybe she's a witch,' his companion whispered.

'She's pretty enough to be one,' the first boy replied loudly, forcing me to bite back a smile as I gathered up my healing pack.

'You've stolen my line,' came a sharp feminine voice from behind me, followed by the crack of a ripe apple being bitten. I rose to my feet in surprise, the boys darting away at the newcomer's arrival.

Leaning on the stair rail mere inches away was a tall, lean woman. She wore a man's shirt that hung provocatively off one shoulder, revealing skin covered in all manner of dark ink marks. The shirt was tucked into a mass of skirts, one side tucked into her belt, showing her worn, high leather boots.

Her auburn hair was braided back from her face and left to cascade down her back. She was clearly unbothered by the cold weather, considering me carefully before taking another bite of the fruit.

'Are you one of the healers in charge?' I asked, wondering where her apron was, or if she wasn't a healer, what she was doing lingering around healing houses.

'I hope not.' She grinned, her amber eyes, heavily lined with dark makeup, flared a little brighter with amusement. 'I see Emrys has finally arrived to cause trouble for us all.'

'Do you want to speak to Lord Blackthorn?' I frowned, unsure how she knew he was here.

'He wouldn't like that.' She grinned wickedly, revealing that two of her teeth were fanged in the way some ancient feys were. 'Besides, if I wanted to listen to lies, I'd listen to my own.'

Her words tangled inside my mind. A clear warning pressed between them.

Here, came whispered on the wind, turning my head sharply to consider the forest, seeing the strangeness to the trees and remembering the boy's injury. Mort bark shouldn't be here.

'Who are you?' I asked, turning back to the woman. But there was nobody there. Just an apple core on the ground where she had stood.

If she was ever there at all. My heart thudded in my chest with unease but I didn't have time for her riddles as I moved across the village clearing to the beginning of the forest where the boys had pointed. I reached the wall of trees and had to pick up my skirts to avoid the brambles that had overtaken the grassy ground.

These trees were different to the others. Instead of dark trunks and luscious green leaves that would survive even through this winter, the bark was twisted and pale, aged beyond its years.

I'd seen erosion like this before, on trees too close to the sea and salty air. Only something else was eating at these, something stronger than salt and sand.

My father had spoken of a time before the wars, that no matter how far he moved from the centre of Elysior, he couldn't escape a feeling that chased him on the wind. A strange sensation of wrongness, a fear in him that couldn't be quelled. Something brewing like a storm he couldn't see, only for it to break in the form of a war.

I'd believed it to be a story, but now I knew it wasn't.

Despite my instinct to flee, I moved even closer. The trees pressed together so tightly that beyond was nothing but darkness. An endless gloom that seemed colder than the rest of the village settled here.

I laid my palm against the bark, feeling it crumble beneath the slightest pressure, the dust catching on the breeze. Dead.

I crouched down, rummaging in my bag for my sample jars, picking up what twigs and soil I could. Each left a strange sensation against my skin, a cold sting that didn't go away even as I tried to rub some warmth back into my fingertips.

A bitter wind tore past me, forcing me to turn out of it only to feel it snag at my hair, plucking strands of it free with its ferocity. I reached back with disappointment to find my ribbon gone.

'Do you ever stay in one place?' Emrys sighed, sounding flustered from behind me.

He stood amongst the trees, somehow more imposing than even them. A reserved expression on his face and the stormy nature of his eyes as he came to a stop next to me.

165

'Something is wrong with this forest. I—' The rest of the words died on my lips as I saw my ribbon caught in his fist. His hand extended towards me in offering.

Beware of demons in the woods offering gifts of silk and stone. The fable whispered through my mind. Taunting me. Stories of maidens lured with forbidden kisses to dwell in the deep with their dark lovers.

'Thank you.' I took it gently, ignoring the warm brush of his fingers. Averting my gaze and hating the warm treacherous flush of my cheeks. But as I dipped my chin to consider the damp earth between us, all warmth abandoned me.

A dead folk lay just before my boot.

A horrid cold grief washed over me at the cruelty of it. Carefully I crouched, gently letting the small creature roll into my palm. Its head was made of a small bird's skull, its limbs of moss and small stones. All tinged grey, so cold as if formed of ice, the magic that had made it dead.

'*Marov,*' I whispered in Kysillian. *Rest now.*

I ran my thumb over the skull, knowing it was too late for comfort as the creature became nothing but dirt in my palm, slipping easily through my fingers. Blinking back my childish tears, I looked to the hollow trunks of the wood, where they liked to hide.

'Kat.' Emrys reached for my arm cautiously.

'I can't see any more of them.' I looked up at him, my fingers trembling, unable to wipe away the remains of what that small creature had been.

'They're . . . not fond of my presence,' he replied carefully, dark eyes guarded.

I let him help me back to my feet before cautiously moving further into the wood. Emrys following silently like a dark shadow, reaching out to move the low branches for me and helping me over the thick tangle of roots. His firm hands brushing my waist, making our cold dismal surroundings more apparent compared to the warmth of his nearness.

I only stopped our wandering when I saw something peeking through the misty wood: the rubble of stone temples pressing through damp earth, runes carved on the smooth mossy stones. The ruins of sacred grounds. Fey temples.

They wouldn't have been here in the times of the Kysillian Kings. Kysillians wouldn't take kindly to worship of anything but their queen's blood. To the chaos they wielded.

No, these ruins came after the ancient wars between chaos and death. Between Kysillian and Verr. Before the mortals arrived with their saintly King and corrupted the world.

This was a sacred place for fey to ask their ancestors for protection.

Yet unease crept through me as I moved through the over-growth, seeing a simple flat stone of what remained of the altar. Fresh offerings still placed there. Animal bones, blessed crystals and herb bundles.

A shiver rushed down my spine that had nothing to do with the damp air. A chill not even the warmth of Emrys's proximity could chase away.

'Fey don't leave their sacred grounds,' I whispered, seeing that empty village and the evidence of how many had already abandoned it. Not unless all hope had failed. Just as folk didn't just drop dead on soil that was made to protect them. 'Something is wrong.'

Wrong with the earth. Wrong with the very creatures that lived upon it. Something in them turning from an unseen enemy. Something that didn't exist in me. No, because I'd come before this. My blood knew too many things, know-ledge it couldn't give me with words.

Emrys stood there, and I knew whatever was in his blood must be as ancient as my own. Must be to endure this. To try and unravel the mystery we'd been left.

Yet there was an unease in him, eyes too sharp, like a sinner stepping onto blessed territory.

'You've been to ruins before?' I frowned, following his gaze to see what had put him on edge.

'Not those belonging to the fey.' There was a caution to his words and in the deep grey of his eyes. 'The lords liked to hold their meetings in the most . . . unseemly of places.'

Of course. In the times of the Mage King, those lords had been just as submerged in the worship of the dark as their king had been. Including Emrys's father, even if it had been a pretence.

'Were you ever introduced to him?' The question I shouldn't ask. The name I wouldn't say. The heart of all this cruelty, another man who'd torn this world apart for nothing but greed and darkness. Torn apart my life so easily despite being nothing but a story to me.

Emrys was silent for a long moment, the winter wind ruffling his hair as he considered me . . . as if trying to work something out.

'No,' he finally said, expression pensive. 'I was seventeen when the lords rebelled. When they finally sprang their trap. Blood vows were made to him at eighteen.'

When his life had been plunged into the war. I would have been seven. Still safe in that cottage with my parents, tucked away from all of it.

Seventeen years, he'd lived under that king's rule, or his family had. Seventeen years, they'd played that game, had to stomach it before finally they could act.

'Too late,' he added, reading every thought in my head. They'd acted too late. 'They'd already sold their souls.'

Hurt gnawed at my chest but I forced myself to feel the cold breeze and smell the rot of the forest, to consider the chipped stone before me.

Something urged me closer to the stone, as Emrys moved with me, crouching before the long grass. He moved it aside, revealing another Nox offering. I reached out for his arm, stopping him from touching it. He watched me with mild concern, somehow sensing my fear. Not at the doll but at the words carved into that stone around it. Over and over again. Each gouging deeper than the one before.

Ancient prayers. Only they all said the same thing.

Temez. A word I knew. Deep in my heart I knew but I couldn't remember it. Not here surrounded by so much fear.

'They're afraid.' Afraid didn't seem a strong enough word for what had settled over this place, what lingered in the dark beyond the wood, chilling my blood.

'They have a right to be.' His dark gaze dropped to consider the ashy ground. 'This is worse than I first predicted.'

He reached into his pocket, pulling out a small stack of torn and mud-speckled papers. He turned them over, showing them to be partially charred.

'Some children found these while playing in the woods,' he stood, taking my arm to guide us back the way we'd come. As if sensing the unease that had draped itself over me and wanting me away from those ruins.

I wasn't paying attention to anything other than the burned papers he'd given me. The incantations written there were dark, scrawled and filled with hate. Wishes meant for the dark's ear. Forbidden worship I hadn't seen in years.

'They're bargains.' Someone was asking for things from the earth. And fey were going missing.

'I've visited two locations like this previously. The town of Maris and a Beven settlement.'

'What happened?'

'They're not there anymore,' he replied. 'They were consumed, and any survivors fled to other settlements or died en route. The Council dismissed it as a case of hysteria.'

Of course they did. My hands grasped at my skirts to contain my magic's flare of rage.

'Those creatures are too dark to be here by mistake.' I hated the helplessness that began to overwhelm me in response to his words. Such creatures needed *permission* to exist and only the darkest of spells could give it to them.

He pulled in a deep breath, looking at the wood once more. 'We're lucky we got here before rebel scouts. They recruit best in places where people are desperate enough to join the cause.'

'The Council should act more quickly then.' However, the Council and the rebellion had more in common than they thought. Both wanting beings at their weakest points to mould them into the perfect followers, gathering up broken men and lost children and trapping them in whatever roles they deemed fit.

'The minute you say a rebellion vow, you're as guilty as the Council already deem you to be.' Emrys's words were filled with a dark truth that unsettled me as he continued to lead us back through the wood. The Council was allowing the rebellion to grow because they knew they could cull it easily.

'Those are dangerous words,' I found myself whispering. Dangerous words that might not get *him* killed, but they had greater implications for me.

'I've been told that before.' He smiled without amusement as we emerged from the wood, back into the clearing of the village. 'Come on, we—'

'Kat!' someone shouted, the call echoing across the empty village from the healing house's doorway.

Our attention turned to the main entrance just as William almost tumbled down the steps, hair in disarray from the rush of the portal's magic. Breath panted though his lips as he came to a skidding halt, kicking up dirt, eyes wide with fear.

'William?' Emrys called, striding towards the boy with alarm.

'It's Alma . . .' He half stuttered. I didn't let him finish, picking up my skirts and racing across the distance between us. Emrys called my name but I didn't stop. Couldn't.

I'd failed her again.

Chapter Sixteen

There was once a boy, cursed to become a beast, marvelled over as one blessed by the Old Gods.

Then man wished to be blessed too, so they hunted him like the beast he pretended to be. Skinned his many pelts, ate his flesh, and sucked the marrow from his bones. Finding no magic in their bellies, only hunger for all the things they could never be.

– Fables of the Old Beasts, 1374

'Alma?!' I called, tripping over the clutter of the study as I skidded into the hallway and up the stairs of Blackthorn Manor, following a strange crying sound coming from down the hall. The trinkets on the walls rattling in the direction I needed to go, stairs clattering with warning as I flew around another corner. The floor covered in papers and books – a sideboard had fallen over as if something had crashed into it, causing the drawers and cupboards to be thrown open.

Beneath all the mess was Alma in human form. Eyes wide and bloodshot, panting wildly as she convulsed, dark curls matted and stuck to her damp face. Her usually warm skin was horribly pale, her naked body curled into a foetal position.

'Alma!' I pushed the sideboard off her with little effort, my arms sweeping papers out of the way, dropping to my knees to pull her clammy and unstable form into my arms.

Blood coated her lips as she coughed weakly, breaths wheezed from between her teeth. Another convulsion took over her, an animalistic wail caught in her throat. I pressed the back of my hand against her forehead, too warm despite how violently her teeth chattered.

'S-s-orry,' she panted, trying to breathe, the spasming of her muscles making her curl in on herself to try and conceal her naked form.

I tore off my jacket, stitches popping with the haste as I pressed it against her feverish skin, trying to cover her.

'It's going to be all right,' I soothed as she tried to hold on to me, fingers clumsy with weakness.

She was back and I had to stop the sting of tears coming to my eyes with relief as I took in the lavender-and-rosemary scent of her.

'Kat?' Emrys called, coming to a skidding halt before all the mess. His attention solely focused on me, his grey eyes dark with worry.

'She hasn't stayed in one form so long before,' I said, stumbling over my words, unsure for a moment if I should hide her from his gaze or ask for help. As Alma trembled vulnerably in my arms, the choice seemed made, her skin changing from feathers to fur and back again as the spasms overtook her once more.

There was a ripping sound, as Emrys pulled a threadbare, priceless tapestry from the wall and laid the rough fabric over her. As if it was no more than a blanket.

Our noses almost brushed with the closeness of him. His gaze met mine, awaiting command.

'I . . . I need my things.' My voice broke as I tried to shift Alma's weight in my arms.

'Let's get her to your room.' He nodded, reaching out to take her gently from me. Strangely, I let him, as he effortlessly picked her up, curling her in that tapestry to cover her completely. He had her cradled securely in his arms just as William came to the end of the hall, out of breath and panicked.

'Bloody saints, is she all right?' he asked, running a hand over his horns in distress.

'William, boil some water please. We'll need a brewing cup,' I said. The boy turned on his heel and ran back down the stairs without another word.

Emrys moved past me and over the mess with ease towards my room. I struggled to match his pace, skirts bundled in my arms.

'Her convulsions don't usually last this long.' I squeezed past him in the narrow hallway to get the bedroom door open, throwing it wide as I crossed to the bed and pulled the sheets back.

He deposited her on it gently without question as another convulsion made her back arch. Her breath panted through her lips, the skin of her face becoming scaled before settling back to flesh with an odd greenish hue.

'Oh, Alma.' I pushed her damp, sweat-matted hair off her face and pressed my fingers to her neck to check her pulse, which was hammering ridiculously fast.

'I'm sorry,' she whispered again before it turned into another string of tremors that stole her breath.

I kissed her damp forehead, brushing her wild curls back. 'It's not your fault. Although my hair is mighty pleased you're back.'

The remark made her laugh quietly before she winced, her hand finding my own where it rested at the back of her head. As if she could hold onto mortal form by anchoring herself to me.

'Her breathing is too erratic,' Emrys commented as he pressed his fingers against her pulse on her other wrist, where her hand gripped the sheets in a white-knuckled hold.

The door flew open and William entered with a pot of steaming water and a stack of towels balanced on his shoulder, an extra healing pack dangling precariously from his fingers.

'Put it on the side here, William.' Emrys moved around the bed as Alma continued to shift unwillingly.

Once relived of the tray, William went to stand awkwardly in the corner, eyes wide with concern as Alma continued to writhe on the bed.

I gently untangled myself from her and moved to my desk, opening my bag. I pulled the cursed root out of its container, measuring the right amount and putting it in the pot to brew. Then I added the rest of the concoction, releasing a horridly sweet smell into the room as I carried the pot towards the bed.

I was startled to see Emrys had pressed a damp cloth to Alma's forehead, and she was holding onto his wrist as if it was me, her eyes closed tightly as she dragged in deep breaths. He seemed unbothered by the razor-sharp claws that would emerge sporadically from her fingertips.

Then I realised where his gaze was focused: the skin of her wrists. Heavily scarred skin, still pink despite the years that had passed. Deep gouges and marks from chains left to chafe too long.

Marks I'd forgotten about because we had other dangers to fret over than where she'd come from. How the menagerie had chained her so she didn't escape and how desperately she'd struggled against those chains . . . leaving reminders she could never forget.

Emrys turned to see me, his eyes dark, knowing, and yet his face giving nothing away.

I couldn't contemplate the consequences of revealing those truths, not now. I quickly poured the concoction into a cup and brought it to Alma's lips.

'Alma, drink this and we'll get you settled,' I ordered softly, her trembling so great she spilled most of it, but I got her to swallow a healthy amount. Emrys was waiting to take the empty cup from my hands as another tremor moved through her.

'It hurts,' she whispered, tears running down her cheeks as she hiccupped and fought for breath.

'It's all right,' I soothed, holding onto her, pressing my palms against her burning cheeks, taking up the icy cloth Emrys handed me. He'd pressed an enchantment into the fabric to keep it cold.

Her hands formed claws, movements erratic as I felt the tearing of my sleeve, but I didn't let her go as she cried out from the pain of it. I pulled her closer, knowing she could hurt me, but I didn't care.

'You're safe with me,' I whispered into her ear as her back bowed. Holding her tighter so she knew I wouldn't let her go. I wouldn't leave her.

A promise made on a cold winter's night between two lost girls who needed each other: that I wouldn't leave her behind. Not then. Not now.

I closed my eyes, seeing her in my memory, skinny and shivering in the corner of the room, where the guard had dumped her. Wounds on her wrist bleeding with infection, feet blue with the cold as I extended my hand to her. She'd been fearful, with pain in her eyes and the expectance of cruelty, and I'd never wished to banish a demon more.

With trembling fingers she'd taken my hand, her grip weak and frail as I promised to take care of her right there, in the middle of that freezing dormitory in a cruel place neither of us should have been. Yet, after all this time, the guilt remained that I still couldn't save her from herself.

'Kat,' Emrys called softly, making me open my eyes to see how closely he watched me. How deeply concern darkened his gaze.

'She's fine.' The words barely a whisper as Alma grew heavier in my arms as the mixture took hold.

Emrys waited a moment, to be sure. Then he nodded.

'Come William, let's give them some privacy.'

I almost sagged in relief, feeling Alma's calmer breath against the curve of my neck as I heard the door click shut with their departure.

'I wish I was stronger,' she barely murmured, her words slurred with tiredness. The small spasms of her muscles lessened and her breaths deepened as the colour crept back into her cheeks. The cursed root was doing its job.

'You're the strongest person I know.' I wished more than anything she believed that truth.

'I . . . I hope Blackthorn isn't too angry,' she whispered as I pressed her gently back into the pillows, watching the twitch of her nose and restless movement of her eyes behind her closed lids.

'He can deal with me if he is,' I reasoned as I tucked her in, but she was already asleep. I made the fire roar in the hearth with the barest summoning so the heat of it brushed over her.

Then I retreated to the edge of the bed and let my head fall into my hands, exhausted with all the things I couldn't change.

Too many things had gone unsaid between me and Emrys. I'd put him at a disadvantage, taking the truths he offered, but still keeping my own secrets. Alma's change making a mess of his hallway was something I also needed to see to before the house took it personally.

My eyes fell to that tapestry, now discarded on the floor. The gold stitching and deep green threads hinted at expensive. By the shape of the figures and the Ridion language, I suspected it was an artifact of the twelfth century, and he'd used it like a blanket. For me. Because I needed his help.

He'd come to help me when he should have been turning me in for the liar I was.

Rising from my perch on the bed, I moved to the door, taking a moment to pull in a steady breath before I ventured back out into the strange reality of this world.

Emrys lingered in the shadowy hall, head bowed in thought. His coat was missing and sleeves rolled up as if expecting another healing job at any moment. From his fingers hung my jacket.

The door clicking shut behind me made him look up, those eyes pitch black in the dim hallway. I pressed my hands behind my back so he wouldn't see them tremble.

'Cursed root.' His head tipped up as he watched me cautiously. 'That was used to help bind slaves in the Mage King's reign.'

'It quietens her power enough for her to heal,' I said. 'Three days is sufficient.' It was the only thing I'd found that worked so far.'

No matter how hard I worked, the solution for helping Alma still eluded me, making it only more evident why they called transfiguration a curse. Why most beings who possessed it had been killed out of mercy.

'Wild magic.' He sighed. Those two words had been so deadly for so long, and yet they were so cautious and soft from his lips. 'The secrets of beast transfiguration were lost for a reason.'

Because they were deadly to those who wielded the magic. Caught and used. Tangled in blood bargains to make them weapons against mortal kings by the rebellion. That menagerie had used Alma for entertainment . . . and a few centuries before she would have been used for sport.

'Those were shackle marks.' He considered me carefully, anticipating any lie that would leave my lips as he held my jacket a little tighter in his fist.

I should have been scared but I saw no danger in Emrys's eyes, only a challenge. If I lied, Alma would be safer, but I'd put everything I'd built here at risk. I'd hidden everything for so long, fearful of the consequences, but I couldn't live another day of lies. I needed to be braver than my fear.

Only fear can bind your hands. My father's words came back to me, just when I needed them. I knew I needed to finally trust in this partnership.

Then there were Emrys's words that night. When he could have turned me in for keeping a ghoul as some demented pet. *When you realise how brilliant you are, Croinn, I think we'll all be in trouble.* The memory of them dissipated my fear, my hands coming out from behind my back. My decision was made.

'The Council patrol found her in a menagerie,' I began. 'She was kept for amusement as a child. It isn't my story to tell but I made her a promise to keep her safe,' I began, trying to work out which part of the tale *was* mine to tell. 'She was too sick to make it to the fey healing houses in the north. They already saw her as a lost cause, and . . . Daunton was closer.'

On the coldest of nights, I'd forced her to live. Bullied her into surviving, perhaps selfishly because my fear of being alone was greater than my fear of failure.

'She's the reason you wrote about septime weed,' Emrys summarised, gathering that fact from the words I hadn't spoken.

'I wouldn't let her die like that,' I admitted. No matter the punishment I'd been given for it, the marks that still covered my back. 'Couldn't. The only thing that divides us is the fragility of luck, and we both know I am anything but lucky.'

He'd seen how the Council treated me and he'd seen firsthand the brutality of this world. No, I wasn't lucky, but then again, considering him and his scarred skin, maybe he wasn't either.

'I'm sorry about the mess in the hall,' I offered weakly, unsure how to navigate this new dynamic between us. 'I—'

'She's the luckiest being in the world to have a protector as fearless as you,' he cut in matter-of-factly as he considered me with clear eyes.

'Stubborn is a better word.' I smiled weakly.

'Stubborn then.' He nodded, coming even closer to offer me my jacket, only for me to wince as I reached for it. A horrid burning pain seared up my arm.

Emrys took my forearm carefully, his gaze darkening as he turned my arm, revealing a blood-soaked sleeve and a deep gash from one of Alma's stray claws.

'That needs looking at.' His lips were tight with displeasure.

'I can do it.' I sighed, annoyed with myself for not noticing sooner as I tried to see the extent of it. The red drips on my dark skirts and on the hallway floor were another unpleasant surprise.

Gently, a single finger came beneath my chin, forcing me to look up at him, a softness to his features that diminished any arguments I could form.

It wasn't the worst thing to be cared for, I thought. I'd allowed myself to forget that.

'I think you've done enough for today, Croinn,' he replied, a small smile lingering at the corner of his mouth. And then I realised: I didn't want to sit alone putting myself back together like all the times before.

'Okay,' I whispered, some quiet agreement beginning between us.

Chapter Seventeen

I should have stopped him, shouldn't have wanted his comfort, but I was too exhausted with the turbulence of my own emotions.

Alma was back, but for how long? This magic was beyond us both, and the answers didn't dwell in any books.

I was quiet, occupied by my chaotic thoughts as I found myself sat before the fire in the study. Emrys asked permission to examine my arm, rolling up the ruined sleeve of my shirt. I did my best to ignore the gentle drag of his fingers as he checked for any further wounds.

He worked silently, with mortal instruments, no spells, or incantations, just a numbing ointment, healing balm, needle, thread and bandages.

There was a slight hesitation to each of his movements, indicating his reluctance to hurt me. His brow furrowed with concentration. Then perhaps my tiredness made me delirious in human form. I imagined smoothing out that frown with my fingertips.

'I thought healing wasn't your specialty?' I asked, mesmerised by the grace and speed of his work.

'War wounds are,' he replied in the businesslike tone of a healer considering how much to charge for their services as he gently cleaned the wound.

The firelight played off the textured scarring of his skin. Every small movement of expression seemed to pull at the tight skin, but he remained unbothered. I was drawn to the sharpness of his features. The scars did little to distort his handsomeness.

Then again, I feared every intelligent word out of his mouth was more attractive to me than anything else.

Then I wondered how such a quiet and studious man had been thrust into that life of bloodshed and war.

He wrapped the wound, then stood and moved to the sideboard, the cotton of his shirt almost sheer in the firelight as the muscles played across the expanse of his back with every small movement.

I shouldn't have noticed. Perhaps it was the exhaustion conjuring such wanton thoughts.

'You have an affinity for healing.' He moved to the small drink stand tucked in next to the bookcase and picked up a decanter filled with amber liquid. He gripped two glasses in one hand, placing them on top of a large priceless book on the side table and pouring a generous measure into each before holding one out to me.

I took it, and settled back in my seat, watching him drink deeply from his own. I followed suit, needing it more than I was willing to admit. My attention was once again drawn to the scars on the one side of his face and how they twisted down the strong line of his throat.

'A gift from my mother,' I smiled sadly, instantly rewarded with the memory of her smile. The softness of it, the endless kindness in her eyes.

'She was a healer?'

'A natural one. Her family didn't approve of . . . magic.' I swallowed awkwardly around the words, the hint of a lie. 'Of fey either.'

Despised would have been a better word. Enough to make her run and never look back. I could feel the intensity of Emrys's eyes, trying to work out what I wasn't saying, so I pressed on, offering what truths I could.

'She taught me, until she became too sick.' I swallowed another sip of drink. Letting it burn a path through me. Refusing to take myself back to the night she went. The night a part of myself died too.

'You must have been young.' Emrys's words were almost lost in the crackle of the fire.

'I was eleven.' I turned to see him, a hardness to the grey in his eyes. Emotions I couldn't understand. 'I thought that was the worst thing that would ever happen to me. Losing them. I suppose this world endeavoured to prove me wrong.'

A silence came between us, one filled with exhaustion and doubt. Then the revelations of the day came back to me. The papers he'd shown me, the incantations on them, and the depth of the sickness that had worked its way through the land.

'The darkness infecting that wood is old,' I said, frowning. 'Old enough to scare beings who've been settled for centuries.'

'So is the greed that summons it from beneath the earth,' Emrys replied, sounding as exhausted as I felt, but there was a small smile on his lips as he tapped the scarred side of his cheek. 'From personal experience, I fear this won't end well.'

My attention was focused on those marks, the depth and brutality of them, leaving me to wonder how someone could survive such things.

'You want to ask about it,' he surmised, working out every curious thought in my head, sending heat flaring to my cheeks.

'I shouldn't.'

'You won't offend me.' He rolled his own drink, the liquid turning gold as it caught the light.

'It isn't that.' I dropped my gaze to my own glass. No. It was because wondering how he survived forced me to wonder why my father hadn't. Fearful of the power of whatever beast could have kept him from coming back to us.

I shook the thought away, looking up once more to see him studying me over the rim of his glass.

'How did you end up in the middle of all this?' I asked, braver with the drink at my lips.

'A lord's job is to serve his king and any son in his line.' He shrugged, downing his drink as if to chase the bitterness of the words from his tongue before sitting forward and bracing his elbows on his knees to finish the story. 'But this house could serve him no longer when he sold his soul to the Old Gods. My father dedicated his life to fighting this darkness. Since he's not here, I owe it to him to continue.'

'Even with the Council being so difficult?' I frowned, knowing he could have easily abandoned all of this and the Council's hypocrisy. There was nothing in it for him apart from frustration and the agonising torment of watching the world fall apart.

'They have no choice,' he replied. 'The dark leaves a mark on all of us, even them. They need me, unless they want the demons they sold their souls to for a king's love to come and collect payment.' His gaze drifted to the fire, uncomfortable with the admission. 'I made a promise.'

I finished my own drink, trying not to cough at the burning sensation in my throat.

'I'm sorry I ruined the investigation at Paxton Fields.' I sighed.

'We got everything of value from the excursion.' He reached out to take my glass, a strange foolish rush moving through me at the barest brush of our fingers.

'I haven't seen ruins like that in a very long time.' I leant back in the chair, trying to behave myself as I forced my aching shoulders to relax. 'My father took me to the Kysillian temples when I was six for my blessing.'

'That must have been a sight.' Interest lit his features, his head tilting to show the strong line of his throat. 'The Kysillians guard their temples well from the stories.'

I smiled. Deep in the north was where the Kysillians were said to have settled now. Out of reach of the Council rules and oppressive laws.

'I can barely remember it now.' I rubbed a circle against my palm, remembering the rough feel of the statues, of the ancient pillars and the burn of the magic encased in stone. 'It feels like no more than a dream.'

To be loved. To be safe.

'You said he fought.' A darkness fell over Emrys's expression. An understanding. 'He was there until the end.'

There. In those killing fields.

I nodded, swallowing around the sadness clogging my throat. 'He didn't have a choice.'

No. He was nothing but fodder for their cannons.

'Those Kysillians in the settlements in the north never came for you?' he asked, those curious grey eyes fixed on nothing but me.

I frowned. 'Why would they? I'm mortal-touched.'

The Kysillian elders would see me as a half-breed, no better than a mortal or lesser fey, despite how dominant my Kysillian blood would always be. I would never look mortal. Neither would any children I produced, if I was capable.

Darkness seeped into the corners of Emrys's gaze. 'Their misfortune.'

'From my records of misconduct . . . maybe a blessing to them,' I countered, inclining my head, unable to stop the self-mocking smile that came to my lips.

He blinked as if I'd surprised him. My reward was watching that darkness slowly leave his expression as he returned my smile, so easily I felt it soothe something raw inside of me.

'My misfortune then,' he corrected wryly.

A comfortable silence fell between us, filled by nothing but the crackling nothing but the crackling hearth. I watched the fire shift ravenously, as if performing under my assessment of it.

'I should get back to her.' I sighed, knowing I was doing myself little good getting too attached to Emrys's company. The calmness and chaos he supplied all at once. I had too much to think about and all of it was impossible when he was looking at me.

'I have something to help.' He stood, moving to his desk and opening the drawer. He came back to me with a vial of liquid that glowed with its own light, shifting from blue to green.

A strange substance I'd recognise anywhere.

'Transfiguration draught,' I breathed.

His smile was sharp with amusement. 'Not many would recognise it.'

'Where did you get this?' I asked, still stunned as I felt the heat of the potion against my palm. The secret to brewing transfiguration potion had been lost for years.

'William found one of Emmaline's old potion notes. He thought it could help,' he replied easily, turning his attention back to his desk, hiding his expression from me.

'What did she need it for?' I wondered if he would tell me that truth. Surprisingly, he turned back to me, leaning against his desk with his arms crossed.

'To become a man. Emmaline had many schemes, but changing form to antagonise our father was her favourite.' There was a challenge in his eyes that accompanied those words.

Testing me. If he thought I'd be offended by beings changing gender and form, he evidently hadn't read my notes clearly.

His eyes moved almost reluctantly to my desk, the carvings beneath and the person he used to see sitting there. I didn't know how that must feel, to be reminded every day of what you lost, for this house to bring nothing but that pain, and yet he remained.

'How did she die?' The question left me before I could consider the rudeness of asking.

'In the wars. One of the skirmishes. At least that's the story that they told.'

The wars. The image of her sunk beneath a muddy battle-field or tossed into a pit as nothing but a rebellious nuisance made me sick, especially because I knew my father would be right there with her.

'She's out there somewhere, in an unmarked grave. Lost like all the rest of them.' There was a depth to the guilt that coated his words. As if the entire war was of his own making, despite him being young when it had begun.

No matter his guilt, we couldn't change the course of history. No matter how many times I had willed my father to run, to keep running and survive, that wasn't the story his life was destined to tell.

'And what was it all for? We didn't change anything.' Coldness coated his words, and as he looked into the fire, a hardness came over him that made me realise just why the Council feared him. A ruthlessness that lay beneath. It should have unsettled me, but I was too familiar with the ravenous emotions of grief and rage.

Wondering if he wished for privacy, I moved to leave, only for him to catch my hand – gently – but it was enough to hold me in place.

'It's hard to remember it happened when some of us carry it so well . . . others crumble and then some simply act as if it never happened,' he whispered, his voice suddenly coarse.

'I don't know which one I am,' I answered, feeling the emotion well in my throat. I'd never had my pain sit before me so vividly.

His eyes were jet black as they considered me, raw with too many emotions. 'None of them, Croinn. You haven't stopped fighting.'

Every day. I was fighting every day. It was why exhaustion clung to my bones, why every day felt like a trial all its own.

'I didn't realise I was, too, until you crossed my path.' His smile was faint, but his eyes remained dark. 'It reminded me of something I'd forgotten.'

'Not to leave cursed books open?'

His answering smile was sharp and devious, making my magic rise for a different reason.

'To fight. I could see the jaws closing around you . . . saw you standing right in the centre of it, not begging or bargaining for a way out. No. You were looking right at the beast. Daring it to bite.' That warm and uneven smile came back to his lips. 'Ready to take down the whole Council despite knowing you'd never win.'

'I suppose it's nice to have company in the madness,' I whispered, accepting my pain and his.

'I suppose it is.' He nodded, as he let my fingers go, in a dismissal that hurt worse than any word.

That sting remained as I reached the doorway and took myself off to bed.

Chapter Eighteen

When morning came, I made my way to the kitchen for breakfast only to find a pensive William absorbed in reading a paper, as he absently stirred his tea, brow furrowed in concentration and hair a wild mess around his horns.

'William?' I asked, only for him to almost jump a foot in the air, dropping the paper and bashing both his knees on the underside.

'Bloody saints!' he cursed, eyes wide with surprise as he bent forward to rub his injured knees. 'You move like a wraith, Kat!'

'Are you all right?' I tried to conceal my laugh.

'Me? How is Alma?' He glanced at the doorway behind me as if she was about to make an appearance, eyes scanning the floor in case she'd reverted to her previous form.

'She'll be better after a long rest,' I lied. The truth was I never knew how Alma would be after a change. But no change had ever lasted this long, and she hadn't jumped to multiple forms before so effortlessly.

'What are you reading?' I asked, rubbing my temples against the threat of a headache as I considered the mess of papers scattered across the table.

'*The Crow's Foot.*'

'I've heard its nothing but salacious gossip and scaremongering.' I frowned. A way for rebellion sympathisers to spread fear, so I was surprised to see William so engrossed in it.

'You sound like Emrys,' he replied dryly, slapping the pages in protest as he laid them flat and pointed to a section at the bottom of the page. 'They've run a piece on Paxton Fields, about the incidents there.'

'The illnesses?' I leant closer, turning the page to see it better. Since when did mortals care about dark illness?

'No, the missing beings. Two went missing from a village further south and another from a fey settlement to the west. Maris and Beven I believe. They're hysterical enough to even claim a vesper demon is to blame.'

My stomach dropped to my boots.

Maris and Beven, the two places Emrys said he visited. It had been in his notes, but he'd said nothing about missing beings.

I pulled the paper closer, scanning over the words. Maris and Beven both had Council-run homes for women, similar to Daunton. Hale had spoken about them before. He'd run campaigns to try and help fey settlements in both areas.

Something was very wrong. Breaches, sickness and now missing fey. All in the same areas. That wasn't a coincidence; it was the beginning of something.

If I wanted to be told lies, I'd listen to my own. The memory of that strange woman outside the healing house mocked me as I looked over the paper again. I would be a fool to trust a stranger blindly, but this wasn't coincidence, and Emrys wasn't the type to forget such details.

'Kat?' William laid his palm flat on the paper to catch my attention.

'Sorry, William.' I shook my head. I needed to check on Mr Thrombi. Emrys hadn't mentioned his condition and hopefully he was slightly more recovered now.

Hopefully recovered enough to tell us something about the anthrux.

'You should have some breakfast,' he cautioned.

'In a minute, I just need to check on something.' I moved to leave before catching sight of William's crate of healing tonics by the door. The bottles empty, ready for cleaning.

'You don't happen to have any olus weed, do you?' I asked absently, eyes turning back to the boy where he had resumed reading his paper. Olus weed was rare but powerful in its ability to repel dark sickness. If anyone had some, it would be William.

'I can check. I did brew a tonic that needed it a few weeks ago.' He got to his feet to check his inventory immediately.

'Thank you, William.' I tried to find some relief in his support of my madness, but again, dark sickness shouldn't be here at all. I moved to leave, only for that crumpled page Emrys had found on Mr Thrombi's body to come back to the forefront of my mind.

Reimor. Impossible lost things.

Troubled, I went back upstairs to find the study. It revealed itself where I presumed a guest bathroom was once located. I was relieved to fill my lungs with the comforting smell of books, relishing the heavy air and the quiet of the house after such a chaotic night.

Sickness from contaminated earth wasn't unheard of, but an anthrux bite was worrying, as was the forest in Paxton Village. I might have seen many cursed illnesses, my mother's coming to mind most vividly, but she had died at the end of the war when there were still skirmishes involving dark magic.

This land was supposed to have been cleansed long ago – the Council prided themselves on it – but if there were anthrux, dead folk, missing fey and a need for Emrys to investigate, it appeared the Council were just telling more lies.

No wonder Emrys hardly ever appeared in their meetings; he didn't have time to waste on their games.

I found myself at my desk, flicking through pages of notes. I'd come here to complete my studies, find a cure and graduate – only, I couldn't focus on anything. That word coming back to me over and over again.

Reimor.

There was something here darker than I could have ever feared. Fey needed my help now, no matter how inconsequential my assistance to Emrys was. I had to help them.

If I wanted answers, the first place I needed to start was Thornfield, and Mr Thrombi.

I moved in the direction of the Portium door, shelves shifting for me, anticipating my foolishness. I was relieved to see the portal was already running to Thornfield. I hoped Emrys was on the other side with answers, but as I stepped through, I found myself in Mr Thrombi's room, not the hallway like last time.

Perhaps I had just missed Emrys after all. Mr Thrombi was still unconscious, but his fever had come back. Perplexed, I mixed up a stronger dose of the treatment. Waiting only a moment to see it finally work, the man pulling in an almost relieved breath.

I checked his bandages and saw that he'd been bathed, and the sheets changed, but his skin was oddly cold, strange grey marks had appeared beneath the flesh close to the wound, as if someone had run coal-covered fingers across his pale flesh.

I needed Emrys. This was his area of expertise, after all.

Turning on my heel I opened the healing door, stepping through and raising my foot to meet with the worn wooden floor of the study.

Instead, my boot met with an elaborate rug and I was enveloped by the comforting scent of beasam bark. A warm dampness lingered in the air, as if someone had just finished having a bath.

My head shot up to see a room similar to my own, only far more worn and in disarray. Dark, masculine furniture accented with thick, navy velvet, with fixtures carved to show mythical beasts in battle rather than wildwoods and ancient plants.

Emrys was standing by a large window as the warm morning light spilled over him, catching on the toned contours of his chest and the webbing of silver scars that stretched across his broad shoulders and down his side as he pulled a shirt over his muscular back, the cotton sticking to his still-damp skin. The early-morning light brushed over the streaks of scarring across his chest and throat, tracing a path down his abdomen. Some curving around the indentations of his muscles, others cutting harshly through them. A strange map that went right down to the waistband of his half-unbuttoned trousers and probably further.

A treacherous gasp slipped from my lips, sounding more like a wanton cry in the stillness of the room.

He turned towards the sound the same moment I tried to dart back out the door, only to trip over my own feet, tumbling out into the hallway, crashing into the opposite wall. An involuntary shriek left my lips as cupboards in the hallway rattled with the house's laughter.

'Kat?' Emrys voice was gruff, caught somewhere between confusion and amusement.

A moment earlier and I could have caught him bathing or, worse, naked. My cheeks flamed at the thought as I grasped foolishly for words, rolling over to get my knees beneath me as I continued to be tangled in my own blasted skirts.

'I . . . I was coming to find you.' I pushed stray strands of hair behind my ears as I looked up to see him filling his bedroom doorway, his shirt still mercilessly open.

'The house likes to play tricks.' He crouched before me, hand extended to help me up. Wet hair falling across his forehead, his eyes soft grey, a wicked grin on his lips making him appear almost boyish.

'I didn't know . . . I wouldn't have . . .' A foolish tangled mess of words fell from my lips, cheeks burning. 'I'm sorry. I was thinking about—'

You. Thankfully I swallowed that word down to avoid any further mortification.

'I've had worse surprises,' he commented, taking my hand and pulling me up effortlessly. 'Releasing beasts from books and now charging into bedchambers. Maybe you're more dangerous than I first thought.'

The casual playfulness of him in undress stunned me, and I seemed unable to release his hand as I pondered if I'd hit my head.

'I should be more cautious. There are terrible stories of fates suffered by those who fall victim to fey charms.' The wickedness in his gaze was something I had to be imagining.

'They usually exclude Kysillians,' I replied dryly. Most deeming Kysillians to be too brutish to have any seductive qualities.

'More fool them,' he muttered. 'What seems to be the problem the house thinks needs my attention so intensely?'

'Mr Thrombi is getting worse. I couldn't understand the new markings that—'

'New markings?' He frowned, something about the severity of the words reminding him of his current state of undress. He buttoned up his shirt and ran a worried hand through his hair.

'Yes, there are—' Before I could finish, a ringing started that made Emrys go completely still. His eyes darkening like ink spilling across fresh parchment.

'Those are the study warning bells,' he said.

Chapter Nineteen

If I had any doubts of Emrys's status as a renowned fighter in the wars, they were all erased as he bolted down the hallway, giving me no choice but to run after him. I lifted my skirts to an inappropriate height, catching up with him just as he jumped the banister of the main staircase, landing with the grace of a cat on the steps below.

Despite my natural urge to copy him, I flew down the stairs instead, gripping onto the banister and using it to launch myself down the hallway after him.

Even with my Kysillian blood, he was somehow faster. A crash and thud echoed down the narrow corridor, followed by a cry of alarm as the bells continued to chime. The repetitive slamming sound of a door guiding me until I turned the final corner to see the study doors opening and closing erratically.

Emrys skidded to a halt before me, flinging his arm out to brace it on the wood panelling, blocking my path as I ran into his forearm, almost winding myself where it caught my ribs. I held onto his shoulder and tried to catch my breath.

Then William was flung out through the study doorway, crashing into the wood panelling just in front of us before slumping painfully to the tiled floor.

'William!' I cried, ducking under Emrys's arm and dropping to help the boy up.

'I think something is wrong with Mr Thrombi,' he groaned, rubbing his neck. Emrys came to my side, quickly assessing that William was all in one piece.

'Are you all right?' I worried.

'Just need to catch my breath.' His face was pale as he tried to drag in a deep breath while clutching at his side.

'You should go and—' My words died on my lips as something changed in the air. A horrid cold tension, a strange whistling as the bells silenced. Strong arms were around my waist and I was wrenched around, my feet leaving the floor momentarily only to stumble into the panelling on the other side of the study entrance. A loud crash and the sound of wood splitting filled the air along with another startled cry from William.

My back pressed against the wall, Emrys's arms caging me in, his breath brushing against my cheekbone, one arm braced on the wall next to my head, the other still around my waist. His head was dipped, dark hair falling across his brow, and his eyes were so dark even the whites weren't visible as he looked at me. I was suddenly unsure if it was just *him* inside there. My hands pressed against the bare warm skin of his chest where his shirt had parted.

'Bloody saints!' William cried, fracturing my thoughts, and I yanked my hands back and rose to my tiptoes to see over Emrys's shoulder.

Three ceremonial swords from one of the display cabinets at the back of the study were now embedded in the wood panelling. Right where I'd been standing.

'I don't . . .' I began breathlessly, holding onto Emrys's arm, trying to find the answer to what was happening – only to see him looking down at me, his eyes nothing but darkness

197

swirled with grey like a storm on a winter's night. A chill ran over my flesh from the volatile nature of the magic seeping from his skin.

His brows were creased, fighting to understand something before he pushed away from me. The air was colder in his absence as I ran my hands over my arms, checking that I was indeed all in one piece.

'Whatever it is, it's really pissed off,' William offered as the study door continued to slam. The crashing carried on inside those bells chiming wildly.

Emrys reached into his trouser pocket, pulling out a round metal contraption no bigger than an apple, rusted and engraved with long strokes of a craftsman's tool.

A containment orb. An object I'd only ever seen in a history tome. A piece of ancient technology made to stun dark magic into remaining in one form for a short period of time.

'Did you stitch an endless charm into your trousers?' I accused, confused by how else it could have fit in there with how snug they fit against his muscular thighs.

'We can discuss my trousers later, Croinn,' he commented dryly, turning sharply towards the study doors.

'It's not going to like that,' William warned with a grimace, looking down at the containment orb, but it was quite clear Emrys was beyond caring. He twisted the metal orb twice, a clicking of gears began as he waited for a gap in the doors and tossed it carelessly into the study.

There was a moment of silence in the chaos before bright white light burst through the gaps in the door, forcing me to avert my eyes. Then the screeching began.

The study doors were thrown open, spots dancing in my vision as I leant around Emrys, and there in the centre of the library was Mr Thrombi.

Or what had once been Mr Thrombi.

His body was hunched and convulsing. The crack of bone sounded with each jerked motion. His limbs longer than natural, with taloned claws, the fur around his hoofed legs peeling away, his skin unnaturally trying to shed.

Dark foam dripped from a mouth filled with too many sharp teeth as the creature continued to scream, clawing at its eyes as if the light had injured it. Tendrils of smoke rose from its greyish flesh, evidence of its dark power.

Books and papers lay across the floor in disarray, all the destruction leading to the shelves where the Portium door was hidden. Where he'd come from.

'A tallet,' Emrys said.

A tallet. A curse come back to life. A formless being that possessed weakened prey. Stronger than death, as it sunk into the victims very bones.

Emrys turned to me, his lips thin and face drawn. 'Did you use magic in that healing?'

'Only a spark,' I replied, confused as to how that would cause this. But before I could contemplate it further, the tallet dropped its hands, its beady black eyes focused on us, and roared. The bells on the chains guarding the darker texts began to jangle furiously, books slid across the room of their own accord towards the beast.

'It's trying to open the books!' William lurched forward, catching three of the tomes and pushing them under his body so they couldn't move towards the creature.

I shook my head. A tallet was a lesser demon. It wouldn't know how to feast on the remains of dark magic.

'It isn't clever enough for that,' Emrys replied, opening his palm. Appearing there in a wisp of smoke was a thin, sharp blade.

A shadowsbane. A magical blade forged to contain the demonic.

'*Am I not?*' the creature replied with a clacking of teeth, the wisps around its body growing darker.

Emrys froze, a tension rippling over him.

Dark fiends didn't speak.

'It shouldn't be—' I began, trying to understand, but it roared, dark wisps shooting out towards us. Emrys didn't move to block the summoning. No, he pushed me out of its path. I went tumbling over my skirts and William's sprawled legs where he still fought with the books that appeared to suddenly have a will of their own.

The tallet's attack caught Emrys across his chest, throwing him back through the study doors, which were rendered to nothing but a splintered mess with the impact.

'Emrys!' William cried out as he struggled to catch more books. I pushed myself up, slipping on papers as I faced the creature just as it gave another victorious roar, spittle flying from its lips.

I pressed my palms together, allowing my magic to surge. Not my summoning glow but the wild flames, forming a crackling sphere of chaotic magic that was difficult to hold. But I needed to control it a moment longer, to make it unable to miss its target.

Sweat beaded my brow, but just as I felt the strain in my arms of holding it, the creature laughed and vanished.

Silence filled the space, the library creaking with unease and the roar of my magic in my blood the only sound. I moved cautiously further into the room, turning wildly in a circle, watching dust motes dance in the sunlight pouring in from the window.

'Kat?' William scrambled to his feet, books clutched to his chest as he panted for breath. 'That's . . . it can't have . . .'

Run. A voice mocked in the back of my head.

The warning was enough. A horrid sensation brushed my neck like icy fingers, turning me, but it was too late. The thing had barely reformed in a swirl of black, acrid smoke, a laugh echoing in my ear, as dark energy struck me.

My feet left the ground, a cry escaping my lips as I felt solid impact and the shattering of glass. I hit hard ground, my momentum sending me rolling.

Grass tickled my nose and a horrid ache shot down my spine as I pushed myself up onto my forearms and shook glass from my hair.

Panting, I looked up to see the ruined study window. The bastard had thrown me through it.

Pain radiated through my limbs as I groaned and forced myself to my feet. Regretting every decision I'd ever made, I watched helplessly as the dark form of the tallet appeared at the shattered window, clinging to the frame, and with a hiss launched itself at me.

Faster than I thought possible, the thing made impact, sending me tumbling back to the earth. A tangle of limbs, a swirl of demonic smoke and the snapping of its teeth.

A scream filled my ears, shrill and feral. The creature's claws scraped at the earth either side of me, its razor-sharp teeth gnashing too close to my nose. I pressed my palm against its face to hold it back. Its rotten breath washing over me.

I brought my foot up, managing to catch it in its middle. Kicking it off and over my head with a frustrated scream, I rolled and tried to get my bag open to get my sword.

'*Kyvor Mor*,' it hissed as it scuttled and twisted across the ground. My stomach dropped, fear freezing me in place. Kysillian words.

I watched it run its horrid grey tongue over its lip, smeared with red blood. I glanced down to see my palm covered in blood. My blood.

Kyvor Mor. Curse Killer. An ancient magic my father commanded, that he'd passed on to me. One this dark couldn't know. Shouldn't know.

The ground shook and before I could find my sanity, the soil erupted and a thick root wrapped with deadly thorns emerged from beneath, swatting the creature away from me.

William crouched a few feet away, hands pressed against the grass just beyond the window, sweat coating his brow. The pale freckled skin of his hands stained green with the ferocity of his magic.

The tallet clawed at the earth to catch itself, bones cracking as its head twisted unnaturally and it screeched again. It held itself low to the ground, ready for another attack.

The wind changed, growing sharper at my back. The ground rumbling beneath my boots – nothing to do with the earth or William's magic, but something deeper. Older. The bitterness of old spells and forsaken curses echoed in my mind, almost in warning, forcing me to turn towards that feeling, only to see Emrys jump down from the ruined window frame with a lethal grace.

His shirt was torn, but there was not a mark on him . . . but those eyes were intent with fury. He threw out his hand and bright white energy left his fingers to strike the creature in the centre of its chest like a lightning bolt, sending it rolling across the loose earth, scattering it into nothing but dark shards of bone and dust.

The wind roared past me, almost dragging me across the distance and closer to Emrys, as if under his command, but the remains of the creature bounced, cracking and twisting back into formation, across the grassy earth.

'It's not dying!' cried William as he flung his arm, another great root surging from the ground to try and trap the pieces of the creature before it could reform, but they darted past in smoke form, twisting violently in the air with a crackling hiss.

'I can see that, William!' Emrys snapped, that ethereal glow consuming his hands.

A dark fiend that couldn't be killed with fey magic.

There was a dark magic long ago that fed on fey magic, and used it to become stronger, one that was supposed to be dead, buried beneath those Kysillian Kings' seals. Just like that anthrux should have been.

Reimor. This creature should be beneath the earth.

I looked down at my muddy palms, seeing the glow of my magic waiting there, the heat of it still not content even with what it had already done.

I shouldn't be able to resurrect a cursed being with nothing more than a flare of energy. My hands curled into fists as I forced myself to remember the things I longed to forget.

They hunted us for a reason. We are a being without limit, and if you show them such limitlessness, they'll come for you too.

A warning I'd promised myself to never forget. I'd given it that strength from my magic, from the endlessness of it. But magic wasn't the only gift I possessed.

I reached for my bag, rummaging for the sword just as another screech filled the air . . . one not of a demon. The sun was blocked out for a mere moment as a long shadow moved across the uneven grass.

'Is that a wrywing!?' William called in disbelief.

The dark scaled body of a wrywing came diving from the skies, landing between us and the creature. The dark scales rippling across its body like armour and its wings flared wide, deadly sharp talons at the point of each joint catching the sunlight. The ground shook as the wrywing's large, clawed feet dug into the turf, its wings slapping behind it in threat. The updraught almost sent me tumbling backwards.

It roared and turned its head, looking down its lethal scaled body at me with familiar green eyes. The spiked tail swishing from side to side with annoyance. Sharp teeth bared in its large snout as scaled nostrils flared with irritation.

'A-Alma?' I whispered in horrified confusion.

The wrywing form of Alma turned its attention back to the tallet as it charged again – only the wrywing was ready, and the pair becoming nothing but a whirl of scales and smoke as they fought. A wrywing: a natural enemy of the dark, able to devour dark spells and creatures made of it.

'Kat!' William cried, giving me just enough time to duck as another large root soared past to help the wrywing, knocking the tallet back so Alma's deadly jaws could snap around its clawed hand.

The dark fiend screamed as I raced across to Emrys, ducking and dodging as clumps of earth and roots sailed past me.

'She hasn't been that big before!' I half screamed in hysteria, stumbling to his side.

'I'm slightly occupied right now, Croinn,' he growled back as he ducked to avoid another surge of dark energy from the tallet, dragging me down with him.

'What if she can't turn back!' I worried. Ignoring the current chaos and the dart of dark magic that barely missed my ear as I continued to watch the beastly form of Alma snap and wrestle with the dark being.

'Just give me a minute and we'll sort it out,' Emrys hissed through tight lips.

Alma threw the tallet to the ground, sending dirt into the air as roots protruded, wrapping around its limbs to trap it with William's help.

Except it untangled itself too easily. Knew the magic, was somehow stronger than . . .

Emrys had asked if I used magic in my healing. My magic. Not a summoning.

A tallet, a curse that possessed and fed off the magic it found. I'd fed it my own. It wouldn't die because there was no power stronger than a Kysillian flame. Only that which was trapped beneath.

The wrywing gave out an annoyed cry as another of its bites did nothing. Then I realised just how useless my fear had made me. I pulled my father's blade from my bag, the hilt glowing hot against my palm.

Magic isn't the only gift we possess. Those words came back to me so softly on the wind, like breath against the shell of my ear. The sword heavy and waiting for command.

As if sensing something shifting within me, I felt Emrys's dark eyes roaming over my face.

'What are you—' he began, but I was already running, faster than I ever had in my life, ducking and sliding beneath the large monstrous roots to reach the centre, where William's magic was struggling to contain the tallet as Alma's sharp tail failed to land another killing blow.

I allowed my magic to streak down my arm, to wrap around my very bones, giving me strength as I felt the blade shift, becoming a throwing knife. I released it. Let it whistle like a flaming arrow through the carnage to bury itself in the creature's chest right where its heart should be. Dark, sour ichor seeped from the wound and down its grey flesh.

It froze mid screech, those demonic eyes fixed on me, mouth open as it tried to roar. I hurtled into it, hand closing around that knife as its teeth snapped an inch from my face. I yanked the knife free. The creature hissed and fell back, smoke rising to try and escape, but the blade lengthened once more just as I turned, raised it and in one clean swipe slashed deeply across its middle, making its clumsy body heave and pulsate.

I drew my arm back for another strike, only for Emrys to be there, bright white light between his palms and wrapping around the creature, it screamed but glowed with that same light.

Emry's eyes blazed ethereal white for the barest moment, a word I couldn't hear leaving his lips, and then the body of the cursed creature crumbled in on itself to become nothing but dust between us.

Unmade by him.

I lowered the blade, that horrid bitter dust coating my lips as I panted for breath. Looking down at the sword in my grasp, as it shone in muted sunlight. Another piece of my chaotically dangerous magic and the legacy of my blood. Something the dark should never know, and I'd given it away foolishly.

Kyvor Mor.

'Kat.' Emrys took hold of my arm, turning me harshly towards him. Expression stony as his now dark eyes ran over every inch of my face. No traces of that strange magic.

'An anthrux bite doesn't possess the power to summon a tallet,' I whispered, watching the dust of the creature catch on the breeze over his shoulder.

'A tharox does,' he replied carefully, that tension still not leaving him, displeasure pressing his lips together as he took in the tears in my clothing.

'They haven't been seen since the second age of the fey rulings.' I frowned. 'He shouldn't have died like that.'

Carefully, Emrys pressed two fingers under my chin. There was an icy chill from the remnants of his magic that made my breath catch, mud flecks in his hair and tension in his jaw.

'You have a scratch on your cheek.' His thumb ran gently over the edge of my jaw. There was a stillness to him.

'I'll survive,' I whispered unsteadily. 'Why does this feel worse than we could have anticipated?'

'Because you're too clever to fool.' He considered me for a long moment, lips parting as if he wished to say more, before a strange expression crossed his face. His eyes dipping to my hand where it hung at my side.

He captured it gently, turning it over to see the slice from the glass. The blood that the tallet had tasted. His eyes appeared wholly black again in a moment.

A whoosh came from above, breaking us apart before the wrywing made impact with the earth, its whole body trembling as its wings snapped shut.

'Bloody saints!' William cried, as the earth trembled with the force of the landing, making him stumble and land on his backside in the long grass. The roots he'd summoned were withering and slipping back beneath the earth like serpents.

'Alma.' Her name left my mouth in a breath of relief, only to be twisted into tight-chested fear as I rushed for her, seeing her begin to morph and change in a painful twisting of flesh and bone.

The sharpness of her naked spine was stark as she remained on all fours, retching. Her clawed fingers digging into the soft earth as she choked for breath. The long grass hiding most of her.

Her dark hair in disarray, curls stuck to her temples and skin glistening with sweat as she dragged in deep uneven breaths.

'Alma?' I dropped to my knees at her side, my sword – now nothing more than a hilt again – tumbling across the grass as I took hold of her arms. Watching with bated breath as her head came up, eyes luminous but mortal, cheeks rosy with exertion, the impression of dark scales still just under the skin's surface, but her wobbly, exhausted smile of relief stood out most of all.

'I think you fixed me again,' she winced. I threw my arms around her as a relieved sob crawled up my throat.

'No. You fixed yourself,' I whispered into her hair, trying my best not to crush her as she held on. Thankful to whichever ancestors were watching over us as I took in the carnage before us, the unturned earth slowly seeping back into place under William's influence, the large gouges from her claws growing new grass.

'You changed form!' I laughed, unable to help my excitement.

'Let's not do it again for a while.' She grimaced. 'I'm nothing if not efficient at cleaning up your messes.'

'I should be taking care of you,' I argued, pressing my hand against her chilled forehead.

'Please don't. I'll be dead by the end of the week,' she quipped, sounding annoyed by the mere suggestion as she tried to sag weakly back towards the ground as if content to sleep there curled up like a stoat. 'Where are my chocolates?'

I couldn't help the laugh that escaped my lips as I held her even tighter.

William came to a skidding stop before me, his gaze darting between us in confusion. Of course, he'd only seen Alma as a cat or a mouse, not a mythical beast. His cheeks flared bright red when he came to his senses, and pulled his long work coat from his shoulders, crouching to drape it over her.

'Hello, Alma,' he greeted a bit sheepishly, the wind playing in his copper hair.

'Hello, William,' she replied, forcing her tired limbs into the sleeves of his coat, and I was thankful she was petite enough for it to cover everything.

'Are you all right, William?' I asked, concerned about his dishevelment and damp brow; the streak of mud across his cheek and the red welt underneath.

'Nothing a good rejuvenation tonic can't fix.' He smirked. 'You must be famished, Alma. Let's get you something from the kitchen. Some bone broth should do the trick.'

He held out his arm, and to my surprise Alma took it easily, steadier on her feet than I had expected as she rose.

'I think we all might need something a bit stronger than broth, William,' Emrys added, suddenly at my side, moving forward to help Alma. 'Miss Darcy,' he greeted with the politeness of a dinner guest.

'Lord Blackthorn,' she replied, and in true Alma fashion, despite being without her clothes, and with the indentations of those scales still on her cheek, she raised her chin in challenge, boldly meeting his eye.

'We better get inside before the house locks us out.' William sighed with a grimace as he surveyed the damage. 'I'm sure it's furious.'

'I'll have a word,' Emrys muttered with genuine exhaustion. Offering his arm to help Alma, she took it despite the claws that remained on her own. William moved to support her other side as they made their way across the uneven terrain.

I bent to retrieve my father's sword, smiling as I heard William already engaging Alma in a conversation about wrywings, and she didn't appear to be in too much distress about it as Emrys guided them through the debris.

Kyvor Mor, came whispered into my mind. Almost as if on the wind.

Unease ran down my spine, but as I turned there was nothing but grey dust tumbling through the long grass. The remains of the creature that had taken over Mr Thrombi were quickly disappearing. The remains of something that shouldn't exist. Something too dangerous for this world.

Just like me.

Chapter Twenty

Fools will tell you to court fear. They will tell you it makes you stronger, but all it does is rot you from your bones out. What do beings like us have to fear? We, the creatures who hold chaos in our hearts and destruction in their will.

— The Ballad of Kysillia — Unknown

Those ancient myths pierced through my thoughts as I sat in the warmth of the kitchen, hands curled around another cup of tea. At ease slightly now that Alma slept soundly upstairs, exhausted from being an ancient dark-fiend-eating beast. The biggest she'd been. Just how monstrous could her magic be and how many impossible, forbidden things could it do?

It was the reason they'd hunted her and why they would hunt her again.

I kept those worries buried at the back of my mind as my eyes drifted over the notes I'd spread across the table. Looking for anything to distract myself with but still that unease didn't dissipate.

Then came the brush of Emrys's magic over my skin, a moment before the dark form of him ducked into the kitchen, his eyes moving to me first as if I was the only thing he was looking for.

He'd changed. His shirt buttoned to the collar and cravat in place. Sleeves fastened at his wrists, but his waistcoat was open.

'Are you going somewhere?' I asked with a frown. Despite there being no windows down here, I knew it must have been late.

He shook his head with a small smile, moving to sit opposite me, our knees brushing beneath the table. 'How is Miss Darcy?'

'Recovering.' I sighed, rubbing my brow. She'd managed to devour one chocolate against my advice before she fell asleep, clutching the box. 'I've given her the transfiguration tonic. So let us hope it works for her.'

'I've never seen a being change that easily,' he said carefully, cautious of how I'd take his interest in those secrets.

'You've seen one before?'

He shook his head, dark hair falling onto his worried brow. 'Only lesser fey, and larger folk that could change shape in defence. Or Verr beings when they twist their summoning curse.'

Unease flooded through me as I took another sip of tea to try and get the lump out of my throat. Not knowing exactly what Alma was or the origin of her power.

'My father told stories of beings in the Western Mountains that could take on the form of dragons and other winged beasts,' Emrys continued softly, reaching to move some of the small notes I'd been reading. Notes I'd read far too many times about transfiguration. 'I think even they had limits.'

Then he moved one hand, holding his palm to face the ceiling. Without command a book apparated, resting there, the old brown leather cover creased, buckles cracked and peeling. The pages curling with age.

Stunned, I could have sworn I saw phantom tendrils of black smoke weave between his fingers, but in a blink they were gone. Just shadows from the fire perhaps?

He held it out to me. The clasps were heavy but lifted easily enough and as I turned the page, the faded ink showed depictions of the Western Mountains and beings that took on the form of scaled beasts.

'Did he have any more books like this?' My voice was quiet with wonder as I turned over the pages, running my fingers down the illustrations as a man took monstrous form with wings.

'We can look.'

We. The word brought a smile to my lips at just how much more trouble we could find, how much we'd already stumbled into already and how unbothered by it all he seemed.

'How did you keep her hidden?' His voice was guarded, eyes an unsure stormy grey. As if worried such a subject would bring me nothing but pain.

'Master Hale offered to take her in if I agreed to be included in the treaty. He didn't know the full extent of her powers then.' I let my shoulders droop into a shrug. It sounded so much worse when I said it out loud 'Nobody is going to look twice at a fey maid. I think the other maids were too scared of her temper to question anything.'

The truth was harder. That when men came wandering drunk from the Councilmen's parties seeking maids to fondle, they had the misfortune of running into Alma.

Turned out men who needed to save their purse by marrying a lord's daughter didn't want to explain to their new wife how they were no longer in possession of their bollocks; losing them to a maid who grew claws in the shadows of the stairwell.

Word must have travelled fast because no men wandered the kitchens anymore, and the maids gave Alma a wide berth, either scared that the story was true or that she was mad enough to make it up.

Emrys's gaze moved back to my notes, and he gave a small smile as if sensing Alma's cunning. 'More unsavoury reading?'

He moved the papers aside, revealing the cover of the numerous copies of *The Crow's Foot* I'd piled together, looking for clues.

'William thinks there could be a vesper demon killing lords.' I sighed, leaning forward to look again at the articles covering the missing lords, none of whom had been heard of since the war. They could all be in hiding perhaps, or all murdered in conspicuous ways. 'However, there is nothing to say their ring fingers are missing.'

Vesper demons loved trophies. Ring fingers being their favourite, wearing the bones like jewels around their necks. It seemed bad luck was the only reason for the lords' murders. One had been killed in a brawl, another for gambling debts and the third by an enraged mistress. Nothing had been taken from the bodies. However, the lack of the Council's care about it sent a shiver down my spine.

I looked, waiting for Emrys's dry remark about William's reading material, only to see his face blank, jaw tense and eyes darker than before. Gaze locked on those pages.

'Emrys?' A sudden icy chill had seeped into the warm bricks of the kitchen. The fire sat lower in the hearth as shadows seemed to stretch from the corners of the room.

'That creature spoke.' His voice was as cold as the air, distant as those dark eyes met my own. 'What did it say to you?'

Kyvor Mor. The words hissed through my mind in that cruel mocking voice.

'I didn't learn all my Kysillian words. Not the ancient ones,' I lied too easily.

Guilt gnawed away at my ribs but I wrapped my arms around myself, rubbing my forearms as my eyes fell back to the horror in those papers between us.

'Poor Mr Thrombi.' I sighed, hating that he didn't have a chance. That none of them did. 'He didn't deserve to die like that.'

'None of them do.'

I moved the papers aside to pull the file from beneath. 'I wrote up my half of the report about it but I know it won't do anything.' It had felt better to write it all down. But Emrys didn't reach to take it from me.

'This is darker than I anticipated,' he said. 'You shouldn't—' He shook his head, moving to leave, the rest of the words lost in the tension that had taken over him.

Forgetting myself, I reached across the table, taking hold of his hand and stopping his retreat.

'Please, Emrys,' I whispered, as he paused, looking at only where I touched him. 'I want to help.'

Something moved through his eyes, a tension in his jaw as if he'd refuse, but then he relaxed back into his seat. Before I could apologise and pull it back, he turned my hand gently in his own.

His focus was on the small bandage around my palm from where the window's glass had cut me. His thumb ran over the small scars on my fingers from being caught by a training blade. Small insignificant things. Marks I'd seen catch the light on his own hands. Fighter's marks. Reminders of how my mother would tend to them, while singing folk tales of the north. Then how Alma had to do it instead after our sparring sessions.

'You fought remarkably.' He offered the compliment quietly, as if it was the most ordinary thing in the world to say.

'My father taught me.' I smiled, hoping he couldn't feel the uneven nature of my pulse, unsteady at the rough feel of his thumb against my skin. 'You don't have to keep complimenting me.'

His attention came back to my face, tracing every inch of it so carefully.

'Stop impressing me then,' he challenged, his crooked smile almost boyish. A warmth sweeping through my chest, a comforting swell just like that my magic offered.

'I'll try my best.' I smirked, for once allowing his words to nestle into some quiet lost place inside of me.

'You drew these?' He asked, turning around another open book. An old journal filled with the stories I'd written from memory. The Kysillian histories, describing how Kysillia had battled the Old Gods, the Alder Kings and the endless night. How she had won these lands. The Kings of her blood following in her teachings, the rising of the Verr and the sealing of the earth.

'With the first pen and paper I managed to get hold of.' I smiled at the rough and rushed nature to some of them. 'I suppose I was afraid I'd forget.'

All the tales. From the First Queen, Kysillia, who was gifted chaos and flame from the heavens, all the way through to the Seven Kings of old, the kingdoms that stretched across Elysior and all the magic that had been here.

Stories lost after the Kysillian Kings fell centuries ago and the world tumbled into chaos with mortal power. When most captured Kysillians were chained in mines, including my father's mother. Forced to work until their bodies gave up. That's why they called us trolls, for how long we were forced to exist in the dark.

The illustrations accompanying the stories had got better over time, closer to the ones I remembered, no matter how the pages curled with age or the misspellings and mistakes.

I'd kept it because it was all I had. The memory of those stories. The voice of my father telling me them.

I'd told every single one to Alma, whispered in the dead of night at Daunton. Making her promise to tell them if she made it out instead of me. To make sure they escaped even if I didn't.

I shook away the darkness of the thought. Focusing on the warmth of Emrys's calloused hand against my own. It was then I noticed a smudge of grey at the cuff of his shirt, perhaps a nasty bruise forming.

'You have—' I began, leaning forward to better see the mark, but he suddenly remembered himself and let go.

'I should go. We'll look for those books in the morning.' He cleared his throat, fingers raking through his hair.

'We should be focusing on the tallet,' I pointed out, despite how my other hand lingered on the pages of the book he'd given me. Eager to read every word.

'After.' There was a slight command to that word. Reminding me of the balance to this darkness. Indulging too long wasn't good for either of us.

As if knowing he'd won that tiny battle, he slipped from the bench, checking his pocket-watch as he crossed the kitchen.

'Goodnight, Emrys,' I called quietly after him. He paused on the stairs, looking back at me almost reluctantly.

'Goodnight, Croinn.' His voice was hoarse with his response before he left me there, tracing the shape of those dragons from ancient tales, none of the words going in when all I could think of was him.

Chapter Twenty-One

Morning came, but Emrys was gone. Which was evident as I stood in the middle of the study that had miraculously returned to its former cluttered self. William had explained that the room held a magic of its own, which was why the tallet didn't get far with its attack, why the room had a window again and not a gaping hole. Not even a smear on the glass to evidence our battle.

I wasn't greeted by William, but by a small paper bird waiting atop a stack of books on my desk, drenched in a stream of soft winter morning light and fluttering its wings in excitement at my arrival.

'Do you have something for me?' I smiled, holding out my palm as I reached my desk. The magical paper hopped up into my hand and unfurled instantly.

Croinn,
These were the ones I thought you'd find most useful.
I hope they are.
Emrys

Foolish emotion welled in my throat. It'd been late last night when he'd left the kitchen. Had he stayed up to find these for me? The note folded itself back up and I tucked it into my pocket before letting my fingers run over the weathered spines of the books piled on my desk, ancient tomes of transfiguration and the shifting of Verr, still dusty from disuse.

Books I could only have dreamt of stumbling upon in the Institute, and Emrys leaving them for me was an act of kindness I was too unfamiliar with, unearthing strange emotions from a secret quiet place inside of me.

'Thank you.' The words seemed important despite the fact he wasn't here to hear them.

I pulled the tome on transfiguration he'd given me last night from my bag, my numerous notes sticking out from the pages, and put it with the others.

Only I couldn't sit and focus on books I'd longed to read. Not when I was burdened with everything that had come the day before. The words of that tallet still echoing in my mind. *Kyvor Mor.* Words it shouldn't be able to speak.

If dark sickness was returning to the earth, there had to be a starting point. The village by Paxton Fields had fey who were desperate enough to leave, to abandon their sacred grounds, but it didn't point to a darkness this powerful originating there. Which meant it had come from somewhere else. Somewhere close enough for a fiend to travel without feasting too often.

Emrys's absence plagued me. Something about it felt wrong. The look on his face at those pages in *The Crow's Foot*, the darkness that shouldn't be there.

I wandered around the shelves, extracting the newest maps I could find, noting that Paxton Fields was a cluster of farms in the south, on a narrow strip of flat land between the South Wood and the lands of Fairfax Manor.

I opened older maps of the south and laid them flat, finding no such place as Paxton Fields or Fairfax Manor, just wastelands where the Battle of the South Wood had taken place centuries before. The lands must have been redistributed after the event, making me wonder what they'd been before, and why darkness would choose to manifest there.

I ventured further into the shelves, rummaging for war logs and Verr surges. I gathered the darkest and heaviest volumes in my arms and laid them out.

The Battle of the South Wood had been a massacre in the ancient tales. They said the ground split and such darkness poured free it was almost impossible to contain. Master Hale had his own historical records of it and some fragments of a surviving tapestry that depicted it.

I didn't know much about the Fairfax family. They weren't mages, at least not anymore. They were one of the older families who built its wealth on the backs of fey enslavement and the wars, having little skill or merit of their own. Now, they'd apparently chosen cursed earth to settle their name upon.

I turned another page, not understanding why someone would settle on ground willing to kill them. Grounds where darkness lurked closer to the surface. Unless, of course, that was exactly what they wanted.

An anthrux wasn't just a consequence of the earth and its creations; a spell had summoned it, and now I needed to work out which one. If someone in Fairfax was summoning, what were they summoning for?

There my theories took a manic turn as I pulled out all my notebooks and emptied my bag to see if any samples I'd collected from that cursed wood could hold an answer to the puzzle.

Yet I was unable to escape the guilt that if I hadn't used my magic, maybe Mr Thrombi would still be here, maybe none of this would have happened.

Those thoughts plagued me, my shoulders becoming stiff as the study grew dimmer and dimmer. The books darker in matter. More fragmented history of the Verr, the ancient enemy of the Kysillians. Of the Verr's dark deeds, their vicious will, and the cruel Old Gods they worshipped.

A simple tale. Perhaps too simple. For if darkness was returning, maybe such evils could never be beaten after all.

Rain began to pound relentlessly against the window from a storm I hadn't anticipated. Thunder rumbled in the distance as I rubbed my neck. Turning another page to try and decode a brief section of curses before I finally relented. I needed William's chatter to chase away my unease, and as I looked at the gloomy sky I knew I also needed to check on Alma, hoping Emrys's tonic had helped her settle.

A soft rattling of bells came from the back shelves. The weak fire in the hearth flickered as if disturbed by the sound. I turned towards the shadowed maze of bookcases, now somehow more ominous.

'Hello?' I frowned. A silence followed that almost made me think I'd imagined it, but the soft jingle came again. Taunting.

'William?' I called. But only ominous silence answered. A flash of lightning broke overhead, making the shadows between the shelves appear endless.

Picking up the small lantern from my desk, I worked my way through the shelves, following the sound of those bells, worried Alma had changed again and lost her way, or maybe the house wanted to show me something.

I moved further into the gloom, unease prickling against the back of my neck. My breath misting before me halted my steps, the hairs on my arms raising. Books on the shelf next to me began to bounce and shake, creaking deeply with distress.

Then, out of the corner of my eye, I saw something move deep down the shadowy aisle. A centre of darkness that stood out more strongly than the rest, long and thin. I turned with the lamp, light stretching across the narrow passage, but there was nothing there.

Just the endlessness of darkness.

My magic rose in response, hot and relentless as it made my fingertips burn with insistence. Something was here.

'Hello?' I called foolishly, swallowing down my fear as my heart climbed further up my throat.

Breath stuttered through my lips. Magic rolling unsteadily through me as I tried to rationalise my growing anxiety. My magic biting more sharply into my skin. Almost in warning.

That icy sensation streaked down my spine. A prodding pain at the base of my neck, making me grip it.

The crash of a book tumbling from a shelf made me jump, turning me around, and there it was. A long, dark humanoid shadow pressed between another set of shelves, watching me between the volumes.

Terror seeped into my veins as I watched its shadowy fingers curl around the shelf as if to pull itself closer.

'I'm surprised you don't smell of him yet,' came a voice from behind me, harsh in its coldness, that sent me spinning towards it with a cry of alarm. My lamp flew from my grasp to shatter on the hardwood, magic dispersing and plunging us into stormy darkness.

I stumbled backwards into the shelves, knocking free a stack of volumes that tumbled to the ground at my feet.

A roar of thunder and another flash of lightning illuminated the stranger.

Just a man. He had a shock of brown hair that had been slicked back so harshly that it reflected the dim light. His eyes were dark, too harsh in his face. And they were solely focused on me. Something cruel in the severity of his features, too angular to be found handsome. His clothes were pristine, the intensity of his cologne so sharp I should have smelt him before I heard him.

'What are you doing here?' I demanded, forgetting myself as I pressed my trembling palm over my pounding heart.

'How bold.' His thin lips curled in disgust. 'I see Blackthorn's loosened your leash.'

I bristled, my grip on the bookcase behind me tightening as my fingers started to burn in warning. 'I don't know who you are.'

'Oh, but I know you,' he mused bitterly, leering at me. 'Master Hale's little treasure. How sick the old bastard has become with his longing.'

Revulsion rolled through me, my hands squeezing into fists at my side. Then I noticed the pristine cut of his dark clothes, seemingly like a Council uniform but one I didn't recognise.

'I'll summon Lord Blackthorn and he can deal with you himself.' I smiled tightly.

'I wish you would, *pet*.' A cruel smile twisted his face into something not quite human.

Bastard. I tried to move past him as I bit my tongue against a string of curses but he stepped closer, forcing me to back into the shelves. That unease sharpened in my chest. I'd been cornered by enough men to know their intent and no matter how I wished my rage to build, only a small helpless fear manifested in its stead.

My magic burned through my veins in response, painful in its desire to be free. The bells began to ring weakly next to us – not from the books, but because the house willed it.

Relief flared through me that someone would hear them. Hopefully Alma with claws and teeth.

Then that hope was smothered as the vile stranger threw out his hand, some invisible summoning slice cutting through every string until those bells clattered uselessly on the ground.

The house let out a horrid groan as if pained by the spellcasting.

'I didn't permit you to leave.' He assessed me as if I was some form of parasitic creature.

His eyes raked over me with a familiarity that made my skin crawl. A sickness filled my throat, and I wanted nothing more than to vanish.

'However, I'm certain Emrys is already on his way here.' He inclined his head, dark eyes practically gleaming. 'He has a special sense for danger. Haven't you noticed?'

A horrid fear moved through me at his familiarity with Emrys's name. Why did Emrys know this man? Why was he here?

'Though . . . I suppose you've probably been busy with other *things*.' There was a short, disgusted laugh to finish.

Pig. My magic was almost molten now, as sweat gathered on my palms. Begging me to let it go.

I tried to charge past him, not caring what title he might have held. He moved fast, faster than my weary limbs could account for. His hand wrapped around my wrist, pain seared through my flesh, right to my bones. Igniting them with agony.

My knees almost buckled, a horrid desperate cry escaping me as I found myself backed against the bookcase, his hips pressing sharply into my own.

'Careful.' His tongue clicked in disapproval. 'I've heard worrying tales of you, our rebellious little troll.'

My breath was too short. Too desperate. That pain clawing at my skin, making me arch closer to him against my will. Almost begging for it to stop.

Pain I'd felt only once before. At the hands of Daunton.
Beg, little troll.

'Do you know what happens when forsaken iron enters
the blood?' His grip tightened, and I swallowed my scream,
tears filling my eyes as I glanced down to see the familiar
horrid iron forming rings on his fingers. Forsaken iron leaving
merciless red welts on my skin.

With the moment of distraction, he took hold of the loose
hair at the nape of my neck. The smallest mercy was that it was
with his other gloved hand, shifting my head to see me better.
The brutality of his grip almost pulling the hair from my scalp.

His eyes dipped to my trembling lips and lower. He leant
closer, pressing that pain further into my flesh. Tears slipped
from my eyes and down my cheeks. That made him smile.
A smile I'd seen a hundred times before.

Beg, came hissed in my memory, my magic surging painfully
in my veins, mixing with the agony of that iron.

'What big ears you have.' His breath brushed my cheek, the
scent of him burning my nose with its intensity. Reminding
me vividly of saints' herb, the bitterness of it. How Master
Daunton would wear it, and the vulgar nature of his touch.

Beg. Little troll.

In a moment, that agony took me back. So small and weak.
Kneeling at a saint's altar, that horrid metal burning around my
neck as he forced me to wear it. Waiting until I could bear
it no more, until I hit the cold stone so his torment could
begin. Blows swift and cruel. Amusement in his twisted sneer.

Just as it lay in this man's eyes as he leant closer, his breath
brushing upon my face, and I knew I was going to kill him.

My magic a wild thing within my chest, thrashing against
my ribs. Smoke crawled up my throat, the lick of phantom
flames all over my skin. Searching for a way out.

Wishing to boil him inside his skin, just as I had Daunton. *Murderer,* that dark voice hissed inside my head.

No.

Before my magic could seize control, I broke his hold. One sharp shove with all my strength, forsaken iron burning my flesh, but I pushed through the pain, balled my fist and struck him across the face.

He stumbled back, knocking books and a collection of small sample bottles to the ground.

My magic rushed through me as I slumped back against the bookcase, gasping for breath as I forced myself to remain silent. I willed my body to move. To leave. The fear penetrating too deeply for what I'd done. How close I'd come to doing it again. Hands trembling with the agony of those burns.

Murderer, hissed in the back of my mind.

The pain of my magic surging bowed me over, as the shelf I held onto cracked beneath my hold. Panic tightening my chest as I heard the intruder moving, coming closer again, but I couldn't move.

The bookcase rattled and then the largest compendium on the shelf shot free, hitting him in the groin, Doubling him over. Another book tumbled to my feet, where it began to bounce and ruffle its pages in annoyance. Small pieces of paper flying free. I kicked it, sending it skidding in the man's direction, and a clawed hand made of ink and paper reaching out and taking hold of his boot, claws burying themselves in the leather. An annoyed grunt left him, as he tried to kick it away.

I gathered my skirts and ran through the dark shelves towards the safety of the hall, panting as I glanced behind me, only to slam into something hard. A cry peeling from my lips.

I raised my hand to fight, only to find myself pressed against Emrys's chest, my forearms caught as I panted against the exposed scarred skin of his throat. His coat wet from the storm. His eyes black as night.

'Kat?' His brow was creased with worry even before he heard the footsteps behind us. I turned from his hold, spinning myself so I was behind him. I kept moving backwards, clutching my chest as I tried to pull in breath. Tried to push down the urge to let the wickedness in me free.

The shelves around us creaked, a rumble beneath the wood, a tension about to snap.

'You better have a good reason for being here, Montagor.' Emrys's words were as sharp as a knife as the man stepped from the shadows of the shelves, leaning casually against one.

Lord Montagor. The King's bastard. Currently in charge of managing the fight against rebel fighters in the north.

'Your pet hit me, old friend.' The Lord grinned, wiping at his mouth where I'd split his lip as he leant one hand on the side of one of the study pillars, looking down at the blood on his fingertips with amusement.

There was no relief in being away from him, or Emrys being between us as my skin continued to burn.

'She's not my *pet* and we're not friends,' Emrys replied, a coldness to his voice that didn't reassure me. The tightness that had taken hold of Emrys's mouth seemed to consume his whole body. The shelves around us creaked, a rumble beneath the wood, something about to snap.

'How you wound me, dear Emrys.' Montagor grinned, pressing his hand over his heart, his distaste coating every word. 'You can imagine my surprise when you requested the troll.'

Troll. The panic in me continued to rise, my skin flushing as magic shifted in my blood, responding to the burns on my hands.

Disorientated, I pushed myself further from them, unable to breathe, the coldness of fear and the bitterness of my shame for being afraid chasing after me.

I wanted to vanish, to run, but I was unable to move as I pressed my palms to the cold wood of the shelves behind me. The darkness pressing closer and closer with every breath.

'I know you like to play games, Emrys. This is a step too far. Kysillians are highly valuable.'

'Miss Woodrow is under my mentorship and therefore my protection.'

'You lie as badly as your father.' Montagor laughed, the humour sickening as a wave of pain from the rage of my power almost bowed me over. 'We both know the Council wants rid of the creature, why delay the inevitable?'

The truth in his voice only ignited that inferno inside of me.

Stupid, ugly troll. Those words always came back to me, that pain always came back. As bitter and sharp as the sting of a lashing. My breath stuttered through my lips, my magic surging.

I was losing control again. Another rush and my knees almost buckled from the energy of trying to contain it. Tears filled my eyes as the echoes of screams came back to me.

Stop. I bit down on an anguished sob and ran. Stumbling over my own feet, heat flushing my skin, ripples of pain searing through my chest. Catching myself on one of the last shelves, which had lowered itself – as if to assist me. The house creaking with unease.

'Please,' I whispered, overcome with a terrible childlike panic that made my blood run cold. Nauseous with my energy as it built.

Moving weakly for another passage amongst the shelves, only to find myself stumbling into my room. The house putting me where I needed to be most.

A relieved sob slipped from my lips, my trembling legs finally giving way as I crawled to the hearth like a wounded creature.

Thrusting my hands into the newly stacked wood, a horrid cry leaving my lips – the hearth engulfed in bright blue flames. Surging from me violently, scorching the mantelpiece as they tore up the chimney, brutal in their intensity.

Kysillian fire that left me gasping for breath as my now trembling palms rested against the cold tiles before the fire. The iron burns on my wrist throbbed but I couldn't catch my breath long enough to care.

Of all the things I'd suffered, I wanted to press the feelings down. To bury all my emotions. But they poured through me, horrid and bitter. I'd allowed fear to make me mad. Make me subservient and weak. I'd allowed them to win.

No matter what I did, I couldn't escape the guilt. What I'd allowed myself to become.

Through tear-filled eyes I looked down at the burns on my wrist. No balm would heal them, only time, and I'd just have to suffer until it did.

Just like all the times before.

It was all just a game. I'd forgotten that no matter what I did, nothing would change. I was lesser than them and I always would be.

'Kat?' Alma called, her worry sounding so distant to me, but suddenly she was there, crouched before me. Her cool hands a blessing against my cheeks.

Those green eyes so wide with distress. 'What happened?'

'I . . . I don't know,' I sobbed, wilting in her arms as the horrid wailing left me, muffled only by her shoulder. Again. I'd almost done it again. Allowed myself to be consumed by the rage of the fire. Felt it simmer so close to surface, knowing if I let go there would be nothing left.

'It's all right,' she whispered in my ear, her hold tight and firm as she began to rock us. The intense heat of the fire was unbearable but she stayed. 'I'm here.'

Here. She always had been. In this nightmare with me that only made me hold her tighter.

'Montagor is here,' I whispered, like a child afraid of a shadow, my breath catching on my sobs.

'Montagor?' She pulled back, pupils lengthening to resemble those of a snake. 'I thought he was busy raiding fey villages in the north on one of his witch hunts.'

'I don't know.' I shook my head, unable to understand any of it. Another tremor ripping through me as I pulled from her grip, dragging myself closer to the fire.

Fearful I'd lose control again. Needing the release.

There was movement and then the running of water. I dragged shallow breaths in through my teeth, holding onto the cold stone, bowing over to rest my flushed brow against it.

Please, I begged helplessly in my mind, uselessly, knowing there was nobody listening.

Then Alma's hands were a firm pressure on my back, soothing circles until she gripped under my arms.

'Come on,' she urged, trying to get me up, but my limbs trembled too wildly. As if I was about to come out of my skin. Losing control in my panic.

I shook my head but those hands became claws, a commanding pinch in their hold.

'Up,' she demanded, stronger now as she pulled me gently to my feet.

I didn't feel any of it, strangely numb as she quickly got me out my confining day dress, stripped me down to my slip, but my trembling became so bad she put me in the cold bath still wearing it. My hands curled into fists around the wet fabric, sucking in short breaths through my teeth. The water warmed quickly with my burning skin and steam rose before me. I focused on it, on anything but the wildness of my magic as it streaked through my veins.

I bent over my knees as I let those tears drip into the water.

Alma's hand found mine where it gripped my shin beneath the surface, as she rested her cheek on the tub. Simply waiting. Taking watch like an ancient wyvern over a precious nest.

I found my eyes fixed on the shadows of the room beyond, making sure they moved with the firelight. Not knowing if what I saw in the study was real. But eventually I relaxed enough to rest my head on the side of the tub next to hers, exhaustion almost dragging me to sleep.

A distant knocking made me flinch. Alma cursed sharply under her breath as she moved to the door.

'She's resting,' her voice drifted back to me, harsh and sharp, even though it was whispered.

'I need to speak with her,' Emrys responded and I flinched at the pain that seeped through me, curling further into my knees. 'Miss Darcy, I need to—' There was a sternness in those words that should have silenced anyone, but Alma wasn't just anyone.

'You've done enough,' she seethed and I could imagine the threat in her vivid virescent eyes. 'Next time, send your *friends* in my direction.'

'I came back as soon as—'

'Too late,' Alma snapped. Then there was a click of the door shutting and Alma's hurried steps back to me as muttered curses fell from her lips.

'Let's get you into bed.' She brushed a clawed hand over my hair, scales catching on a few loose strands.

I didn't move.

'Kat?' she asked softly.

'I heard his voice in my head.' Those words came broken from my lips, hating the weakness of my fear. How it seemed to echo off the bathroom tiles. 'Master Daunton.'

She was closer instantly, her arms around me despite how wet and unstable I was.

'He's dead, Kat.' She ran her hand over my damp hair again, those claws sharper now.

Murderer, that voice came back, and it was right. It would be right again. The smell of burning flesh almost made me retch before I could shake the memory away.

'I can hear them still,' I whispered, unable to stop the painful nature of that guilt. 'That was a full house of lost children just like us . . . and I burned it down for nothing more than rage. Every night, I can hear them.'

'They were dying,' she protested gently, but the words were somehow still too loud in the cavernous bathroom. As if it mattered. I'd killed them all the same.

'You don't know that.' She couldn't know that. We hadn't been in the dank basement that day, hadn't seen how many lay there without care. How many were fighting to survive against all the odds, how many I'd stolen that choice from in one moment of rage.

How many were still alive when I'd lost control. How many couldn't get out.

She took hold of my trembling hands and I let her despite the burns, needing her more than I ever had before. Leaning down so our foreheads met, and I was forced to look into her vibrant and truthful eyes.

'Whatever monster you wish yourself to be, I'll still be here, loving you.' Her words were wrapped in steel. A challenge. Willing me to call her a liar, so she could prove just how much she meant them. 'I'm here because of you, Kat. Only you.'

Her for them. The choice I'd made. Alma for the rest of them. The choice Daunton had forced me to make, battered and broken as I was.

'I won't spend my life haunted by my death,' she warned, a fierceness coming over her. 'Neither will you.'

Those words sat like a promise between us.

All I could do was nod, swallowing past the lump in my throat. She was right. She always was. If I hadn't unleashed such chaos, Alma would be back with the menagerie. She'd be dead by now, and I don't know what would have become of me.

Slowly, as the water cooled again, she coaxed me from the bath, dried me and put me into a nightgown. That numbness not leaving me despite the fierce nature of her words.

She forced one of her precious chocolates between my lips before bullying me into bed and climbed into it too with her dress and shoes still on, wrapping herself around me. Not tight enough, though, as the coldness of my fear seeped into my flesh.

A heavy silence fell with just the cracking of the wood as the fire devoured it, while still she held on. Like she always had.

'Of all the things I've endured, I regret not a moment of that pain because it led me right here,' she whispered, voice catching on the words with the rawness of her emotions. 'Right here to you, Kat, and there is nowhere else I wish to be.'

I wanted to smile, but all that left me were tears as I held onto her.

Chapter Twenty-Two

You belong to this suffering, Woodrow. You created it and your blood deserves the penance that comes your way.

The memory of those words struck me like a blow. So sharp I could taste blood. Master Daunton's words.

A ravenous heat bubbled through me. I wrenched myself free of the darkness of sleep, waking in a cold sweat, tangled in the bed sheets, unable to catch my breath. I buried my head in my hands, a breathless sob leaving my lips.

He deserved it, I knew he did, and yet it didn't stop it hurting. That death was on my soul, no matter how valid the act was.

Silent tears escaped my eyes, a trembling in my hands as I tried to catch my breath. I couldn't stay here. Couldn't suffer the silence of the night. Alma was curled up next to me. Still fully dressed as if unable to leave my side.

A tapping came against the window, drawing me towards it, just where it was cracked slightly to let the breeze in. Sharp and relentless as it whistled through the gap.

There was a tiny bird pecking at the glass. Only this bird was made of paper, its pecks becoming more insistent with the streaks of rain that began to appear on the window.

I let it in, the bird hopping onto the ledge. Flapping its wings in annoyance where a few raindrops had made it soggy.

An enchanted message.

I held out my hand, letting it hop into my palm, and just as expected, it unfurled into a note.

Kat, forgive me.
Emrys

The burns on my wrist ached at the words. At just how foolish I'd been in trusting anyone. I let the message curl and turn itself into ash in my palm. Montagor was a game I didn't have the strength to play, and Emrys seemed to be a mystery I couldn't trust. No matter the horrid gnawing pain that consumed my chest at the thought.

I let the ash slip through my fingertips, refusing to let it distract me as I pulled on one of my simpler dresses, grabbed my bag and headed to the study, intending to work through my frustrations. I would finally go through the ledger on pox that Emrys had given me, ignoring the kindness of the favour.

I entered the study, hearing the room creak as if in concern. I pressed my hand against the doorframe. Feeling the ancient hum of the magic within.

I brought my forehead to rest against it, taking a deep breath as a sad smile came to my lips.

'Thank you,' I whispered, knowing the house had helped me. That it had hurt with me. It groaned in answer as I released it and moved soundlessly to my desk. Rage guiding me as I pulled a piece of paper free, writing Master Hale's name at the top. Suddenly overcome with the need to demand the truth from him. Why he'd lied. Why he'd kept these hideous secrets from me, secrets of dark fiends and fey deaths.

I tried but I only managed to write one word on the page. *Liar.*

I tore the letter up, letting it scatter across my papers.

Dark things hide in the darkest wood. The story echoed in the back of my mind. Of course they did. That's why they couldn't be found. My focus shifted to my notes, flipping through them to see the map again, to see how close the woods of Paxton Fields were to Fairfax Manor. A natural barrier between his lands and the villages. The perfect cover for the dark to hide. Where nobody was allowed to venture unless by the lord's command.

I remembered the strangeness of the tree bark beneath my palm, the small weight of that dead folk against my skin. The damp press of the foggy air as if weighted with secrets.

Make the bastards pay, Katherine, Master Hale's parting words came back to me. Those painful burns on my wrist almost mocked me as they ached. How powerless I'd been. How powerless Master Hale had allowed me to become.

Liar, that dark voice inside of me hissed. My eyes burned with childish tears. He would have known. Hale would have known about these fey, about the horrors still happening to them on these lands. He'd kept me blind to it all this time and I hated him for it.

Hated more that I'd allowed myself to be blinded. Blinded by a childish desire to be wanted, to be helpful and cared for.

Rage simmered through me and I found myself at the Portium door, not having a moment to hesitate about my foolishness or how the house creaked in protest. Knowing the door reacted to incantations – Emrys used stones to amplify his requests, but pure magic on its own should suffice.

'Please.' I summoned a single flame, pressing it into the space where the crystal was supposed to go. I willed the ancient metal to listen to me. The cogs began to turn and rattle. Light flared beneath the crack of the door before it fell silent.

I turned the knob gently, opening it to see nothing beyond the threshold but the blackness of night, the gloomy mist curled around the base of pale dying trees, and the cries from creatures of the nocturnal wood. Paxton Field, where the missing fey had last been seen.

The portal had formed in the archway of what used to be a stone storage house with only its frame remaining, held together with thick vines and brambles. Breath misted from my lips as I walked further into the wood, leaving the warmth of the portal behind. Trees swayed in the night wind, branches creaking like old bones.

I was cautious of every step. Every crack of a twig beneath my boot, the smell of rot thick in the air, lingering too long. The creatures here were subdued, the bushes not even rustling, so as not to attract beasts on the hunt. The dark seemed almost endless, as moonlight seemed unable to reach down through the thick entanglement of branches above. Seeing a thicket, I knelt down to take a sample of the earth, only to see the stems corrupted and covered in dark spots of infection.

Cursed earth.

My fingers trailed over the dark moss clinging to the tree trunks, finding old carvings into the wood. Familiar fey markers. Prayers to the ancestors to ward off evil.

This was the right place, but I felt no comfort in that.

A cracking of wood made me glance up. There, in the distance, was a pale figure partially obscured by the trees. Her hair was unbound and swept across her face – there was fear in her pale eyes. The translucent quality of her as if formed from moonlight.

A spirit.

There was a sharpness to her features, and a striking point to her ears. She was an aurrak. An ancient being, one of the many descended from Kysillians.

I rose slowly, trying to seem unthreatening, but she still ran. A flare of white in the night, like starlight streaking through the dark of the wood.

'Wait!' I called, hurrying after her, tripping on brambles and rotting wood as I charged headlong into the dark. I'd seen spirits before, but not like her. Not so clear, or so distressed.

I ran until my lungs burned with the night air, lonely puffs of breath before me as I twisted around, only to find myself alone in the vastness of the wood.

She'd been going somewhere, and not back to the village. No. I was too deep in the wood. On the edge of a steep embankment of rocks and roots. The screeching cry of a nocturnal beast made my heart leap into my throat, panic settling in my gut. I didn't know the way back.

The earthy scent of rotting wood weighted every breath.

The cracking of a twig spun me around, magic flaring into my palms with brutal heat as I turned, lavender flames illuminating the startled face of William, a lantern almost slipping from his hand where he stood in the overgrowth, breaths panted, and hair mussed.

'What are you doing?!' I snapped, clenching my fists to extinguish my defensive spell. 'I could have hurt you!'

'Emrys said you'd been hurt,' he protested, eyes wide with confusion. 'He went half bloody mad! Almost put a hole through the study wall!'

I frowned. 'Really?' *Kat, forgive me.* The memory of his note flashed to the forefront of my mind before I shook it away. 'You shouldn't be out here, William.'

'I'm so sorry about Montagor, Kat. I left the portal door unlocked after a delivery. Emrys said—'

I held up my hand, unable to bear any of it right now. 'Please, William, it's dangerous out here.'

'I couldn't agree more,' came the dry, annoyed tone of Alma, making us both jump.

We turned, finding her in a dark cloak, her hair tightly braided. I was even shocked to see she was wearing her sparring attire, arms folded tightly across her chest, cat-like eyes filled with disapproval.

'What are you doing here?' I threw my hands up in annoyance, not only at being caught by William, but Alma too. Both now also in the middle of my foolish mess.

'You're really not as light-footed as you think you are.' She sighed, moving towards us soundlessly. 'What did you do to the doorway?'

'I gave it a new location.' I sighed.

'Can you do that?' William frowned.

'It appears so,' I considered the thick, dark forest surrounding us. 'How did you even find me?'

'You mean the mad woman shouting and running through a wood in the middle of the night?' Alma was still looking like she was about to batter me and was considering using William's lantern to do it. 'Besides, William isn't exactly *discreet* about sneaking off.'

'The bloody house was working against me,' he offered weakly in his defence, cheeks flushed as he turned back to me. 'You're looking into something, aren't you?'

'I saw something in the woods.' I decided to leave it at that.

'A spirit?' Alma asked, her eyes suddenly mortal with concern.

'She was different. She didn't expect me to see her.' Spirits also didn't run.

'Maybe she hasn't accepted it yet,' William reasoned. Only I couldn't shake the feeling it was because her passing was recent.

'If someone is out here, we should go back. Last I checked lords like to make examples of trespassers,' Alma interrupted, stepping between us in warning.

'I'd be more curious as to what a lord was doing wandering the wood to see us?' I smiled, watching annoyance turn her eyes reptilian as they narrowed.

'She has a point. We're already here,' William interrupted, clearly not sensing my impending doom.

Before Alma could turn her rage on the unsuspecting boy, the crack of a branch echoed back to us. I grabbed their arms, dragging them both down behind a thicket. William's lantern tumbled free of his grasp and was extinguished instantly by the damp earth.

'What is it?' he asked, pressing himself closer to my side.

'You really couldn't just go to sleep?' Alma snapped in a whisper, one side of her face covered in dark panther fur.

'Shh,' I breathed, turning to peek over the brambles, and saw a tall, hunched form coming up through the earth. Its snout was long like a dog's, its limbs covered in matted, filthy fur. Its body was skeletally thin, bent over so its long-clawed arms could drag across the damp earth.

'A skelmor,' I whispered.

Skelmor were earth scavengers. The myths said they'd once been fey who refused to join the Old Gods, fight against the ancient Queen Kysillia as she brought chaos to the earth.

The Old Gods had cursed the creatures for their cowardice to be eternally hungry, left to feast on the pain and anguish of the dead.

'A skelmor shouldn't be here,' Alma hissed back.

The creature sniffed desperately at the earth, before a sharp owl's cry caused it to vanish into the dark trees. They were large and powerful creatures, but violence wasn't in their nature.

Yet they also weren't known to waste time on places they didn't need to be. Seeing that girl's spirit suddenly didn't seem to be a coincidence. She'd led me here after all.

I moved out of the undergrowth, hearing Alma snap my name before she followed, William trying to keep up close behind. I crossed to where the creature had been inspecting the ground. Raking my fingers through the dry, dusty soil, feeling the odd gritty texture.

'Something is here.' I followed my instincts, searching through the roots and brambles on my knees until my hands brushed against something hard and cold.

My magic flared, my caution quickly forgotten as bright flames of blue and lavender illuminated the earth and a dark shiny stone that I had uncovered. The stone was carved with intricate warnings for beings like me.

'A Verr stone.' I felt the bitter coldness of the rock, and the sharpness of the carvings on it. A marking stone to lead beings to places of worship. An impossibility, and yet here it stood, struggling to survive amongst the thicket and not be swallowed by the earth.

Verr worship was forbidden. It had been ever since the uprising. The King had indulged and become lost in the darkness of that worship. Yet here stood a marker.

Which meant a Verr temple was close by, or at least what remained of one.

'Verr?' Alma frowned, and I could sense her revulsion. Having been kept in a menagerie, she was well acquainted with mortals that found reverence in the tales of the Verr.

The cruelty of such men, with their duelling hatred of and sinister lust for fey.

Despite the Council's instance of peace, I wasn't foolish enough to believe worship of Verr could be eradicated. Greed was an impossible monster to kill, and it infected faster than any plague.

Every fibre in my being told me to stop. To forget and run. Yet, I moved further into the woods, seeing shards of the strange black, glass-like stone that led the way to a large crack in the muddy earth.

An opening where plants that had grown either side of was now surrounded by nothing but ash. Strange cold air came up from its depths, an odd sweetness to it that didn't fit in the damp forest.

I grabbed a rock from the mud and tossed it into the hole, waiting a moment until it struck hard ground beneath.

'William, what can you sense?' I asked, watching as he dropped to his knee, letting the strange dark soil rest in his palms, fingers glowing faintly green.

A shudder of revulsion rolled through him, eyes almost desperate as they found mine again. 'Something is very wrong, Kat.'

It was here. Whatever it was, it was here. I moved closer to the hole, grabbing the sides to try and see how deep it was.

'Kat!' Alma seized hold of my arm. 'Are you really going to crawl into a hole a dark fiend just came out of?'

'A lesser fiend,' I corrected, 'and I want to know what it was doing.'

'Something it shouldn't have been, which is exactly what we're doing,' she hissed sharply, William nodding enthusiastically in the dark behind her. 'We should tell Emrys, he'll know what to do.'

A relieved sigh left William's lips as if we'd unanimously decided that was indeed the best next step.

Cold emotion pierced my chest at the mention of Emrys. The secrets he kept and the duality of his character. The iron burns on my wrist stung in agreement with my annoyance.

It didn't matter. Emrys's secrets weren't important now and I wasn't foolish enough not to accept I was out my depth.

'I'll get him.' William rushed off into the dark night.

No. He shouldn't be on his own. Not here.

I opened my mouth, stepping forward to follow, but before I could utter a word the damp earth of the embankment gave way beneath William. His cry of alarm pierced the night as he twisted and tumbled over himself.

'William!' Alma shrieked, the pair of us throwing ourselves over the edge too, stumbling and skidding after him. Rocks tumbled free and bushes cracked as the loose earth gave way.

William lay in a heap at the bottom of the steep drop. Filthy, with brambles tangled in his curls and his horns. He held onto his arm as he laid awkwardly on the wet earth.

'Stay still!' I commanded, using the roots protruding from the dry, dead earth to lower myself down to him, landing in a heap of now-ruined skirts.

'Show me where it hurts.' I knelt at his side. Horrid guilt clawing at my insides as I waited for him to gather his breath, finding little relief as Alma landed soundlessly next to me.

'Let me check your head.' Her hand pressed against the boy's forehead, rubbing the dirt from his skin as her other hand went gently to the side of his neck. Fingers already turning into claws with her worry.

'William? Where does it hurt?' I asked, starting my examination with the arm he clutched to his chest, but his lip trembled slightly in response, eyes still straight ahead and his complexion deathly pale.

'K–Kat,' he stuttered.

'I'm sorry. It isn't your—' I shook my head in annoyance.

'Is that a body?' Alma's words were higher in pitch than normal. William nodded his head incessantly, forcing me to follow his gaze, and there, right at his feet, was a body. Milky dead eyes staring right at us, its soil-filled mouth hanging open in an eternal scream.

I recoiled from it, landing next to William, hands buried in the wet earth either side of me.

Here, a voice called in the back of my mind. Ice filled my veins as I felt the strange thickness of the air, the bitterness of the cold, but still my breath didn't mist.

Unnatural. I took hold of William's good hand, feeling it shake, his grip brutally tight with fear.

Only it wasn't fear that seared through me, that twisted like molten liquid in my gut. No, it was rage as I took in another deep breath. Tasting the death and desperation on the damp air. What I'd missed in my panic. The sourness of it coating my lips as the veins in my hands began to glow lilac. The pain of those burns on my wrists not enough to temper it as I finally saw what lay before us.

Dark stone covered in strange grey moss, as if all colour had been drained from it. An arched opening that led to nothing but darkness. Ominous ancient ruins that even the wind didn't dare howl through. Just a deadly silence, the darkness staring back in challenge, watching us. The clouds shifted above, drenching the cursed place in a pale column of moonlight, turning the Verr stone silver.

Beware of the Old Gods who wield silver, demon fire, as bright and endless as moonlight above.

Verr stone was used to contain fey, to limit their power so they could be killed easily. Sacrificed for bad bargains.

A foul place like this was what they saw in their last moments on earth, nothing but darkness and hate. It lingered here still, pressed into the wet mud, leaving a biting cold sensation against my skin.

I felt a single tear roll down my cheek, overwhelmed by the cruelty of this place.

'Kat?' William whispered as he tried to scramble back from the body, only to wince in pain again.

I didn't bother with a summoning charm, knowing the Verr stone would weaken anything I conjured. So, I let my Kysillian flames free, licking across my palm and twining between my fingers. Magic no stone or darkness could snuff out. Something it would remember. I let it twist into a sphere of fiery light, as I released it into the darkness.

Alma called my name in caution, but I was done with warnings as I watched those purple and blue flames illuminate the entrance to that foul place. Looming before us like a giant beast. We stood in its jagged maw made of nothing but cursed stone.

A screeching flurry pierced the night as a swarm of bats fled from that cave and shot into the sky.

Please, seemed to echo in the back of my mind, distant cries lost in time, beings still trapped and wandering the dark in spirit form. Fey.

The fear in that ghost's face moulded my anger into something lethal. The magic in my veins almost humming in satisfaction at the freedom. My hurt at Emrys, anger at Master Hale's lies and the disgusting cruelty of Montagor. My fire glowed brighter with the wildness of my emotions. Flames leapt from the sphere and began to devour the dead leaves around it.

Come and see, the darkness before me seemed to mock.

'*Norac*,' I hissed in response, wrath corrupting my reasoning.

Coward. A language spoken by its blood enemy. The reason for its Old Gods' demise and upon hearing the taunt, it revealed itself.

The earth began to shift, shaking as dirt rained down from the edges of the opening.

'What is that!?' Alma called, pushing herself in front of William's prone form.

The earth before us rose and fell, twisting with the cursed roots beneath. Shards of the dark stone and bleached white bones mixing with it. Scraps of chain and moss-covered rope. Fragments of weapons and the telling curve of jawbones. Formed of nothing but hate and the remains of what had died here. What they'd taken.

That inferno inside of me rose, my hands curling into fists as I bared my teeth, allowing the warrior blood in my veins to sing true.

A waft of dead air and the tartness of old magic carried towards me, as the thing rose, its rock-and-earth body tangled with bones, impossibly tall. Face all sharp angles with stone and thorns, its mouth wide and made with the rusted fragments of forgotten blades – a humanoid form, but the limbs were too long, too jagged as thorny claws scraped at the ground.

A caymor. A creature of nightmares formed to protect cursed earth from those who would wish to take it back. To cleanse it.

The earth shook as the beast roared. William let out a cry of alarm and Alma swore, reminding me I wasn't alone.

I brought my hands together, feeling the fire crackle and build between my palms. The chaos of my magic seeped from my skin as I forced my rage outwards, sending a large fire ball of sacred flame flying towards the creature. The light almost blinding me with its brightness as it took the caymor off its feet, smashing it against the damp wall of the chamber from which it had escaped. Large chunks of soil and rock rained down on top of it.

There was a flash of movement from my right, a ripping and snapping of bone. Alma's clothes fluttered in pieces across the barren ground. In her place before me, blocking the caymor's path, was the silver-scaled wrywing. Its tail was lethally thumping into the wet earth as it considered the darkness. A roar pealing from its razor-sharp jaws.

Alma.

In a moment of clarity, I watched the sharp points on her back as the rumbling from the caymor getting back to its feet echoed through that cavern. I could hear William panting for breath, his pain still restricting his movements.

'Alma!' I called, watching that sharp maw turn in my direction, green eyes gleaming with threat. 'Go and get Emrys,' I commanded, watching her eyes narrow with annoyance. 'William needs help!' I might have been filled with fury, but I wasn't a fool.

She growled in complaint, those beast eyes looking to the boy before she shot skyward with a strong pull of her wings.

Relief eased the tightness of my chest. Emrys would come. All I needed to do now was keep the beast distracted.

While the nightmare still reformed in the darkness, I turned, grabbed the lapel of William's coat and I used my Kysillian strength to toss him back up the steep embankment onto a small outcropping of stone, out of the demon's path. He cried out, tumbling out of view and back into the safety of the wood.

The earth cracked and crumbled, another scream coming from the creature's mouth. Whatever dry leaves had survived the damp were alight. Illuminating the remains of the temple.

Magic erupted from my hands, wrapping around my wrists and licking up my arms. I didn't know much about the workings of a caymor, but I'd kill it. Needed to. Some ancient and feral part of me demanded it.

I withdrew my father's sword from my bag, the blade long and lethal as I remembered who I should be.

Steady is the heart. Swift is the flame. The memory of his voice calmed my breathing just as the monster lurched from the dark in a mess of sharp stone and gleaming metal.

I darted past its attack, one fluid turn, slicing down its rocky back with the glowing blade. It roared, its form shifting as it shed rock and bone. It threw out a clawed hand but I managed to lurch back, only for a rock to detach from its form, colliding with me.

The impact threw me back against the stone ruins, head making painful contact as I dropped to my side, gasping for breath.

'Kat!' William cried as the thing howled, dropping and reshaping into a form closer to a large spider as it scuttled towards me.

Before pouncing to pin me, I rolled away just as those blade teeth sank into the wet earth. Rocks cracking under the power of its bite.

I pressed my free palm to the earth, drawing on my flames, still devouring the leaves around us. Those flames roared across the earth, charring and striking the thing like a molten snake, wrapping around the darkness and trying to restrict it from another change.

It thrashed wildly, almost breaking my hold as I panted.

'I think you've annoyed it,' William called, half leaning over the ledge with a pale face of worry.

'I gathered that, William,' I hissed back, ducking as a newly formed long dark tail swiped close to my head, as it continued to struggle under the power of my flame. Snapping and screaming.

I charged into my own fire, feeling its reassuring heat lick across my exposed skin. Burying the blade in the centre of the creature's chest as it reared back on its hind legs, making my blade slip free.

Then I saw the remnants of the chain in the soil beneath it, tangled completely within its form.

Forsaken iron chain.

Do you know what happens when forsaken iron enters the blood? Montagor's words came back to mock me.

Beg, little troll. That taunting whetted my fear into something else, something deadly.

I let my fire pour from my palms, wrapping around the metal that had trapped my kind long ago. Metal that would burn me just as those rings had. Only, instead of fear, fury ignited my magic, turning the chain molten.

The red-and-orange glow streaked with my lavender flame, made the beast roar in agony as the thick liquid dribbled onto the cursed earth. Hissing as it made contact echoing through the chamber like its own battle cry. The beast screamed as it was slowly unmade, the molten liquid seeping between the rocks and bones that formed it. Killing the spell from the inside, just as its master had unmade those fey. Turning them into nothing but bones.

The thing roared and twisted, crumbling in on itself, seeking any way to escape.

I walked slowly towards it, my sword a lethal weight in my hand. Its stone jaws snapped wildly with desperation. Its head swiveled looking for any mercy from the darkness around it. From its Old Gods.

Mercy it hadn't given those fey it feasted on.

Mercy I wouldn't give it now.

One deadly arch and my blade seared through what was left. Rocks and metal tumbling across the cursed earth. A hiss at the bitterness of the spell being broken filled the air, and what remained of the beast was reduced to nothing but ash that fell to the damp earth, extinguishing most of the fire I'd created.

Kyvor Mor. Curse Killer.

My knees shook as my arm dropped, the blade reducing itself to nothing but a hilt once more.

'Bloody saints!' William practically whooped from somewhere in the thicket. 'You didn't say anything about being able to do that!'

'Bragging isn't an attractive trait, William,' I cautioned, as I pushed the sword into the safety of my bag.

Wiping the sweat from my brow, I sucked in a deeper breath of dead air, trying to calm my rapidly beating heart. Looking at the walls of that cavern, seeing the marks deeply gouged there. I felt a chill. Runes twisted and inverted with cruel intent.

'Neither is trespassing,' came a strange male voice from above and a distant cry from William as he was dragged out of view.

'William!' I called out, running for the embankment on legs too weak and clumsy, only for something to come whistling through the air. There was nothing but white smoke, a horrid sweetness on my tongue as I tried to cough the spell from my lungs.

A subduing draught.

Panicked, I struggled to hold my breath, stumbling and turning to find a way out. But in the end, all I found was myself in a heap in the cold mud as darkness consumed my senses.

Chapter Twenty-Three

There was a high-pitched ringing in my ears, temples pounding with spell withdrawal, tongue dry and stuck to the roof of my mouth. Everything sounded muffled, as if my head was submerged in water.

'Kat!' someone called beside me, making me flinch away from the sound. Even the slightest movement hurt. It was William, calling my name.

'Shhh,' I hissed, opening my eyes, trying to blink the spots from my vision. 'I'm awake, William.'

'Thank the ancestors.'

I blinked the murkiness from my vision, realising I wasn't face down in the dirt of that forest. No. We were both sitting on what appeared to be dining chairs, hands bound in our laps. William was covered in dirt, twigs stuck in his hair and tangled around his horns. His cloak was missing and his shirt torn, face horridly pale with worry and pain.

We were in a large room with sparce bookshelves, a piano and a seating area before a flaring hearth.

The horrid sweetness of saints' oil and incense was thick in the air. I straightened instantly, sensing a threat in the mere presence of such things.

Glass cases were spaced about, as if holding great works of art, but inside they were littered with war artefacts – tapestries and weapons used by various fey tribes, trophies of conquest.

A collection of beautiful ball masks was pinned to the far wall, their ribbons vibrant and intricately embroidered, but the masks themselves were dull and cracked. Fey flesh that had begun to peel and decay with time. Masks the King would commission for his balls.

Repulsed, I turned to the large marble fireplace, only to see the head of a valek mounted on the wall, its beak wide open in an eternal scream of torment.

Maybe this was a nightmare after all. I remembered the caymor, the smoke incantation and the dark coldness of the pit.

I'd allowed them to catch me once more.

'Don't worry about a thing. I'll do the talking.' William dragged in a deep, pained breath. 'Emrys will be here shortly. He has a habit of turning up when you need him.'

Emrys.

My heart sank to the pit of my stomach at his name. Emrys was a mortal man of flesh and blood and not some form of wish-granting spectre who turned up unannounced. No matter how many times he had done it to me recently.

No, we were on our own and in trouble from the look of the two men stood across from us in crisp liveries. Thankfully not Council hunters or guards – they rented out their services to lords who had issues with fey.

'Listen, gentlemen, there has been a terrible misunderstanding,' William began, his smile nervous, as a mere movement made him wince with pain.

'I'm sure there has,' came a cold voice from behind us in response.

A tall, heavyset blond man walked into view. A mere click of his fingers sent our guards away as he stood before us. He had the presence of a lord, but there was nothing remotely attractive or interesting about him. He was ruddy cheeked and wearing a coat that stretched over his bloated belly. Sweat dampened his forehead, blond hair thinning by the second.

'I'm William Roydon, Lord Blackthorn's assistant, and this is—' William started politely, but the man held his hand up to silence him.

'What were you doing in Fairfax Wood?' He folded his arms tightly across his large chest.

In the light of the fire, I saw scarring at the tips of his ears. Someone had cut them to appear mortal. Definitely a lord's son then, and a failed fey breeding experiment by the resentment in his eyes.

Mortals always did hate the shame of being of fey blood and still not possessing a drop of magic, knowing they were unworthy to wield it despite their title and wealth.

Fairfax Wood.

I didn't know much about the Fairfaxes apart from their favour with the King and their lack of presence in the Council chambers following his death.

One more thing I now knew about them – they clearly really didn't like trespassers.

'We're investigating the village outside Paxton Fields,' I explained simply.

'I heard some commotion from the village about a disturbance,' the man mused, his gaze drifting to my face and then the curve of my breast that the tear in my muddy bodice revealed.

'We need to speak to Lord Fairfax.' I sat straighter in the chair, forcing myself to feel less groggy.

'Do you?' He considered me down his nose, as if I was an amusement.

'This land is infected with dark magic. He needs to be informed. It's a matter of great urgency.'

'How well you monstrous beasts lie,' he said. His smile was tight with its cruelty, those bloodshot eyes fixed on my lips.

'She isn't lying, we—' William began, but faster than anticipated, the man grabbed his shoulder in threat. William grimaced, colour draining from his face.

'Leave him alone!' I snapped, leaning forward and almost burning straight through my bonds. Not caring about the consequences. 'He's hurt!'

'Is he?' the man replied. A malicious delight playing behind his eyes as the boy cried out before he released him, William panting through his teeth.

Beg me. That voice came back to me now from the darkest depths of my memory. Fear sparked in my heart the same moment magic flared to meet it, but all I could do was curl my fists.

Attacking a lord was a punishable offence, but the hearth crackled, taunting me as he came close to leer over me. Taking hold of my face, his warm stubby fingers, reeking of tobacco, dug into my cheeks.

'Don't touch me,' I bit out between my clenched teeth. That rage simmering in my veins.

The fire surged behind him as I willed it to live for only a moment, forming a monstrous set of jaws that snapped out at him. He jumped away, but not before the flames could catch on the tail of his jacket. A cry left his lips as he stumbled over himself, smacking at the smouldering fabric.

William gasped, eyes wide.

'Bitch,' the man hissed through his teeth. He lurched towards me, a trail of smoke behind him. I could have broken my bonds, should have, but I was frozen in place. Knowing all the things I wasn't allowed to do. Knowing that if I struck him . . . I wouldn't stop.

I flinched, eyes shut and ready for the strike, certain it wouldn't be close to the worst I'd endured.

William made a noise of surprise, and then there was a large crash. My eyes opened to see the man half sprawled on the chaise across from us, the low table broken and his clothes in disarray.

A chill bit at my skin, the fire in the hearth almost extinguished, and there standing over him, like a beast over prey, was Emrys.

As if I'd conjured him.

His dark coat open, only a loose shirt beneath, plastered to his skin with the rain. His riding trousers and boots were speckled with mud as his hair dripped water onto the carpet. Every annoyed breath from his lips forced the transparent fabric of his shirt to cling to the muscular expanse of his chest.

Maybe this was a dream after all.

'You don't touch her.' Emrys's voice was filled with lethal intent.

'Blackthorn!' The man spluttered using the chaise to push himself up, shoes sliding on the polished floor. 'What on earth are you doing?!'

'You should be grateful I don't maim you further, Lord Percy,' Emrys sneered in response, his voice unfamiliar to me in its rage. A feral nature to his expression and I was glad I was already seated.

'She burnt me,' Lord Percy protested, getting to his feet and tugging at his jacket.

'Count your blessings I don't do worse.' Emrys hands formed fists. Dark tendrils seemed to appear in the air around him, but they vanished when I blinked, making me wonder just how hard I hit my head in those ruins.

'What's happening, Jonathan?' came the croaked call of an old man. He stood in the doorway, weedy and holding onto a cane for support. He was clean shaven, with a shock of bright white hair, and stood hunched over his walking stick. Fine clothes of velvet and gold glimmered under the firelight as he hobbled into the room.

'*Trespassers*, Uncle,' Lord Percy sneered, running an unsteady hand through his thinning hair.

'Lord Blackthorn?' the old man asked, coming to a stop before myself and William. I could only imagine what a sorry sight we both looked, covered in mud, semi-conscious and bound.

'My assistant, Mr Roydon, and my partner mage, Miss Woodrow, Lord Fairfax,' Emrys said, and bowed to the old lord, gesturing to each of us.

The old man took me in with kind, confused eyes, but it did little to settle me.

'There has been a misunderstanding.' William smiled nervously, trying to get comfortable in his chair.

'This all seems a bit much for trespassing, Jonathan.' Fairfax frowned.

'Suspicion of murder too,' Lord Percy pressed, that sly smile coming back as Emrys's stiff gaze darted to his face.

He had a mere moment before his expression shifted to indifference once more.

'Now I'm interested in seeing how you managed that,' Emrys replied dryly, his eyes finally meeting my own, jet black with fury, and I had the good sense to be worried.

'We didn't kill anyone; he was already dead when I landed on him,' William protested, his voice a little higher than I think he intended. 'There was a dark fiend, too.'

'My men didn't see anything when they located the trespassers,' Lord Percy mocked.

'You should be grateful I already contained it.' I glared at Lord Percy, a ferocity he returned. I wondered if I could get away with summoning another fire beast in the present company but decided against it. That might push Emrys over the edge.

'Well, we should be grateful for your help, Miss Woodrow.' Lord Fairfax cleared his throat, stepping forward to address us fully. His gaze then darting to someone behind me in the doorway. 'Show Mr Roydon to the healing room.'

'I'll take care of Mr Roydon, thank you, Lord Fairfax,' Emrys interrupted before any form of servant could enter. 'If you don't mind, I need a moment alone with my partner mage.'

'Of course.' Fairfax tried to bow but his clear ill health hindered him. 'I'll have the guest rooms drawn up immediately.'

'Uncle,' Lord Percy objected, but Fairfax already had his hand up in protest.

'That won't be necessary,' Emrys interjected.

'I insist. Poor Mr Roydon needs his rest and it's the least we can offer as an apology for this misunderstanding. In fact, you can stay as long as you'd like. Surely being in comfort while you investigate such horrid claims is for the best.'

Guest rooms? My focus darted to Emrys, a panic rising in my chest, but he wasn't looking at me. No, he was straight backed and cold faced, considering the lord as if they were at a dinner discussing current affairs.

'Of course,' Emrys relented, although there was a stiffness to his words that told me there was no point in protesting.

'That settles it then.' Fairfax grinned, turning his attention to me. 'A pleasure to meet you, Miss Woodrow.'

I should have said something, but I was still struggling with my disbelief. Emrys couldn't mean we were staying here.

'Come, Jonathan,' Lord Fairfax ordered as he left.

Lord Percy muttered under his breath as he stormed from the room after his elderly uncle.

'I'm sorry Emrys we—' William began, looking like he wished the ground would swallow him up as the door closed behind us. But I wasn't in the mood for grovelling.

'Is Alma all right?' I demanded, remaining in my chair as Emrys's attention focused on me.

'I don't think you're the one who should be asking questions,' he replied coldly, still a threatening figure as he pulled off his coat, letting it drop heavily to the floor as the fire struggled to overcome his arrival. The fabric of his shirt was plastered to his forearms, showing the definition of his biceps and the scars that covered them.

'Don't be too cross with her, Emrys, she's only just been able to wake up,' William threw in, trying to be helpful. 'That fiend didn't half crack her head against the stone.'

Emrys went tense, jaw tight as his hands curled into fists as the fire gutted out. Something working behind his dark eyes at William's words.

I surged to my feet, effortlessly turning my bonds to nothing but ash, which fell to the threadbare carpet. 'Something is wrong with those woods,' I said, 'and I think a dead body justifies our investigation.'

'A body you're a suspect in *murdering,* unless you missed that part,' he fired back, taunting me, and for a moment, I hated him.

'Don't be *absurd.* We didn't murder anybody!' I snapped. 'And if we hadn't found it first, that caymor would have eaten all the evidence.'

'She has a point,' William offered weakly, still clutching his injured arm and looking paler by the second.

Emrys's dark gaze flickered to his assistant, and I stepped forward, going boot to boot with him, forcing him to focus on me. 'Don't you dare be annoyed with William; he's been through enough.'

'Oh, don't worry about that, Miss Woodrow. My annoyance is solely focused on *you*.'

'What else was I supposed to do?' I challenged. If he didn't have horrible unannounced guests that lurked in the dark and made it impossible for me to sleep, I wouldn't have gone looking for trouble.

The thought of Montagor only reminded me just how enraged I was with Emrys now that my wallowing was done. How dare he leave me to that man.

'*Wait?*' His tone remained dry, which only heightened my anger.

'I don't sit awaiting your command. Fey are dying.'

'I doubt you'll be much use to them after getting soul-snatched,' he pressed, leaning closer so I could see every angry speck of darkness in his eyes.

I laughed dryly at the ridiculousness of the suggestion. 'Don't be dramatic. The creature was half asleep.'

'It was an *ancient* being with a hunger for fey blood, and you offered yourself up on a plate.'

'I think the dusty remains of it would disagree with that, *Lord Blackthorn*,' I seethed.

His stern face became flushed as his temper grew. 'Do you know how worried I—'

'I'm much recovered, thank you for the concern!' I shouted back. 'Next time you should give warning in your partnership agreements that you relish hideous guests who you allow to do as they please to whomever they so desire!'

'He wasn't my guest.' He had the audacity to sound offended. 'He came seeking some sick entertainment.'

'And he found it, didn't he?'

'That wasn't supposed to happen.' A softness lay in his voice that I wouldn't allow to distract me. 'If you think I'd let him—'

'Well, you did,' I snapped, not quite able to pull in a measured breath as my voice broke.

He froze at the words, as if they'd physically struck him. His fury guttered out as quickly as the fire. Something else burning in his eyes.

'You think I enjoyed any moment of letting him hurt you like that?' Those words were quiet with regret.

'It wouldn't be the first time someone has.' My breath trembled slightly. A deep pain blossoming in my chest because I didn't know the truth. 'Only I didn't trust them so foolishly.'

I pressed my palm against his wet chest, hoping to push him away, to free myself, but he captured it, keeping it trapped against the hard texture of him, forcing me to remain. To look at him.

His breath brushed my lips with how close we were standing, two hot-headed fools half panting. I wanted to push him away, to shake him and pull truths from his lips, and I knew he wanted the same from me. Could see it in the sorrowful soft grey of his eyes.

'Kat,' he whispered making my name sound like a plea. His free hand moving the hair behind my ear, his eyes at my temple, where the worst of my pain was at present. His jaw tightening, eyes darkening to nothing but black.

'Now isn't this scandalous!' came a cheery male voice.

I stumbled away from Emrys, almost crashing into William as I turned to see a tall, attractive man, shirt partially unbuttoned, but still dressed in evening attire, leaning against the wall next to the closed door. He had tanned skin, dark auburn hair swept back from his perfect face, his strange amber eyes filled with mischief. Like he'd been there the whole time as a witness and loved every minute of it.

259

'Who—' I began but a strange sensation brushed over my skin, stopping me. The furniture in the room seemed to creak as if a storm had come rumbling from above.

'Emrys,' William half groaned in warning. Emrys's eyes were jet black, and his lips slightly curled in fury. In the space of a heartbeat, he had lunged to pin the stranger against the wall, his shirt straining with the ferocity of it. The impact rattled the wall-mounted cabinet above, vulgar fey trophies tumbling to the ground.

'Emrys!' William cried, almost falling over his chair in his haste to stop the brawl. He tried to lurch forward, but bowed over in pain as he gripped at his side.

'William!' I caught him, supporting his weight as he panted for breath.

Emrys and the new arrival didn't notice.

'You've picked the wrong evening to anger me, Thean,' Emrys warned, a vulgar and feral nature to his tone.

'You wouldn't hit a woman, would you, Emrys?' the man taunted, his smile sharp, revealing fanged teeth.

Then he wasn't a man. He shifted effortlessly, in the space of a moment, into a woman with the same wicked grin, one too familiar to me. That red hair now long and cascading over their shoulders, and the shirt that Emrys bunched in his fists almost revealed breasts where the fabric had been torn. Those dark marks, too, I'd seen before on their skin.

'*You*,' I breathed.

Emrys went completely still. A tension rolling off him that should have made me regret the words as he pulled back slowly from the stranger.

'You? How do you know them?' William asked, his eyes darted to my face.

'They . . . she . . . I . . .' I stumbled over my words. Not knowing which pronoun was appropriate to use.

'Call me whatever you like, darling. I'm too old to care,' the stranger half purred, mirth practically gleaming in their gaze.

'They were outside the healing house, by the woods,' I continued, confused by the creature's impossible appearance and Emrys's animosity towards the being.

'I needed to catch your attention somehow.' They grinned wickedly, pressing two palms to Emrys's chest, pushing him back easily. Their grin did not diminish as those bright amber eyes flickered to me once more. 'Maybe I need to get some bigger ears. You seem quite . . . enthralled with them, my lord.'

I felt William's attention come back to my face, and it took everything to control my reaction, to keep my gaze forward.

'What are you doing here, Thean?' William asked, standing upright with my help.

'You're looking well, dear William,' she said, and the creature called Thean grinned suggestively at the boy.

'Don't talk to him.' Emrys's hands formed fists once more. Ready to attack again.

'*Jealous*, darling Emrys?' They teased, relishing in his annoyance, leaning forward to antagonise him further.

'I'm not here to play games, Thean,' he warned.

'You should have listened to me then,' they taunted, head lolling to one side gracefully. 'I told you the reanimations of dead fey would come next. That land has been sick too long.'

There was a sharpness to their smile, the presence of their fangs and the ease of their shifting of forms. Something I should never have missed.

A voyav. A cursed form changer.

'Voyav.' The name left my lips in the old fey language before I could stop it. A changeling, a being without name in mortal tongue, a dark magic that had existed longer than the records. Voyav were a tribe of Verr, devoid of form, who grew tired of war and wickedness, bonding themselves to mortal flesh to survive the sealing of the earth. Beings that could feast off fey blood and pull the magic from it for their own use.

Beings the Verr sought revenge against and that fey had mistrusted for centuries. The closest creature I'd ever found to Alma's own magic. However, voyavs were limited to human forms. Or so the stories said.

Their attention snapped to me, a cruelty coming over those female features as the voyav took me in.

'How do you know that? About the reanimations?' I demanded.

'I was there when it happened last time, darling. Right before the uprising,' They shrugged, their focus returning to Emrys. 'Back when our handsome lord here used to listen to warnings.'

'How did you infiltrate Fairfax's house?' Emrys demanded, his voice returning to the cold disinterest I'd heard him use before.

The voyav leant back on the wall, as if they had all the time in the world to toy with him. Unbothered by those almost exposed breasts. 'I knew you'd come here eventually. Especially when your beautiful Kysillian *friend* set her eyes on that wood. From her Council records she has a habit of causing trouble.'

'Her name is Katherine,' William said sharply, offended on my behalf.

'Oh, I know her name.' Thean smiled, a malice in it I understood instantly. This strange creature shouldn't know anything about me. Voyav were dangerous.

'You'll do well to forget it,' Emrys half growled, stepping closer to them once more, but all it did was sharpen the being's smile.

'Where would be the fun in that?' Thean teased.

Kyvor Mor. That dark fiend's voice came back into my head, warning me with all the secrets I'd already given away.

A knocking came at the door, forcing us all apart and to pretend to have some form of decorum. Everyone but Thean, at least, who still lounged back against the sideboard, breasts almost exposed, before slipping back into male form effortlessly.

A housekeeper entered with a sullen expression and sharp features. Her grey hair brushed harshly from her thin face.

'The room is ready for Miss Woodrow,' was all she said, and I knew in that moment my fate was sealed. We were trapped here.

Chapter Twenty-Four

The housekeeper led me unceremoniously down numerous corridors, each as cold and vacant as the next. Remains of old red candlewax dripped down the peeling walls. Mould speckled high on the ceiling, with cracks appearing in the corners, barely disguised by the thick cobwebs.

I was almost halted by a sprouting of mushrooms that had appeared from the skirting boards beneath a side table, but her pace was unforgiving.

The last thing I bloody needed tonight was to get lost. So, I moved on, greeted only by the unpleasant aroma of stale cigar smoke, saints' incense and the bitter scent of old polish as we made it up a creaking threadbare staircase. I was worried about my muddy boots on the carpet but by the lumpy feel of it, and the crack of weak floorboards, the mud wouldn't make a difference.

I pushed the thought aside as the housekeeper finally came to a stop at a nondescript door, opening it before rushing off without a bow or backwards glance, clearly desperate to be unburdened by my company.

Even mortals far beneath the elite they served still saw fey as being under them, despite our circumstances being so similar.

It took me two deep breaths to find the courage to go inside the bedroom, to accept where this game was going.

There was the faint smell of damp despite the small fire being lit. A small tin tub sat before it, already full of water. The rest of the room was sparsely furnished: a small bed with greyish linens, a wardrobe and a vanity with a chipped porcelain washbowl.

The dark curtains were moth-eaten, covering small, latticed windows.

I crossed the room to open one, allowing in only a crack of air, bracing my hands on the windowsill and dragging deep breaths in. A futile attempt to keep my anxiety at bay.

What had I done? The phantom sting of my true power remained, a slight trembling in my limbs. Knowing the magic in my blood was already hungry for more freedom. To hunt and avenge what it had found in the wood.

'You've survived worse than this,' I reasoned under my breath as I pressed my forehead against the cold glass.

No matter how much I wished to wallow, it wouldn't solve anything.

The mud on my boots was beginning to dry and crumble onto the worn carpet. Then I noticed how much of it was clumped against my skirt, how torn and filthy the fabric was. I stripped off my ruined clothes, slightly horrified to notice the bodice of my dress was so torn my corset had been visible the whole time. No wonder the voyav was grinning. I shuddered as I got into the small, lukewarm tub beside the hearth.

There was a lump of brown soap on the side, along with a rough washcloth. I used it until my skin was pink and the water turned murky with dirt from those ruins. I winced as I sank beneath the water to wash my hair. My temple was tender and aching, along with the rest of my body. It had been too long since I'd used my true strength. Since I'd tested the limits of my body. Since I'd allowed myself to be who I truly was, to access that part of my nature.

Murderer. I shivered in the cooling water. Knowing I couldn't hide there all night I got out, using the rough towel to dry myself. I'd only been left with an ill-fitting nightgown that must have belonged to a guest a few decades before, judging by how frumpy it was. The lace yellowed with age.

Not wanting to suffer any further humiliation of trying to put it on, I rummaged in my bag, reaching deep beneath my notes to find my loose training garb instead, and the spare underthings I carried just in case.

I pulled on the trousers and knotted the tunic, then sat before the fire to comb the knots from my hair with my fingers, not even allowing myself to contemplate what came next. How angry Emrys was, whether William was okay, what Alma would say or who on earth the mysterious voyav had been.

A demon from long ago, a creation of the Old Gods' will, a story. An impossibility, and yet, all those things seemed to be meeting at the same point. Right here in this old rotting house.

Too many things to consider, and I didn't have any remedies in my bag for any of them. No, I simply had to wait for my fate.

A creak coming from the corner of the room turned me sharply to take in the small wardrobe. I didn't usually fear spectres, but in an unfamiliar location the prospect of an uninvited guest turning up didn't sit well with me. Another clatter came, louder this time.

The doors of the wardrobe rattled, the wood squeaking in protest. The latch creaking, unable to open.

I lunged forwards, wrenching the doors open, only for someone to come tumbling through them with a familiar head of dark curls and bright green eyes looking up at me in surprise as they sprawled across the floor in a mess of skirts.

'Alma?' I asked, bewildered by the sight of her on the rug as she jumped to her feet, arms around me instantly.

'Thank the ancestors you're all right!' she snapped, pulling back to strike my arm. 'Bloody listen to me next time you menace!'

'Ow!' I exclaimed, barely having a moment before she pulled me into another embrace.

'You're a pain in my arse,' she seethed against my shoulder, her grip so tight it threatened to squeeze all the breath from me.

'I'm sorry.'

'As you should be.' She pushed out of my hold with an annoyed sigh, turning to consider the room. The lecture I expected didn't arrive, probably because she was too disturbed by my current accommodation. 'This room is abysmal; I'll have to bring over a cleaning enchantment to sort it out.'

Her now-mortal eyes came back to my face. 'Help me with your things. Since we're going through the pretence of you being a guest.'

She turned her attention back to the wardrobe, reaching inside and lugging something towards the entrance. From where the back of the wardrobe was supposed to be, instead there was the strange glow of a portal entrance. A large, battered chest with fabrics trying to burst out of the wooden confines came tumbling through.

'These aren't mine.' I frowned, but still reached for the handle to help her pull it through, dropping the monstrosity onto the worn carpet.

'They're the gowns William found; he wrote down some incantations to help me alter them.' She sighed.

'Why do I need gowns?' A horrid feeling had begun to seep through my chest.

'William mentioned something about a dinner,' she continued, unbothered by my clear distress at the idea, as she popped the lid of the trunk and began to pull out swathes and bundles of extravagant fabric.

'I don't need . . .' I began but realised it wasn't important to argue right now. 'How is William?'

'Emrys was dealing with him.'

Of course he was, probably telling him off when all of this wasn't his fault.

'I should go and check on him.' I tucked my wet hair behind my ears.

'Dressed like that?' she scolded, her eyes flaring, pupils lengthening as a furry pattern appeared on her cheek.

'I've done more scandalous things this evening,' I pointed out dryly. Having my breasts out in a lord's house being one of them.

'True.' She relented, although she wouldn't look at me, giving a scratch on the side of one of the trunks her undivided attention. 'You may need to speak to Emrys for me and make an apology.'

I frowned. 'Why?'

'He wasn't best pleased with how I woke him up,' she muttered, her cheeks flushed, which made me instantly suspicious. Alma didn't get embarrassed.

'He was asleep?' I couldn't imagine Emrys doing anything so remotely mundane.

'He sleeps deeper than you do.'

That instantly made me remember all the demented ways Alma had woken me up in the past.

'What did you do?'

'I'd rather not remember it.' She practically shuddered, clapping her hands together to usher me from the room. 'You'd best get out of my way while I sort out this room.'

Her words brought forward the horrific realisation that I'd actually have to stay in that miserable-looking bed. A maid could come in unannounced at any moment, a spy to see that

268

I was behaving myself. I didn't need the rumours of what it meant to be missing from the bed. The thought unsettled me. I hadn't spent a night apart from Alma since Daunton. The nightmares still prevailed with her company, but it was better than being alone.

Resigned to my punishment, I climbed through the wardrobe, finding myself crouched on the other side, emerging from the Portium door in the back shelves of the library. Dusting off my sparring trousers, I made my way through the labyrinth of bookcases, guided by the orange glow from the hearth.

Wondering why the house hadn't taken me straight to William or the study, I continued on.

I got my answer as I came to a stop between the final shelves.

Bloody bastard house.

Emrys sat before the fire, one leg thrown up on the small footstool and a glass of amber liquid dangling precariously from his fingers as he rolled it with boredom.

He'd changed too, crisp fresh shirt partially undone, sleeves rolled up to show the scarred muscular surface of his forearms and the light dusting of hair that caught the fire's light.

Aware he was being watched, he turned his head lazily to see me. Taking in the bedraggled sight of me – my messy damp hair tangled around my ears, loose training attire and my bare feet on the rug. A tension moved through his jaw, a power to his gaze that unsettled me.

'Have you come to torment me some more, Croinn?' he asked, dropping his foot and finishing his drink before leaning forward to set the glass on a stack of books. He bowed his head to rub the back of his neck. Dark hair falling forward onto his brow.

I stopped at the large table, like a barrier between us, hands fiddling with the edge of my tunic. 'I came to see William. How is he?'

'He has a sprain and some bruising. Both will be healed by morning. I gave him a sleeping draught so the healing incantations work better. Sitting still isn't a skill he possesses.' There was a sharpness in his gaze that told me he was annoyed I possessed the same habit.

'I'm sorry,' I replied.

His dark brow raised. 'For getting caught?'

'I should have waited for you,' I admitted. No matter what had happened with Montagor, I'd been foolish to let fear guide me so recklessly and William had paid the price. 'I was . . . angry with everything.'

Emrys brought his knuckles to his lips, considering me thoughtfully over them. 'It'd take a king's commander years to figure out how to fight magic that dark on its own terms.' There was a lightness to his tone as if I'd impressed him.

'You could say I have a secretly vicious temperament.' I let my gaze drop to the table, considering the vastness of his notes that he'd left out, as if he'd been disturbed from work. The chaotic nature of them as he spoke of Mr Thrombi, of the thing he'd turned into. The ancient nature of the dark.

The impossibility of everything.

'I wouldn't say there is anything secretive about it.' His voice softened, as I felt the weight of his presence where he'd silently come to stand behind me. The power of his warrior's build radiated heat as his hand rested next to my own, the warmth of him travelling down my back.

'Do I want to know why the house is forcing me to crawl through a wardrobe?' I asked over my shoulder, wondering if it was some form of devious punishment.

'At least you can fit through yours,' he offered wryly, and it was then I saw the tear at the shoulder of his shirt. As if he'd caught it trying to do the same thing. 'The house misbehaves in my absence; it also doesn't like competition for my sleeping arrangements.'

'Jealous?' I teased him with a smile, watching his face darken with annoyance as the door behind us creaked loudly with confirmation. I could only agree – I wasn't fond of his absences either.

The sudden desire in that thought chased my mirth away, heating my traitorous cheeks as I turned quickly back to the table.

'That tallet shouldn't have been able to speak.' I swallowed uneasily at all the foolish mistakes I was making. 'Have you seen that before?'

There was a sudden pensive nature to his face as he considered the papers before us. He was so close I could see the fragments of light grey trying to purge that darkness from his eyes, the wickedness of the scar down his cheek.

'Close to a seal during the war.'

'There are no seals in the south.' I frowned, turning to him, ignoring the sting of fear in my chest.

Seals were the ancient points where Kysillians had eradicated the darkness. Most were buried by now, their locations lost to record thanks to one of the many mortal kings' plundering. I didn't know anyone who had seen an ancient seal and lived to tell the tale. Hadn't even heard of one apart from in my father's bedtime tales.

'You didn't tell me you saw Thean at the village.' There was a quietness to his words as he changed the subject. A guarded nature to his expression. His attention moved to my face, focusing on my lips once more. Waiting for a lie.

'I didn't know who they were. What they were. They presented themselves differently. I thought they were looking for you.'

He huffed out an unamused laugh as he moved around the table, putting distance between us. 'I'm sure Thean enjoyed that.'

A chill in the air penetrated the thinness of my training attire with his absence. There was something in the pensive nature of him, a heaviness to his shoulders, troubled deeply by his own thoughts.

'A voyav isn't good company to keep,' I warned. 'Who is Thean Page?'

'The less you know about the voyav, the better.' He ran a hand through his messy dark hair, letting it fall back across his brow.

'Yes, because naivety always works out well in the end,' I argued, watching his expression shut down, a cold mask of indifference slipping into place. The mask of a lord who somehow knew Montagor on unfriendly terms and kept cursed voyavs as acquaintances. Who was he?

I could see the lies working behind his eyes, trying to find a way to spin it. Saving him the effort, I moved from the table with a huff of annoyance, striding back towards the dark shelves that led to the portal.

'Kat.' He caught my wrist, but the barest contact made me recoil with a surprised cry. The burns I'd forgotten stung in response to the barest hint of his magic. My wrist clutched tightly to my chest, I faced him once more.

A tension came over him as he stood deathly still, the fire in the hearth dimming.

He reached out gently for my wrist. A part of me didn't want him to see the weakness on my flesh, didn't want his pity, but I let him take it anyway, revealing the horrid raised pink flesh beneath the sleeve of my tunic.

'Montagor's rings.' The words left his lips, but they didn't sound right. They didn't sound like him.

'It'll fade,' I whispered, not knowing why it filled me with embarrassment.

His eyes closed tightly, as he dragged in a deep, almost painful breath, his hold on me tightening ever so slightly. As if searching for some sort of restraint.

'He shouldn't have come anywhere near you.' The deep regret pressed between those words reminded me of the urgency in his voice when he'd come to find me.

Forgive me. The words he'd left for me.

'You wanted to see me.' My breath wasn't quite steady as the words left me.

'I was fully prepared to grovel at your feet.' His thumb dragged over the unhurt skin of my hand. Across my knuckles, following those faint training scars.

'Alma wasn't . . .'

'I'd take the disembowelment.' He grimaced, eyes lifting to my own before drifting to the side of my face where it ached at my temple. 'I'm sorry, Kat.'

I felt that strange bite of his magic, almost as if brushing back my hair to see better. I watched as those grey eyes darkened to black, as if ink had been spilt across a page with the turmoil of his emotions.

'I know,' I whispered, seeing a protective softness take over his features, the slight drop of his shoulders with relief. I might not have known all his secrets, but I knew regret too well to distrust him.

In the quiet, with only the crackling hearth, I looked down again at those welts on my skin. Evidence of all the cruelty in this world. Pain those fey had felt too.

'I was angry with Master Hale.' I sighed, hating the burning sting in my eyes. 'Angry at all the lies I allowed myself to believe.'

That any of this was over.

'I can feel them.' The confession left me so easily. Perhaps it was the closeness of him, the gentle nature to his hold or the understanding I knew I'd find in his eyes. 'In those ruins, all I could feel was their pain. Just like those artefacts the Council keep.'

I let my head tip up, swallowing down that sadness. 'It's like they're still calling out for help, even after all this time.'

His gaze was so dark, patient and focused on nothing other than me.

'I can feel it, too.' His hand shifted gently to avoid those burns, to hold onto my fingers in firm comfort.

In that moment I didn't feel so alone. Not while burdened with the grief of it.

I swallowed. 'He should have told me.' Understanding now why Hale hadn't. Why would he? When he didn't need to? I had no choice but to remain.

'Perhaps he didn't wish for you to be burdened with it.'

I smiled sadly at his effort to be convincing. 'You don't have to make excuses for him, Emrys.'

Those troubled grey eyes dragged over every inch of my face. 'It's not for him.'

Something sparked in my chest. No. It was for me. Trying to find a way to comfort me, to make it better – if only for a moment.

'You should get some sleep. A scout will take us to the ruins in the morning.' The words were gentle as he let me go, forcing himself to take a step back. Hands flexing into fists at his side.

'Ruins?' I pulled back in confusion, my fingers colder in the absence of his touch.

'The Fairfax family moved their residence a century before the war.' He rubbed the back of his neck. 'It's connected to the remains of that pit you found. So, the source could be there.'

'Why would someone be trying to unsettle what darkness rests here?' I wrapped my arms around myself, unsure why the mention of such things made my magic churn uncertainly in my blood.

He shrugged. 'Fairfax claims to have no enemies.'

'You don't believe him.'

'Everyone has enemies. You even made one an hour ago.' His gaze sharpened with his words. Of course, Lord Percy.

'He was hurting William,' I challenged, knowing I was right, but that wasn't the main point I needed to get to. 'How did you get there so quickly?'

'I rode from Paxton Fields, which gave me a great opportunity to see something we'd missed.' He reached into his pocket, producing a charred piece of wood between his thumb and forefinger. 'The west wing has been consumed by fire, which Fairfax claims is due to a maid's carelessness with a candle.'

I took the shard from him, letting it rest in the centre of my palm. It didn't crumble upon contact, but it did irritate my skin with the summoning still present in the wood.

'These are magical burns.' I turned the piece over. Magic burned down part of Fairfax's house and, judging by Emrys's lack of surprise, he already suspected such. 'Why wouldn't a lord report a magical surge?' Especially when it was in connection to damage of his property, and especially in times when lords weren't as wealthy as they pretended to be.

'They don't want anyone to know.' Emrys observed.

Surges of this magnitude were reported often. Some fey were unable to contain their magic, the lack of elders for guidance causing them to become lost. Most losing control, causing deadly surges that could decimate entire villages. The Council hadn't captured any such dangerous beings recently.

'How do we know it wasn't a rebel attack?' I challenged.

'He would have reported it. Lord Percy wouldn't have hesitated and I'm certain Thean would be gloating about it.'

'Not if they had a good enough reason to attack him,' I corrected, holding the shard back out to him. There weren't many fire-wielding beings left, their destructive nature put them top of the list for culling in the King's opinion during the war.

Emrys took the shard from me, my magic warming my fingertips at the barest touch from him. As if curious, demanding his attention, too.

'I found something else you might find useful.' He pushed the shard back into his pocket and pulled out a small velvet pouch embroidered with silver ivy leaves. He held it out to me and I took it gingerly with confusion.

What spilled out of it was a long silver chain with a beautiful glistening crystal wrapped in detailed filigree made to look like vines with small thorns. The stone glowing ever so slightly with an iridescent light. My magic flared soft lavender at my fingertips in interest.

'A wishing stone,' I breathed, unsure if he could even hear me as I ran my finger over the metal to check it was real. An ancient gem with the power to trap magic, just enough of it to come in useful for protection. From the glow, it was already imbued with a wish.

'I took the liberty of testing to see if it was still viable.' Emrys cleared his throat, fussing with the fold of his shirt sleeve.

'Thank you.' I hoped he knew just how much I meant those words. Not just for this gift, but for helping with Alma, for all of it. 'I'm sorry for more than just getting caught.'

His broad shoulders gave the barest shrug as a soft smile came to his lips. Those strange eyes now crystalline. 'We would have ended up here anyway.'

I found myself smiling back. 'By less dramatic means, surely?'

'Perhaps.' He nodded, his focus remaining on my face. 'You don't have to stay over there.'

'I'd rather not have the maids gossiping about why I'm missing from my bed,' I challenged lightly, reaching back to rub my shoulder and finally admit to the exhaustion in my limbs as I made my retreat back to the portal. Looking forward to seeing what trouble Alma had got up to in that awful room.

'Anyway, you should follow your own advice,' I called over my shoulder, seeing how he watched my retreat. His arms folded, expression troubled once more.

'Croinn,' he muttered under his breath, focus shifting to the piles of papers on the table. Despite all the things I wished to say, I tightened my grip on the gift he'd given me, worried it might slip from my grasp.

'Goodnight,' I whispered as I left, but he didn't reply.

Chapter Twenty-Five

*There is an ancient witch in the west. A blood seeker, luring children
into the night and binding their blood to her cause. To her rebellion
which seeks to decimate our world. Killing innocents and purging
Elysior back into war. Pray to the saint the stories are wrong, for her
greed and desire for power will ruin us all.*

— Recovered Council correspondence to the southern fields — 1835

The land beyond Fairfax Manor was nothing but a green smear
through the filthy glass of my bedroom window. I glanced to
the dusty clock in the corner, which clearly hadn't worked
in years, before pressing my palms against my tired eyes and
wishing, for once, I could have a peaceful night's sleep.

However, the horrid lumpy mattress and the draughty room
were my own fault. I'd woken numerous times during the
night fearful I'd somehow ended up back in the Institute's
cramped quarters.

Unable to bear the discomfort of the bed much longer,
I'd got up, but the cramped confines of the room still felt
stifling. I lingered at the uneven dressing table and considered
the items I'd dumped there. All the papers and notes for the
things I should be doing, and yet all I could think about was
that horrid cavern forgotten in the woods.

The dark scrawl of runes on the inside, the bitter taste of fear in the air. The screech of that creature and all the cruel things it was made of.

The chaos of that darkness, how vicious it remained after centuries. How my palms still ached with the power of my magic, how feral my flames had been. Then my thoughts wandered, remembering the firmness of Emrys's chest beneath my palm. The strong thrum of his heartbeat and the teasing bite of his magic. The strong erratic nature of him and just how dark his eyes went the closer I got.

Croinn. The subtle playfulness in his tone. Unwilling to let me go.

I let my fingers drag across my collarbone before catching on the chain around my neck. The weight of the gift he'd given me was a strong comfort as I pulled it from where it rested between my breasts and let the stone sit in my palm.

A wishing stone. Old magic. How beautiful it was, delicately made and kept safe all these years. How the stone glowed radiantly against my skin, reminding me of that troublesome dust sprite in those ruins. The little cretin that had started all this.

Maybe I needed to go back and thank the beast.

'Good, you're up,' came Alma's sharp greeting, making me jump and knock my knees painfully into the dressing table.

'Alma,' I hissed, flushing as I tucked the necklace back into my nightgown. 'You could have warned me.'

She stood with clothes freshly pressed and folded over her arms, her eyebrow raised disapprovingly – knowing every scandalous thought in my head.

'I wasn't in the mood to summon a necromancer to rouse your corpse,' she drawled, crossing the room to lay my clothes on the bed.

'I don't sleep *that* deeply.'

Something shot from the still-open wardrobe, tiny and white, its wings fluttered impatiently. It landed on Alma's shoulder and pecked at her hair to get her attention.

'Shoo,' she slapped it in my direction. 'That bastard thing clearly can't operate the portal on its own.'

I held out my hand as the message in tiny bird form tumbled but caught itself, fluttering over to land in my cupped palms before unfurling.

> *Croinn,*
> *I've acquired some horses.*
> *I'll meet you at the stables at ten o'clock.*
> *—Emrys.*

'Why is he calling you a witch?' Alma asked nosily over my shoulder.

'Never mind that.' I shook my head, slipping the note onto the dressing table, ignoring her suspicious stare as I walked around the moth-eaten changing screen to put on my chemise. 'How is William?'

'Sulking, considering Emrys has forced him to rest for the day.' I could hear the clatter of her re-tidying the vanity as I emerged from behind the screen.

'I should have gone to see him.'

Alma waited with the corset, frowning as her gaze locked on my chest.

'What is that?' she asked. I looked down to see the wishing stone dangling free.

'Emrys gave it to me.' I tucked the chain back inside my chemise and turned before she could examine it any further as she fit the corset and went to work.

'How *chivalrous* of him.' Her lacing motions were tighter than usual. 'Was this before or after his horrid guest arrived?'

'That wasn't his fault.' Montagor's sick amusements were his own. The house had tried to warn me, and as always, I hadn't listened.

'Fine,' she huffed, blowing an errant strand of dark hair from her face as she turned me around to offer me my shirt. 'Was it before or after you accosted him while he was half undressed then?'

'I didn't!' I protested, ignoring the burn of my cheeks. Remembering the hard planes of that chest and just how it had caught the morning's light.

'William said he barely had a shirt on,' she continued, ruthless as ever, as she held the riding skirt for me to step into. 'His trousers were unbuttoned too.'

'They were not.' I scowled as she laughed at the flush that had taken hold of my face. 'William is a terrible gossip.'

I went to step into the skirt. Then I saw there were two leg holes.

'Are they trousers?' I asked, trying to pull the skirt apart to see, but she slapped my hands away, tugging it up my legs.

'*Secret* trousers, and you better not tell anyone,' she half muttered, yanking at the fastenings with more force than necessary.

I moved my legs, feeling the fabric between them, but looking at my reflection, the garment looked like an ordinary travelling skirt.

'I love them.' Not knowing it was possible to have both comfort and propriety, but of course, Alma found a way.

'Hopefully that means you'll take care of them.' She sighed, holding out the matching jacket for me to slip my arms into. Something in her teasing expression reminded me I had my own questions to ask.

'What were you doing in Emrys's room?' I asked as she bullied me to sit before the misty, aged mirror, starting on my hair.

'Looking for secrets.' She shrugged as I watched her work in the reflection.

'Did you find any?'

A mischievous glint came to her eyes. 'No, but there is still time.'

Time. What Mr Thrombi had run out of quicker than the rest of us. Because of me. That truth was harder to swallow than the rest. I looked down at my hands.

'Do you trust him?' Alma's voice was quiet, as if sensing the direction of my thoughts. Leaning down to rest her hands on my shoulders, her head next to my own as she watched me carefully in the mirror. That stone against my breastbone warmed in comfort.

'Master Hale does.'

'I'm not asking Master Hale.' She raised a dark brow in challenge, but there was a softness in her eyes. Cautious of my emotions.

I should have thought about it, but all I could see was the warmth of William's smile, his ease with the house, Emrys's work to heal Mr Thrombi, his disdain for the Council and how easily he'd forgiven me for almost killing him with a ghoul.

'Yes.' The word left me without doubt. I did trust him. Maybe foolishly, but perhaps I was tired of suspicion, tired of running and fearing everyone's motives.

'Fine.' She smiled reluctantly, before leaving me to find my boots. 'I'll forgive him then.'

I laced up my boots as she tidied up the room and grumbled something about the horrid bed. I watched her, the ease of her movements, the natural flush in her cheeks. No longer weakened by her transformations, despite the fact she'd had one mere hours ago.

'How did you do it?' I asked. Watching her sharp eyes turn to me, not needing to ask what I meant.

'It wasn't a choice. Or perhaps the racket you were all making irritated me enough to test my limits.' She smiled, running a palm over the horrid bedspread to smooth it into place. 'Just as you killed those dark things so effortlessly. I think there is something in me that wants to . . . change.' She contemplated her words for a quiet moment. 'Something that wants to be free at last.'

My magic shifted within me, a warm rush in agreement that made me ball my hands into fists to hold it back.

'That doesn't scare you?' Did it scare her as it did me? To be everything that had been forbidden for so long?

She crossed the small space to stand before me, such vulnerability in her suddenly feline eyes as she looked up at me, reminding me how much smaller she was. Yet there was nobody stronger or more imposing than Alma. Maybe Emrys.

'What do we have to be afraid of, Kat?' The was such a gentle strength to those words, I found my fingers interlaced with her own.

Nothing. There was nothing left to fear now. We'd seen it all. Survived it all.

Then a wretched knocking came on the chamber door.

'Don't get soul-snatched!' Alma snapped before ducking through the wardrobe, the doors closing behind her of their own accord.

Being soul-snatched appeared to be the least of my problems as I opened the door to another dour-looking servant. This one was younger but held the disposition of someone twice her age as she turned sharply on her heel and forced me to follow at pace.

We went down the creaking stairs to the quiet, dim halls, where the scent of tobacco lingered and the wallpaper was threatening to peel.

It was unusual for lords to let their houses sink into such disrepair, then again, by the job Lord Percy was doing monitoring the lands, it shouldn't have been that much of a surprise.

I was led past a busy kitchen to the back of the house and out onto a gravel path to a carriage house. A familiar figure stood there, dressed in dark grey riding attire cut close to the imposing form of him as he fixed his gloves, surveying two grazing horses.

The maid left me without a word – chased back inside by the cold – and I was suddenly grateful for the thickness of my jacket as I made my way over to Emrys.

His riding coat was a fine suede, trousers the same, and boots had not a mark on them, despite the muddiness of the ground surrounding the stable.

'I don't suppose Hale taught you how to ride a horse when he was planting a seed of rebellion in you?' He smiled in way of greeting, the breeze forcing his hair onto his brow. Out in the sunlight I was momentarily startled by the handsomeness of the man, and just how oblivious he was to it.

'I know how to ride.' I stepped around him to assess the dark horse I'd been given. At least it was tall enough for me. I lifted the saddle to check the girth, tugging on the straps before dropping my attention to the stirrups.

'My father used to rescue and raise perrybons,' I added over my shoulder, watching with interest as he stroked the side of his own mare.

I remembered the ancient creature with deep affection, their shape similar to a horse, except larger and with small twisting antlers, closer in appearance to deer. Wild and fearless animals that demanded respect, not control.

'I don't think I've ever seen a perrybon,' he mused.

'There are hundreds on the northern islands to the south, if you know where to look.' Too wild to be coaxed onto ships and I often wondered how they were getting on, undisturbed now, since most beings had abandoned the islands after the wars.

'You'll have to show me,' he replied easily.

It felt like a promise, as if there would be time after all this. Time he wished to spend in my company. His eyes said the same, an intensity to them genuinely awaiting my answer.

'My Lord.' A young serving boy emerged from the stables with his own smaller, and far less impressive, mount. The old beast looked like it would keel over at any moment, but the boy mounted it anyway.

Emrys nodded. I assumed this was the scout.

'Come on, before the weather changes.' Emrys moved closer to help but I ignored his chivalrous offer.

The animal shook its head in annoyance as I mounted, shifting beneath my weight, but I was thankful for my trousers as I settled, and watched Emrys mount his own horse in one effortless motion.

The boy moved off, compelling us to follow down the rest of the path and into the vast muddy lands. I patted the horse's neck as it resisted slightly, uncertain of the path. The wind picked up, forcing me to turn my face out of it, glancing behind to see the imposing structure of Fairfax Manor in the distance for the first time.

A grand structure of stone, bold and out of place in the enormity of the nature that surrounded it. I could also see the extent of the damage the fire had caused. What Emrys had warned me about.

Half the building was gone, hollow and dark. What little remained clawed up towards the sky in sharp charred points.

The devastation shocked me, and yet the lord inside pretended there was nothing wrong with his home. Oblivious to the scent of smoke even now. Emrys followed my gaze, a troubled expression on his face. As if the madness of the old man's grief hadn't missed his attention either.

'Lord Fairfax knows you.' I was curious to know just how deep his connection with higher society went before the uprising.

'I was at the Institute with his son,' Emrys replied distantly as he returned his attention to the mud path, steering his mare round a deep divot.

'What happened to him?' I asked, despite knowing from the gloom that lingered around Fairfax the tale didn't have a happy ending.

'I killed him.'

'What?' I almost slipped in my saddle. Unsure if I'd misheard him or he'd lost his mind. 'Does Fairfax know?'

'That his son became one of the dark fiends he worshipped? No. I saved the old bastard that at least.' His response was devoid of emotion, and where that could have pointed to cruelty in some, I'd learnt it pointed to a depth of emotion in Emrys.

A hesitance lingered in his voice, cautious of sharing. As if these events had taken place in a different lifetime. To a different Emrys.

'Richard wasn't as strong as he thought he was. He believed that he could be smarter than the darkness, use its power against it. He didn't stand a chance.' A bitterness accompanied those final words.

I considered the troubled profile of him, this lonely, strange being.

We manoeuvred the steep land and came to the opening of the woods, the trees bleached of colour, their branches like sharp claws tangling with each other high above. No leaves on the ground, and the smell of rot was prominent in the barren surroundings.

He'd made me forget with his words and attention that there was a war happening. That there was an Emrys long before he strode across my path. An Emrys with secrets and a past. Perhaps even darker than my own.

I fixed my gaze ahead, unsure if I was more worried about what those things could be, or how little they bothered me.

'It's easy to misjudge how well a being can fight the temptation of the dark.' Emrys's words were softer with caution, his gaze straight ahead. Monitoring the dark press of trees for a lingering threat, but I could see the stiffness in his jaw and hear coldness in his voice.

'Not me.' No, because what could it offer me? This world had already taken everything and that was the dark thought that burdened me.

Emrys was silent.

We pressed deeper into the forest, the horses protesting as they stepped over large roots and maneuvered the undulating trail that was barely visible. The trees were green despite the winter season, and thick mud covered the ground. There was no evidence of the darkness consuming this earth, despite it devouring it so viciously on the other side around Paxton Fields.

'Fairfax seems open to our interference here,' I observed.

'I wouldn't find too much comfort in that. He's half mad, talking to the dead and telling the servants his son has returned,' he commented wryly.

'Grief is a potent monster.' A demon all its own and one that could never be exorcised.

Emrys looked at me with that dark knowing gaze, his lips parting, but no words left him.

'Here you are, my lord,' the boy called, jumping down from his mount. He fixed his cap as he crossed the path, ducking into the thicket to indicate a narrower and more overgrown passage. There was stone hidden beneath the moss – ruins of what used to stand there. The remains of metal gates merged with the great trunk of an oak tree. 'The trail is too narrow now for the horses.'

'Thank you,' Emrys replied, flicking a silver coin to the boy, who caught it and rushed back to his horse, turning swiftly and guiding it back down the precarious path. Clearly he'd decided we wouldn't need a guide back.

Emrys dismounted with a smooth kick, landing easily. I followed with a little less grace. The horses moved aside to graze on the grass that protruded from the uneven stone ground as I ducked under a low hanging branch to reach Emrys's side.

There was a worn, cobbled footpath concealed under a blanket of moss. Through the thicket, the remains of a manor house, or the ruins of what used to be one, sat deep in the woods before us. Statues of saints watched from the darkness between the press of trees.

We were here.

Chapter Twenty-Six

Beware of the places the world forgets. For the memories that remain there are creatures all their own. Feral with their despair and looking to share misery with their bite.

— Myths of the Damned, 1645

Words from a book that had filled me with nothing but horrid unease as I'd read it, however, nowhere near to the unease I felt looking at the remains of what stood before me.

'This was Fairfax Manor?' I wondered just in what century the family had abandoned the house and why.

'What's left of it,' Emrys corrected as we climbed over large roots and up uneven stone steps, passing warped metal gates that led to the front door, or what little remained of one. 'They clearly have a habit of ruining their houses.'

The forest had claimed the house. A thicket and vines tangled with wood and stone until it was almost impossible to distinguish the two. A large tree sprouted up from where the entrance door had once stood. The space was too packed with bark and crumbled stone to get through.

There was a window frame to the side of the entrance, half collapsed, but a snarled branch was keeping the rest of it upright. I moved up the steps, climbing over the ancient roots and around to the window at the side, pressing myself close to the crumbling stone.

'Kat,' Emrys muttered in annoyance as I reached for the shattered window, pushing the ivy aside to lean in and see the drop on the other side. It appeared to have once been the main hall. Morning light streamed through a gaping hole in the ceiling as birds roosting above flapped their wings in annoyance of our presence. A rusted corpse of a chandelier lay in the centre of the room, the gems that had survived throwing multicoloured shapes into the darkness.

Emrys climbed up next to me, our shoulders pressing together as he peered in. A curse slipped from his lips and he grasped the window frame to climb through. I caught his arm.

'Do you think that floor will hold?' I frowned.

'Only one way to find out.' He sighed, taking hold of the window frame and using a gap in the bricks to get his foot on the windowsill, barely fitting through the space before he dropped to the other side as silently as a cat. I had to lean in again to check he hadn't gone straight through the floor.

No, he stood looking up at me in the dismal dark, trying to rub a moss stain off his sleeve. I was instantly grateful to Alma for my trousers as I hoisted myself up and used the ledge to lower myself as far as possible before I let go. Emrys caught my waist as I landed, my back pressed against the warmth of his chest as I struggled to steady my feet on the uneven floorboards. His hands gently cupping my elbows until I was balanced.

'Thank you,' I whispered, turning, but he was already moving into the gloom.

The air was thick with damp. The space was vast and circular in shape, with only threads remaining of curtains that had once clung to the windows, walls now crumbling, and thick vines and roots growing over them. Archways surrounded us. There was nothing but a dense darkness beyond.

The remains of glass cracked under my boot as I followed Emrys across the room, avoiding loose planks in the floor. The aftermath of the night's rain seeped through holes in the roof. Most of the upper rooms had collapsed, visible through holes in the ceiling above us that had been painted once with what appeared to be a grand mural, now overrun with foliage.

The place teamed with life. Nothing like the darkness that consumed Paxton Fields or that horrid verr pit in the woods. This didn't seem like the hiding place of a monster. No, just a forgotten manor in a hungry wood.

'There isn't anything here.' I was overwhelmed by the lack of relief I felt at those words. Only because, if such dark things weren't dwelling here, they were dwelling somewhere else.

'Looks can be deceiving,' Emrys replied, a hesitation in his voice. This wasn't his first inspection after all.

He moved through one of the sagging archways, unbothered by the cobwebs, seeming to know the layout without having to glance at which way to turn, despite the fact I was certain nobody had been in these halls in the last century. I let him guide me through doorways threatening to collapse and over precarious gaps in the floor until we came to a more protected room. The ruins of a library, judging by what bookshelves remained.

Books and papers were left to rot in a strange pulp on the floor. Amongst the mess was the gleam of golden coins from Elysior, currency during one of the old Kings' rule. Tarnished with the centuries that had passed. Wealth that had killed the world.

'They left in a hurry,' I observed, kicking over a small wooden chest with my boot. More of the garish bright coins spilling onto the floor, rolling until they dropped through the gaps to whatever abyss lay beneath us.

The disarray confused me, as did the remainder of valuable items. What had stopped them coming back to plunder it?

'Dark magic has a habit of consuming when it's left unchecked.' Emrys' response held apprehension, making me feel this place wasn't as safe as I'd first anticipated.

It was then that I noticed how the coins gleamed brighter out of the corner of my eye, trying to attract my attention. Cursed artefacts, holding a great price for those greedy enough to take them.

'There are curses here,' I whispered; cautious they were listening even now.

Emrys moved closer to my side, brow furrowed in confusion. 'You can see them?'

'My mother was mortal.' Her blood allowed me to see the things that would drive mortals mad, yet my Kysillian side protected me from being fooled by it.

'I forget sometimes,' Emrys murmured, more to himself, turning to consider the mess at his feet.

I weaved carefully through the damp, ignoring the ruined fey trinkets, shattered furniture, and the curses trying to lure me into madness. Towards a small pile of books in the corner, overcome with rot and moss.

One stood out more than the others, left on a table as if it had only just finished being read. The gold embossing still visible under the grime. I took hold of it carefully, allowing my palms to heat ever so slightly, remembering the lyrical mix of the incantation at the back of my mind, a song that didn't need words to be formed.

Slowly, with a crack and the blue hue of my magic, the complete volume came back to life in my palm.

'What are you doing?' Emrys asked at my shoulder, curiosity overriding his concern.

'Reformation.' I smiled, holding the book out for him to see as I peeled the cover open, the crisp pages turning effortlessly.

'How did you come up with that?' His eyes were bright and clear with his confused amazement.

'I took apart a looping spell and . . .' I began, but something in his expression stopped me, something that felt more intense than simple admiration.

'Never mind.' I shook my head, turning my attention to the page of the book before me, finding it full of scrawls, sharp dark markings and demonic wishes. The ink had a strange red hue in parts. My magic rose in recognition of it without even touching the ink. Blood ink, made with fey sacrifice.

I recoiled, the book tumbling from my hands, falling to the earth as nothing more than a moss-covered piece of rot.

Here. The word brushed calmly over my shoulder. A comfort in it. Something small caught my eye in the dim light. Something brighter than all the other earth-toned colours around it.

'Emrys.' My hand reached out, catching his sleeve before I moved towards the corner of the room, right by the doorway into another. A small Nox offering leant there, next to an upturned volume of a book. Not a piece of damp on it.

I picked the book up, flicking through the pages to see one torn. Remembering the shape of the note Emrys had been left, I turned to him. 'He was here. Thrombi was here.'

A darkness passed over Emrys's expression that could have been a trick of the light. 'Which means so is the anthrux,' he said. 'It's a perfect nest. Enough dark spells to feast on.'

He frowned at the mess, troubled. A cold breeze swept through the room, rolling papers and leaves over our boots. I shivered, but Emrys's head snapped to the side, facing down the hall as if someone had called his name.

He moved past me to the doorway to consider the darkness beyond. Frozen in place, his face bleached of colour, those scars more prominent down the side of his face, an odd tension coming over his limbs. Shadows seeming to pass over his skin.

'Emrys?' I asked.

But he didn't move, no recognition that he'd even heard me. I reached out for his arm. He flinched at my touch, turning towards me, eyes impossibly dark.

'Something else is here.' Those words left his lips softly but there was a fear moulded into them that turned my blood cold. The dark played games with the truth. I remembered that.

'We need to go,' I urged.

He shook his head slightly, his hand dropping to capture my own as he turned and pulled me back the way we had come.

There was an urgency to him that made me hesitant to argue as we wandered back through the rooms, a horrid coldness following that had nothing to do with the wind. There was a pattering of footsteps that weren't our own, a creaking of the trees but nothing lurking on their branches. The shadows became longer and darker.

The shattering of glass echoed down the hallway, stopping us as we reached the main hall. Emrys released his hold on me to turn towards the sound.

The birds above took flight, small feathers and dust rained down, making patterns in the sunlight. But there was nothing else. Silence from the shadows.

The stone around my neck burned with an intense warning that my magic followed.

The dark played games, wishing us foolish enough to let it feast. My father's voice echoed through my memories as I slipped my hand into my bag, finding his hilt. I took it out, let it slip into a small blade against my palm, warm and ready. My magic welcoming it.

Steady is the heart. Swift is the flame.

I heard the slightest creak and tap of something on the wood. My magic barely rose in warning before I turned, forcing all my energy into my arm as I threw the blade. It sailed effortlessly through the air like an arrow, nothing but the sheen of metal as it travelled through the stream of sunlight straight into the dark. A loud thwack the only evidence it had made contact, and then came the screech and the scuttling of limbs.

Attached to the wall and hidden in the shadow was the creature. Covered in putrid grey scales, long and flat with arachnid limbs. No bigger than a city rat. It curled into itself with a cracking of thin bone, black blood dripping to the ground before it shifted to nothing but ash. The Kysillian blade protruded from the wall, gleaming in the limited rays of sunlight.

That horrid feeling dissipated, the light a little brighter as the stone around my neck went silent once more. I moved to retrieve my blade, having to jump over the gaps in the floor, listening to it groan in protest.

'Remind me never to piss you off, Croinn,' Emrys offered wryly, considering the darkness around us, hand extended to coax me back to him.

Only there was no relief in his amusement.

'It should be more difficult than that.' I moved closer to the dark where the thing had hidden. Beings of such power didn't need to hide, not when they should be ravenous with a will to live.

'Ancient things don't tend to do well in modern times, dormancy weakens them tremendously.' Emrys' voice echoed across the space.

It was something more than that. I pulled the blade from the wall, letting it turn dormant once again as I pushed the hilt back in my bag.

I crouched to run my fingers through the dark ash the creature had left behind, confirming by the gritty texture it was as ancient as I believed it to be. 'I don't understand how it survived. There isn't anything here to feed on.'

'It must have come from somewhere else.'

If the house was connected to the Verr pit, whatever was causing this must have been hiding between. We needed to find out where this had begun, and the only thing effective in hunting the dark was the magic it craved. I kept some of the dark ash in my palm, causing my magic to flare with irritation, I rolled a small spark against my skin and manipulated it into a shape.

'*Zeltu*,' I ordered, watching the spell flare in recognition before forming a hard glass-like orb with a faint glow. I opened my hand, letting it roll off the tips of my fingers. It bounced and spun of its own accord across the rotting floor, vanishing through a hole in the wall.

A hunting orb.

'What did you tell it?' Emrys asked, watching the path the strange spell had taken.

'To go to the beginning.' I smiled at him, watching how the rainbowed light from the scattered chandelier gems reflected off his darkness. 'All we have to do is follow.'

'Croinn.' He smiled, but there was something lingering in his features, a slight unease that surprised me. As if the distance between us was something he couldn't quite bear.

My confusion lasted a mere moment as a sharp crack made us both go still.

'Kat,' he said, lips parted to give me an order, but the floor gave in beneath me before I could hear it.

Chapter Twenty-Seven

Darkness and dust consumed me as I tumbled through nothingness, striking numerous things on the way down. My cries echoed back to me, damp rotting roots slipping through my fingers, slowing my descent, but when I met the ground, I hit with winding impact. The force sent me rolling until I bounced off a brick wall, dirt coating my lips.

Wood rained down, forcing me to duck into a ball, hands over my head as I was showered with debris. I choked on dust, retching as the creak of the ruins settling once more echoed around me. I pushed most of the wreckage off me, shattered pieces of rot-eaten wood and dry roots. Spitting the grittiness from my mouth, as I started to right myself. Damp leaves clung to my walking suit, thankfully carpeting the ground enough to break my fall.

The wishing stone hung free from my dress, thrumming like a heartbeat. Bathing the confined space in a soft silvery light.

I pressed my palms against damp earth, weeds sliding between my fingers as I dragged myself unsteadily to my feet.

'Emrys?' I coughed, squinting in the darkness, weak light streaming from the hole I'd come through a few floors above. Trying to blink the dirt from my eyes, shaking my head only to shower myself in more.

Circular brick walls surrounded me, as if I stood in the base of a tower. A lone door opposite me was obstructed by debris that had come down with me.

The only sound was a distant drip of water, echoed ominously back to me and the groaning of the wooden supports above.

I needed to find Emrys. He didn't have the fallback of possessing Kysillian blood and being annoyingly difficult to maim after all.

Seeing no other way out, I dragged myself over the larger chunks of wood, moving towards the warped door. Finally making it to the wall, my fingers tangled with thick ivy, pulling it away from the frame in search of the handle.

My hand closed around it. Ignoring the ache in my shoulders, I gave it a sharp turn, pushing against the wood, only for the rusted lump to come apart in my hand. I'd only managed to push the door a mere inch from the frame. Annoyed, I tossed the remains of the handle aside, forcing the door the rest of the way open with my shoulder, only to be assaulted by stale air and cobwebs. The darkness beyond containing nothing but a bitter cold.

I summoned an illumination orb, allowing it to leave my hand and hover in the dark, barely lighting a few feet before me as the darkness devoured the light. Rats scurried from one shadow to another, the density of the damp making me cough as I pulled thick cobwebs from my path.

I'd spent most of my time at the Institute in the ruins beneath it, unbothered by the decay of lost places, and yet, something about this place felt wrong.

The orb moved further into the gloom, but there were only collapsed rooms and roots. A maze of decay and dark tunnels with arched doorways made from thick stone.

Old. This place was too old. A creaking sound echoed through the darkness, making my heart climb further up my throat.

'Bats,' I reasoned quietly to myself, taking another step, eyes desperately searching the darkness beyond for any sliver of light.

Something in me shifted restlessly. The stone around my neck flickered faster, copying the panicked beat of my heart.

A hiss brushed my ear, turning me around only to see the dark I'd come from. A strange distant scuttling followed, echoing from one of the archways I'd passed. The orb moved, bathing the dark in pale light, revealing nothing but puddles and grime.

Nothing there.

Ignoring my childish imagination, I quickened my steps, grasping onto the stone around my neck, letting the warmth of it reassure me as I followed the orb, ducking under roots and shrivelled vines.

'Emrys?' I called again, trying not to sound too desperate as the foulness of this place pressed closer. The air thicker, my heart pounding painfully against my ribs.

I turned another corner, boots sinking into a puddle of stagnant water. Then I felt it. Ice cold, almost burning with its intensity, like a frosty breath against the nape of my neck.

A searing pain wrapped around my wrist, a curse slipping from my lips as I grabbed it. The burns Montagor had given me throbbed painfully. The orb dispersed with my distress.

The stone around my neck became blinding with its brightness, casting long, sharp shadows down the dark, ruined hallway.

Run, a quiet voice whispered in my mind. Small and scared.

Something was wrong. A strange pressure in the air told me I wasn't alone. That scuttling came back, something changing in the darkness, moving in the shadows out of the corner of my eye.

Little troll. The pain in my hand intensified with the memory of that voice, almost taking my knees from beneath me. I panted as I stumbled into the dank wall.

No. That wasn't real.

I shook the memory away, screwing my eyes shut to push it further into the back of my mind. Then I heard it. The familiar click of heeled boots and the intensity of his stride. The sound of his cane as he slapped it against the dorm doors. A warning.

A sick game of chance as he taunted his next victim.

My head shot up, heart pounding as I watched the gloom before me, feeling the vicious bite of that dark in the silence. Something watching. Lurking.

Run, that warning whispered again. Desperate.

I followed its command, turning back the way I'd come only to crash into a brick wall that hadn't been there before. My fingers curling against the damp stone.

No.

That memory of that stinging bite came back to the nape of my neck, slipping down my spine.

'Little troll,' came that taunting voice from over my shoulder. My whole body trembled and my vision dimmed, making my head spin as bile crawled up my throat.

'S-stop,' I begged. Just as I'd begged back then.

Those steps still came, a figure walking towards me from the darkness, swinging its cane, a strange smoke rising from it as the horrid stench of burning flesh met my nose.

'Little troll,' he called in the bitterly cheery way he always had, stepping into the dim light so I could see the charred remains of him: lips peeled back, black flesh, and hollow pits for eyes, his remains still smoldering as he continued to move towards me.

I could smell him, feel the heat of his charred flesh. He was real.

A broken sob escaped my lips. Shaking overtook my limbs, fear taking control of everything else as I slipped onto my knees. The air too thick.

Please! A horrid screaming filled the air, bowling me over. Shattering my heart.

Alma. That was Alma.

'Stop,' I begged, a weak, childish whimper leaving me as I pressed my palms over my ears, shaking my head. It wasn't real. It wasn't real.

Then those screams came again. Louder as I tried desperately to get to my feet. As I clawed at the rough stone wall but my legs wouldn't work.

I needed to find her. Needed to stop it.

My magic ignited in my veins, brutal and wild. Ravenous to be free. To unleash its molten rage upon him just as it had once before. As I tried to reach down into that chaotic well inside of me.

Not real. This wasn't real.

'No!' I curled my hands against my chest, refusing to let out my magic, to let it consume me. The pain of it bowed me over, body trembling with the ferocity of it. I shook my head wildly, trying to hold on to my sanity.

It wasn't real. It couldn't be. Magic burned my flesh and agony turned my limbs against me as his laugh came back through the darkness.

Smoke gathered in my lungs, making it impossible to breathe. All I could feel was the callous, cruel nature of his touch, the pain of my hunger and the brutality of their punishments.

My back stung with a sharp cutting pain I knew too well, right at the base of my spine, where those lash marks remained even now. The pain stealing my breath and making me scream.

Run. Another phantom pain streaked my back, bending me over as I grabbed onto the roots and vines. They turned to ash beneath my heated palms. I recoiled, forcing myself up onto my weak legs, tumbling into rough brick and using it to push myself further into the dark.

I ran, letting the sharp roots claw at my skin, only for them to become small, charred hands emerging between the cracks of the brick around me, grasping and pulling.

Then came their screams. Desperate and shrill.

Those hands came from the fractures in the stone floor, wrapping around my ankles and dragging me down. My chin made painful impact with the stone. I kicked and screamed as I felt something cut into my calf, deep and sharp like claws. I kicked again, breaking free with a painful sob, crawling into the dark but unable to look away. Unable to stop listening to the screaming.

Another phantom pain of a lash came to my back, knocking me to the cold floor, more hands grasping and pulling at my hair and throat. Too many, pulling me against the wall.

A hideous sharp tightness took hold of my chest. The ferocity of my magic bowed me over. I tried to hold onto the damp stone, tried to ground myself, but there was nothing but smoke in my lungs and the sound of him coming closer.

Little troll.

'No!' I screamed. My hands erupted. The narrow passageway devoured in blue-and-purple flames, the force of it turning any plant life to ash, erasing those hands that held me in place. Silencing their screams. A storm of chaotic wildfire. Smoke crawled up my throat as weakness consumed my limbs. But he remained in the centre of it. Dark and crumbling, aflame as he had been once before.

The damp air smothered that fire in a moment. The darkness eating it whole.

Then those screams started again.

Beg. The charred remains of Master Daunton leered closer. Ready to kill me again.

'No!' I panted, my magic burning through my veins to protect me from the impossible: the brutality of my mistakes. My eyes screwed shut as I pressed my palms against my ears, trying to push it out. To wake up. To make the nightmare go away.

Alma's screaming echoed all around me, followed by all the others, louder than the roar of my flames . . . louder than anything else.

'Stop!' the agonised cry left my lips, my body trembling as I tried to hold on. To stop those flames consuming me too. I curled into myself, painfully pressing down on my ears, trying to block it out.

Kat, another voice called. But I shook my head.

There was just smoke and fear. Cold, familiar magic swept around me like a breeze, flooding my lungs with air.

Something touched my arm. I cried out, eyes screwed tight as I kicked and fought.

'Kat.' The cold leather of Emrys's gloves pressed against my cheeks as he held my face, unbothered as my fists struck his arms.

I was frozen in place by the deep concern in his dark eyes as he crouched before me, but there was no relief as I panted for breath, tasting the tears on my lips as I struggled to pull in enough air. Drowning in the pain of it.

I shook my head. He wasn't here. He hadn't come.

Nobody had.

Yet, as my hands circled his wrists, he remained before me. The darkness of his eyes reflected the suddenly soft glow from the wishing stone between us.

His thumbs dragged gently across my cheeks. The rich scent of beasam bark chased everything else away as I uncurled my trembling fingers to take hold of his ruined jacket lapel, to feel the thick familiar material of it. The warmth of him, the brutal strength of his hold.

Real. He was real.

He was here.

A weak sob clawed its way up my throat, but there was no relief as my palms continued to burn with the evidence of what I'd done. Ash rained down around us, gathering on his broad shoulders and in his hair. I could have killed him. I'd allowed my nightmare to ignite the chaos in my veins. Allowed it to consume everything. I would have killed him for nothing more than childish fear.

Murderer, that voice hissed and I felt tears slide down my burning cheeks that he caught with his thumb. He leant forward, gathering me closer to him. As if his body was a shield against the horror of this world. Against that darkness behind him.

'It's not real, Kat,' he whispered against my skin, the ghost of a kiss against the side of my ruined hair. His hands gently moving down my stiff back, still tender with those phantom pains, but I didn't pull away.

Couldn't.

I trembled, unable to stop shaking, holding him tighter as I let the comfort of his magic soothe my flushed skin.

'It's all right.' His hand moved to the back of my head, a reverence in his touch that I leant into.

I never thought it would be okay again. I thought I'd die, my magic continuing to churn viciously in my stomach.

Emrys pulled back gently to root around in his pocket for something, a cylindrical crystal he tossed carelessly to the ground.

'Come on.' His arm went beneath my legs, another around my waist as he scooped me up easily. My arms looped around his neck in fear he'd drop me once he fully gauged my weight.

His foot came down on the crystal, a dark grey smoke rose and with another step we weren't in the dank darkness anymore. Both slightly breathless and covered in mud, we were greeted by the comforting smell of old books. The study of Blackthorn Manor. *Home.*

Emrys tried to put me down gently, but the moment my right leg touched the ground, a hissed breath left my lips. My calf burned with pain as I felt a wetness running down my ankle, and I was back in his arms.

He moved to his desk, sweeping the contents to the side as he placed me on top of it. Books, pages of notes and samples clattering uselessly to the ground.

'You shouldn't—' I began but the pain in my chest made me stop. Heat flared in my veins and stole my voice. I leant forward, hands curling around the edge of the desk as the agony of suppressing my magic came over me again, forcing me to tense every inch of my body to keep it contained.

'You're trembling.' His hands came to the side of my throat, trying to see me, but I couldn't raise my head. Couldn't be distracted by him.

'How did you bring us here?' I asked through clenched teeth.

'Portal stone,' he answered dismissively. Of course. A stone that had been banned in one of the first centuries, but he was in possession of it.

'The—' I began before I clamped my mouth shut, another wash of pain coming over me. Breath hissed between my lips, and I wondered if I could make it to the hearth.

'Beings die from suppression, Kat.' There was a warning in his voice, but I was in too much pain to contemplate it.

Suppression. Restricting wild magic until it consumed a being from the inside out. Usually starting with their mind.

'It will pass in a minute.' I shook my head and tried to drag in another deep breath through my tight throat.

He took hold of my wrists, pulling them from the desk and gently forcing my burning palms to lay flat against his own. His gloves missing. The strange irregular thumping of his pulse and the magic deep in his blood. Wild and waiting, just like mine. Cooler, stranger, but the same.

The pain faded on that realisation, my magic too curious to attack, to even remember what had unsettled it as I felt Emrys's pulse beat chaotically against my skin.

Something about it, the ancient part of my own magic recognised. Recognised it enough to go silent. My head tipped back to see his handsome face. To see how worry creased his brow, and how those storm-grey eyes were focused on nothing but my lips. As if every breath that passed through them mattered to him.

'Better?' he asked, so softly.

I could only nod.

A stillness passed between us as his gaze moved to focus on my eyes, his jaw tightening on whatever he saw there. Yet he didn't break his focus on me, not until he was satisfied, I wasn't going to hurt myself.

'Let's get you cleaned up, Croinn.'

Chapter Twenty-Eight

Emrys released me slowly, making certain I was settled enough before he moved about his desk. Pulling off his filthy ruined coat and dropping it onto his chair. Dislodging some books as he rummaged for something.

My limbs began to tremble again, teeth chattering as if my body was reacting to his absence. My fears threatened to return. As if sensing it, he came back, crouching before me where my feet dangled off the desk, propping my injured foot gently on his muscular thigh.

'W-what are you doing?' I tried to pull my foot back but that pain made my breath catch again. There was a healing kit on the ground next to his knee, his sleeves rolled up over strong forearms, ready for work.

'Sit still,' he commanded, unbothered by my squirming as he unlaced my boot and rolled down my stocking with the efficiency of a lady's maid, which forced my mind to wonder just how many stockings he'd rolled down how many legs.

My face burned. His hands were cold, making me acutely aware of every single touch as my fingers curled around the wooden lip of the desk with a white-knuckled hold.

'Are these trousers?' His brow rose, head tipping back to see me.

'Alma told me not to tell anyone,' I answered weakly, hoping she wouldn't be too cross at the state of me.

'Scandalous.' His grin was uneven as his gaze dropped once more to my ankle. I saw the mud specks in his hair and a streak of it on his cheek.

He assessed my leg with the efficiency of a battle surgeon. 'This is small but deep. Did you see what cut you?'

Those dark eyes were filled with a soft patience, but all I could do was shake my head as I wrapped my arms around myself in some form of protection. A nightmare did it, but I couldn't let those words leave me. I'd lost my mind. Somewhere in those ruins I'd gone mad.

A muscle moved in his jaw with my silence, as if it unsettled him, before he returned to focus on my leg. He worked carefully, cleansing his hands before wiping my wound with healing tonic that stung, then bandaged the injury cautiously.

The strong callous brush of his fingers against my skin raised gooseflesh, making strange forbidden emotions swoop through me. My breath became uneven for a very different reason.

'It will need re-wrapping in a few hours,' he continued oblivious to the torment he was causing. 'Does it hurt?'

I shook my head.

He stood slowly, wary, as if I could bolt at any moment, then braced his hands on the desk, either side of my hips, his hair falling across his brow as he studied me.

All I could smell was beasam bark as it chased away the reek of smoke and the horrid memory of that place.

I'd never felt small; I was always too large and boisterous. I found a strange comfort in the size of him. The potency of his magic, the silent chaos of it, reminded my own it was in safe company and that none of my mistakes could hurt me here. There was a calmness between us that I hadn't felt before as I considered the beautiful disarray of him.

His fingers brushed something off the edge of my jaw. Gentle but hesitant as if he couldn't resist. Then he must have seen something he didn't like, those eyes going so dark, and he retrieved a jar of healing balm and began to gently wipe it on my chin and the curve of my cheek.

So tenderly, as if he could hurt me with the barest motion.

'You came.' The words were so small from my lips, freezing him in place for a moment, before his thumb brushed my cheek once more, eyes gentle.

'Of course, Croinn.'

Of course. As if there was no other option for him. That I mattered that much. Mattered enough to be found.

Forgetting myself, I reached up to brush the hair from his brow, revealing a faint trace of blood at his hairline and the beginning of a bruise. There was such a stillness in him, and I wasn't quite certain he was breathing.

'I got myself knocked unconscious,' he said. A frown furrowed his brow and I traced my finger over the corner of it as if to smooth it out.

'I won't tell anyone,' I tried to tease, but it came out too quiet. 'I have something for it.'

I dropped my attention to my bag, opening it and reaching for my healing case, pulling out a fresh cotton square and bottle of tonic.

He didn't move, considering every action of my hands like it was something profound. I let a few drops of the tonic soak into the cotton before I lightly placed my fingers underneath his chin, turning him towards the light as I dabbed at the area.

He let me fuss over him, almost sensing how much I needed my hands to stop trembling by doing something mundane.

'You should take better care of yourself,' I chided softly; the fact he hadn't even seemed to notice he'd been hurt sat uneasily with me. The rich, almost intoxicating scent of him was perhaps the reason why such stupid words kept tumbling from my lips.

'I didn't choose to fall through the floor, Croinn.' His response was dry and something about it caused a laugh to escape my lips. I felt my cheeks hurt with the fullness of my smile.

His stoic, serious eyes suddenly focused on my lips and then I wasn't laughing anymore. The imposing nature of him made me want to move closer. To be made to feel safe for even the smallest moment.

'Tell me you're all right.' The command was so gentle. Spoken like a confession.

'I'm all right,' I whispered in the small space between us, unsteady. I was overcome with the foolish urge to kiss him, and the equally foolish thought that he might kiss me back. To taste him like I'd never wanted to taste anything before.

Deep relief in those strange eyes as they shifted to a stormy grey.

He'd come looking for me. In a way nobody had before. This impossible man who still held too many secrets. Yet I found myself unable to care about any of them as my fingers curled around the collar of his ruined shirt and I pressed my lips gently against the scarred side of his cheek, feeling the rough texture of his stubble beneath the chaste kiss along with the slight tension in his jaw.

His hand came to settle at the curve of my waist, head turning the barest inch, so our noses touched. His breath was unsteady and his eyes pitch black as his full bottom lip barely brushed my own.

The strong hand at my waist curled around me to follow the line of my spine. His other hand gently cupping my jaw as my palms came to rest against the broad expanse of his chest. Feeling his warmth through the thin cotton. My breath stuttered through my lips with anticipation, as my fingers curled into his shirt.

His thumb glided across my flush-stained cheekbone with reverence before he found the curve and soft point of my ear. Following the shape as if it was something beautifully delicate.

'Kat.' My name sounded like a prayer from his lips, settling in some forbidden place inside of me. Warm and tempting.

Then a horrid crashing commotion echoed through the study, making him go rigid in my hold.

'Blackthorn!' an unfamiliar voice shouted down the hallway. Another crash drew us apart, as a cry of alarm and a beastly roar rang out. Emrys turned with a curse and strode for the study doorway with murderous intent.

I slid off the desk, lightly limping after him. The sting in my leg was nothing but a dull ache by now but still, it wasn't happy bearing too much weight.

I rounded the door, holding onto it, and there, sprawled on the floor of the entryway, was Thean Page. Pinning them to the tiles with bared teeth stood a manticore. The stinger of its tail hovered over its shoulder, threatening to bury itself into what appeared to be a genuinely distressed voyav.

The eyes of the beast were a familiar bright green.

'Alma,' I breathed, somehow both fearful and overwhelmed by the sight of her.

Her enormous head turned to consider me with irritation, as if I'd personally let the intruder in. She growled low in her throat, carefully moving off Thean, paws making the floor creak with the sheer size of her.

Thean scrambled to their feet, annoyed breaths escaping their lips. Alma turned with another growl, shifting into her tiny tabby cat form in the blink of an eye as she trotted down the hall and darted into one of the rooms. An extra little bounce in her step.

'You better have a damn good reason for being here, Thean.' Emrys's tone was clipped and practically murderous, as he crossed his arms and leant back against the doorframe next to me.

'Interrupt something, did I?' The voyav grinned, smoothing their dark auburn hair, looking between myself and Emrys with a knowing glint in their eye.

Thankfully, there was a sharp slam before a barefoot Alma came padding back down the hall, finishing tying the belt of a threadbare and bobbled housecoat that was far too big for her, dust clinging to its shoulders. A deathly scowl on her face.

'Maids used to be more agreeable.' Thean grinned as they fixed their elaborate maroon jacket, gaudy red and silver beads stitched at the shoulders. The silk frill of their shirt billowing over the collar.

'You shouldn't enter people's houses unannounced!' Alma snapped, bracing her clawed hands on her hips in warning.

'I couldn't agree more, Miss Darcy,' Emrys added darkly.

'What a fine collection of oddities you've acquired, Emrys,' Thean mocked, watching Alma stiffen in response.

'Charming,' she sneered. 'Why don't I make you squeal again?'

'I'll squeal for you anytime, sweetheart, just as long as you have two legs next time.' The voyav winked, leering.

Alma curled her lip with disgust, turning her attention sharply to me, finally taking both myself and Emrys in. What a sorry sight we must have been. 'What on earth happened to you both?'

'It's a long story,' Emrys replied through clenched teeth, still glaring at Thean.

'If it doesn't involve debauchery, save us the boredom.' Thean sighed, folding their arms with impatience.

It had almost involved debauchery and, at that thought, the voyav's eyes came to my flushed face, their smile devious.

'Who is this vulgar guest and why am I burdened with his presence?' Alma pressed, looking at Emrys expectantly, who was still too busy glaring.

'Thean!' William called cheerily, coming around the corner right on cue, a stack of books in his arms and a welcoming smile on his face. 'Would you like something to drink?'

'They're not staying,' Emrys said coldly.

'Oh.' William stopped with a frown. 'What are you doing here then?'

'How wonderful for you to ask, William,' Thean practically preened, turning to address the boy. 'I had a feeling Emrys might stumble upon something . . . unpleasant in the ruins and need some help.'

'You knew something was there?' I asked, aghast.

'I had a sense something was off about the place.' The voyav shrugged, but something about their smile told me it was more about playing a game with Emrys than anything else.

'What was there?' Alma asked, her tone short with the annoyance of not knowing something.

'Something . . .' I tried to get the words out, but that horrid feeling tightened my chest. 'I don't know.'

'Miss Darcy, if you could take Miss Woodrow to her room. She needs to rest.' Emrys's words were curt, and he seemed to struggle to remain still as his hands formed fists at his sides.

'With the state of her she'll be late for this dreadful dinner,' Alma argued, clearly not sensing the darkness that was creeping in around Emrys.

'She isn't going,' he replied off-handedly, barely looking at the pair of us. 'We found a bad collection of dark spells at the ruins.'

'I'm perfectly fine,' I insisted before Alma could fully process her shock at the revelation.

'I don't think it's wise.' Emrys finally turned to me, something in his tone trying to be gently persuasive, but the tightness of the words ruined the effect.

Of course, he was ashamed of how overfamiliar he'd just been and was trying to put distance between us. Through revulsion probably.

'Neither is being anywhere near Fairfax Manor, *clearly*,' I argued, folding my arms, unbothered by the darkness of his gaze. 'I came here to solve this. Not hide in that horrid guest room.'

'On this one occasion I think you should seriously consider listening to me,' he pressed, an authority to his tone that made me straighten my back.

'I'm not the one who got knocked unconscious,' I challenged, watching his eyes narrow in warning.

'Don't argue with her, Emrys, the little beast might get you,' Thean mocked, straightening the frilled cuff of their shirt with little care. A rumbling came from deep within Alma's chest that sounded close to a growl.

'Kat,' Emrys said too gently, turning me so I was closer to him. So, there was only us and his words. That worry in his dark gaze.

'I'm fine,' I lied. However, the sooner we solved this and left Fairfax, the better.

That was all that mattered. All that had to matter.

Sensing he'd lost the fight, he let me go, running a hand through his dark hair before he turned back to the voyav. 'Thean, you're coming with me.'

'What?' My mouth hung open in shock. After all the warnings he'd tried to give me about the voyav. 'You can't go back there.'

'Worried?' he challenged, his dark brow raised with teasing.

Of course. I'd dismissed his worry for me so why couldn't he do the same thing? A dark amusement lay in his grey eyes, ignoring how my heartbeat quickened at the intensity of his attention.

'*Fine*. But if you leave me to attend this wretched dinner on my own, I'll reanimate your corpse and make you regret it,' I warned ominously, trying not to care as I turned on my still-aching leg and made a dignified exit.

'Where is your shoe?' Alma asked, tucking her curls behind her ears as she fell into step with me.

'It was confiscated by an *idiot*.' I took her arm, letting her lead us back to the portal and my room in Fairfax, however I was certain I heard someone laugh in response.

Chapter Twenty-Nine

You are a beauty without end, a fire that cannot be smothered by something as fickle as men.

My mother would say those words as she tucked my hair behind my ears. Over and over, as if forging a blade. Building something within me, knowing perhaps I'd need those words when she couldn't give them to me anymore.

I needed them tonight as my heavy hair, which refused to do anything but curl in unruly waves, was braided and pinned delicately. Dried flowers were woven into the hair at the side of my head. William was beyond excited to have something to do with his stash of preserved wildflowers.

Tiredness draped over my shoulder like a heavy cape, my hands still trembling despite how I balled them into fists.

I'd dealt with the Council lords before, but there was something different about being trapped in a house with them. A house surrounded by such horrid things.

My hands ran anxiously over the thick, lavender fabric of my dress. Thanks to Alma's new impressive skill of manipulating fabrics that William had supplied, I was in a stunning dress. However, the colour would make my eyes stand out, and that was the last thing I needed at a lords' dinner.

'It's so beautiful!' Alma clasped her hands together in excitement as she made me turn before the mirror.

'It's too tight.' I struggled to pull in a deep breath. My waist was much smaller than I remembered and my breasts suspiciously fuller as they almost spilled over the top of the bodice.

'It's supposed to be tight.' She slapped my hands away as I tried to tug the bodice up before she began to mess with the underskirts.

'Are you sure this is appropriate?' I asked, the chill of the room seemed to nip at the top of my exposed breasts.

'You know they have different rules for ladies at dinner,' came her muffled reply from under a ridiculous number of petticoats.

'The point is to fit in,' I countered. A nice dark blue or grey would have sufficed. Formal and plain.

'It hasn't happened yet.' She reemerged, grabbing my shoulders to turn me towards the large mirror she'd somehow dragged through the wardrobe with her.

The dress was wrapped beautifully around my fuller frame, the neckline just resting off my shoulders but covering enough of my back. It was trimmed with delicate lace, not garish at all. Simple and softly beautiful – almost fooling me into thinking I couldn't possibly be the murderous, monstrous being I was.

Silver flowers were embroidered around the bodice and the tiny sleeves, curving around my waist and down the skirts. My gloved fingers traced the shape of the flowers before I really looked at myself.

Then came the pain. How for a moment I saw my mother looking back at me. My Kysillian features made it hard to see her sometimes, my lavender eyes and strange golden skin taking over everything else. Yet, with my unruly brown hair like this, a softness had come over me, my harsh fear of the world fading away so I could see her.

How her beautiful chestnut hair gleamed, the sharp wit in her eyes, the same freckles across her nose and the humorous nature to her smile. Despite all she'd endured, she didn't wear it like I did.

Lanthor. Echoed in my mind, a word she had whispered on her deathbed as I held onto her. *Forgive them* in Kysillian. Her last request as she lay dying in my arms. Her punishment for daring to love my father being death.

Yet she still wanted me to forgive this world for its cruelty. The sadness of that grief consumed me viciously, gnawing at my very bones. A hollow ache taking up place in my chest, a longing for her that had never gone away.

'Kat?' Alma took my arm gently, worry in her expression.

'I don't want to go down there,' I admitted, giving her part of the truth. She didn't need to be burdened with my fears.

'Emrys will be there.' She took hold of my hand. Things really must be bad if Alma was putting her faith in Emrys.

He hadn't sent any word about how the ruins had gone. Maybe he was already a dark fiend's food by now, or whatever foulness lurked in those ruins.

Troll. That voice echoed through my mind, mocking me with the painful reminder of how far it had driven me to madness mere hours ago.

A knock came at the door, stopping any further wallowing.

'It'll be all right. I'll be here when you get back.' She squeezed my fingers in reassurance before rushing to the wardrobe. I waited for the doors to shut tightly before I opened the bedroom one, finding a male servant with a sour expression.

'I've been sent to escort you, Miss.' He bowed, stepped back, and walked down the hall before I was even ready.

I doubted he cared for my thanks as I shut my door and hurried after him, trying my best to keep my skirt pleats straight for Alma's sake.

The way to the ballroom was nothing but a maze of warped hallways. Lamps flickered weakly against the walls, black smears where the smoke had stained the peeling wallpaper. The stench of old oil mixed with stale potpourri made my stomach churn.

The grand portraits seemed to sag on the walls, dust gathered in their corners and cobwebs strung above them on the mould-speckled ceiling. The garish dark wallpaper made my eyes hurt; the more I looked at the pattern, the more I saw things looking back at me.

The servant led me right to the grand glass doors of a ballroom. The echo of forced laughter, dull conversation and low music only solidified my dread.

The lamps were brighter inside, warm against the floral wallpaper. The gold decorations were dulled with time, just as the marble floor was covered in scratches and stains from overuse. Women in brightly coloured gowns flitted between the men, who stood tall in dark evening attire. The heavy stench of perfume and cologne only intensified my disgust.

The servant left me standing there in the shadows, as I tried to build up the courage to go inside.

'Miss Woodrow,' came the sharp voice over my shoulder. Dread sinking further into my gut as I turned to see the form of Lord Percy, wearing an ill-fitting dark dinner jacket, a scowl on his liquor-rosy face.

'Lord Percy.' I bowed, tucking my balled fists behind my back.

'I was seeking your master.' He glowered down at my breasts with disdain as if they'd personally offended him.

'Then it's no wonder you've struggled to find something I don't possess.' I smiled tightly, refusing to play his vulgar game.

'You can remind him he's here for no other purpose than a mad old man's grief.' He half spat the words under his breath, a hideous wash of sour drink reaching my nose.

'The ruins stand as testament that that's not entirely true,' I pointed out carefully.

'More fey seeking revenge,' he snapped, his lip curling and an unfocused nature to his eyes.

'Lord Percy, you should wait for a dance to stare so intently at a lady,' came the cheery voice of Thean Page. I turned, stunned to see the voyav dressed in a pristine grey velvet suit, heavy black beading at the collar and cuffs. A glass of wine in their hand and their hair was brushed back harshly, fangs on display.

However, there was a slight distortion from the glamour they'd wrapped around themself to fool a mortal eye.

'Master Gladstone.' Lord Percy bowed sharply with annoyance. 'If you'll excuse me.'

Lord Percy thankfully left us as quickly as he appeared. Suddenly tight lipped like the coward I suspected him of being.

'Who does he think you are?' I asked, watching Thean's predatory amber eyes track the lord's retreat into the ballroom.

'The architect to repair the house.' They smiled sharply, offering me their arm.

'Do you know anything about architecture?' I frowned, letting them guide me into the ballroom. It probably wasn't wise, but I fancied my chances better with the mysterious voyav than a priggish lord. I had no reason to maim Thean. At least not yet.

'Enough to fool a fool.' They winked, and if I wasn't so cautious and annoyed by their presence, I could have considered them to be a handsome being. Although clearly not scarred, brooding and secretive enough for my current foolish tastes.

'He'll notice when you haven't repaired his house,' I pointed out.

'Will he?' There was a sharp seductive nature to their answering smile that I could see working on someone more reserved than myself.

I turned my attention to the room, regretting it immediately. The ladies fluttered feather fans, intensifying the thickness of perfume in the air. Bosoms were powdered and jewels reflected the lamplight to throw shapes about the room.

Crowds of people occupied the hall, none of whom had noticed I'd arrived. I looked for Emrys, and finally saw him standing in the centre of the crowd, at ease and in deep conversation, a glass of wine in his hand. Not a strand of his raven hair was out of place. His dark suit, embroidered with silver, was in fashion and tailored perfectly to his imposing physique. He looked like a beautiful holy demon, the type the saints spoke about, who lurked in murky woods to persuade maidens to raise darkness from the earth with their blood.

Only, I preferred him the way he normally was, disheveled and trying to make sense of madness. This version only reminded me of the different worlds we came from and just how comfortably he had settled back into his own.

A young woman stood close at his side, rosy cheeked with blonde curls elaborately arranged. Her ruffled pink dress was decorated with jewels and bows, and she hung off his every word. Soft and demure.

'What did you discover?' I swallowed painfully, shifting my attention back to Thean, ignoring the sinking feeling in the centre of my chest at the sight of Emrys with that woman.

'You're supposed to start conversation a little slower than that, darling,' they teased, stepping closer with a mocking lift to their eyebrow.

'Who is that woman?' I asked before I even knew I wanted an answer.

'Lady Constance Lovell,' Thean replied conversationally, clearly caring more for gossip than Emrys's privacy. 'There were rumours of an engagement brewing between them, but she found a new suitor while Emrys was serving in the wars. Her husband developed a wasting disease and it's said she's looking to improve her circumstances, now her mourning period is over.'

I pushed down the strange, horrid pang in my chest, reminding myself Emrys had a life before I stumbled across his path. 'You mean now her wealth has run out.'

'Women have to make different bargains to men,' Thean countered, a strange sympathy in the words I couldn't argue with.

'Some do it far too comfortably,' I hated the thought instantly, it felt like a betrayal to myself and everything I thought I believed in. My anger was childish and beneath me, but I couldn't help myself.

'That's pretty.' I felt the voyav's finger slide along the collar of my dress, catching the chain of the wishing stone hidden deep in my corset.

I slapped their hand away, or attempted to. They pulled it back faster than I anticipated. 'Keep your hands to yourself.'

'You know you shouldn't take gifts from dark beings,' they taunted darkly.

'At this point I'll take all the protection I can get,' I countered sharply, watching their grin turn wicked. Impressed. 'What happened at the ruins?'

Thean rocked back on their heels, waving a servant over to present them with a glass of wine. 'Don't remind me, my ears are still ringing from the lecture.'

'Did you find the creature?'

They shook their head, unimpressed with their new wine, as the servant hurried away. 'No, Emrys said something about needing a powerful cleansing charm. I became bored and stopped listening.'

I frowned. 'There was something there.' I knew there was. 'It vanished as quickly as it came. When Emrys arrived, it was gone.'

'Of course. It probably didn't like the competition.' The voyav smirked.

'Why would a lord have such a creature dwelling on his lands?' One that old and made of fear.

'You expect me to tell the truth?' They considered me carefully, amber eyes sharp.

'You're quite happy to let a grief-stricken old man's house fall down around him, so you clearly have no love for the lords here. Therefore, I don't see the harm in you giving the answer to me,' I countered.

'Clever girl,' they half purred. 'Creatures with that much power are born, not cast. Which means somebody has been performing very *naughty* spells.'

'For what purpose?' I didn't know spells powerful enough to awaken such a darkness. Nobody's greed could be that vile, could it?

'The desperate only need a meagre one,' Thean replied dryly, just as a man and his wife passed in their finery, nodding to the voyav in greeting. Obviously seeing whatever they were projecting for them to see.

It reminded me that everything in this world held a hint of a lie, a trick and a game. Everything was struggling to survive, and some did it more wickedly than others.

'Do you think this house is strange?' I asked as another wave of unease came over me, causing me to look behind me. Yet, I found nothing there.

'Everything about mortals is strange,' Thean said. 'However, I will say just how stunning you look, Kat.' They smiled, wicked fangs visible as that dark auburn hair curled onto their brow, amber eyes glinting with mischief. 'When you don't frown so much, you're quite beautiful.'

'If you're trying to seduce me, you're terrible at it,' I replied dryly.

They chuckled softly, tracing the summoning mark inked on the side of their neck, deep in thought. 'Darling, you're not my type.'

'In full possession of my senses?'

'*Tall*,' they replied wryly, and perhaps it was the humour of the response, or the impending sense of doom, but I laughed, startling both Thean and myself.

'I was being serious.' They sounded affronted. 'Now, your little maid on the other hand . . .'

'She's not my maid,' I countered. Shame washed over me that anyone ever had cause to think that Alma was my servant.

'You seem to have found unpleasant company, Miss Woodrow.' The dark drawl of Emrys's voice brushed my ear as he came to my side. His handsome face was one of indifference as he took in Thean.

'Charming, my lord.' Thean winked.

With Emrys so close, all I could remember was our proximity in the study. The warm solid nature of him. The feel of his cheek beneath my lips. The drag of his rough, calloused hands down my throat.

'D–did you discover anything from the guests?' I flushed at my own traitorous thoughts.

Emrys's attention dropped to me, lingering at the side of my head where Alma had arranged the flowers behind my ear, before he finally met my eyes.

'Nothing. Everyone appears aggressively tight lipped.' He reached out to take two glasses from one of the passing servants, handing one to me.

'I'm sure they're loose skirted enough,' Thean commented, almost making me choke on the sip I'd taken. 'If you'll excuse me, I'm too sober for my liking.'

Emrys watched the voyav go, a tension in his limbs that gave me a warning without words. Whatever Thean's game was, it was dangerous, and yet, I was kept at arm's length about just how bad that danger could be.

'I see you survived.' The words left my lips before I could fully consider what I was saying. 'Maybe I should have taken your advice and remained abed. If you've brought me here to help you shop for a wife, I'll happily march myself back to the Institute.'

Emrys's irritated gaze swung back to me; brow furrowed. Probably wondering if I'd lost my mind. Maybe I had.

'That would have been preferable considering every man in this ballroom is giving me nothing and only interested in debaucherous arrangements,' he muttered, taking a deep drink of his wine.

'With whom?' I frowned, looking to find Thean, wondering what the voyav had been up to.

'You.'

'Me? Don't be absurd.' I rolled my eyes with a breathless laugh. 'They've said nothing? Not even about the bodies? The upper classes usually love gossip.'

He gave me a frustrated glance, his eyes seeming to get even darker as he ignored my question, looking at my skirts

325

with suspicion before taking another deep drink from his glass. 'Where did you get that dress?'

'William gave it to Alma.' I huffed in exasperation, wondering if something had happened to his memory and just how long he'd been drinking.

'Remind me to have a word with him,' he grumbled murderously.

'What?' I frowned. 'Alma spruced it up. I think she did a wonderful job.'

He continued to consider me uneasily, eyes moving to where the sleeves rested at my bare shoulder, drifting to my collarbone, tracing the thin chain of the wishing stone, before returning his gaze to the room. The tension in him made me wonder if he'd lost his mind too.

'Lord Blackthorn, how wonderful you're here,' a male voice announced as we found ourselves joined by a young man, short and large with circular glasses perched on the end of his nose and stark blond hair. 'I thought it would take a miracle to get you out into society again.'

It was unclear if his mirth was genuine or from the wine.

'Mr Canthorp.' Emrys bowed. 'May I introduce my partner mage, Miss Woodrow.'

'What a lovely companion. No wonder you're monopolising her attention, Lord Blackthorn.' He grinned.

'Pleasure to meet you, Mr Canthorp.' I bowed respectfully, but he already had his hand out, forcing me to surrender my own.

'The pleasure is all mine.' He smiled, kissing the back of my hand. His lips were repulsively wet even with my gloves on; there to cover up the horrid welts on my wrists. Thankfully, his grip was loose enough for me to pull myself free, his lips puckering slightly in disappointment as he straightened, returning his attention to Emrys.

'Lord Fairfax said you found the man's body in the wood by the old ruins,' Canthorp stated, more of an accusation than a question. 'Unsecure ground, one wrong step and it would be a long way down. Nobody really knows how far those ruins have sunk.'

I went still at his words. Emrys hadn't said the victim was a man, or where I had found him, at least not in my company. So why would Canthorp assume it was the ruins?

'Perhaps, but its best to be cautious in such turbulent times.' Emrys's smile was tight, too tight.

'What are you talking about so excitedly, Mr Canthorp?' came the high-pitched voice of the woman Emrys had been talking to. Lady Lovell. Her arm was looped through that of a very annoyed-looking Lord Percy.

'The discovery in the ruins, Lady Lovell.' Canthorp bowed respectfully.

'How dreadful.' She practically swooned before her eyes reluctantly moved to me. She considered me like some horrid inconvenience, smile faltering as she noted where Emrys's arm brushed against my own with his proximity.

'Of course, the quieter we can keep the tragedy, the better. We know how feral the fey can be, don't you agree, Miss Woodrow?' Canthorp continued with a laugh.

'Miss Woodrow discovered the corpse after trespassing on these lands,' Lord Percy interjected before I could speak, making Mr Canthorp choke on his mirth. 'Quite scandalous.'

'Fey lands,' I corrected. A silence followed the words as I felt the intensity of Lord Percy's gaze come back to me.

'Excuse me?' he bit out, tone barely remaining polite.

'The original lands of Fairfax surround the ruins. Any lord who abandons his ancestral home for longer than a century surrenders that land back to the fey who had once inhabited it. It's written in clause thirty-four of the King's Agreement. Or in section four of the Peace Agreement.' I smiled, surge of Emrys's magic brushed my side. An intensity to it that had nothing to do with warning.

Canthorp's mouth fell open, Lovell looked stunned and Lord Percy considered me as nothing more than an insect beneath his boot.

'I assumed that was why you stopped providing provisions for Paxton Fields? With the moving of the borderlands?' I pushed further than I knew was smart, just enjoying his eyes narrowing.

'I see everyone had the same idea,' Lord Fairfax announced, breaking the tension as he approached slowly, his leg seeming to pain him as he joined our gathering. 'You've fallen right back into step with society, Lord Blackthorn. We feared we'd lost you to your investigations forever.'

'It must be exhausting chasing the same ghosts and finding nothing,' Lord Percy drawled, anger still simmering in his gaze.

'You should be chasing women, not ghosts. I'm sure the ladies have missed a bachelor as strapping as yourself, Blackthorn.' Canthorp laughed, his nervous gaze flicking in my direction.

I wanted the ground to swallow me whole. Thankfully a servant stepped forward to disrupt the odious conversation.

'My lord,' he said, dropping into an overly low bow, holding out a letter. 'A message for you.'

The deep burgundy letter caught my eye, the wax seal holding a golden hue. The same that Emrys had received that first day when he'd shown me the study.

I wanted to catch Emrys's reaction, but something passed over Lord Percy's expression that stopped me as he reached out to take it from the servant, quickly stuffing it into his pocket as Canthorp continued to witter, drawing most of the gathering's attention to him, even the horrid Lord Percy's.

'Don't stare too hard, they'll know you know something,' came a whisper to my ear. It was Thean at my other side, smiling around the rim of another glass of wine.

Suspicious that they knew what was going on and who the letter was from, I turned to give them my full attention.

'I thought you were looking for a drink?' I asked under my breath.

'I got distracted.' They shrugged, 'besides, it appears you're the entertainment.'

There was a sharpness to their gaze as it focused on something beyond me. I turned to see Emrys watching us both, his expression guarded, and I had a strange feeling I was in the centre of a very different game. Emrys's energy brushing my skin like tendrils of icy smoke with his annoyance, as if I'd caused some great disturbance within him.

Thankfully, a bell rang, and a servant announced that dinner was served.

'Come, Miss Woodrow.' Thean held out their arm, proclaiming too loudly for me to refuse as I slipped my own into theirs. Their head ducked ever so slightly to whisper in my ear. 'Let us see how monsters entertain themselves.'

Chapter Thirty

I was wrong when I thought the ruins of Fairfax Manor held my worst nightmares. This dinner was another one. There was no William and no Alma to reassure me.

Emrys was across from me, but it felt like a world away. Especially when his mask of indifference had slipped into place, a tightness to his lips that told me he'd rather be anywhere else but here. My finger ran over small holes in the discoloured white tablecloth as the candlelight cut through the chipped crystal glasses.

I'd put us in this situation, and I was still struggling to see how we were going to get out of it.

Emrys's familiarity with the people at this table was another concern. Despite his reclusive lifestyle, I'd forgotten his position before the wars. I suppose I'd convinced myself it didn't matter. I'd learnt long ago there was a duality to this world.

Good people did bad things for better outcomes, but would I be so forgiving if it wasn't Emrys?

'How delighted we are to have your company for a whole evening, Lord Blackthorn.' One of the older ladies seated close to Emrys grinned. With her modest red ballgown, ears adorned with fey sapphires from the eastlands and over-powdered grey hair. 'What blessed creatures we must be.'

The table began to laugh, an air of amusement I found sinister.

'How blessed indeed,' smiled Lady Lovell, who was sat next to Emrys, leaning forward to take his arm with familiarity.

I kept my expression blank, conscious of Thean's amusement from a few places away, as they sipped another wine and reclined impolitely, ignoring the old man next to them.

I let my gaze fall on my silverware as the soup was served, only to instantly regret that decision. The silver was intricately decorated, the handles bright white, glistening like stone, but I could see the different hues. They were made from bone. Valeks were the only creatures whose skeletons were stained by their magic. The fracture marks through the bone like expensive marble, adding to their sacred nature, and here they were using them as decoration.

Repulsion rolled through me as I realised the mortal men sitting either side of me had normal cutlery. It was a game, and I'd been foolish enough not to anticipate it.

Making me eat with the bones of monsters they deemed me no better than.

Torments from Daunton came back to me vividly. How my food would burn my tongue with excess salt, my cutlery blunted to make me seem like an animal. So thirsty I'd have no choice but to drink the sour water they gave me.

Little troll – the words echoed through my mind, trying to force me to remember what I'd seen in those ruins. I shut my eyes and pulled in the deepest breath my corset would allow. Yet, when I opened them, my silverware was plain, undescriptive and I was certain I'd used it in Emrys's kitchen.

I glanced up to see him watching me, an intensity to his gaze. As if silently trying to convey something with the darkness of its anger. As if he hated this as much as I did.

'It's wonderful to have such a dear friend of my Robert back in our company.' Lord Fairfax's words pierced the moment, turning us both to see the old man smiling, his eyes teary with his words. 'You've been away too long, dear boy.'

I felt that sadness like a physical thing, clogging the air. The poor man couldn't let go and I wondered if the truth of it might make his grief better.

I killed him. Emrys's admission cut through me. The coldness of how he'd said it. The lack of choice in those words.

'You're just in time to give us some gossip about the Southwest Territory conflict,' Canthorp boomed, nudging the pale thin man next to him, who spilled his wine as a result.

'My time on territorial disputes has long passed,' Emrys replied formally. The brutality of his scars seemed starker under the candlelight, the sadness in his profile. To exist different to the rest of this world.

'What a marvel Miss Woodrow must be to have gained such a partnership,' Lord Percy joined in, turning the table's attention in my direction. 'I heard you turned down the Marquess d'Alene's heir for her, Blackthorn.'

'The Marquess d'Alene?' one of the women gasped. 'Saints above, perhaps you are mad after all, Lord Blackthorn.'

'There is more to a partnership than a title, Lord Percy,' Emrys replied, his smile tight, which sent the ladies into disarray.

'Well, Miss Woodrow, don't you have some wonderful gossip for us all?' Lord Canthorp pressed, returning everyone's eyes to me, and silencing the surrounding conversations.

'Unfortunately, the lord is almost as secretive in his own home as he is here.' I smiled politely, trying to make myself seem as small as possible.

'How well trained she is.' Lady Lovell chuckled, making me bristle. My magic coiling deep in my gut, willing me to strike.

Thean let out a devious laugh, arms folded with an amused smirk on those lips, waiting for me to break. Emrys had gone very still, that dark gaze focused on my own.

'Where did you receive your start in education, Miss Woodrow?' Lord Fairfax asked, with genuine interest. The madness of his grief making him blind to the tension rippling about the table. 'It must have been tremendous to have got you so far?'

'I was taught by my mother in the northlands.' I kept my tone polite, not allowing my grief to slip into the words. It belonged to me, not them.

'Unusual,' Lord Percy commented. 'Kysillians aren't renowned for their literacy, are they? More their . . . brutality.'

The candlelight flickered harshly. That cold bite of Emrys's magic seeming to brush across my exposed collarbone as if it could shield me from the slight.

'My mother was mortal,' I corrected, not missing the shocked glances that were now focused solely on my face, trying to see it. The disgust and pursed lips at how one of their own had debased themselves.

'Abandoned after the rutting, I assume,' Lord Percy continued without pause.

A shocked gasp came from my right, along with a clatter of cutlery. The table creaked slightly and the cold, tumultuous nature of Emrys's power made the man next to me shiver.

Only I didn't need Emrys to defend me from this weasel.

'My parents were sworn to each other. My father was with us until the wars.' I kept my voice bored, expression disinterested. 'I don't believe Lord Blackthorn mentioned serving with *you*, Lord Percy?'

The lord jolted at that, cheeks flushing to match his ruddy nose at the silence that claimed the table at my response.

333

'Unfortunately, my nephew didn't pass the . . . *requirements*,' Lord Fairfax added, an edge of distaste touching his words, but I heard everything they didn't say.

'Unfortunate indeed,' I mused coldly, taking a deep drink of my wine.

'From Miss Woodrow's records, she studied at Daunton until she was selected for the Institute, Uncle,' Lord Percy added through his teeth, his grip on his spoon white-knuckled.

'Daunton?' Canthorp asked.

My heart began to beat erratically within my chest. Breaths became more difficult to draw between my lips that had nothing to do with Alma's ruthless corset lacing.

'How terrible what happened there.' Lady Lovell sighed, reaching for her glass of watered-down wine to soften her distress.

'What happened?' Mr Canthorp asked, and the question felt like a physical blow against my skin.

You killed him, that voice whispered in the back of my mind, taunting me with its cruelty. My magic flared in response to the memory, in recognition of that pain.

'A terrible fire killed him, burned half the house to the ground,' Lovell continued. Of course that would be the answer she gave. Nothing about the fey children who had died there. 'How dreadful for such a man who dedicated his life to helping those creatures, to suffer so.'

'I heard there were bodies beneath the floors,' another man at the table said, seeming intrigued, which did little to quell my nausea.

Don't let them take me, came a young Alma's whispered plea in my ear, desperate as she held onto me. Willing herself to live. The creak of those wheelbarrows as they took more bodies into the wood. The horrid echo of screams and the choking potency of saints' smoke.

334

The wishing stone fluttered against my breastbone as if in comfort. Almost making me reach for it.

'Penance comes in many strange forms,' Emrys commented sinisterly, a sharpness to his gaze as he looked at me, somehow sensing my distress.

'How could such a holy man have anything to do with that? What scandalous rebellious rumours you believe.' Lovell laughed, fluttering her lashes and leaning towards him.

'Some say the most wicked of us hide in plain sight,' Emrys reasoned, the sharpness of his gaze meeting my own. I felt reassured by it, but he didn't know how true his words were, that I was just as wicked as them.

The power of a Kysillian wasn't just their ability to harness destructive magic, but to possess such a power and not use it in a moment of weakness. My father had told me that, and right now I wished he hadn't. Setting the table alight seemed like a wonderful way to end the horrid affair.

'On to more pleasant topics, please,' one of the women declared as the next course came, and I made a point to finish every glass of wine I was given before they added water to it.

However, despite the edge the sour wine had taken off the evening, the table clearly wasn't finished with my discomfort.

'Did you hear of *another* rebellion attack in the west at the ports?' One of the guests tutted.

'They just need to concede and accept it's better for them,' Lady Lovell drawled, her nails clinking against her glass as she took another demure sip, eyes slipping back in Emrys's direction. 'Thank the saints you've been saved from such impropriety, Miss Woodrow.'

'Indeed, what sent you on the path of your discipline?' Lord Fairfax asked. 'My Robert was fascinated by the old tales. He loved the Kysillian ones most of all.'

'The Kysillian is one of the peace children of Master Hale's vision,' Lord Percy interjected, answering for me.

'That old bat.' Lord Canthorp laughed, much to the amusement of his companion, a small unimpressive brown-haired man called Mr Branner.

'Strange you should choose the occult, Miss Woodrow,' Lord Percy continued, his sharp gaze meeting my own across the table. 'Surely a woman seeking to find her way in that world can find a more . . . *advantageous* position?'

I didn't even want to imagine what positions he was thinking of.

'There is much we still don't know,' I smiled politely, resisting the urge to bare my teeth at the swine.

'Magic is boorish and too aggressive for female sensibilities. We're too emotional for it,' Lady Lovell reasoned, her tone sparking a rise in false laughter that irritated me more than normal stupidity.

'There is much left to understand. Especially in the north-lands. Who knows what the fey are hiding over there?' Canthorp mused.

'We won the war, what else is there to know?' Lovell tilted her head demurely to the side, the light catching on the stone around her neck. I knew what it was the moment I saw her. Another trophy, only she was too unintelligent to understand.

We won the war. Her stupid words seared through me. At the cost of fey blood. Their freedom. Rage burned in my gut more viciously than any magic I could summon.

Demure. Quiet. Still. Master Hale's favourite command came back to me.

Sod that.

'What a lovely stone, Lady Lovell.' I smiled, leaning forward to gesture to the gleaming red gem around the lady's throat. The ridiculousness of it.

'An admirer gifted it to me.' She ran her gloved fingertips over it, tilting her head to tease the other guests.

Something burned in me I had never experienced, watching her gaze try to catch Emrys's attention. He was watching me, so intently, almost trying to communicate something with a single look. Maybe sensing I'd lost complete control of my senses.

'I haven't seen a Malac stone before,' I spoke clearly, catching the table's attention. 'Only heard stories.'

'A Malac stone?' Lord Canthorp asked, eyes alight with fascination. 'What does that mean?'

'The Malac were great warriors of ancient magic. They commanded beasts who breathed fire more vibrant than the sun. They believed the stone held the same power as that fire.'

'A wonderful gift.' One of the ladies grinned in encouragement to Lady Lovell, while sending a sour glance my way.

'The leaders would wear it around their penis in celebration of a great victory,' I finished, watching the colour drain from Lady Lovell's features.

Someone dropped their cutlery, a glass smashed, and there was a dramatic wail from the end of the table as Thean almost choked on their wine.

'H-how . . . fascinating.' Lord Fairfax laughed. 'Miss Woodrow, you should do an inventory for me. I'd hate to cause such offence.'

The rest of the table awkwardly joined in with his mirth after a pause, and thankfully, they brought another course out in that moment.

I expected to feel the heat of Emrys's gaze, and his impatience to chastise me. Instead, every time I glimpsed him, someone was trying to get his attention, but he was grinning at his dinner, endlessly amused.

Chapter Thirty-One

Hate is a poisonous thing. A calling to the darkness beneath. Rotting and sour as it forms us into something we never wished to be. One of the Old Gods' curses on this world, to make their summonings easier. To weather our hearts so their offers relieve us of the pain of our own destruction.

– An Introduction to Ancient Curses, 1289

Thankfully, everyone seemed to have forgotten I existed through the rest of the dinner and afterwards. Enough for me to linger by the window, looking out at the dark gardens as I held a glass of wine, rolling it between my palms. Waiting for the torture of the evening to be over. Before I was overcome with the urge to bludgeon Lord Percy to death with a wine bottle.

I turned to look out at the darkness beyond the window, part of me wondering if anything was looking back. The moon a pale silver disk against the blackness.

Yet, as I glared at my own reflection in the grimy glass, I couldn't stop my attention being drawn to the cackles of laughter coming from the far corner, where the loudest guests had gathered, Emrys pulled deep into the fray, either by choice or obliged, I didn't know. Shouldn't care.

A flare of light in the darkness beyond the window caught my eye, just by the trees at the side of the house. I leant closer to the window, holding my breath so it didn't fog the glass as I tried to focus on the shape. A small spectre, from what I could make out. Maybe the same one from Paxton Fields. But it darted around the other side of the house.

My temples ached with the threat of a headache, like a creature clawing at my mind. I put my wine down on the sideboard, turning sharply to try and find where the spectre went, wondering if the gardens were still open as I ran head-first into something solid.

'Good gracious, Miss Woodrow. Are you all right?' Lord Fairfax asked, breathless with my assault.

'I'm so sorry,' I blurted out, pulling back and trying to steady the old man. I could have knocked him clean off his feet but thankfully he remained upright, smiling as he fixed his grey hair with trembling fingers.

'It's no trouble. I came to see if you were enjoying the evening.'

'Of course, they don't offer such entertainment at the Institute.'

'No, I wouldn't say they do. How dour they've all become since they took power.' He nodded, tired blue eyes taking in the room. As if wanting to be anywhere but here.

'I don't have any complaints,' I replied easily. Not falling into the trap of disrespecting the Council to a stranger.

'Really?' he pressed, a playfulness in his eyes that had little to do with kindness. 'You seem startled.'

'Sorry, I thought I saw something outside.' I shook my head, unsure how I'd lost control of myself so easily.

'This is an old house; spirits are bound to dwell,' he reasoned, but his politeness didn't distract me from the lie in his words.

Fey spirits didn't dwell in places like this. Not unless they were trapped. 'Robert found it easy enough to find his way back to me.'

Robert. His son. The potency of that grief, the glimmer of tears in the man's eye, made my stomach knot. Pain at his loss, at how much I understood it. I didn't want to. Wanted no connection to this lord and all the horrid secrets his house kept.

'I'm glad.' I smiled, even if it was nothing but madness. I was glad he had that comfort if nothing else.

'Come.' He offered his arm gently, giving me no chance to refuse. 'You'll find this interesting.'

Unease brushed across my bare shoulders, hoping he wasn't about to show me some petrified creature, only for him to move to an alcove bookcase with a small seating area before it – off to the side where I imagine guests would play cards. The dusty chairs clustered together for privacy.

'My father was a great lover of the game.' He waved his hand to the small table, where a game board was set up. 'Despite his other . . . reserved beliefs.'

My heart dropped within my chest, sinking into a horrid coldness of my own grief. All the sound seemed to fade away and all I could see was that board. The small stone pieces carved with a different creature.

Lo Karun. The Game of Beasts.

A fey game from the wilder lands. One my father taught me; one I hadn't seen since. Not beyond the memories of my childhood. I could feel the rough callouses of my father's hands as he curled my fingers around the dice. Hear the deep echo of his laugh. My mother's soft hands would be on my shoulders, the tickle of her breath at my ear as she showed me the best way to beat him.

No cheating, Eria. He'd warn her with a laugh. How it would fill the whole room.

Eria – 'my love' in Kysillian. How much tenderness he could press into the word.

Memories buried too long. Ones I'd almost forgotten that seared my chest with the pain of them. As if Lord Fairfax had fished down deep into my soul and found something I missed the most.

'I haven't seen one of these in a very long time,' I barely whispered. Unable to swallow down that horrid weakness in my voice.

'Do you play?' Fairfax asked, that kind smile still in place.

'Not since I was a child.' I shook my head, blinking hard to stop the fall of tears. How something so small could unman me so easily.

'I'm sorry, I didn't mean to upset you, Miss Woodrow.' He reached out for my arm cautiously.

'You haven't.' I ran my hands over my skirts in an attempt to stifle my grief. 'I'm just tired from the day.'

'Perhaps I could interest you in a quiet game?' His voice was so soft and alluring. Speaking to that weaker part inside of me that needed it. 'In the library if the noise is too much?'

I wanted to say yes, for a moment to go back. To hear that laughter again, but out of the corner of my eye, there was something wrong with his face. His smile too sharp, eyes too intent and the skin beneath them rimmed grey. I blinked and it was gone. Just a kind old man waiting for company.

That wishing stone against my skin fluttered quickly before falling silent once more.

I'd definitely drunk too much.

'I would . . .' A strange sensation washed over my skin, the same moment that wishing stone against my breastbone began to flutter again. Insistently. Pinpricks of icy pain were running down my arms, turning me to see the entrance to the hall, but there was no threat there. Just a gathering of people conversing drunkenly.

My eyes moved around the room, finding . . . Lord Percy surveying me with suspicion from the corner of the room, Thean surrounded by flushed ladies as Emrys watched me cautiously from the shadows, seeming to ignore every word from Lady Lovell, who chatted endlessly next to him.

Please, whispered through my mind, telling me it wasn't a mistake. The wishing stone almost vibrating against my skin, forcing my hand to rest on my chest, feeling it beneath my dress. Turning me back towards the main doors just as something rushed past them. I could have mistaken it for a trick of the eye, but I knew it wasn't.

Something inside of me grew unsettled by that darkness beyond the ballroom, as if something was watching from that hallway.

'Miss Woodrow?' Lord Fairfax asked gently, almost making me jump as I turned to see his concerned expression.

'I'm afraid all the entertainment has taken it out of me tonight.' I tried my best to smile, to shake off the feeling, but I couldn't.

Please, it whispered against my ear, as soft as breath, turning me in the direction of the doors of the main ballroom again. There sat a small tabby cat with familiar green eyes and one ginger leg.

Alma.

She turned and ran off into the darkness, fear constricting my chest. She shouldn't be here.

'Excuse me,' I mumbled, working my way quickly across the room, trying not to run as I pressed passed the other guests. I ignored their sneers as I slipped into the dark hallway, the lamps struggling under the damp darkness. I pressed my hand

342

to the cracked wood panelling, letting my fingers drag across it as I heard the cry of a cat, pulling me further into the dark.

'Alma?' I hissed, checking under the side tables. Finding nothing but cobwebs as I moved further down the hall. I hitched up my skirts and raced further down the hall after the sound, not caring if any servants saw. Past rooms illuminated with nothing but moonlight, doors creaking in a breeze as the sheet-covered furniture made odd, foreboding shapes.

Deeper and deeper down mould-speckled corridors I hurried, until nothing but a covered mirror stood before me at a dead end. All the peeling doors closed. Nowhere she could have gone.

The sheet hanging over the mirror rippled, something moving beneath. I lurched forward, pulling it free. Dust swirled in the disturbance, only to see a reflection of myself and the endless darkness behind me. Rust consumed the outer filigreed edge. The roses looked like skulls before I leant closer. That ache in my temples deepening making me wonder if I'd imagined the movement as I studied my own confused expression.

'Behave,' I whispered, frustrated with my own foolishness as I looked at the ground and surrounding walls for a crack or hole a cat version of Alma could have gone through, only for the small tabby shape to dart behind me in the reflection.

The echo of her cry came once more. I turned, hearing the distant clatter of movement, something drifting across piano keys that were out of tune from a distant room.

'Alma,' I hissed as I moved back the way I'd come, wondering if I'd missed her in one of the rooms. Only to take a different turn to end up in a dark hallway, walls stained with soot, what remained of the wallpaper curling away. No lamps, just the bitterness of winter air as I grasped my elbows,

343

breath misting before me.

Faced not with the rest of the hallway, but hanging fabric that billowed, covering the wooden scaffolding beyond in the ruined section of the house.

'Alma?' I called out. The cloth flapped sharply, almost beckoning in the breeze.

I grasped the fabric, seeing nothing but the charred remains beyond. Sharp burnt wood and darkness. A piano leaning drunkenly to one side with only two legs.

Here, the wind hissed past me, brushing my skin like a physical, icy touch. A sniggered hiss of laugher followed. A scuttle that reminded me of those ruins.

I dropped the fabric, turning, but there was nothing.

My heart pounded against my ribs as I reached out to touch the charred wood panelling next to me. Feeling the same bite of that magic I'd felt earlier when Emrys had given the wood chip to me, the roughness of where the fire had tried to devour it but there was something else.

A horrid consuming pain, agony streaking through my fingertips that didn't belong to me.

A wetness ran between my fingers and a hideous groaning, almost human, sent me stumbling from the charred wood as I looked down at my hand. Smears of red covered my white gloves and the copper tang of blood filled my nose.

The shadowy soot-coated wall seeped with it, catching in the cobwebs before it dripped down to the ash covered floorboards.

Run.

'Miss.'

A short cry left my lips, and I spun round to see the decrepit, stooped housekeeper, hands clasped before her. 'Is everything all right?'

I panted, eyes darting to my hands, almost holding them out

344

in a silent plea for help, only to see they were just trembling. No blood. No pain. Just white satin.

I turned back to the wall. Nothing but charred wood and dust. I was losing my mind.

'You shouldn't be in this section of the house. It's dangerous,' she continued sharply. Oblivious or uncaring of my madness.

'S-sorry,' I stuttered, feeling the wetness of tears as they ran down my cheeks. Mad. I'd gone mad.

Ashamed, I rushed past her. Back the way I'd come, uncaring as I started to run, finding the stairs and taking them two at a time. Not slowing until I found my room, entered, and locked the door before clambering through the wardrobe, uncaring that my gown snagged on the old wood.

I rushed out into the study, the house leading me to the kitchen stairs. I tripped on my skirts getting down them, desperately following the murmur of voices, skidding to a halt at the bottom.

'Alma.' Her name left me like a plea. Seeing her sat before the fire, smiling at something William had said. Dark curls were pinned in a relaxed fashion on top of her head, wearing her simple grey day dress over her very mortal form.

'Kat?' She frowned, standing and dropping her mending back into the basket at her feet. 'What's wrong?'

I charged towards her, unable to catch my breath until I had hold of her.

'Why were you over there?' I demanded, hurt burning in my chest that she'd play such games. Those foolish tears blurring my vision.

'Over where?' She frowned, eyes darting to the cluttered kitchen table next to us, pages scattered across it. The remains of a small dinner, still-steaming cups of tea and slices of cake.

I shook my head. 'I – I saw . . .'

What did I see? Nothing.

'Sit down, Kat, you're terribly pale.' William suddenly had hold of my arm, trying to pull me down, but I shrugged him off.

'I saw you in Fairfax Manor,' I accused. 'You were there.'

Her eyes went wider with worry as she shook her head. 'I've been here, Kat. William has been helping me with all the notes you left.' She indicated to the table.

I shook my head, unable to understand. It was Alma, I knew it was and yet, her eyes were clear and mortal with her truth.

I'd seen her. Just as I'd felt that pain. Just as I'd seen that blood.

Grief was a monster all its own. I'd forgotten that.

'I'm sorry,' I whispered breathlessly, exhausted with my fear as I sagged onto the bench.

'It's no bother,' William said, and patted my shoulder gently 'I'll make some tea.'

'Thank you, William.' Alma smiled, crouching before me. Those feline eyes running over me with concern as she reached up to wipe my tears away. I should have resisted with my shame. With all the fuss I'd caused, but my limbs felt heavy as the pounding of my heart slowed. Unable to understand any of it.

'Are you sure you won't be missed?' William asked carefully as he began to mess with the tea pot.

I gave him a pointed look as I pulled off my gloves and he quickly went back to making the tea.

'I've been studying those earth samples Emrys gave me from the ruins. I think I'll have some results in the morning.' He continued to talk as he worked, filling the silence with conversation as Alma led me to the table.

'What happened, Kat?' Alma asked, taking my trembling hands between her own as she remained before me.

'I'm probably just tired.' I smiled weakly, my throat burning with all the things I wanted to say, to tell her about the horrid things I'd seen, but what good would it do to give my nightmares to someone else?

Daunton and the foul things that haunted me.

She frowned, leaning closer to gauge my expression. 'It's not like you to make mistakes.'

Perhaps I just didn't know myself anymore. Not like I thought I did. Breaking my own heart with foolish thoughts and thinking I could play games that were way beyond me.

'Kat,' Alma whispered, her grip on my hands tightened as if sensing that darkness in my thoughts. 'I'm here.'

A promise she'd made me before, when Daunton's blood was still on my hands and the madness still in my veins. She'd held me even when it had burned her. Knowing the danger but staying anyway.

I pulled her into an embrace, finally letting an even breath slip between my lips as her hands made soothing circles at my back.

Here. That voice whispered in my mind. Too real and I was fearful that not even Alma's reassurance could chase it away. As if something had followed me from that darkness.

Chapter Thirty-Two

Please.

The ghost of that word occupied my thoughts in the dark of the night. Desperation pressed into it. Then that pain that had overwhelmed me, the warmth of blood between my fingers.

Real. It had been so real.

Rolling over in the lumpy bed, there was nothing but the damp darkness and the pounding of the night rain rattling the thin window to greet me. Weak, cloudy moonlight seeped through the threadbare sections of the curtains. Shadows slid ominously across the walls as trees swayed in the storm winds beyond the house.

Alma had asked if I wanted her to stay, even if she had to be as small as a mouse not to get caught by a maid, but I didn't want her suffering the dank confines of Fairfax Manor. This was my own punishment for bringing us all here.

Unable to bear another moment of my own restlessness, I got out of bed and found my robe. Thankful at least that I had a way back to the study through the wardrobe.

I wandered easily through the study bookshelves in the darkness, only stopping as the muted orange light of the fire reached me. It appeared I wasn't the only one struggling to sleep, haunted by too many things I couldn't change.

The familiar form of Emrys was slumped in a chair before the fire. His eyes narrowed at my presence, seemingly awaiting my arrival. As if there was a meeting I'd missed.

'You've decided to torment me some more then, Croinn?' he called conversationally, continuing to enjoy his drink. His untucked white shirt was rolled to his forearms and unbuttoned so the firelight could play off the sparse dusting of hair on his chest.

'Are you drunk?' I asked, moving further into the room to stand at the cluttered table at its centre.

'Unfortunately not.' A dry, mirthless laugh left his lips. 'Tonight served as a reminder how blessed I should be for the war in saving me from such an existence.'

'They appeared pleased to have you back.' He was nothing but a pillar of moody charm and confidence mere hours ago.

'Fools are easily pleased.' There was a sharpness to his smile as he continued to watch me with caution, as if I'd brought some form of danger with me.

'Lady Lovell seemed especially entertained.' I hated the words the minute they left my lips.

His gaze sharpened, but he simply took another sip of his drink, eyes moving to the fire. I should have left him then, but my feet didn't move. Couldn't, when there was such a sadness lingering around him, a loneliness I knew too well.

All I could see was him crouched before me in those horrid ruins. Feel the brush of his thumb against my cheek.

It's not real, Kat. The softness of those words. Unbothered that I'd struck him, that my fear had driven me mad. Staying with me in that darkness so my demons wouldn't feast. I wouldn't now leave him with his own.

'My father used to send me to dinners like that to spy for him. Setting up matches to gain their trust.' His words were

349

blunt, half murmured, and I wondered if he knew I was still here, lingering in the dark, listening. 'I became so good at it I almost forgot what parts were for his game.'

His eyes came back to me, burdened with that sorrow. 'A useful pawn in all this madness. A willing traitor, an easy whore and a brutal killer. How proud he must have been.'

A small, haunted smile came to his lips as he took me in, standing in disarray in my robe. Those dark eyes moving from my bare feet to where my loose hair was tangled around the points of my ears.

'Perhaps Master Hale hasn't forgiven me at all and you're his final revenge against me.' He pushed himself to his feet with graceful ease, leaving his drink behind as he crossed the distance to stand before me, ducking his head to look into my eyes. 'Sending you to torment me, Croinn.'

'You really are drunk,' I replied calmly, despite the rapid beating of my heart under the intensity of his gaze and his proximity. The horrid things he'd just confessed, the pain that lingered in those words as I dropped my gaze to the table next to me, seeing it littered with samples and notes.

'What are you looking at?' I moved around him, considering the mess, the files littered across the surface he'd just finished working on.

'The body from that Verr pit.' He reached around me, turning over a file and showing me the notes. 'Mr Peter Catron. He's a threll. He wrote numerous articles.' He nodded towards another paper, an article from *The Crow's Foot*. 'He was adamant he'd seen a dark entity. Claimed it came from the soil and shadow.'

My eyes scanned the new notes. Thrells were ancient beings, as ancient as Kysillians or Verr. Elemental summoners. They held water magic, able to command storms and rains for harvest, though I hadn't heard of any being able to command such feats anymore.

'Zorval,' I whispered, reading the word twice to make sure I hadn't made it up in his report.

A poison to fey, made to show their true potential during one of the old mortal king's purges centuries ago. If you held ancient blood, you survived the poison, only to be killed by the King's order. Mercy for the madness of the magic you possessed. It was how they'd eradicated most of the Kysillians centuries before.

Only the poison didn't kill Mr Catron, which meant he had ancient blood. Ancient enough to be worth something.

The cause of death suddenly didn't matter to me, not when I noted Emrys's lack of surprise.

'You've seen it before?' I asked. A being with ancient blood was dangerous in the wrong hands, especially if a Verr could feed from them.

The image of that ghost-girl came back to me so clearly, the sadness in her eyes. A being who should be nowhere near land this cursed. Something making her stay.

'What about an aurrak?' I pressed, catching Emrys's attention at the ancient name.

His brow furrowed, eyes darkening as they moved about my face in confusion. 'How do you know that?'

'You've found one,' I pressed; he must have. 'She's here. I've seen her. In the forest.'

He returned his attention to the table, pulling at papers until he passed me a journal. A small magical sketch of the girl. She'd sat for it in her serving attire, as many fey did for advertisements at large households.

It was her. The same solemn eyes, striking features and straight hair.

'Drained of blood. Her body was found dumped at one of the borders a few months ago,' he said, and I felt that pain deep in my heart. Felt the warmth of it running through my fingers.

'Blood worship fuels the Verr,' I whispered, closing the journal, unable to look at her anymore.

Verr were nothing more than a story. A fear the rebellion peddled in their gossip sheets to draw more fey and mortals to their cause. That was what the Council said, but faced with the truth, I couldn't deny their lies went deeper than even I had anticipated. The Nox offering at the forest's edge was attracting fiends, not deterring them, because this type of darkness was half starved of magic. Just like the fiend in that book in the library. Those fey never stood a chance.

'It's only going to get worse.' I looked at the mass of cases on the table. It was a sign we were on the brink of an abyss, only this time nobody was paying attention.

'Lord Percy has a very expensive mistress and has run his inheritance into the ground. He moved in with his uncle under the guise of being the executor of his will. The west wing burnt not a month later.'

I turned to him, troubled. 'You think he's summoning for wealth?'

'All the fey that can be connected, died of blood draining or heart failure. All could be creature-summoning related.' A sadness weighted his shoulders with the words. 'One more badly cast spell on these lands and we could all be in trouble.'

'How would you stop that?'

'I have all the evidence I need to perform a cleansing charm.' His sharp gaze came back to my face. 'We'll need to cleanse the ruins, hopefully obtain and trap a piece of that darkness that will show its connection to Lord Percy.'

We. I ignored the sudden importance of that one word to me. Letting my fingers run over the small journal with that picture of that poor girl inside.

Unease tightened my chest. From the dark fiends I'd come in contact with, I'd be surprised if we had days. Especially if Lord Percy was still making offerings to the dark, despite our presence.

I turned to the papers, trying to pull them into some form of order when a brightness of ink caught my eye. The delicate marks and beautiful illustrations I'd recognise anywhere. I pulled the aged map from the bottom of the pile.

'I haven't seen an original fey map for a long time.' My voice was soft as my fingertips traced the illustrations of this world and the beasts that had been sketched around the outskirts of the map.

'One of my father's. He loved the North Islands. That's where he met my mother.' He leant around me, his finger tracing the border of the wildlands, almost touching my hand where it rested on the map. Right over the cluster of islands in the north.

'The Isle of Beasts,' I whispered, knowing I shouldn't have drawn attention to it, to my connection to such a beautiful place, but I couldn't control my emotion at seeing it again, even in a map form.

The Council maps never went that far north, or diminished the sacred islands to nothing but an irrelevant drop of ink just off the coast.

'Tauria,' Emrys replied softly, as if he said it every day.

The sound of my true name on his lips made my breath stutter. It'd been so long since I'd heard it said in such a way, with reverence and beauty. The heart-island of the north. Named after the lost, ancient Kysillian queen. The sacred name from my bloodline.

'My father gave me that name,' I confessed before I could fully contemplate the danger of that secret. Could worry about how easily I'd given it to him.

'I thought only members of the Kysillian Kings' line could carry sacred names.' There was a weight to Emrys response, a closeness to him, like he didn't want to miss a single word from my lips.

I smiled weakly, looking back to the map. 'Perhaps my father believed there was nobody left to care about tradition.'

'Do you think there is?' I felt his magic gently brushing my skin with curiosity, as if trying to sense my emotions. I felt the comforting warmth from the sheer presence of him at my back.

'If there is anyone, they're cleverer than me not to get caught.' I considered the lands in the north that had once been a haven, running my finger down the aged page, ignoring its tremble.

'I don't think anyone on this earth is as clever as you, Croinn,' he replied. A tenderness to the compliment.

A heat rolled through me that had nothing to do with magic. I turned, our noses almost brushing, seeing that darkness in his eyes. How it reflected the bright lavender of my own.

The mere presence of him, the anticipation that he might touch me. Seeing one of his rare smiles, the way his eyes shifted colour when he looked at me. The smell of forbidden herbs and old books whenever he was around. How carefully he handled me, like I was something that needed care.

All of it, and perhaps that was the most terrifying thing of all. There was a strange vulnerability to him in the dark, an intimacy to his closeness and too many things I wanted to know.

'Tell me what happened in those ruins, Kat,' he asked so quietly, yet still I felt the fear claw at me.

What haunted me even now. How I'd allowed that fear to drive me to near madness after that horrid dinner.

'I . . .' I swallowed around the word, shaking my head. 'I can't . . .'

Couldn't risk making it real. Summoning that pain here to ruin everything else.

I thought he'd pull back in frustration, at the secrets I kept when faced with the truths he offered. But no, he came closer, gently tipping my chin with his thumb. A comforting softness lingering in the corners of his gaze. Unburdened by anything else but their sincerity.

His fingers dragged along the edge of my jaw, until he could trace the shape of my ear. 'No matter what comes next, I won't leave you to that darkness.'

My breath caught, lip trembling, but his thumb came back to drag across it. I understood that he didn't mean only the darkness that had dwelled in those ruins, but perhaps the one that lingered within me too. A vicious monster of fear and grief.

'I'll find you, Kat,' he whispered, but the intensity remained. The truth of it. 'I promise you that.'

It was impossible. Yet I allowed those words to fill part of that hollow place inside of me as I leant into his touch, pressing myself into his waiting arms like it was the most natural thing in the world to curve my hands around his back. To feel the powerful strength of him beneath the cotton of his shirt, relishing the firm strength of his arms around me in that forbidden embrace.

'Tauria,' he whispered into my hair and I felt that word resonate in my soul. My name. My magic flared in response, raising on command from his lips. Seeking its own truth.

'Tauria died a long time ago,' I spoke quietly against his shoulder, afraid of my own voice. She died on a stormy night with her mother. Consumed by the fire and ash. Carried away on a storm wind.

'Impossible.' He shook his head, pulling back so I could see the dark hair fall onto his brow. 'She's before me, as unattainable to me as she was to mortal men.'

I felt the caress of his magic as it washed over me, chilling the potency of my own, matching it so it didn't have to be afraid anymore.

'Starlight,' he whispered against the curve of my cheek, breath sweet from the brandy. 'Chaos of the heavens.'

'Emrys,' I warned, my voice trembling slightly with anticipation.

'The perfect revenge.' A sadness tinged his response, as my heart stuttered in my chest. 'What a wicked thing you've done, Kat. To make it so I only dream of you.'

Then he kissed me softly, as if concerned it would scare me away. His other hand dropping to my waist, curling me closer to him. Patient and waiting.

I'd been kissed before, once by a messenger boy behind the hay shed, but it wasn't like this. Not with this impossible longing.

It wasn't quick and cautious as if fulfilling some dare. No, he kissed me desperately like he never wished to stop. A depth to it that felt endless.

As if he could press secrets against my lips.

My fingers curled into his shirt. Needing the delicious press of the hardness of his body against me. The demanding power of his magic swept over my skin with the gentle caution of a lover's caress.

My hands dragged upwards over his powerful chest, melting into the firm nature of his touch. I savoured the tightness of his hold, the soft moan that left him as he nipped gently at my bottom lip, commanding me to open my mouth, and then his tongue followed.

My fingers slid into the thick softness of his hair, devouring him with the same intensity. He dragged me closer, hands clutching at the fabric of my robe like he could tear it from me. I wished he would.

My skin was too tight. Needing more attention from him. Needing him. Wanting to be needed like this.

I arched into him, wanting something I didn't fully understand as his lips ran along my jaw and down the line of my throat, nipping at my pulse. Tasting the wildness of it against his lips.

My hand slid beneath his shirt, feeling the warm hardness of his skin. The uneven texture of the scars there, my fingers heating with my magic, hungry to experience the madness of him too. His hands captured my face, pulling back for the barest moment so I could see the bright violet of my eyes reflected in the endless dark of his.

His thumb traced my bottom lip, swollen from his kisses, before he leant in again, softly. Slowing our pace once more, delicately savouring every moment of it. Kissing my mouth from one corner to the other, fingers tangled in the heavy fall of my hair.

Desire coiled low in my abdomen at the warm hardness of him through the thin fabric of my nightgown where my robe had slipped open.

My fingers dragged down his front, feeling the tension in each muscle all the way to the waistband of his trousers. The evidence of his passion for me.

'Emrys,' I whispered against his lips, begging weakly for more.

Only for the sound to freeze him in place, dousing us both in the icy realisation of what we were doing.

He pulled himself harshly back from me, breath unsteady. My cheeks heated with shame as I settled back into reality, instantly fixing my slipping robe with numb fingers as he turned his back.

A tension across his shoulders as he straightened his shirt. 'I'm sorry, Kat.'

Of course.

He'd been drinking and I'd been a fool to think any of it had been real. The words left a hollowness I'd never felt before, different to all the others, chasing away any warmth I'd gained in his arms.

Unwanted. Yet, in a different, more brutal way as he moved to the fire across the room.

Stupid, ugly troll.

'You should go,' he said coldly. His hands curled into fists at his sides, knuckles white. 'The Council put boundaries between—'

He didn't need to finish. Boundaries between partner mages and master, but between mortals and fey too. How forbidden it was. Montagor's mocking words about impropriety burning through me and leaving nothing behind but the brutal pain of that truth. How fragile this safety was, no matter how much I wanted it.

'You don't have to remind me of all the things I can't do, Emrys,' I answered tartly, unable to keep the burn of my tears out of my words. Unsure if he flinched, as I left him to his demons.

Chapter Thirty-Three

Do not wander too far into the night, seeking a glimpse of me in moonlight, for I am not there. I have gone where you cannot follow, and the more you call my name, the more you tether me to a place I can no longer be.

— The Wandering Tales of Amrock, 1572

It was the story my father told on stormy nights, of beings driven mad by grief; a reasoning for why spirits existed. Trapped because those who loved them grieved too much. A story of magic that couldn't find its way back to the earth. It took too much energy for a spirit to manifest, most waited years for a bare moment for someone to see them.

Yet, that girl had wished for me to see her and I couldn't get her out of my mind. I'd seen her twice and I couldn't shake the feeling she needed something.

Now she stood in the outline of the forest, nothing but a faint glow in the distance between the thicket of trees drenched in morning light. Again, trying to catch my eye. As if waiting for me, knowing she'd captured my curiosity.

The loud calls of the birds echoed through the barren wood as the cold morning air sent leaves rolling across the muddy ground.

A rustle and crack of twigs made me turn to see a small beast emerge from beneath the undergrowth.

Some would incorrectly call it a goblin. The creature's skin was a pallid green, its stout, small body covered in sparse fur like a boar. It had a pointed snout, belly low to the ground and short stubby legs. Its clawed feet curling into the dirt as a thick tail dragged behind it through the thicket. Its familiar annoyed bottle-green eyes squinted up at me as a long, forked tongue licked out to taste the damp air.

It was indeed a rare creature called a rot badger.

'You said you want to build up a tolerance,' I teased. Alma had been repulsed by the idea, but it was the only *pleasant* creature I could think of that had a good nose for darkness.

Don't remind me. Her sharp hiss seemed to say before she darted off into the shrubbery. Surprisingly fast for such a chubby little creature, chasing any trace of a scent that could help us.

Alma had come across to Fairfax Manor early with a pot of tea, as if she too couldn't sleep. Or that she was worried about me as always. Wanting to know what troublesome plans I had for the day.

So here we were, back at the Verr pit in the middle of Fairfax Wood, trying to make sense of more madness. I took in the hideous cavern, still dark, even in the morning sunlight that trickled through the thick canopy of twisted branches above.

The house guests had left for a hunting trip, the maid had reluctantly informed me. I didn't press her further to ask if Emrys had also gone, didn't dare mention anything to Alma about last night. I didn't know what was more dangerous, letting myself get tangled with a lord, or keeping a ghoul beneath my bed.

He'd sent no note. I didn't think I could have stomached the shame if he'd tried to apologise. I shouldn't care.

There were other things that needed my attention, such as the wrongness of Fairfax Manor.

Pushing the thoughts of Emrys's warm solid body pressed so close to mine, the sounds in the back of his throat and the demanding thoroughness of his kisses, to the back of my mind as I moved to stand in the entrance of the forsaken ruins.

The cavern was nothing but a cruel ancient beast as I stood in its maw. Only it didn't have teeth anymore, just the hollow remains of all the terrible things that had come before. All the things this world had forgotten. What its hatred had allowed to happen.

The myths exist in your veins, Tauria. Nobody can take them from you, nobody can diminish them, only you can by forgetting. My father's words seemed louder in the silence of this cavern.

I moved further inside, kicking at the clumps of earth and stone. Moving them to see the shattered remains of metal chain beneath, the fragments of bone now stained with ash.

Then a gleam of white caught my eye. I crouched down, pulling out my blade and letting it shift into a pocket knife as I dug the thing out of the earth, which seemed reluctant to let it go. The large piece too pale, ice cold to the touch and veined with dark. Like a piece of marble.

It was nothing more than a fragment, but I saw the symbols carved on the smooth surface, how yellow they were with age. A Verr summoning charm.

A fresh summoning rune carved on top. What had called that Caymor. Someone had put this here. Buried it recently.

A crack came from behind me, too loud to be a rot badger. I lurched to my feet, turning with my blade twisted outwards, only to be greeted with the sharp amber eyes and sly grin of Thean Page. Their auburn hair falling over their shoulder, the ridiculous frill of their lace collar catching the sharp breeze. The fabric was thin enough to see they hadn't bothered to bind their breasts. Or wear a cloak against the winter chill.

'I could have hurt you,' I snapped, brushing errant strands of hair out of my face as I lowered the knife.

'I'd love to see you try, darling,' they taunted, brushing their fingers down their britches. A luxurious dark green suede, completely impractical. Gold stitching in the shape of vines curved around the inside of their thighs, almost inviting someone to trace the pattern with their hand.

I scanned the forest, annoyed I hadn't heard them creeping up on me as I pushed my blade and the cursed summoning fragment into my bag. I knew I shouldn't keep cursed items on my person but I didn't want to linger in a wood with a voyav that was clearly up to no good.

I turned back to that cavernous dark. Feeling the sadness of the place clinging to my skin. Reluctant to let me go. Unbothered by Thean's presence as I touched my forehead and the space over my heart in the Kysillian tradition of respect. Just as my father had taught me, hoping that whatever poor souls had suffered here could feel it. Feel my regret that those Kysillian Kings weren't here now to keep them safe as they promised.

That they'd failed. That I'd failed them too.

'You are not as I expected you to be,' Thean said softly from behind me, almost confused by the admission.

Because I was Kysillian.

'I am not yours to expect things of.' I met their gaze with my own sharpness. I had nothing more to say, so moved back towards the wood. The voyav might wish to punish themselves by dwelling here, but I didn't.

'If you look any more forlorn, those mortals will start to gossip,' they taunted.

I sighed, continuing through the wood. 'Unless you want to learn why they hunted the Kysillians so ruthlessly, you'll mind your business.' A tension coiled in me, rage needing a way out. It'd been too long since I'd sparred. Too long since I'd allowed my body that freedom.

'Darling, I'm not the one you're mad at,' they goaded, unfortunately still following.

I should have been worried about their company but the stone around my neck remained silent. Whatever threat Thean Page was, they weren't here for me.

'You're here to stalk Emrys, remember, not me,' I snapped over my shoulder, only for them to slip into step with me, humming softly as their hands slid into their pockets. Those immortal amber eyes surveying the surrounding wood with boredom.

I wondered why, of all the things they had to do, they were bothering me. However, those thoughts only led to their worrying familiarity with Emrys, which almost stopped my retreat.

'How do you know Emrys?' I pressed, wondering if they'd even entertain that conversation.

They eyed me cautiously. 'Careful. Secrets from my lips may cost you things you cannot give, little Kysillian.'

'Try me.' I turned, stopping them in their tracks. The last few days had tempered my will and I refused to be afraid.

Their head tilted slightly in contemplation, red hair cascading over their shoulder, showing streaks of gold in the sunlight and revealing the summoning runes down the side of their neck, curving down the low plunge of their shirt.

'Three questions in exchange for a favour.' They held out their slender hand, runes curled around their finger, one shaped like an eye sat in the centre of their palm.

I could have said no, but again, the stone around my neck was silent.

'Deal.' I took their hand, squeezing it harder than needed.

'Emmaline,' I began ruthlessly.

Thean's amber eyes hardened instantly, their fingers slipping free from my grip and they continued to walk.

'She was in service with me.' There was a coldness to the words, as if they were sharing a simple fact.

'To the rebellion?' The confession almost made me stumble over my own feet.

'Fulfilling the last of their mother's oath. That's how the rebellion keeps itself supplied with willing participants. They bind them with blood oaths.'

'Lady Blackthorn was a member of the rebels?' My mind was racing too viciously to make better use of my questions. Lord Blackthorn was a king's mage. He'd been so close in his ranks and yet he was married to a member of the darkest part of the rebellion.

A willing traitor, an easy whore and a brutal killer. Emrys's words came back to me, the bitterness lingering in them. Just how deep did Blackthorn allow his children to go into those games, and his own wife?

'She was many things before she was Lady Blackthorn, darling. A sorceress beyond limit, a clever spy and a deadly assassin. She was sent to Blackthorn's bed to kill him. I think you can gather how that went.' Thean raised a dark brow with insinuation. 'It seems like a family trait to desire forbidden things.'

I ignored their taunt.

'Rebels don't break their vows,' I warned. They couldn't. They were blood sworn.

'She didn't. Lord Blackthorn is dead and her love led him down that path.' Thean's words were careful, weighted perfectly like a warning as their slender shoulders lifted with a shrug.

A cold dread shot down my spine but I persevered. Foolish as always. 'Why are you here?'

'I have debts to pay that cannot be ignored.' A weight came with those words as the voyav was suddenly occupied with the lace of their collar that the wind had disturbed.

Avoiding that truth. A debt. One that had led them to watch over Emrys like a hawk. To try to warn him of this.

'Emmaline asked something of you?' I stopped in the middle of the wood, seeing the pain hidden in the voyav's expression. They knew Emmaline, and she had asked them for something. Something beyond a blood vow.

The voyav simply gave me an irritated glance over their shoulder. 'That's four.'

I didn't need the answer. Thean had already given it by being here. They had been following Emrys; they knew the things that were happening. Did Emrys see the warning in the voyav's presence? If Emmaline had commanded them, they had no choice.

You can't break a dead being's vow.

'He's in danger here,' I murmured softly, too afraid to speak the words any louder.

'He's always in danger, darling, mostly from himself,' Thean replied. They somehow seemed mortal and exhausted by the revelation before their eyes turned sharp again. 'Something else you both have in common.'

We'd come to the small clearing where the portal door had formed in that crumbling archway. Only I was rooted in place by the weight of all the truths I'd asked for.

'Of course, you had to find some other form of bloody trouble,' came the irritated words from Alma as she emerged from the wood, arms tightly folded across her chest. Re-dressed in her simple dark day dress, errant leaves and twigs in her hair, her cheeks flushed with exertion.

'Just when I thought my day was looking rather dull.' Thean crossed their arms, the words a lover's purr from their throat, smile wicked. 'Good morning, darling.'

Alma ignored them, placing her hands on her hips and scowling at me. 'Why are they here?'

'Riddles,' was the only answer I could give.

'If I'd known you were naked, sweetheart, I would have come sooner.' Thean grinned, eyes dragging over Alma's rumpled skirts.

Knowing by the sudden stiffness of Alma's spine this wasn't going to end well, I left them to it.

Alma hissed something about disembowelling the voyav, but the rest of the brutal threat was thankfully lost as I stepped into the portal.

It seems like a family trait to desire forbidden things.

Sat at one of the tables hidden deep in the library shelves, I turned Thean's words over in my mind. The very thin line the Blackthorns had walked. Secrets that had led them to the grave.

I turned the white Verr summoning charm over in my hands, thumb running over the carved runes. Refusing to allow myself to be cowed by them.

More evidence of the Council's lies. Of Master Hale's. How they preached there was no darkness in this world to worry about. I couldn't get that girl's face out of my mind. The fear in her eyes. Left in the dirt like nothing but discarded waste.

I let the cursed object tumble from my fingers, clattering to the table as I pushed myself to my feet in disgust. Anger coiled tightly in my gut as I gripped the shelves. How foolish I'd been to believe any of it. To allow them to keep me locked in that institute, to gorge myself on their lies.

I pulled a few more books about ancient ground curses from the shelves. The sideboard next to me rattling its drawers in question.

'I'm fine.' I sighed, turning back to the table and dumping my new collection on top. Then I took all the small soil samples I'd taken in the wood for William out of my bag.

If you look any more forlorn, those mortals will start to gossip, Thean's words taunted in my memory.

'*Forlorn,*' I scoffed under my breath at the ridiculousness of it. It was just a stupid kiss.

Annoyed I'd let the voyav goad me, I opened one of the heavy tomes to see what lay inside. The thin time-stained pages crackled in greeting. My other hand moved to play with the chain around my neck as I tried to concentrate.

Chaos of the heavens. Emrys's words whispered through my mind, as soft as any caress. Making me bite my lip. Consumed with the foolishness of that desire. Then came the memory of the alluring scent of him, the teasing bite of his magic as it had run temptingly down my throat in the absence of his lips. Following my unspoken command for more.

'You need to stop doing that,' came his dark voice over my shoulder, making me jump.

I turned to see him, regretting it instantly. The dark handsome disarray of him. Like I'd summoned him with the barest thought.

'R-reading?' I stuttered, ignoring how my stomach dipped with his closeness, his hand mere inches from my own where they curled over the lip of the table. 'I thought you were hunting.'

'No, opening cursed books,' he clarified, reaching over me to flip the cover closed. 'And I don't hunt innocent creatures.'

I looked to the book, reminding myself of the night I'd seen him first in the moonlight. How far away that was now. How many things had changed.

I cleared my throat. 'You shouldn't own so many,' I said, annoyed by my own breathlessness.

The shelves had shifted into a circular shape, concealing us. The vaulted ceiling, adorned with stone carvings like one of the saint halls for worship. Bright with long arched windows allowing morning sunlight to pour down on us.

'You wouldn't find me half as interesting if I didn't.' His gaze was cautious as it traced my face. 'You shouldn't go wandering those woods, Croinn. Not until we figure this out.'

I pulled back, ignoring the fact that he knew my latest scheme. 'Is that why you sent Thean to spy on me?'

'Thean?' His eyes darkened immediately, his frown deep. 'The last thing you need is to catch the rebellion's attention, Kat.'

'I doubt they're recruiting at a lord's dinner party,' I countered tartly. The rebellion wouldn't want a member as chaotic and undisciplined as me.

'I don't know. It appears Thean's seduction tactics work wonderfully on you.' He said the words so dryly and there was no missing the envy in his gaze.

'I'm surprised you noticed,' I observed coldly, his focus sharpening with almost deadly intent. 'You think the rebellion care about a dead Kysillian bloodline?'

I pressed my hand to his chest to move him back so I could make my departure. 'I'm in no danger from Thean. They're here for *you*, not me.'

His dark brow rose, the hint of a smile at the corner of his scarred mouth almost mocking as he captured my hand so gently, keeping me close. 'Really? You think a Kysillian with full range of her magic wouldn't catch their eye?'

'Jealous?' I snapped irrationally.

Something shifted in his expression, almost in warning. 'Let's just say it isn't in my nature to share.'

'You're just annoyed someone else is trying to take advantage of my usefulness before you can.' I broke, letting that bitterness out of me. Ready to be done with the game as I tugged my hand free of his hold.

If he was offended by the slight, he didn't show it, no, he did something worse. He leant closer, a softness in his features that unsettled my heart. 'That's not why I chose you, Kat.'

'Why else would you?' I hated the hurt that burned in my chest at that truth. I was here because I was *useful*, and I wouldn't fool myself otherwise. I pushed him back, moving past him to leave. 'Call him an old bastard all you want, at least Master Hale was honest about his intentions.'

Liar. That voice hissed in the back of my mind.

'Getting you killed for nothing more than his pride?' He teased bitterly behind me.

I spun back to face him, hearing the shelves around us creak, displeased with our fighting. 'Master Hale was trying to help.'

'Help? By trapping you there?'

'Where else was I supposed to go, Emrys?' I threw my arms wide with frustration. 'To the fey traffickers? The workhouse? Or the streets?'

Each word struck him like a blow but I didn't care. Ignoring the sting of tears with my irritation, I charged back to him, finger pointed to ram it into the centre of his chest, Council regulations about partnership conduct forgotten.

'We both know the rebels won't have me. I'm even too cursed for the likes of them.' I prodded the space right over his heart. 'Whatever *debt* Hale owed you—'

'Debt?' He cut me off, the question as sharp as a blade, but it was his fingers that captured my wrist, pulling me closer until we were flush.

My palm was flat against his chest, feeling the calming, steady beat of his heart. His head ducked to meet my eye, an intensity resting in the stormy grey of them.

'I once read a paper so beautifully written, it was like I was learning magic was real for the first time.'

My next words stuck in my throat, breath escaping me too softly.

'Like seeing it rise from my own flesh, feeling it move through my veins. Proving I was real. I was alive,' he whispered, like we were sharing a secret. 'Magic survives, no matter how weak or thin its threads become. Unashamed of its weakness, consumed by its relentless will to live. It survives and we forgive it for its viciousness in doing so. We'd forgive it anything, and yet we never forgive ourselves.'

My words. They were my words.

Tears escaped my eyes; I shook my head. Unwilling to believe it, but he captured my face so gently between his palms.

'I hunted down the author, only to discover they lied. And so did the next, and the next. Months it took me to find the crumpled and stolen source material in one of the old record halls. Papers on healing curses, the beauty of mythical beasts and the nature of the darkness we should fear.'

I couldn't quite breathe, but ruthless as always, Emrys didn't stop.

'Then Hale asked for my help. As if Fate were pushing me to an answer.' He stopped there for a moment, eyes clear and full of a strange longing pain. 'Then I saw you. Trapped. That sadness in your eyes. Their endless cruel games, and yet, you didn't cower.'

I tried to see myself that way but I couldn't. I was too far from that version of myself now. He'd brought me too far.

'I chose you because I needed you, Kat.' His voice was steel, unequivocal, and firm. 'Not because you're Kysillian, not because of Hale or for being the apparent scourge of the Institute.'

His head dipped until our foreheads touched and I found myself leaning into the warmth of him, foolishly wanting things I shouldn't from him.

'I needed *you*.' His eyes closed as if pained.

You. The single word broke my heart, to be something more than the magic inside of me. More than their bargaining chip. More than my foolish fate.

I'd needed him too. The moment I'd pressed my words to those pages, I needed someone to read them, to know it was real before they took everything I had left.

His magic brushed my skin in comfort, reminding me too vividly of the seduction of his touch as he began to pull back.

'I won't take things from you you've worked so hard for, Kat. They'd ruin you for it, for my weakness in not letting you go.' His eyes drifted to my lips before he corrected himself, jaw hard with restraint.

'I was ruined the moment I was born, Emrys.' I allowed the pain of that truth to consume me. The bitterness towards my parents for trying to teach me any differently. 'If you think I care what those old bastards think of me, you haven't been paying attention. I make my own decisions. No matter how much you regret yours.'

'Regret.' He repeated the word sinisterly.

'Shame, remorse, regret – pick a term. I'm certain it will fit,' I mocked, moving to turn, to flee – only for his arms to come around me, to bring me back against his front.

'You'd be very wrong, Kat.' His words were a wicked thing that brushed my ear. 'Wrong for thinking I haven't wanted to kiss you every day since you set that ghoul on me.'

'I didn't set it on you.' I wanted to snap but my voice didn't sound steady as I turned to glare up at him, finding our fingers interlaced at my waist. 'However, you're giving me wonderful ideas.'

I wouldn't mind setting a ghoul on him right now.

'You're under my house. My protection. I'm not going to—'

'I wouldn't say the house likes you very much at the moment,' I interrupted, and to emphasise the point, the drawer beneath the table opened to whack into his hip, making him mutter a curse at the furniture, but he still didn't let me go.

'And I can protect myself just fine.' I turned in his arms, knowing I'd proven that. Perhaps finally proven it to myself most of all.

'It was just a kiss, Emrys,' I finished, unable to focus on anything other than where his hands still rested at my waist, how my own had somehow curved around his forearms. 'A moment of madness.'

'You're a terrible liar, Croinn.' His head tilted, smile devious.

'Then what a wicked pair we make,' I taunted, leaning forward with my ferocity, only for one of his hands to capture the side of my face again with such gentle reverence I felt my anger slipping from my grasp.

'I can't lie to you.' There was a desperate longing to the quietness of those words. 'For once in my life I wish I could.'

'Really?' A huff of a bitter laugh left me, only to be stifled as he ducked his head closer. His thumb dragged across my bottom lip. 'What are you doing?'

'Having another moment of madness.' That teasing smile was still there as I watched his eyes bleed to complete darkness.

'I'm still angry with you,' I whispered, almost desperately trying to find my will.

'I know, Croinn,' he answered, barely brushing a kiss at the corner of my mouth. My fingers curled into his shirt as I felt his smile sharpen at the tremble in my lip.

'Out of all the punishments I've endured, why is being forbidden to have you the worst of them all?' he whispered against my cheek, such desperate sadness pressed into each word it made my heart break.

'Emrys—' I barely breathed, before a clattering crash stole all other words from me, making me jump out of Emrys's arms as he stepped back. Leaving me feeling oddly hollow.

'Bloody saints!' came a yell from between the bookcases, whatever awful stupor had consumed us vanishing.

'William?' I rushed around the corner, finding him looking down sadly at a ruined breakfast tray in the doorway to the study, the contents scattered across the entryway.

'Half the sodding floor just came up!' he groused. 'I could have broken my neck!'

'Here.' I dropped to a crouch, turning the tray over and gathering up the shattered remains of plates and cups. I could have used my magic but my hands weren't quite steady yet.

'Bloody house,' William muttered, pulling a rag from his apron and trying to stop the tea from seeping down a large crack in the floorboards. Then his head darted up just as I felt the brush of Emrys's magic down my spine.

'This came under your guest-room door from Fairfax. I think Lord Percy is looking for you.' William held a small letter out from his apron. Emrys took it carefully, his face troubled once more as he considered the mess before us.

'You should go,' I offered softly, those grey eyes coming to me instantly. 'The last thing we need is them asking questions.'

'Kat can help me with the cleansing charm. I think I've found something that will work with the soil,' grinned in agreement, oblivious to the intensity in Emrys' tense form.

Emrys remained silent, that letter curled into his fist. Hesitant. Too many things unfinished and unsaid.

'I'm certain I'll find you later.' I smiled as I got back to my feet, something about the offer seemed to make the decision for him as he excused himself and left us. I tried to ignore the stinging bite of longing in my chest.

'Where is Alma?' William asked curiously, trying to balance all the shattered remains back on the tray.

'Probably gutting Thean.' I sighed, knowing I should probably be more worried for her, but Alma could handle a nosy voyav better than I could.

'Thean?' William's eyebrows shot up, but I was already turning him by his shoulders back to the kitchen.

'Never mind.' I sighed, not wanting to think about any more of my mistakes. 'We should get to work. The sooner this is over the better.'

Chapter Thirty-Four

A storm arrived late afternoon that forced the hunting party back to the house. Lord Fairfax – in a joyous mood – had started the evening entertainment early, drinks poured, the band was filling the dilapidated ballroom with music, the guest's laughter excruciatingly loud.

After the drama of yesterday, everyone was quick to pretend I didn't exist and I noticed noticed most of the ladies had refrained from wearing jewellery.

I'd kept myself aloof, especially when Emrys had appeared. Mainly so I didn't think about what had happened in the study. Madness indeed.

I touched the flowers Alma had woven into the braid at the back of my hair, trying to give my scalp some reprieve as I looked down at my beautiful deep indigo dress, feeling sad it had been so wasted with how eager I was to drop it onto my bedroom floor, sink between the sheets and forget about another horrid day.

I let my eyes drift over the bland landscape paintings on the walls of the ballroom more interested in how the dust collected in the corners of the frames. Small mortal pieces, colours muted and grey. Letting my fingers drag across the peeling picture rail, as I moved to one of the large alcoves with a few measly books on the shelves.

My boredom was replaced with a horrid stinging cold at what stood before me. A collection of display frames. Pinned there by their small beetle wings, dull and dusty with decay, was a small display of folk. Their tiny acorn heads and moss bodies trapped inside the frames.

Something hurt so deep inside me, buried in the marrow of my bones. How something so innocent and free of malice could be hurt so viciously. How endlessly cruel this world could be to creatures that were filled with nothing but innocence and hope.

Please, a younger voice pleaded in my memory so desperately. My own.

As I looked at those little creatures, all I saw was Alma's small pale bruised hand reaching for me across filthy stone. The creaking wood of those wheelbarrows as they took more small bodies into the wood outside Daunton. The reek of damp soil and decay. Only to be chased away by the finality of flame and smoke I could still taste on my tongue.

Haunted by how I could save none of them.

I was too late once again. So slowly I rested my finger against the dusty glass, taking in every sharp bite of the little things' pain.

'*Marov*,' I whispered. *Rest now* in the old tongue. The last blessing as the smallest lick of flame from my finger turned the remains to ash that glistened as if made of glass at the bottom of the frame.

Free.

'Strange little things, aren't they?' The brittle voice of Lord Fairfax came from behind me as I let my hand fall to my side, forcing my anger down to sour in my gut along with the cheap wine.

'They were,' was all I could let out, anger darkening my voice.

'My grandfather's collection,' the old lord mused softly. 'He was fascinated by the wildness of the world. Too cruel and short of temper to read about it or study for the answers he wanted.'

A small glimmer of hope rested in those words. Of regret.

Lanthor. Forgive them. My mother's words came back to me. Guiding me even now.

'I should have let them go, but Robert used to care for them. They were why he wished to be a mage, why he wanted to study the folk in the north.' His words broke apart with the depths of that grief. 'He was bright, like you. Clever.'

Something unsettled me with those words. How easily he compared us, like we could ever be equal. A mortal lord and a Kysillian. Too much distance between us, a gaping wound that couldn't be filled, and my mind instantly started thinking of Emrys.

'I'm sorry you lost him.' I was, because despite all this death and cruelty, I was too familiar with grief to sneer at it in others.

'He's come back to me.' Fairfax smiled softly, as if it was just our secret. 'Like in the tales of those bone collectors and their many spells.'

Necromancers and wraiths. Dark things that deserved to be forgotten, to be lost to dust and myth.

Maybe he was as mad as Emrys suspected.

'There are some old books I thought you might enjoy, they were Robert's,' he continued, extending his hand to lead the way. It was then I could see his shirt was on inside out, his dinner jacket worn thin at the shoulders. A jam stain on the lapel. 'They're in the back library.'

As I watched the lord, the strangeness of his movements, battered by his grief and the weight of his words, I understood. There was a different way to trap creatures and pin them in place, and Lord Percy was doing a perfect job.

That stone against my breastbone flickered in small warning, but all it did was remind me of all that had come before. That pit and the body. Mr Catron had been here.

'Lord Fairfax . . .' I asked carefully, keeping my voice light. 'Do you remember a gentleman by the name of Mr Peter Catron?'

His brow furrowed deeply, his thin fingers coming up to rub his temple, like the motion could bring the memory to the forefront of his mind.

'I don't want to trouble you with it,' I pressed quietly, unsettled by his distress as I reached out to touch his arm. That stone around my neck burned sharply with warning.

'No I . . .' His gaze went distant for a moment before he turned those old eyes to my face. 'I believe . . . a threll gentleman did come by the house.'

I moved closer, desperate to coax more from him.

'Something to do with land disputes.' He shook his head, his laugh soft. 'I believe Richard spoke to him.'

'Richard?' I asked uneasily, that sinking feeling consuming my chest. His dead son.

'Yes, they were talking about—'

'Uncle,' Lord Percy interrupted sharply, drawing us apart to see his dour expression. 'The Mattersons wish to see you.'

Fairfax pulled back, a small laugh slipping through his thin lips with surprise. 'When did they get here?'

'Last week,' Lord Percy answered coldly, not really paying attention as the old man glanced about the room before limping off, leaving me with his horrid nephew.

'You made quite an impression during your time here.' Lord Percy shifted his weight uncomfortably.

'That was a curt interruption, Lord Percy.' I smiled tightly, tone sharp with accusation. 'I hope Lord Fairfax wasn't about to say too much.'

'Mr Matterson had some interesting theories on the ruins you trespassed into,' he half sneered, clearly not able to restrain his temper. 'Apparently the stone of them is supposed to weaken fey magic.'

My heart sank to the stained marble floor between us.

There was a feral glee in his bloodshot eyes. 'Yet you managed to make quite a mess.'

My heart then began to pound wildly at the words, but I kept my features blank, forcing myself into the same defensive boredom that had saved me from the Council's accusations.

'You know an awful lot about restricting fey magic, Lord Percy,' I countered politely. 'Is it a subject of interest for you?'

He stiffened at that, so tense I could almost hear the grinding of his teeth.

'You should count your blessings I managed to survive the ordeal,' I continued, my smile sweet and demure enough to enrage him further. 'I'm certain you wouldn't want your negligence to be the reason the Peace Agreements failed.'

His face had gone purple with rage, his breath uneven and his fist white-knuckled at his side.

I leaned closer, letting my smile sharpen into something vicious. 'However, I would love to see how you deal with the rebellion at your throat. Since one woman seems to have rendered you . . . quite impotent.'

Disgusted, I moved to push past him, but he seized my arm, pushing me back against the alcove with a speed I didn't expect. He stepped into my space, his bitter drink-filled breath striking my face.

'I'd be careful with your temper, *Miss Woodrow*,' he bit out, and I could smell nothing but the putrid stink of him. 'The Council only need hear of the *familiarity* between yourself and Blackthorn and you'll be on the streets. From gossip, patrons would pay good money for a fey bitch like you in heat.'

Heat. Like an animal.

His grin was cruel as my heart hammered against my ribs, a coldness streaking through me as I remembered Emrys's lips on my own.

They'd ruin me for it.

My magic rolled through my limbs, the lamps surrounding us flaring brighter in response to me, revealing the grotesque decay of the ballroom walls. Then I saw the scarring of his ears. Evidence of his shame. That he was fey-born and still possessed no magic.

'Like your mother?' I smiled in response, a harshness to the words. Almost willing him to touch me again. To let me break his nose. The Kysillian in me vicious for the blood of it.

The glass in his other hand shattered, wine spilling down his front as he stumbled back. My breath came in short pants as I looked at my hands, not seeing the flare of brightness in my veins. It hadn't been me.

'It appears you've had an accident, Lord Percy,' came the annoyed voice of Thean, who had stepped close to my side, weaving their arm effortlessly through mine and pulling me away further into the room.

'I didn't—' I began, turning to the voyav, but they were already glaring down at me.

'If you could refrain from almost causing a massacre, I'd appreciate it.' Their bored tone had returned as they stole a glass of wine from a passing maid and led me away. 'Eaveshaw lace is difficult to clean blood out of.' They indicated the ridiculous shirt they wore beneath their embroidered evening jacket, the silk collar slightly ruffled in a fashion a few centuries out of date.

'The horrible bastard came over to *me*.' I confiscated the glass from them and contemplated throwing it over the voyav. However, I found I needed the drink more than the drama to settle my nerves. I downed it, letting it chase away the bitter bile from Lord Percy's threat.

'I meant for wearing that dress.' Thean's eyes dragged up my skirts with annoyance as they plucked the empty wineglass from my hand and held it out to a passing servant.

'Alma picked it.' I ran my hand over the bodice, the perfect shade of midnight. Simply beautiful as it curved around my waist and rested demurely at the edge of my shoulders. No adornments needed. However, Alma's ruthless lacing meant far more of me was on show than I appreciated, but considering I'd decided to linger in the shadows, it hadn't bothered me that much.

'Of course the little nightmare did.' They let out an irritated breath, their gaze locking on something over my shoulder.

'You have two options,' they commented wryly. 'You can dance with me or with the greasy man over there that seems intent on asking you.'

Dread made me shudder.

'Lead,' I snapped, taking the voyav's hand before they could offer it. Thankfully the music started with a slow and short waltz. It had been a long time since I'd danced, and I was glad for the distraction of having to focus on my feet and the music that swelled around us. Watching the other couples laugh and dance as they moved across the floor, most giving me a sharp irritated glance.

'Are you all right, darling?' Thean asked quietly, making me look into those amber eyes and seeing they'd lost their sharp edge.

'I should ask you the same thing, I'm surprised Alma let you live.' I sighed, not needing to give away any more weaknesses.

'I think she's quite fond of me,' they teased, manoeuvring us effortlessly into another turn.

'Did the claws at your throat give you that impression?' I asked, unable to stop the mocking smile that came to my lips.

'She should be flattered I let her catch me.' They winked, and then I did laugh. At the ridiculousness of it. As if they stood a chance against Alma.

However, it appeared the voyav wasn't playing games, their face becoming quite pensive as he considered me. 'What hunts those ruins takes its toll. You should tell your dark protector about it.'

'What was it?' I asked. Watching the sharp planes of their face, the mischievous glint in those amber eyes dampened slightly.

'You should have asked that earlier,' they taunted, but that softness remained in their expression. 'It isn't anything you can't handle. You who commands deadly creatures with ease.'

'That's not true.' I shook my head as we turned again.

'One look at Emrys should prove my point, dear,' they added darkly, turning us to emphasise their point. There, over their shoulder, at the far corner of the room, was Emrys, watching us over the rim of his wine glass with deadly focus before Thean spun me again, further across the dance floor.

'You're causing trouble,' I warned, remembering Emrys's earlier irritation at the voyav's presence.

'Trouble is my second name,' they taunted, their smile sly. 'Depravity is my third.'

They brought us into the final turn, to stop at the edge of the dance floor as the room applauded weakly with the break in music. I couldn't clap, too focused on the dark form of Emrys coming towards us. Ignoring two lords who tried to step into his path to get his attention.

'This should be fun,' Thean purred quietly in satisfaction over my shoulder. 'Darling Emrys, something important you wish to share?'

'I've promised Miss Woodrow a dance,' Emrys replied frostily with his annoyance. I was stuck between the pair of them, quite certain every single guest was staring right at us.

Bastards. The pair of them were bastards but there was no room for my irritation as Emrys held out his gloved hand, Thean's soft chuckle mocking over my shoulder.

Despite the audience and the foolishness of it, I took Emrys's hand. I'd done so before, but this felt different, too public and evocative of a statement. Lord Percy's vile words seared through my thoughts but I pushed them all away, needing every ounce of concentration to deal with the lord before me.

Clearly fate was laughing at me as wickedly as Thean was from the edge of the dance floor as the next song began.

"The Midnight Rendezvous". A song written for one of the mortal kings, a dance performed at his balls. One for when he attempted to find one of his many queens. A flirtatious and scandalous melody with many tales to accompany it.

Emrys stepped effortlessly into the dance, drawing me in. His hold tighter and closer than Thean's had been. I fell into step easily, remembering the movements as if it was just yesterday that I had done them, waltzing around a small cottage in a different time, with my mother's laughter in my ear.

The well of emotion distracted me from the danger of being in Emrys's arms and how securely he held me. The luxurious feel of the wool of his jacket beneath my hand, how his strong limbs filled it out, the shifting of his muscles beneath. The luring scent of him, how close his jaw was, the shadow of stubble there. Remembering how rough it had felt against my skin, awakening things I didn't think it was possible to feel.

'You're making a spectacle,' I whispered sinisterly, hoping he took it seriously, because I was a moment away from crushing his toes.

'I thought you were used to that, Croinn?' His words brushed my cheek as I kept my face politely turned away, watching the other dancers. The swell of the music surrounding us.

'What did Lord Percy want?' he pressed, a warning creeping into his quiet tone.

'It isn't worth repeating.' I turned my head at the right moment, seeing him waiting to meet my eye as the dance's pace picked up. Those eyes storm grey and filled with a mix of fury and worry.

'Kat—'

'It's the same nonsense I've dealt with many times before. I don't need you brooding about it,' I added tartly, allowing him to turn us sharply as I tried to keep my breathing steady.

'"The Midnight Rendezvous" was only taught in the King's courts. Did you anticipate me embarrassing myself?' I tried to distract him, only for the sight of him to stop my heart for a mere moment. How that dark hair fell onto his brow, the teasing nature to his eyes and the curve of his lip. The allure of his closeness, the strength of his hold on my waist and the imposing nature of him. The firmness of his shoulder beneath my hand as our palms met. Even wearing gloves, my skin prickled with the cool nature of his magic, always present. Always seeking out my attention.

'I would have led you through it,' he turned me again, bringing me back closer than before, his words brushed my ear as we pressed tightly together. 'Do I even want to know what Thean was up to?'

'*Helping.* Which might be more unsettling than anything else.' I sighed, feeling the press of his fingers as they dragged down the fastening at the back of my dress. 'Lord Fairfax said Mr Catron came here. He said Robert spoke to him.'

My hold on his forearms tightened as his dark gaze looked over every inch of my face, sensing that unease in me. 'You let those creatures rest.'

The folk in the case. He'd seen that foolishness too, then.

'Maybe I have lost my mind.' I kept my voice low, annoyed at myself for the weakness of it. 'First the ruins, the voices, and then the walls . . .'

'What walls?' He frowned, somehow bringing me even closer, noses almost brushing.

'It doesn't matter.' I shook my head, 'I don't need you being annoyed with me. If this is about Thean—'

'I'm not annoyed,' he interrupted as he spun me, only to draw me back to his front, our hands laced together at my waist. Breath uneven as my breasts straining against my bodice, and from that darkness in his eyes, I knew he missed none of it.

His hands dragging seductively across my middle as he turned me again.

'Really?' I laughed quietly, seeing the tension in his jaw as those dark eyes moved down to me once more. He contemplated the small smile on my lips for a silent moment before ducking closer as if it was only us in this cursed ballroom. His hand rested so firmly against the curve of my waist.

'I'm furious.' The soft lethal nature to those words brushed my ear. 'Furious you have to spend a moment in their presence.

385

That you have to breathe the same air as beings as unpleasant as this and I hate the darkness it puts in your eyes.'

'It was my fault. I brought us—'

'I don't care.' His answer was harsh with deadly intent. I felt the cool brush of his magic against the curve of my throat in reassurance, soothing the hammering of my pulse, making my breath stutter through my lips. A wildness in him that pressed me closer. Something equally wild in me wanting free.

'Did you break that glass?' I ran my hand from the curve of his elbow to the strong line of his shoulder.

'He should be grateful that's all I did.' Such a vicious coldness in his words. I feared I could ask him anything and he'd do it. Just as Thean had mocked.

'It'll be over soon. We'll be home,' was the only soft reassurance I could give, allowing it to spread a comforting warmth through my chest.

Home. The word settled in the small space between us and there was nothing deadly about that new light seeping into his eyes.

I wasn't quite able to breathe as those eyes bled into a darkness without end that had nothing to do with anger or threat, but something more primal. Here in the circle of his arms I couldn't lie to myself any longer. How the Kysillian instincts in me rose to the challenge, wanting all his strength closer. Wanting it as I'd wanted nothing else.

'Tell me how to survive you, Kat.' Those words brushed my ear like a secret, and I heard his anguish. Felt it in the pull of his magic, softly brushing my skin. Cautious of hurting me as it swept over my collarbone with reverence, knowing it could never have the hold it wanted. That it could never have me.

The music reached its final swell as I felt his fingers curl into the lacings at the back of my dress. The reluctance to let me go, making me tighten my hold on him. Uncaring that it was wrong. That it was dangerous.

'I'm right here, Emrys,' I barely whispered against the edge of his jaw. My own challenge, letting those dark eyes settle on me once more.

A clattering of applause drew us slowly from our embrace as he hesitantly let me go. The swell of people overtook us again, some of the ladies pushing forward to mob him. Clearly seeing Emrys dancing unmanned not only me.

That thought brought a stinging flush to my cheeks, making me retreat to the windows. Needing the cool air on my skin, to hide once again in the dusty alcoves before I got myself in more trouble. I quickened my steps as another song began, pressing my fingers against my brow for any relief, only to collide with someone.

The cold chill of rain on their coat, the shock of blond hair and the pure searing hatred twisting their face into something repulsive, shocking me into a stumbling halt.

'Finneaus?' I demanded, forgetting myself, unable to understand how Ainsworth's son was before me. But those pointy rodent-like features could only belong to him. 'What are you doing here?'

'Watch your mouth, troll,' he half sneered in response, reaching for me with the same barbarity Lord Percy had.

'Creative as always.' I slapped his hand off me with too much strength, making him yelp like the mongrel he was. The stone tucked in my corset burned with warning.

'I'd be careful, Mr Ainsworth, Miss Woodrow isn't fond of surprise guests,' a voice called coldly over my shoulder. Dread sunk like a stone in my gut as I turned to see the predatory face. Hair smoothed back, fixing the dark gloves that covered his hands. His navy riding coat damp at the shoulders from the night rain.

Montagor.

Chapter Thirty-Five

You can burn down this world if you wish, but that is not our way.

The memory of my father's voice came back to soothe me, and for once I hated the reasoning in it as my hands curled into fists. My fingers burned with the urge to summon flame. To burn the reptile and his master.

This was a nightmare, one come real, for these men to be here now. Still coldly handsome, Montagor had an ugly fading bruise down one side of his face that I knew I hadn't given him.

'I see no introductions are necessary,' Lord Percy mused, joining our horrid new gathering.

'Unfortunately, I've run into the Institute's *pet* before, Lord Percy,' Montagor replied, the ruthlessness of his smile not losing its sharp edge.

'I suppose you wish to see Lord Blackthorn too?' Lord Percy added with a respectful bow, confirming my suspicion that he was a spineless worm.

Montagor didn't even glance in his direction – no, his focus was intently on me. His eyes flicked down to my chest, not out of interest, but like he could see that stone where I felt its warmth against my skin. 'If I know anything about dear Emrys, I'm certain he's already on his way here.'

Fear chilled my blood. Of all the things he shouldn't see. The familiarity between myself and Emrys. That weakness to be wanted that I'd allowed myself to foolishly indulge in. Just how viciously this could all end.

'Leave us,' Montagor commanded softly, my heart rioting within my chest, but I refused to let it show. Refused to be cowed by this monster. 'You seem surprised by my presence, Miss Woodrow.'

'I didn't think a rumoured haunting and a case of hysteria would be important enough for your attention, *my lord*,' I replied bitingly, gathering my hands before me like the perfect dinner guest, ignoring the feel of everyone's gaze coming to settle on us, their focus like sharp pinpricks against my skin.

'No,' he mused, placing a finger against his lip in contemplation. 'However, a Kysillian straining too far from her leash might be.'

Finneaus shifted behind Montagor uneasily, and then I felt the brutal chill of Emrys's magic at my back. Curving over my bare shoulders like night mist, the intensity of it making Montagor stand taller as Finneaus took another step back.

'Just in time, Emrys.' Montagor's smile was thin and vicious in greeting. 'Shall we?' He indicated to one of the shadowed passages that led off from the ballroom and made straight for it, as if he knew the house. Finneaus scuttling after him.

Emrys's hand barely brushed my arm, giving what little comfort he could offer as the dark tense form of him led the way, leaving me no choice but to follow.

The damp air of the Fairfax house was more stifling than usual as we found ourselves in a small sitting room. The carpet threadbare, bookshelves plundered long ago for anything of worth. Dark marks on the walls where pictures had once hung. A horrid, dusty collection of artifacts left on the shelves. Petrified scale samples, gilded feathers and other repulsive oddities won in conquest. The fire was lit but the smell of damp remained, stifling.

'Mr Ainsworth has told me some interesting things, Miss Woodrow,' Montagor began, stopping before the fire as he leant back against the mantel. 'Some *oversights* that Blackthorn might have made where your magic is concerned.'

My heart began to pound uneasily against my ribs. The Fifth Library. Finneaus had been there. He'd seen it all.

'Unless you want another mark, Montagor, I suggest you leave.' Emrys's voice wasn't one I recognised. Too cold and quiet. Laced with a malice that made the small hairs at my nape stand on end. '*Now.*'

A cluster of teeth sat in a murky jar on the shelf next to me, suddenly jumping and clattering together almost in fear as they hit the glass. The remaining books slipped themselves further into the bookcase as a collection of crystals rolled across the shelf, as far from the threat of Emrys and his magic as they could get. A viciousness in it I'd never felt before, not even in the council chamber.

'Unfortunately, this isn't your house.' Montagor's answering smile was hard with calculation. As he ran a gloved finger down his bruised cheek, confirming my suspicion of just who had given him that mark. 'Maybe you do have the *crude* tastes of your father after all.'

My cheeks flushed at the insinuation. That Emrys's mother was rumoured to be a witch.

'You'll be pleased to know I've already put in my recommendation,' Montagor continued as he picked at a piece of lint on his sleeve, unbothered by the tumultuous rage seeping from Emrys. 'About the rebel activity at Paxton Fields.'

'I'll enjoy seeing how you'll spin that lie.' Emrys's response came with harsh brutality, dimming the lamps with its force.

'Of course, Miss Woodrow will have to answer to the Council for her trespassing.' Montagor ignored his words, hateful gaze full of challenge as it met mine over Emrys's shoulder. 'I hear a cleansing is on the cards for her. I doubt her kind can survive long without their magic.'

'Lord Fairfax—' I began, but Montagor wasn't about to listen to the truth. Not from me.

'Is half mad.' Montagor smiled thinly. 'Vulnerable with his illness, only made more *uncomfortable* by such a destructive presence I'd wager.'

'So would I.' Finneaus grinned.

'Careful, *Finneaus*, you might piss yourself again,' I taunted, watching his face pale before it burned red with embarrassment.

He bared his teeth, leering right at me. 'You heathen little bi—'

Only Finneaus didn't get to finish. He was pushed back by an invisible force, slamming back into the sideboard and knocking cheap ornaments onto the carpet as he wheezed weakly in pain.

'Careful, Emrys, I'm certain your beast can defend herself.' Montagor smiled, unmoved and unbothered by the assault on Finneaus as the boy struggled to drag in a breath. 'She certainly has a foul enough mouth. Then again, our sort are rumoured to have a weakness for depraved tastes.'

There was menacing intent in Emrys's responding silence, something working behind his dark eyes and the tension in his jaw.

'I found the summoning scrawl the rebels left in that wood.' Montagor's lip curled in revulsion. 'Once the stones have been destroyed, there will be nothing left to draw the dark.'

Destroyed. All that history. All those prayers. A home those fey could never return to.

'You can't.' The words left me desperately with the horror of what he intended. 'Those temples are peaceful remains—'

'What would a Kysillian brute know of peace?' He laughed bitterly at me.

I wasn't surprised. It didn't burn or shame me. No, it simply fired the rage simmering in my veins.

'Clearly more than you.' My voice was filled with the venom of my fury. 'Section thirteen prohibits the destruction of fey burial sites.'

'Nice try, *pet*,' Montagor pressed, pushing away from the struggling fire, closer to us. 'Temples hold no burials.'

'Rudocc sites do. The runes would have told you that.' Rudocc were ancient fey that lived long before what we were now. They were how folk could exist so easily on that soil. Why the prayers were so desperate. 'Earth blessed by bone magic.'

'You can't touch them without a vote from three elders of that settlement,' Emrys added menacingly behind me, without hesitation, trusting every word I gave.

Elders Montagor would never find, not that far north. The Council didn't have that control. He could burn and plunder all he wished, but there was nothing fey protected more than those who came before.

'I'll save you the hassle of trying to find them,' I interrupted, bringing his hateful glare back to me. 'If you seek the truth. You should have this.'

There was a clatter as the cursed thing from my pocket bounced across the low table between us. The stark white fragment that left an icy bite on my fingertips. The pain nothing in comparison to the viciousness of my temper.

The fragment I'd found in the Verr pit.

'The markings are fresh. You can reanimate it if you don't believe me,' I told him. I could almost hear the grinding of Montagor's teeth at the evidence. Finneaus stumbled back at the potency of the thing on the table, the danger it promised. The sting it should have left on my skin. It *had* stung but I'd suffered worse than a brush with a cursed bone. Suffered worse than *him*.

'I'm certain Lord Percy would be pleased to have it returned, and the Council would love to see how far this darkness goes. How undeniable it is.' My voice was calm with that truth.

Montagor's murderous dark gaze had pinned itself to my face and I felt the responding wrath of Emrys's magic at my back. Like phantom hands curling around my forearms to drag me back.

'But, you already know that. Don't you?' I leant closer, unafraid of him and his games. Emboldened after seeing all those things pinned and dead in that ballroom. After feeling those ruins. Feeling what monsters like him did.

Just as I'd seen that ghost. Those sheet-covered bodies of other fey students on the Institute floor. The smaller bodies deep beneath careless mounds in Daunton's wood.

I'd seen it all and I would not be silent. Not anymore. Heat wove itself between my ribs, volatile and hungry. Vicious in its hunt for vengeance, just as my ancestors would have been.

The fire behind him surged with a roar as it climbed up the chimney, sending Finneaus scrambling from it with a singed sleeve. Yet it was the monster before me I focused my ire on. Not a foolish boy who knew nothing better than hate.

I let my magic bite. Relished the hissed curse from Montagor's lips as he pulled back from me and tore his coat open, ripping the pocket-watch from inside and letting it clatter onto the threadbare carpet, glowing and warped with my molten rage. His hand pressed over his chest, breath hissing through his teeth. The smell of burning fabric lingered in the space between us.

Something flickered on Montagor's face. I could have sworn there were shadows rippling beneath his skin, but in a blink, it was gone. Before I could question my sanity, he moved for me.

Instead of a strike, I was suddenly at Emrys's broad back, unable to understand how he'd got in front of me so fast.

'Karuk.' The word seemed to rumble from somewhere deep in Emrys's chest. A horrid cold bit into the room as the fire went out, plunging us into a darkness only pierced by the stark moonlight seeping through windows behind me. The dark made Montagor's features more predatory, as the thunder rumbled above in warning of the coming storm.

That word was like a physical thing, a shadow lingering, familiar and foreign at the same time.

'Careful, Emrys.' Montagor sounded breathless, discomfort flashing across his features. 'You could be seen to be *bewitched* by the creature.'

'I'll remind you once more.' Emrys's voice held a deadly calm, a strange tension moving through his limbs. 'She's under the protection of my name. Unless you want me to show you again what happens when you breach our rules?'

Finneaus looked wildly between the two lords, who seemed willing to brawl right there. A horrid pressure built, as if the storm from outside had made its way into the tiny room.

'In the morning,' Montagor offered in a smooth and lethal voice as he drew back, almost against his will, fists tight at his side. 'I'm certain all will be . . . revealed.'

The words were clumsy through his lips, as if he was failing to swallow them back down. His murderous gaze stuck on

Emrys. He sent a sharp glance at Finneaus, who scrambled to pick up the cursed shard from the low table, hissing as the icy thing touched his skin. Then carefully picking up the charred pocket watch, looking quite pale as he followed his new master out of the room.

There was a sharp finality to the slamming of the door, as I pressed my fingers to my chest, skin still chilled despite the ruthless heat of my magic.

'Emrys.' I needed his name on my lips, just to taste something less bitter. He turned immediately to me.

Those eyes pits of darkness. There was a stiffness to him, a colder chill to his magic. Something strange and new. He took hold of me, forehead coming down to rest against my own, breath brushing my lips.

His knuckles traced the edge of my jaw. Tentatively. The chill from his magic against my skin, needing to feel that I was real.

'That word,' I shook my head with confusion. 'I haven't—'

I thought he'd explain, be urgent with warnings and regret. No, he kissed me instead. His lips were dangerous. A mere brush and I wished to tell him every secret I knew. Unlace them from my very being as quickly as I wished he'd unlace this dress.

Forbidden, maddening thoughts. The back of his knuckles grazed the edge of my bodice, barely touching the skin, but my breath caught. Something wild flared in my abdomen, pleasure I'd tempered for too long. Desire as chaotic as my magic.

He deepened the kiss, seeming to sense it. Wanting to taste it as my fingers found their way to his jacket buttons, wanting it gone.

A small growl of pleasure against my lips as he backed me effortlessly to the bookcase, crystals and tomes clattering to the floor. His hands at either side of my face, tipping it back to demand more from my mouth.

The stinging burn of magic was still against my fingertips as he shuddered in response to it. Something heightened the crazed need between us as his hands slid to my waist, lifting me to rest on the bookcase lip. He fit easily between my spread legs. Clearly annoyed with the mass of my skirts being in his way, he pushed them up, the coolness of the room nipping at my calves.

One hand going beneath, he hitched my leg higher, closer. The rough callous texture of his hands torturous against such soft skin. Pleasure rippled through me as my slippers dropped from my feet.

I gasped, clutching at his hair, head falling back against the shelves as his mouth fell to the curve of my breast, tracing the edge of my bodice, nipping softly at the sensitive flesh.

His thumb discovered the edge of my garter. Wicked and knowing. My nails dug into his back, feeling his muscles tense under my touch, and all I could do was moan his name as his tongue and teeth traced a path up the side of my throat to take my lips once more.

'Kat?' he asked, beseeching a command. Perhaps some sanity, but I couldn't give him any.

'Yes,' I begged, desire chasing my fear from me as I kissed him again. I bit his lip, freeing him from the rest of his restraint, and his hand slipped further up my thigh. The warmth and solidness of him caged me in. His magic slipping around me in another phantom embrace, across any bare skin it could find. My back arched in silent command for it to have more.

His lips ran along my jaw, making my head fall to the side, giving him more access, only to open my eyes and see a flash of red curls run past the dark window.

William.

With what I could swear was a tabby cat clutched in his arms.

'Emrys!' I snapped, grasping desperately at his shoulders. He stopped instantly, letting me slide down his body until my bare feet were back on the floor, skirts still rumpled between us, breaths unsteady.

Fear streaked through me at the thought that I was seeing things again. That this house was playing awful tricks. I grabbed Emrys's chin, turning his face to the glass just as the figure darted off the garden path and back into the house.

'Please tell me that's not William?' My breath caught, panic constricting my chest that it wasn't real. Only for Emrys to go very still, his jaw tense beneath my grasp.

'Bloody little . . .' Emrys began to curse, but I didn't hear the rest as I ducked out of his hold, grabbing my shoes and racing for the door. Hopping on one foot to get my shoes back on, I darted into the hall that led to the garden passage. I heard a door slam, then a murmur of familiar voices ahead, before another door shut.

I turned around another dilapidated corner to almost run headfirst into Thean Page. Their grin wicked as they leant against the wall, the peeling wallpaper almost brushing the luxurious green suede of their ostentatious suit.

'Interesting meeting?' The voyav raised a brow, those amber eyes taking in the creases in my skirts that I hadn't slapped out sufficiently enough and the curls of my hair that had slid free. My cheeks were red and my breath was barely steady. My bodice had also slipped down inappropriately.

'Wonderful,' I snapped, tugging my bodice up.

Then the voyav's amusement slid to the large cupboard next to them, as a clatter of movement and a curse came from within. Effortlessly, they pulled the door open and William tumbled out, hands pressed over his eyes as he fell into a startled heap on the floor. Peering up at us through his fingers.

'Debauchery!' Thean grinned, eyes gleaming with malicious delight as they draped themself against the doorframe. 'I didn't think you had it in you, dear William.'

'I d-didn't . . .' William stuttered, seemingly struggling to remember how to form sentences as his face went scarlet. 'I don't like breasts.'

'Leave him alone.' Alma emerged from the crammed cupboard, stepping over William's prone form to glare up at the voyav as she laced the front of her maid's dress with military precision. Even as her fingers remained faintly in the shape of claws. Clearly unbothered that her breasts were one deep breath away from being exposed.

Something which only served to heighten Thean's predatory delight.

'How . . . *possessive*,' the voyav goaded, leaning closer with a smile so sharp those fangs gleamed. 'A tumble is supposed to take the edge off, darling. Maybe you weren't doing it right.'

The responding sound from deep in Alma's throat could only be described as a growl.

'Thean,' Emrys cautioned, arms folded tightly across his chest, dark gaze drifting between a red-faced William and the voyav.

'We weren't . . .' William struggled to get to his feet, hair tangled around his horns. 'I didn't . . . We went looking through the lord's chambers while they were distracted . . .'

William pulled a bag from inside his coat. It rattled and clanked as he pulled out a handful of scrawled papers, dark crystals and dried fey skin totems wrapped with string. 'Alma helped. It was full of really weird—'

'Shit,' Alma finished for him . He winced as she took the papers from him and held them out to me, still glaring at Thean as if imagining her next attack.

'Rummaging through people's, bed chambers? I didn't know you were so . . . devious,' Thean teased. Unbothered by the horror William had just exposed.

Alma's eyes narrowed, turning cold-blooded with her rage. 'They were in his office, *actually*.'

'I leave you alone for five minutes and you're—' I began, snatching the papers, but the sight of them stopped any further complaint. '*Septus mor.*'

A dark calling. The crumpled and partially charred papers sent a wave of dread through me. Each one asked for the same thing in the dark language of Verr worship. Summoning spells.

The press of Emrys's warmth against my back was my only comfort as I heard him distantly give a command to Thean. Something about leaving.

'No,' I barely breathed, reaching for Emrys's hand. All their focus shifted back to me, but none more intently than Emrys's. 'Montagor will be expecting you to leave.'

'Montagor?' Alma turned to me, eyes wide, pupils as large as an owl's.

'Lord Percy's latest guest,' Emrys offered darkly, but his focus didn't shift from my face, as if testing how I'd respond to the word uttered from Alma's lips. 'He's brought Ainsworth's son along with him too.'

'Finneaus?!' Alma hissed, making me look to her as her skin shifted slightly so scales rippled down her throat. 'That little rat.'

Then she turned on me, clawed finger pointed, eyes deadly and tongue slightly forked. 'I told you to leave him to that sodding demon.'

'Something we agree on, Miss Darcy,' Emrys added menacingly, making me turn to see him. Only to note the indentation at his bottom lip caused by my fervent kisses.

'I'm going to gut the pig,' Alma hissed, bringing me back to reality as she rooted around in that cupboard for her shoes, hopping with fury as she put them on.

'As entertaining as that would be . . .' Thean grinned, clearly thrilled as Alma's vicious glare returned to them, 'Montagor won't be put off his task for long.'

'He won't be doing anything tonight.' Emrys's words were cold, something in them having more sting than a winter wind. William grasped his coat a little tighter, but it was the voyav's reaction that worried me.

'What did you do?' Thean asked, all traces of amusement gone. Studying Emrys carefully, like he was a lingering threat.

'That smell . . .' Alma murmured, interrupting Thean's interrogation as she moved suddenly for me. Grabbing my forearms. Nostrils flaring. 'That's the smell from that wood.'

'I washed,' I objected, but she was already shaking her head, dislodging her dark curls, brow furrowed.

'Not you,' she snapped with exasperation, stepping away from our gathering, closer to the passage that led to the ball-room. 'It's here. Close.'

'We need to go back in the hall,' I said. 'Try and see who it could be before they come up with any more gossip about Montagor's arrival or—' I couldn't finish. Knowing they'd be talking about what exactly Lord Blackthorn was up to with his partner mage being absent from the ballroom.

'I wouldn't worry about that; they're all talking about those old coins.' William rocked back on his heels, hands running through his unruly curls.

'What coins?' I demanded, a horrid terror seeping through my limbs, but I didn't need William to answer. That unease I'd felt before came back to me now. Sharply.

Why Alma could smell something. It was here.

'Kat!' Emrys warned, but I was already running.

Chapter Thirty-Six

The darkness devours the wildest things first. Feasts off their hunger for this life, the power buried in their bones and the chaos in their soul.
— The Book of Mort, 1247

Useless warnings raced through my mind as I pushed and elbowed my way through the lace- and silk-adorned crowd, past dancers who sneered at me. I followed that horrid sensation rushing across my skin, making my magic claw ruthlessly inside of me, until I stumbled to a stop at the far edge of the ballroom, where the card table was set up in the adjoining room. Lord Canthorp was holding court, a gleam coming from the table before him. A gold coin sat amongst the mess of abandoned cards and glasses of wine. It darkened and twisted in shape out the corner of my eye. One of those cursed coins from the ruins.

No.

'Beautiful, aren't they?' Mr Canthorp crowed as Lady Lovell fluttered her fan over his shoulder. 'After Lord Percy mentioned the ruins, our curiosity was piqued—'

A demonic hiss of laughter clawed through my skull, making me wince just as Canthorp jumped to his feet, clutching his hand. The gold coin slipped from his grasp to roll across the floor.

'Good heavens, it's sharp.' He laughed, the guests joining in like a cruel chorus of fiends. The blood-coated thing started to roll further into the centre of the room. Guests stepping back out of its path.

'Miss Woodrow, what are your thoughts on such a—' Canthorp asked as he spotted me amongst his audience, but I didn't give him the chance to finish.

'Run.' The word barely escaped my lips, fear too potent as they watched me in confusion. It didn't matter, it was too late. The icy pain ran down my back. Something was here, waiting. Watching.

There was a horrific moment of calm before darkness surged from the coin with a deafening scream. The intensity of the blast sent me off my feet, hitting the floor. The furniture was thrown towards the walls, people screaming as they took cover.

Canthorp tumbled over himself as he came to a stop next to me. A horrid sulphurous stench filled the space, as a demonic wind howled with enough force to almost steal my breath. Just like the Insidious creature in the Fifth Library. The portraits on the wall clattered to the floor. The windows shattered letting the night storm in.

I stumbled to my feet, grabbing Canthorp by the scruff of the neck, flinging him carelessly towards the grand doorway with my Kysillian strength, the same direction as all the other guests were running. Not caring if he was trampled as a horrid screaming filled the space.

'Bloody Nora!' William cried, horridly pale as he stood amongst the chaos, Alma next to him with wide eyes.

'Get them out, William!' Emrys barked the command, his body tense and ready for battle as he cut through the guests with little effort. I watched for a moment as William and Alma scrambled to drag and push the guests from the hall.

'Thean!' Emrys tore off his jacket, gaze locked on the creature manifesting in the centre of the room with feral intent.

'This is *Ishvarian* suede,' Thean's tone was clipped with irritation as they ran a hand down their flawless dinner jacket. 'And that is a fucking verbius entity.'

Verbius. Darkness without form that could conceal itself in any object. As ancient and dangerous as the caymor. Just as impossible. The dark smoke leaching from the coin began to form shapes, flashes of claws and teeth, a storm of its own making as the coin that housed it continued to bounce wildly.

The turbulent storm of cursed magic pulled my hair free as it suffocated the room with its intensity. The old house almost whining under the force of it.

Without thinking I summoned my fire, fingers glowing as I twisted it into a lethal blow. Unleashing the ferocious heat. It hit the dark thing at its centre, making it twist and scream against the flames but still – the darkness didn't stop.

I gasped with the effort of it, only for the wind to pick up, mirroring my spell. The creature undulated, now tangled with lavender and indigo flames, before it forced the fireball right back at me.

There wasn't a moment to throw up a shield. The impact of Emrys hitting my side took me down to the floor as the fire roared over us. Hitting the wall behind, igniting the drapes and peeling wallpaper.

'Thean!' Emrys snapped over me, glaring at the voyav through the wreckage.

'Try yelling at the one who taught it fire!' Thean bit back, glaring spitefully at me where I lay prone on the ground, seeing then the flames had charred the voyav's precious jacket.

I didn't have time to apologise before Thean summoned shadows into their palms that turned into lethal blades that caught that darkness's attention as it shifted into a perfect copy of the voyav, shrouded in smoke.

It wasn't just a verbius entity, it was a mimyk. A changeling of the dark. An Insidious being.

'Come on then, you handsome bastard,' Thean taunted, flipping those shadow blades in their hands. The creature's head tilted before it made its hands into sharp blades to copy, ready to fight.

I rolled, grasping onto Emrys shoulders as he started to pull us up.

'It's an Insidious—'

A screech filled the room, cutting me off as the wrywing form of Alma smashed through what remained of the large windows, almost taking out the wall. Rubble and glass slid across the hardwood floor, along with the wrywings deadly claws, making deep gouges in the wood.

She roared, swishing her rain-drenched tail before she slammed into the dark form of Thean, taking it down with such ferocity the floor cracked and splintered. Her sharp teeth went right for its smoky throat, to devour the darkness whole.

Emrys barely moved his hands, but a summoning I didn't understand made a barrier around us. A wall of darkness surrounding the room, cutting off the exits and shrouding us from the prying eyes of any guests that remained.

I didn't know of any summoning that powerful or spell that dark. Reminding me of that blinding white energy he'd also summoned, the same that was concealed in the wishing stone around my neck, fluttering wildly against my chest. It matched that strange crystalline shade of his eyes now.

'Will you all stop interrupting!' Thean seethed, clearly willing to go toe-to-toe with a wrywing as well as the demon.

Then the voyav froze, the same moment I heard it. Even making the beastly form of Alma pause where she had the mimyk pinned beneath her claws.

A demented screeching laugh pealed from its darkness. The rumbling of gold coins as they began to spill out of the endless darkness of the ancient fiend, hitting the wood and twisting and splitting into another and another. They multiplied as they rolled across the room. Hundreds of them. They leapt and turned to a dark mass, sprouting sharp yellow teeth and jagged claws, scuttling across the ground.

'Emrys.' The only word I could say, the only word that would comfort me as the stone around my neck began to burn with blinding white light where it had slipped free of my corset. A warning for what lurked here. Too late. Too many cursed things.

Then another blast of demonic energy tore through the room. Alma was thrown backwards, the beastly form of her taking out the far wall. The force spread the wild flames I'd created up the walls as they crumbled. I curled into myself against the blast, feeling the weight of Emrys at my back, pressing me against the floor as the room fell apart and the storm rains poured down upon us.

One more badly cast spell on these lands and we could all be in trouble. Emrys's warning came back to me as we now faced that reckoning. How powerful this darkness had been allowed to become. The fey blood that had paid for it.

A pattering of water at my cheek made me squint up to see the ceiling was almost completely gone, shreds of wood and glass hanging down. The flames consuming the ballroom.

That dark smoke surged in the centre of the room, popping and snapping as it twisted itself into wrywing form. Those wings lethal and wide, tearing effortlessly through the walls.

'Bastard!' Thean seethed, those shadow blades cut through the new dark formations that swarmed for the voyav, sensing he was something they knew: Verr, a piece of darkness they could devour too.

The weight of Emrys's defence left my back as he rose.

'*Lavrov*,' he seethed, voice too dark. Too strange. That white light between his palms surged as the creature roared, coins bounding as the dark fanged things it made surged for him.

The room trembled, more debris coming down as the howling intensified. Sharp bright white light shot across the distance, the familiarity of Emrys's energy wrapping around the creature, consuming it just as he'd unmade the tallet. Pinning the demon down.

Only I saw the glow, the manifestation beginning to form within the Insidious thing. Thean was right. I'd taught it fire, but not just any fire. Kysillian flames. I saw it glow, giving me the barest moment before it erupted, sending those flames right for Emrys.

Kysillian flames. Flames no magic could smother. Volatile and ravenous.

A feral scream left me as I threw out my own power, pain searing through my limbs with the force of it, stopping the killing blow and sending the inferno of it to the other side of the room, turning the shattered furniture to ash and clouding the room with acrid smoke. The barely formed demon turned to me. A shriek of warning. Emrys called my name desperately as the dark sent another firestorm right at me.

I threw my arms out, fire roaring from my palms as I formed it into a barrier between myself and the darkness, using all my strength to push it back, my feet slipping on broken glass and rubble as sweat beaded my brow.

The roar of those flames, the sharp snapping crackle as they consumed me, pain searing up my forearms with the force to push it back. Muscles I hadn't used in too long. Too weakened from pretending to be all the things I wasn't.

Smoke clawed down my throat, too tight. Too close. A wildness awakened in me I hadn't felt since . . .

A different pain consumed my chest, a creature made of ravenous grief and fear.

Suddenly I wasn't in the ballroom. I was home. Feeling the cottage burn around me, feeling my mother's hand turn to ash in my grasp. Watching her vanish into nothing but embers.

Unmade.

Tauria. Her voice so soft, now so loud in my head. Letting my control slip enough. The mimyk's blow made it through, hitting me in the chest and sending me back. Forcing me to my knees as it hit right into the heart of me, a direct challenge to the magic in my blood. Breaking the rest of my control.

I panted wildly, clawing at the floor for breath, but there was only smoke pouring down my throat and the ravenous hunger of my magic as it burned in my veins.

Too tight. Too panicked. I'd let too much out. Felt it seeping through my defences, beyond my will. Someone was calling my name. Emrys.

Little troll.

I screamed. My palms burned, bowing me over, but there was no holding it in. Smoke and rage and grief consumed me. The image of my mother burned before me.

Murderer, that dark voice taunted.

'Stop,' I wanted to scream, but the word came panted through my teeth.

Whatever monster you wish yourself to be, I'll still be here, loving you. The soft truth in those words chased the fear away.

Alma.

I squinted through the smoke to see a bedraggled William stumbling to his feet from the rubble, a cat clutched in his arms. Those feline eyes watching me.

Here. She'd always been here. Right in this nightmare with me.

I'll keep us safe. Words I'd whispered to her as my monstrous magic devoured that nightmare of Daunton. How viciously it had swelled inside me. Just as it swelled now and all I could do was clutch my chest, try and drag in air, try to press it down.

It was too late and she saw it. In all her forms she could see it. See the monster in me.

She changed in a moment. Wings taking out the remaining garish pillars. She barely gave Thean a moment of warning before one claw gripped the back of that lace shirt, the other grabbing William's jacket, and she shot skyward into the stormy night through the ruined roof.

The darkness swelled and screamed, sensing another attack. The dark form of Emrys was before me, crouched in the ruins and drenched by that rain.

Desperate, I threw my arms around him, sending us both to the ground, and then I was on top of him, making a cage of my body. I imagined a shield my flames couldn't touch. Imagined something beyond their reach.

I felt it build, felt Emrys shout my name, the coolness of his fingers against my cheeks, but all I could do was give in, not caring if the guests had made it out.

Molten heat burned my limbs, reaching a crescendo of chaotic oblivion until I flung my arms outwards. The ruthlessness of it whooshing from me in a flare of devastating heat.

I devoured the room in chaotic fire. A scream of exhaustion left me, a roar of command, spreading outwards from around

409

us and rendering everything to ash. The cursed creature had barely a moment to shriek as I devoured it too, turning those cursed coins to nothing but molten liquid that wrapped around the darkness and kept it contained.

I kept the chaos away from Emrys. Exhaustion ate into my trembling limbs as I cast a perfect sphere around us, the flames unable to touch the things I protected the most.

My deadly focus remained on the fiend as it curled into itself with thick black smoke, trying to change, trying to become the fire itself. I'd given it my flames, but I'd take them back.

It was my divine right to command that fire.

'*Accvern!*' I screamed. *Return.* I pressed those flames tighter and closer around the mimyk's withering form. Peeling them from the walls and ceiling, forcing them tighter and tighter until that darkness had nowhere left to go but back into that one remaining coin gleaming on the ground.

The force of it causing me to scream. Ash coating my tongue and smoke filled my lungs.

Too late, something dark mocked in my mind.

Desperate and almost pleading. So hopeless that confusion clouded everything else as I sagged. The ferocity of my magic abandoned me as I collapsed.

Embers drifted down slowly, the intensity of what I'd just done potent in the air between Emrys and I. Death was too close with the power of the spell.

The sweetness of a burned curse and the persistence of beasam bark was all I could smell. My eyes opened to see Emrys beneath me, the impropriety of our position, how my breasts strained against my ruined bodice with the panting of my breath as I watched that one lone remaining coin roll across the ruined floor.

Desperate and seeking, as it avoided every smouldering piece of the ruins. Coming to land between the feet of a very pale and very guilty-looking Lord Percy where he waited in the sagging, ruined doorway to the ballroom . . . barely visible through the smoke.

The forbidden things always return to their master in the end.

It had returned to him.

Chapter Thirty-Seven

There are princes who sleep beneath the earth made of nightmares and endless dark. Children of the Old Gods. Creatures of death and all the things that should never have been. Be wary of their calling to return curses to the world above, to drag everything beneath. For the night to be king once more under the endless crescent moon.

– An ode to the Old Gods – Unknown

Too late. That horrid voice mocked in the back of my mind as I looked down at my fingers, aching from the chaos I'd set free.

The most monstrous part of me. The hideous taste of that acrid smoke mixed with the sweetness of magic on my lips. Things not even the warmth of being sat in Blackthorn Manor could chase away.

'Alma's fast asleep,' William's soft voice brought me back to the present as he crouched before me. 'Remind me to put in another order for some chocolates from the village.'

All I could do was nod, my smile too weak as I rolled the porcelain cup of cold tea between my palms. Unable to move, to dare think of how badly I'd ruined everything.

The aftermath blurred into nothing but a smear of colour and sound in my memory. The cries of the guests, in too much shock. The protests of Lord Percy as Emrys and Thean dealt with him. The calming touch of Alma as her and William made sure we slipped away in the chaos of the aftermath. How Alma had collapsed with exhaustion, how putting her to bed had become my new priority. Unable to face the weight of everything else.

Sensing the deepening of my despair, William placed his hand to rest over mine, where it clung childishly to the stupid cup, forcing me to look up into his kind, brown eyes. To see the smear of soot on his cheek, the torn collar of his shirt and the knotted tangles of his curls.

'It'll be better in the morning.' His smile didn't falter, nor that endless kindness in his eyes. 'Emrys will fix it. It's not the first time he's dealt with a wild fiend.'

Emrys. That one word seemed more painful than all the others. How could he? How could he fix what I'd exposed? The ruthless wildness of my magic. Nothing could fix me. All I could see were those dark eyes beneath me filled with warning and rage, no matter how gentle his touch had been in the aftermath.

I was a forbidden thing and I knew what happened to forbidden things. What happened to Kysillians who held a deadly flame.

'Thank you, William.' I took his hand, trying not to make it sound like goodbye. I glanced to the clock, seeing how horribly late it had got. 'You should get some sleep.'

He hesitated, his eyes moving to the corner where the portal rested beyond. 'Only if you're sure?'

'I'm sure.' I smiled, trying not to wince around the lie.

He left me reluctantly, the house releasing a comforting creak to spur him on. Seeming to understand I needed to be alone.

The Blackthorn study felt ominously quiet after the chaos, even as the house creaked and groaned, trying to converse with me in my loneliness.

How simple everything had been. How guilty Lord Percy was, standing in that doorway, how easy for Emrys to detain him, as the servants rushed to put out the flames.

The guests had fled Fairfax Manor like rats from a sinking ship as the ballroom turned to cinders. Too fearful to even question how it had all come to pass.

I should have gone back into my bedroom upstairs. Tucked myself next to Alma and pretended to sleep. To hide.

Only I knew this wasn't over. No matter how badly my limbs trembled, how content my magic was inside of me. Peaceful after its chaotic hunger had devoured that darkness.

I'd used my old bedroom to be rid of my ruined ballgown, to wash the stench of smoke off me and change into a thin nightdress. Skin too heated to be comfortable in anything else as I combed the ash from my hair that now hung loose over my shoulders.

I knew I needed to go back to Fairfax. Sit in that horrid room and wait for morning. Pretend I wasn't unravelling, that I hadn't let all my secrets out. To wait for the reckoning that would come from the Council.

Too late, that creature mocked inside my mind, and it wasn't wrong. I'd always been too late.

Finneaus knew. He was in league with Montagor and he would have told him everything. He'd seen it. I'd burned him with it in my anger. The same wildness I should never have let the dark see.

Just as Lord Percy had mocked me with the same truth. How I could use magic when faced with Verr stone. Now what remained of Fairfax Manor was the proof they needed. No matter how that darkness had tried to return to Lord Percy. No matter how swiftly Emrys had acted.

It was too late. Just as the dark said.

My tears dripped into the teacup, a hollowness consuming my chest. Kysillians were vessels for Kysillia's rage. The First Queen. Nothing but destruction encased within flesh, a last resort in case the darkness rose again. This was the reason those mortal kings and their saints had hunted us so fervently.

How they'd hunt me now. Just as my father said.

I got to my feet, pushed the untouched tea across the table and wiped at my useless tears. Before I pressed my palms against the tabletop, I looked down at all those papers scattered across it. All the things I should have done. All the things I could never be.

The exhaustion of defeat made me bow my head, ready to give up . . . before I felt him. A sharpness to the air, a slight flicker of the fire. How the chill of his power manifested in the strange way it always did. An icy sensation drifting over my skin, turning me to the shadowed corner of the room to see him.

His shirt was torn open from the battle, hair swept onto his brow in disarray with ash smudges on his cheek. A hard set of defiance to his jaw.

'You're back.' The words were too quiet, too foolish from my lips.

'There wasn't much to do,' Emrys said. 'The Council won't be alerted until the morning.' Emrys ran a hand through his dishevelled hair, moving easily through the room and towards me, but there was something distant about him. Something colder than I'd ever seen.

'They'll know soon enough.' I straightened, curling my arms around myself. Knowing I had nobody to blame but myself as I looked to the fire. Worrying my lip as I tried to think of a way to twist the truth, to change the facts.

'They can't prove anything.' His words were terse with defence. Unwavering. 'A verbius is unpredictable in how it summons chaos. Elemental calling isn't—'

'You think Montagor needs proof?' My words were sharp with disgust. None of them needed proof. I'd been born guilty. Too much chaotic magic in my blood and it wouldn't be silenced now.

I'd been existing on nothing but borrowed time and bad luck.

'They will listen to me, Kat.' He strode towards me, hands curling into fists, as if resisting the urge to touch me.

I looked to the marks on his knuckles from striking something, hopefully Lord Percy's face. I wondered just how he'd gotten the guards' agreement. Wondered just how far he'd go. How easily he'd dismissed Montagor. He had power I didn't understand, but it didn't frighten me. Not as everything had before I'd come here. Before this strange forsaken thing between us.

'They'll . . .' Fear clogged my throat. They'd test me again, call the Truth Seeker and then they'd cleanse me of my magic. Those where the consequences I'd ignored. The ones I'd seen numerous times before.

My struggle for words stopped as the warm stone flickered at my chest. Not as a warning but to catch my attention.

To remind me. How similar the glow of that stone was to the magic Emrys summoned, unfamiliar to me. My hand clutched it, a strange chill against my palm.

'What did you wish for?' I asked, wondering if he'd tell me. The stone didn't have magic of its own. He'd given it something.

'To keep you safe.' There was no hesitation in those words, like he had no hope of keeping anything from me.

The stone couldn't do that. Couldn't protect me like that. No, but he could.

It had warned him. Every time. It was how he'd known to find me in those ruins. He'd known because he wouldn't let me be hurt again. Just as he said.

Sensing my thoughts, something painful moved through his expression, his jaw tense before he turned to his desk, looking for something. A file he found at the bottom of the mess, holding it out to me but averting his gaze.

'There was also this, for when the Council quieten down.' His attention was locked on the fire, too distant from me and giving me no choice but to take that file from him. 'I should have given it to you sooner.'

I flipped it open, only a few pages inside, all marked the same. The fey delegation symbol of the Kai, the golden winged bird of the north wrapped in the ancient runes of the earth.

Then my hand began to tremble, making the words not quite clear. Travel papers to the Northern Fields and anywhere beyond. Access to the teaching houses in the fey settlements, signed off by the remaining elders there.

Away from here.

'You'd . . . send me away?' I whispered, unable to bear the pain spreading too rapidly through my chest. The ground was not quite steady. Like it was crumbling beneath me, just like in those ruins.

'It's for the best.' There was a distance in his voice I hated more than anything else. A stiffness to his shoulders, as if it took all his will not to look at me. He gave me his back, head bowed with more than just exhaustion.

'I thought you said you couldn't lie,' I challenged coldly.

There was a warning in his stillness. 'It's safer, Kat.'

Safer. I shook my head, almost laughing at the cruelty of that lie. There was nowhere safe for me. 'Tell me the truth, Emrys.'

'The truth?' His words were bitter as he ran a hand through his hair in frustration, looking at me darkly over his shoulder. 'The truth is that I hate the fact you were safer in that Institute than you are with me.'

'That isn't—'

'*Croinn.*' The word was breathless from his lips as he cut me off, his eyes filled with defeat as he turned to me. I knew what he saw, the remnants of a scratch on my cheek from that darkness, the disarray of my hair and the tiredness in my eyes. Evidence of everything I'd done.

My gaze fell back to the papers in my hands. Everything I wanted. Everything I'd ever dreamed of away from all of this.

Only I didn't want it anymore. I wasn't the same person I had been. I'd come too far, seen too much.

I didn't want to run. Not as much as I wanted this delicate and strange thing between us. Not as I wanted him.

I dropped the papers onto the table, unable to bear the weight of them.

'They're letting those fey die, Emrys,' I said quietly, my voice whetted into something stronger. 'I'm not going to run.'

Couldn't. Not when I'd tasted that pain. Tasted what the Council ignored.

'So you wish to stay and be the next victim?' There was a thread of panic in those cold words, concealed in his anger. 'This is beyond Council games, Kat.'

I levelled a glare at him. 'I'm well aware.'

'I didn't suggest it was up for discussion.' His words were terse with irritation as he made his way to the door, ignoring me as I called his name, striding into the dark hallway away from me, his hands flexed as his side as if quelling the urge to destroy something on his way.

'Emrys!' I snapped again as I followed, planning on chasing him around the whole bloody house if I needed to. The house, however, saved me the effort. The doorway shifted as he stepped through it. Not to the hallway but his room. Trapping him.

'The house seems to have decided we're not finished,' I mocked icily, coming to rest inside the doorway. 'For once I agree with it.'

His glared at the doorframe behind me with murderous intent. However, the house was clearly unimpressed as the door slammed shut. I didn't need to turn to see it had vanished completely, I could see it in the tense lines of Emrys's body.

There was a rigid invisible cord between us, filled with unspoken things, and it was ready to snap. I could feel it like a dark cloud overburdened with the storm it had been forced to carry.

'Kat, I need you to—'

'My father ran because he wanted my mother more than he wanted a warrior's death.' My words were sharp with that truth, brutal and painful as they tore at my heart. 'He went to the north to keep her safe from this world.'

Emrys watched me so carefully, taking in every piece I offered him. Every piece of me as if all my secrets were tiny trinkets beyond value to be collected.

'He's dead.' I was unable to hold back the break in my voice. The truth I'd never been brave enough to admit to myself. Never voiced aloud. Always hoping he was just lost. Lost and trying to find me.

Now I understood. It was me that had been lost all this time.

'He's dead, Emrys. Along with everything he wanted to protect.' My mother. That life. Me. It was all gone.

The horrid images of our cottage aflame came back to me, but I shook them away. I wasn't what my father had wanted me to be. Instead, I was nothing but a pawn in a game he never wished me to play.

'I am not my father,' I admitted. The sting of magic against my palms as proof. Wild and deadly with lack of control. 'No matter how much I wish to be.'

Brave, kind and strong. I couldn't be him. Couldn't live with this pain like he did.

'There is nowhere in this world for me.' I couldn't go back. Couldn't hide. 'Nowhere but right here.'

'Kat.' He seemed unable to say anything but my name with the depth of brutal emotion cutting across his dark expression.

'You're angry with me?' I watched the tense line of his jaw, his reluctance to look at me. 'I didn't mean for any of this to happen. *Please*. I didn't mean to put William at risk. To—'

He moved instantly across the room to me with brutal intent. The firelight playing harshly off the scars on his face. Caging me against the door. 'You don't put yourself at risk for *me*.' A rough warning lay in his voice as he came even closer, his energy washing over me with a comforting strength. Giving away his desires. 'That could have killed you.'

Anger was pressed into each word, a wildness to him I hadn't anticipated. Not for dragging him or William into all of this. Or for bringing Montagor here.

'It didn't.' My voice broke on the words, the slight lie they contained. It could have killed me. Just as it almost had before.

'What if it did?' There was a wild wrath in him. Eyes dark with it. Darker than I'd ever seen them before. 'What was I supposed to do, Kat?'

The shadows in the room lengthened, responding to him in a way I didn't understand, threatening to suffocate the flames in the hearth. His rage was from fear, not anger. Those midnight eyes took me in, refusing to let me go.

'What was I supposed to do?' he beseeched me helplessly. Powerless before me.

420

I knew that fear. How easily everything could be taken. My eyes dropped to his throat, to the strange scarring there, evidence of the brutality of what he'd survived, but also of what he'd lost.

Now a few smears of ash from everything I'd done covered the marks. I reached for his collar gently, running my fingertips over it to wipe it away, to feel the relentlessness of his pulse beneath my fingertips.

The faint sweet, earthy scent of beasam bark was there between us, but also smoke, and the bitterness of wild magic. My chaos all over him.

Mine, that voice inside of me claimed. The teasing drag of his magic over my skin, curling around my limbs to seek comfort. Wishing to hold me when its master wouldn't.

'I can't bear it, Kat.' His words were hoarse, weighted with discomfort. Eyes such a solemn pale grey. '*Please*. Let me let you go.'

No. The ferocity of my magic curled in my gut, filling me with a strength I needed. To fight for what I wanted. To stay. How ravenously I wanted to stay, desperate in the aftermath of all that destruction. As the fear of what could have happened, of never having him, spurred on that hunger. That need for this forsaken thing between us. No matter the cost.

I rested my palm against his chest, feeling the pounding of his heart beneath his ruined shirt, still damp from that rain. He didn't reach for me, didn't hold me to him. No, I wasn't quite sure he was breathing as I let my hand drag to the line of buttons.

Slowly I undid each one, eyes lifting to catch his just as his shirt fell open. I found his eyes to be pitch-black with predatory focus as my hands slid across the warm contours of him. The softness of his skin stretched over the ruthless hard muscle. The smooth slashes of scars colder under my fingertips as I traced them.

'You said you needed me.' The words stuck around the lump in my throat as my fingers traced the wicked lines up his abdomen, over his ribs and across the muscular surface of his chest, until I rested my palm over his heart once more. Over a mess of silver scars there too, curved as if trying to form another strange crescent moon. 'What if I need you too, Emrys?'

'Nobody needs this, Kat.' He shook his head, voice rough and filled with such loss. Such loneliness that I felt it call to a lost part of my soul. Searching for something in his. I'd always been lost, but he'd found me, just as he promised.

The thought made my breath unsteady as my hand moved upwards, brushing the strong column of his throat until I touched his cheek, watching as he leant ever so slightly into that touch.

'I do.' I let my fingers linger at the sharpness of his jaw, feeling the roughness of the scar that came to the edge of his mouth. Tracing softly the shape of his bottom lip.

'I need you, Emrys.' Needed his steady will, his interest and his temper. I needed his smile, the darkness of his eyes, the gentle nature of his hold. I needed his hesitancy, that longing in his gaze. Every part of it.

The depth of my words broke some spell over him, as he finally reached for me. His hands gliding down either side of my throat, a slow, gentle reverence about his touch as he ducked his head to catch my ear. Breath not quite steady.

'You're the most chaotically beautiful thing I've ever seen, Katherine Woodrow.' A faint smile tugged at his mouth with his surrender.

Mine. Something in my very bones sighed in response. I might have been chaos, might have been haunted by the cruel brutality of this world, but I was safe with him.

Finally. Right here. I was safe.

I wasn't that clever with words, so I kissed him instead. Gently brushing his lips with my own, refusing to let fear or inexperience hinder me. The warmth of my desire spread through me as ruthlessly as my magic, commanding me to take my fill. He returned the kiss instantly, softly at first. Guiding and patient.

I wrapped my arms around his shoulders, pressing myself closer. Skin flushed, biting at his lip and commanding him to open his mouth. To give me everything. To be rougher with his claiming as his hand dragged greedily across my waist, holding tightly as if I could slip away. Impatience mingled with a ravenous hunger.

My hands curled into his hair, thick and soft between my fingers. My lips parted and his tongue was inside, ruthlessly seeking more of me. I clutched at the muscled expanse of his back, hands dragging across the powerful enormity of him.

The bed post was suddenly at my back as my hands tore his open shirt off his shoulders. Fingers burning with the feral urge to touch him. Everywhere. Something in me needing to know he was all there. That it was real. That he was mine.

He broke away from the kiss with a curse, breath ragged.

'Kat.' The word was soft with breathlessness. Cautious. Trying to gift me back some sanity, despite how tightly he held onto my waist, despite the hunger in his gaze. 'This is dangerous.'

I didn't stop, my lips dragging across his jaw, down his throat. My hand tracing a line down his abdomen to the waistband of his trousers.

423

'When has that stopped me before?' I teased darkly, letting my tongue and teeth drag across his collarbone, tasting salt, chaos and the richness of his magic on his skin. Watching those eyes go liquid with desire as I undid the first buttons of his trousers.

'Croinn,' he cursed, and that one word snapped whatever loose hold remained on his gentleman's restraint. I found myself up in his arms, bare calves locking around his hips. His hand was in my hair, tugging ruthlessly to have my mouth back on his. Something primal in me bent to his will in response. Hands roaming the hard broad planes of his shoulders, nails digging in with command for more.

His hands dragged over the skin of my backside where my nightdress had ridden up, the rough callouses of his fingers making a wanton whimper leave my lips. My head fell back against the bedpost, as the ruthless focus of those lips fell to my throat, down to the barest curve of my breast that my nightgown revealed.

I arched my hips, silently demanding him to move his hands, needing them between us. My movements made my nightgown slip off my shoulder, exposing more of me.

Then we fell to the bed as Emrys's lips continued their torturous exploration of my skin. The cage of his body around me. My bent knees either side of his hips as I panted, fingers curling in his hair, but he pulled back the barest inch, only for his thumb to drag across my bottom lip. Savouring every one of my trembling breaths as he considered the disarray of me. Teasing.

That hunger in his gaze was of my making. Mine. So, I closed my lips around the pad of his thumb, biting it softly in demand.

Then he wasn't teasing anymore as he captured my chin and kissed me again. The hard weight of him pressed me into the bed, the rough drag of his trousers against the inside of my thigh excited me. Warnings tried to fill my mind about fey girls and the things lords wanted from them, but I was far beyond warnings.

'Kat,' he whispered against my neck, as I panted for breath, his hands moving up my thighs as if we were sharing secrets. Unsteady, on the brink of something but afraid to tumble off. Giving me the power once more. Refusing to take it from me.

I tugged his hair so his eyes came back to mine, just as his hands reached my bare hips. I looked into the darkness of his gaze before I kissed him again.

I copied what he'd taught me, biting his lip and tightening my grip on his shoulders. He groaned into it, harder and deeper. His hold intensified as he lifted my knee higher, pulling me closer to his heat. My bare heel dug into the back of his thigh. His hand slid up my calf at a tormenting pace. The roughness of him against such sensitive places fuelled the madness.

His lips slipped down the side of my throat, the rough stubble of his jaw scratching gently at the top of my breasts with his kiss. His mouth found the nipple of my exposed breast and I lost all competent thought. Nothing but heat and desire, bending effortlessly to his will.

One hand fisted in his hair and my other gripped at his back, unable to catch my breath. I dragged my hand across the muscular contours of his skin until I held onto his bicep, feeling the tension beneath. The warmth of his fingers and the teasing drag of them against the sensitive flesh of my inner thigh. A moan escaped my lips before my breath was stolen as his fingers found their way between my legs.

'Emrys,' I pleaded weakly, holding onto him as his attention moved to expose my other breast and taste it too,

His hand pressing and teasing places only I knew. Pleasure streaked through me, making my legs open wider, hips rising, commanding him to add more pressure.

His thumb answered effortlessly as his finger slipped inside, making me gasp, his lips coming back to my own to taste his name as he drew it from me. He curled his fingers with a stroke, his thumb dragging over the most sensitive part of me and I could only raise my hips, feeling the devious nature of his smile. Relentless as he did it again and again.

He watched every breathless plea leave my lips as my head fell back, hair spilling across his bed as that ruthless focus drank me in. Taking his own pleasure at the sight of my disarray. The bright light of the wishing stone around my neck reflected in his eyes.

I was too hot and restricted in my own skin, hands gripping and pulling until I could press my nails into his back. Feeling the tautness of him trembling slightly beneath my touch.

He built me expertly to the brink, only for my whimpered disappointment as he stopped, the cunning nature of his smile as he pulled back to kiss me again. Slowly. His knuckles barely grazing the inside of my thigh.

'What do you want, Kat?' he whispered wickedly against the shell of my ear before taking the lobe between his teeth.

My fingers dragged against the waistband of his trousers, feeling the hardness of his desire against my palm.

'You,' I answered breathlessly against his lips. Driven half to madness with that desire, even if it led me to nothing but ruin.

Pleased with my answer, his hands ran up my bare thighs, over my hips, dragging my nightgown up and over my head, forcing me to let him go. Unburdened with it, I felt the coolness of the room, chased away by the heat of his gaze as he took me in.

He knelt between my spread legs, exposing every inch of me. The chill of his magic brushed down my body like a physical touch, bowing me off the bed with the need for more of it. More of him.

Answering my silent demand, his palm ran from the curve of my neck, possessively dragging down between my breasts, the rough callouses of his fingers calling me towards the sensation as he continued over my stomach, then down lower until a needful sob escaped my lips, his thumb dragging over the aching centre of me. Slow vicious circles, watching every tremor of my pleasure as I bit my lip to stop any more cries leaving me.

He didn't stop, leaning over me, one hand braced in the bed to brush the barest kiss against the top of my breast, right over my heart before his lips moved further down. My hands were in his hair as his mouth ran down my stomach with teasing bites. A torturous dark worship of me as I was spread before him. Then he went lower.

'*Ala Eria*,' he whispered in Kysillian against my hipbone. *My beautiful love.*

I felt those words deep within my soul, real and undeniable as his tongue traced the shape of every curve as he went lower to kiss my thighs.

'Emrys,' I cautioned, unsure of what he was doing, my heartbeat too fast, my skin too flushed. Ignoring me, he nipped the sensitive skin on the inside of my trembling thigh, tongue dragging across the bite as my heart stuttered in my chest. Having no words, no breath.

Then he kissed the centre of me. My back bowed, hands knotting in his hair. Flutters of something in my stomach, stronger than before, unsure what to do and not wanting it to end. Needing more. His hands cupped my backside, fingers digging in as he dragged me closer to his mouth. Devouring me as my other hand grasped hopelessly at the sheets – at the pillow beneath my head, at anything, wondering if you could die from this sensation.

Wildness made me raise my hips, wanting him to give me more as a rumble of a growl left his chest, making the feeling only more forceful. His hand slipped down my calf with knowing authority, pushing my bent leg up so more of me was bared to him. His tongue firmer in its play. Then his fingers joined his mouth. Deep ruthless strokes that stole what was left of my breath.

'Fuck,' I panted from the intensity. I could almost feel him smiling against my skin before he heightened that sensation with another ruthless curl of his fingers deep within me. Feasting wildly on my desire. Deeper and stronger than before.

I was unable to do anything but rise to his command, feeling the mischievous bite of his magic brushing over my bare breasts, wanting more. Curling gently around my wrists to pin me with its torturous play. Touching every inch of me and driving me further into that madness, until a different warmth spread through me.

Rapturous pleasure washed over me. My breath stuttered through my lips as I lay there, unable to do anything but gasp his name. I trembled weakly in the aftermath as it rolled through me, tension leaving my limbs as delicious warmth brushed every inch of my skin. Suddenly too sensitive and limp. Emrys's lips traced the inside of my thigh as his fingers withdrew, his other hand sliding up my calf in reassurance, wet with the wildness of the pleasure he'd drawn from me.

He worked his way carefully back up my body, with lips and teeth. He buried one hand in the bed at my shoulder as he rose over me, eyes considering every inch. From my exposed centre he'd given all his attention, following the flush across my stomach, the glow in my veins from my magic. His eyes were pitch-black, able to reflect the glowing lavender and blue hue from my skin. My magic content and close to the surface.

His knuckles barely grazed the still-exposed centre of me and my breath caught on a moan. The dark wickedness in his smile made me ache all over again. His eyes filled with a satisfied gleam as he watched his fingers drag a teasing trail from my hip, across my stomach and up between my breasts. My back arched in response, needing his attention as he ducked his head to kiss my breasts again, working up to my throat, his hand cupping the side of my face.

Then his fingers ran through the tangle of my hair across his pillows. 'Beautiful.'

I smiled slowly, curling my hands around his forearms to feel the sturdiness of him, raising up onto my elbows so my tongue could trace his bottom lip, tasting what he had. My hand slipped lazily down the contours of his chest, reaching his waistband, fingers slipping over the edge of his trousers to undo the final button.

He kissed me, allowing me to taste all of that passion as a groan rumbled through his chest. His hand dragged around my bare waist to bring me closer. The rough palm moving over the uneven, thick scarring of the mutilated flesh across my lower back. Secrets I'd forgotten in my desire.

He froze above me, feeling it for the first time and the warmth of my need drained from me, replaced by nothing but paralysing terror.

Pink streaks of scarred skin stood out boldly down my back in brutal long strikes, evidence of everything I never wished to think of. Demons in different form, made of memory and pain.

That lazy passion bled from Emrys's gaze to a harder fury and what little fire was left in the hearth was extinguished. My whole body went tight, air seeming impossible to drag into my lungs, the room darkening at the edges with my fear.

Run, that voice hissed in my mind. Dizzy for breath, I snatched my hands back from him, curling them to my chest. Covering myself. Shaking my head as I choked for breath, needing to flee. To run. I lurched forwards but found myself curled into his arms, completely covered by his warmth. Pinned gently with a strength it was impossible for him to possess. A reassurance in the firmness of it, his weight pressing against me, my breaths stuttered against his neck.

'It's all right,' he whispered softly in my ear, hand cradling my head, forcing those panicked breaths against his throat. 'It's all right, Kat.'

I could feel his heart beating against my trembling palms, strong and reassuring. The strangeness of his magic was there too, gently curling around my limbs, cocooning me in the force of him.

Beg, that ghost of a voice hissed sharply in my ear. I flinched, closing my eyes as I tried to breathe through the panic and shame, hands moving to his shoulders. Nails digging in.

Emrys's hold changed as if he could hear the torment in my mind. He tightened his hold as I concentrated on the strange authority of his magic, the coolness of it as it reassured my own. I pulled in a deep breath filled with nothing but beasam bark and forbidden things. Him.

I was here. Not there.

I felt the weight of the memory dissipate, opening my eyes as he tipped his head to see me. Tears leaked from my eyes silently.

'Who did that to you?' There was a feral nature to the quietness of him.

I shook my head. A truth stuck in my throat.

'It's all right.' His voice was soft as he captured my face, pushing my hair back as he leaned forwards, our foreheads touching.

His hands moved gently down my throat to feel the pounding of my pulse, a reassuring sound leaving his lips. I leant into it, feeling the comforting drag of his knuckles across my jaw until my lip stopped trembling. Then his hand found mine, fingers slipping easily between my own, bringing them to his lips to kiss them until they stopped trembling too.

My other hand rested against the small of his back, a tension lingering there, perhaps scared I'd pull away from him. That I'd run.

'Tauria,' he whispered so softly as his lips traced my cheekbone, catching my tears with his lips. 'I'm here.'

I'll find you. That promise he'd given me. He'd found me. I breathed in the sharpness of his scent, forbidden magic and the tart sweetness of mine pressed against his very skin.

Mine, that voice whispered. The soft flutter from the wishing stone was reassuring against my breastbone. Real. This was real. Then my chest didn't feel so tight, the world didn't feel like it was ending and more of me came back with every moment that passed, as he waited each breath with me.

'It doesn't matter.' My voice was so small in the silence. Ashamed of the tremors that rushed through me.

'It matters to me.' There was a steel to his tone that brushed warmly against my ear.

I shook my head, but that thumb dragged softly against my jaw despite still having hold of my hand.

431

'Everything about you matters to me, Kat.' His words were gentle with confession. As devoted as a prayer. It mattered. I mattered.

Daunton. The word I couldn't say. Clogged in my throat. No matter how much I wanted to let it out. Even now I could transport myself back there with such a simple word.

No, because Emrys was here. The warmth of his weight surrounded me and it anchored me enough to feel brave. So, I pressed my palm against his chest, feeling the strong beat of his heart against my skin, tethered myself and then I began with the fear that clawed the most ravenously at my chest.

'Some nights I can still hear her screaming,' I whispered, feeling him go tense beneath my touch.

Alma. Some nights I could convince myself I could still hear her, no matter how quickly I woke to find her sound asleep. 'I didn't care what he did to me. I would have taken anything to make him stop hurting her.'

Emrys had gone very still, but the sharp drag of his magic over my skin was a reassurance that kept me going. The momentum of the painful truth like a stone rolling down a hill, unable to stop.

'I refused their blessings, fell silent for their prayers and spat out their holy bread.' Refused to be tamed. To be unmade. To repent for my wildness. No matter the pain or the endless cruelty from their hands. 'He'd use anything, even iron, but I wouldn't break.'

The room grew darker around us in an instant, a creaking of the wood in warning, not knowing if it was the house or him, but the truth kept seeping from my lips.

'I thought he'd kill me for the amusement of it.' Despite being stronger with my Kysillian body, with the warriors' blood in my veins that knew how to survive. Quicker to heal. 'I begged Alma to be a bird. To fly far away from that place. To leave me behind.'

To forget about me like everyone else. I felt the sting of my tears then, tasted them on my trembling lips. 'She wouldn't go.'

No, because she loved me. A love that had saved me in the end.

'On the coldest nights I imagined the blissful peace of not waking up.' That weakness was the hardest to admit. That I'd wished for my death so easily. So desperate in that darkness. 'I hate him . . . but I hate myself more for that. That I gave up.'

That was what kept me from sleep and chased me in those nightmares to waking. And in the end, I lost. Lost parts of myself I'd never get back. He took them, kept them even now, even though he was nothing but ash.

Emrys was so quiet, his grip unbreakable but still gentle, and maybe it was because of the strength in those arms I could finally say it. The final chapter in that horrid tale.

'I killed him.' So softly the truth escaped me, but the last, darkest piece of that truth remained buried in my heart. That I'd wished it to kill me too.

'Good.' The word was quick and cold from his lips. Like a killing blow. The menace pressed into it didn't frighten me. No, I curled towards it, closer to him.

Murderer, that voice hissed, so loud in my mind I wondered if he could hear it too as he held me tighter. Until all I could smell was the richness of beasam bark, of old magic and him. Warm and solid. Real.

'I heard you, Kat.' Something hollow and painful in his voice told me he'd never forget it. What happened in the ruins of Fairfax. How he'd found me. In the heart of that terror.

'I've hated this world for a long time, but I hate it most for hurting you.' He gathered me closer, my face hidden against his shoulder, my hands running up his back. I felt the uneven texture of scars that started at his shoulders, his marks softer with age.

Absently I traced them as his hand ran through my hair, a calmness between us as I followed the path of marks until I pressed myself back against the pillows to see his throat. The worst of it. The first I'd seen that night when he'd appeared before me like some dark wraith.

He watched me cautiously as I felt the texture beneath my fingertips, raised and red despite the time that had passed.

'I have a habit of being where I shouldn't.' He spoke quietly, hearing the question in my touch – pain hidden in it but no hesitation in telling me his truth. 'I went back into the darkness of battle for Gideon, thinking if I didn't make it, at least we'd all be together.'

The finality of the statement made my heart hurt, that it was possible none of this could have happened. That he would have been lost to me without ever meeting him. Never knowing the beauty of what it was to be found by him.

'He made it,' I whispered, already knowing a part of that story. Wherever he was, Gideon Swift had made it.

'He never forgave me for it,' he replied, continuing to play with the hair that fell against my collarbone.

'I'm sorry.' I was. Sorry for his pain and that he couldn't get better from such grief. That we were all sick with it and would be until the end.

'It's in the past.' He kissed my forehead, a small reassurance that didn't reach that darkness in his eyes.

I lifted myself off the pillow until I could press a kiss against the rough texture of his throat, the most brutal part of this beautiful, impossible man. He captured my face before I could settle, tipping my head and kissing me softly.

There was a lazy seduction to the intimacy of lying here with him until my breathing settled, hands drifting over sensitive flesh as we lay there until I could barely keep my eyes open, half draped across the expanse of him as his fingers traced the shape of me . . . committing it to memory.

I didn't know how long we lay there, or how he moved without me noticing, but I felt the brush of fabric. A silent command as something slipped over me. Soft and filled with the scent of that forsaken bark and smoke. Of my magic and his. Settling me further. I felt his hand tracing shapes along my hip, lulling me to sleep. My head resting on his chest listening to the calm beat of his heart.

'They once used beasam bark to fend off possession of the dark,' I whispered against his skin, unsure if it was a dream. 'My father told me a story once, about Serus and the princes beneath the earth. About wraiths and spirits who serve them.'

He went still for the barest moment, his fingers pausing, digging into my hip before his movements continued. More cautiously than before, but he didn't respond.

'You could be a wraith. You move about like one,' I half mumbled, curling closer into his warmth as I felt the weight of covers coming over us.

'I'm not a wraith.' There was a softness to his voice where I expected humour, a hesitation that confused me as I felt myself become weightless with sleep's arrival.

You'd still want him, that voice mocked, no fear accompanying that truth. I'd want him anyway. In whatever form he came to me.

Chapter Thirty-Eight

Kysillia reigned with a heart of fire, her veins gold with the molten blood of the earth. The endless starlight in her will cast back the darkness beneath. Made the shadows bow and death itself retreat. For she was chaos entire, untethered like the flames she summoned. Flames she used to form ancient blades of her will, so even when she reigned with the ancestors above, her kin would know. She was starlight entire.

— The Song of Kysillia — Unknown

Temez. The ancient word echoed through my mind in the darkness. Eluding me despite how heavily its meaning sat upon my tongue. A calling that sent my magic turning uncomfortably inside me.

Too late, that desperate voice in the darkness whispered, forcing my tired eyes open. The dim morning light streamed through the arched windows, tiny specks of dust dancing in its stream. A peaceful flutter to their movements as I curled my toes, body weighted with deep rest.

A hard warmth along my back, the brush of soft breath at the nape of my neck and the heavy weight of an arm draped across the curve of my waist. Curled so protectively. My eyes ran along the muscular line of his forearm, the pattern of those scars as they caught the soft grey light. How our fingers had intertwined on the bed next to me.

Emrys.

That small crescent moon at his knuckle caught the weak sunrise.

I turned ever so slightly in the tangle of sheets and with the barest motion he fell to his back. I rose on my elbow, expecting to find him considering me with sleepy curiosity, but he was still asleep. The dark shadow of stubble at his jaw, hair falling across his brow. Hand resting on his toned stomach. Breaths even and calm.

I bit my lip against the urge to kiss him as I drank in the sight of him so unarmed. So peaceful. Something sharply protective pierced my heart. Those ash smears remained on his skin. Traces of me.

The brutal nature of his scars as they curved down his body, even beyond the waistband of his trousers, still half unbuttoned after the frenzy of last night. How quickly it had been smothered, but not extinguished. Simply became something else. Gentle and intimate, making my heart ache.

I wanted to stay, but I looked to the creeping grey light of dawn. That feeling didn't go. Didn't dissipate.

Too late, that darkness mocked before I'd silenced it with that killing blow. My muscles were tender with a strange aching I understood. For too long I'd pretended to be mortal, played their game. My body needed more, the Kysillian in me demanded more and I'd ignored it.

Quietly I slipped from the bed, feet soundless on the rug. The cool morning air nipping at my thighs where Emrys's shirt came to rest and I realised that was what he'd covered me in.

My cheeks burned, ignoring how the brush of the fabric had not long ago been his lips. At all the things still unsaid.

How those marks at my lower back ached a little less now, free from the weight of those secrets.

I reached for the door, only for the handle to catch the too-long sleeve of the shirt. Like a child's hand grasping for attention.

'I'm coming back.' I rolled my eyes at the doorframe. Clearly, I was unfinished with its master.

Content with my words, the house opened the door to the study instead of the hallway, letting me slip back into the horrid cold room of Fairfax Manor. The fire was dead in the hearth, thankfully a maid hadn't been. The reek of smoke from the ballroom seeped through the thin floorboards.

I pulled on my robe against the damp bite of the air, knotting it closed and moved to the desk to gather up my things, finding my papers and my bag. I rummaged inside and through my notes on the fey runes. I recalled that I'd identified the runes as Rudocc markings. I'd mocked Montagor with that truth.

Rudocc. The word pierced through the fog in my mind, trying to drag up every story my father told. I found a pencil and I began drawing the symbols. I knew Rudocc. My father had taught me all of it, all the histories entwined with the ancient fey. All the stories they carried.

Too late, that voice mocked so sharply, as if breathing over my shoulder. The pencil clattered from my grip as I looked down at the markings once more, seeing the simplicity of the word repeated. The word I'd missed.

Temez. Salvation. The word they'd carved in that stone. Over and over again. Begging for it. Anything to save them. Something in their blood calling out. Desperately.

I rummaged through those papers again, wild with the ferocity of my thoughts, finding the map of those ruins, of Fairfax and everything beyond, spreading it out across the floor.

How those fey temple ruins curved and stretched across the lands, forming a barrier of ancient sacred stone. The stones placed *exactly* to form the shape of a rune.

The half-star of Kaylin – the seventh Kysillian King. His promise of protection before he led the other kings to seal this earth.

The mark of defence to keep something out. Something older than the fey who came before. Older than Ruddoc. From the time of Kysillia and her battle against the Old Gods. Just like the ruins. Just like the Verr pit.

Too late, that voice mocked.

Here, it had also whispered. That voice in my mind as I stood in the ballroom . . .

I skidded on the map as I lurched to my feet, throwing open the door and rushing down the stairs, racing through the damp and dilapidated hallways, slapping away the sheets that maids and footmen had hung to hide the destruction. Bare feet slid on the ash and rubble as I made it into the ballroom. The room groaned and creaked with the barest gust of wind. I ran right to the centre, until I saw where the floor had cracked, the charred sharp remains where it had started to fall in upon itself.

My magic churned like a wild creature in my chest, pounding against my ribs with unease as that stone around my neck began to flicker weakly. I could see a glint in the darkness, far beneath the house.

Here, that voice mocked with a cruel whisper as a dark chill bit into my skin.

It wasn't possible.

That map, those dark marks on each point. I saw it now. The symbol I'd missed. Why the fey built their temples like that, well before the records began. Markers of their own. Paths that shouldn't be crossed. They weren't temples. They were watch posts. Fortresses against the darkness that slept beyond.

Those marks carved into stone. Prayers for salvation. Something in their blood made them afraid. Made them beg for protectors that no longer existed. Calling for their saviour Kings.

Reimor. The Kings were dead. The Kings had died sealing the earth with their magic. With chaos fire. And here was one of those seals. That's why the Fairfaxes moved their house, to conceal something this dark.

'Miss Woodrow?' came the soft voice of Lord Fairfax from behind me, tinged with a strange, cruel amusement. 'Whatever is the matter, dear?'

I dragged in an unsteady breath, mouth dry with fear. Everything in me was telling me to run, but I was pinned in place by the brutality of what lay before me.

Blood. It had been hunting blood to break the seal. The blood of a creature that had formed it. Ancient blood.

'You wished to see where it all began?' he asked, a small laugh in the words that seemed to crack unnaturally in his throat.

A horrid wave of something strange rushed through my heart. Something I should have sensed. I turned to see him, and there held between his thin fingers was the familiar glow of a spell trapped in an orb. My spell.

Zeltu. The command echoed in the back of my mind. To go to the beginning. So it had come back here because it was all the same. These traps were all the same.

I tasted smoke on my tongue. Felt the ancient rage rumble through me, a storm without end. Magic in that pain that wished for vengeance.

Reimor, came whispered into my ear, tears blurring my vision as I saw her in the corner of my eye. The spirit of that girl with only a spark of the magic she should possess.

A warning I was foolish enough to ignore. Why she hadn't been able to escape. Even in death. The house had devoured her. Why the verbius had tried to flee.

Septus mor wasn't just to summon. It was a command to hide the true potential of the dark. To hide what was real. To hide the evil beneath this place.

My skin was irritated by Fairfax's mere presence. A faint ringing in my ears and my magic rose, surging to my palms until the tips of my fingers glowed. The wishing stone burned against my skin.

I threw out my hand, commanding that spell in the orb to erupt, but the thing in Fairfax crushed it. Scattering the purple aura across the ruined floor.

A cracking of bone, Lord Fairfax's head tilted awkwardly, a hollowness to his eyes. A chalky nature to his flesh, like that of a corpse.

Greed wasn't the only thing that summoned the dark, that could claim a mortal soul and turn it into something else.

Grief could too.

'*Norac*,' I whispered, more to myself than to the creature that dwelled here. Fairfax tried to frown, to seem concerned, but the being inside was too enraged, his face becoming a mangled mix of expressions before it grinned. Skin at the side of his mouth splitting with how wide it stretched, strings of flesh snapping as blood poured from his lips.

A horrid pressure filled the air. My lungs were suddenly too tight, the walls too close. Darkness seeped into my vision. A cracking and popping of limbs, shadows rushing beneath his pale skin. Fanged teeth too big for its mouth appeared as dark liquid ran free from his eyes. Skin hanging loose, revealing muscle and the red of flesh beneath.

'Clever little troll,' it mocked before it lunged across the room with a feral scream. I tried to turn on the rubble-filled ground, tried to run – but the creature was faster, tackling me from behind. The force of it cracked my head against sharp rubble, only for the horrid crashing creak as we tumbled across the ruins, towards that cavernous hole in the centre and the darkness beneath.

'No!' I screamed, clawing at the loose wood and rubble, but there was nothing as we were consumed by that darkness.

Chapter Thirty-Nine

This world isn't finished with you yet, Tauria.
    Live.

Live, the ghost of my mother's voice commanded, just as agony clawed at my body, wrenching me from unconsciousness. A cry left my lips as ashy dry earth coated my tongue. My head pounded but reaching for it hurt worse. Every inch of me resisted with agony.

I shivered, a bitter horrid cold brushing over my limbs. My skin was damp and heavy with it as I opened my eyes. The soft light stung but I forced myself to focus on it, only to discover it was coming from the stone of my necklace, flickering softly in the dirt before me.

I panted against the bitter earth, trying to cough it from my lungs, but with each breath all I could taste was centuries of pain, excruciating and sour in my mouth, pressing down on my weakening limbs.

Deeper and older than should be possible.

I could feel the phantom sting of a blade across my throat. The memory that didn't belong to me. The agony as it cut to the bone, seeking blood for their worship. The burning scrape of that darkness against my skin. All the fey that had died here before. Every single one. I felt it all in a moment.

The horrid grief of it.

Get up, I hissed to myself, spitting ash from my bloody mouth.

Small, sharp and unforgiving things dug into my palm, making me look down to see tiny folk bones pressed into the cursed soil and now my palms. Small bird skulls cracked, little more than dust and ashy shards. I tried to wrench back my hand, as if even now I could be hurting them, only to see the larger fragments mixed with stone and ash across the damp earth.

Jaw bones with teeth, the glisten of magic still trapped in the marrow. Fey bones.

Rage seared through my limbs. Something ancient in my blood responded wildly, giving me enough strength to get my knees beneath me.

'Not so fast,' a voice mocked from the darkness that surrounded me. A jangle of chain made my head jerk up, too late. A gleam as something shot towards me from the dark earth. I raised my arms to protect my head, only for the brutal impact of rusted, forsaken iron chains to wrap around my wrists.

The agony stole every thought from my head, the tormenting burn as the iron seared my skin. I screamed, trying to wrench myself backwards, to pull against the restraints, but they went taut from the other end lost in the dark. With brutal force those chains dragged me across rough broken terrain, fragments of sharp bone and stones ripping at my flesh.

I cried out, kicking and clawing at the wet earth, but there was nothing to stop it. Just the echo of dark laugher and the warmth of something metal beneath me as it finally stopped.

My arms were pulled taut above my head, my back pressed against something smooth.

I squinted into the dark, only aided by weak streaks of light as I tried to work out the origin of the laughter. Trying to pull at the chains around my wrists, despite the agonising weight of them, the tremors that made every muscle contract. I panted and twisted like a wild thing.

The vaulted ceiling was low, made of stone but half collapsed at the centre, letting light stream down. Clumps of dust and ash fell like snow from above.

The ballroom.

The creature that had been Fairfax stepped slowly into view. His eyes were jet black as dark veins bled from them, taking over his face. Head tilted to one side with a crack, operated by something other than himself. Smile too wide, teeth too sharp and cruel. Sharp bumps moved beneath his skin, like a thousand insects trapped beneath the fleshy confines.

It crouched down, picking at its teeth as it considered me. Like it had just finished feasting on the bones scattered across the chamber.

A sharp click of his long dark taloned fingers and light flared in the chamber as torches bolted to the stone walls flickered into life. Harsh, white-grey demonic fire. Brutally cold, tearing at my skin like an icy wind. A warning from my very blood.

Run.

There was a skittering noise, and I looked up to see the shadow of dark fiends crawling across the remains of the ceiling for the cover of shadow, like rats fleeing a disturbed nest.

Too many. Too close. Impossible things that shouldn't be. I panted, panic threatening to overwhelm me. Verr stone lined every inch of the space, reflecting demonic light. This was the sacrificial chamber.

The thing in Fairfax came closer, taunting as it clicked those nails, coated in a metallic sheen that made me recoil. Forsaken iron. Extra fang-like teeth tried to protrude from his jaw as he moved oddly, not familiar with the form. Bones snapped with the slightest movement.

'The old ones told us to fear Kysillia's blood, and yet I remain unimpressed,' he mused, coming closer as I pulled at my restraints again. Nothing but agony rolled through me in response, making my back arch, throat too tight to scream.

'How long we've sought such rich ancient blood,' the creature leered, dropping into an animalistic crouch so its rotten breath washed over my face. 'You may have noticed the damage the last one caused to my trap?'

I twisted, trying to kick it away from me, but the demon was faster. That clawed hand grabbed a fistful of my hair, wrenching my head back to expose my throat. I bit back a scream as the iron of its nails made contact with my scalp. Tears dripped down my cheeks, stinging my raw skin.

'You gave your blood too freely, little troll.' He bared his fanged teeth, watching me squirm and kick like a fish on a hook, gagging on my own urge to beg for it to stop. 'No wonder the Mage King's bastard wanted you so desperately. How you reek of him.'

The thing's clawed hand dragged up the inside of my thigh, burning me as my back bowed, feet kicking helplessly, unable to get away.

Kyvor Mor, it hissed inside my head, making my heart plummet in my chest. Then those nails dug into the soft flesh of my thigh, puncturing to the bone, and the pain entered my blood.

An animalistic scream clawed up my throat. The pain at my scalp was nothing compared to that now pounding through my veins. The warmth of my blood running down my thigh . . . too much . . . too quickly. Panic consumed me but was soon forgotten as another wave of agony overwhelmed me, broken sobs mingling with my screaming.

The stone around my throat burned hot. Something changed in the air before that light grew blinding, shooting from the stone, right into the face of that creature.

It screeched as it was thrown back across the chamber. Its claws had torn free of my flesh as I panted for breath. Choking for air as I tied to roll, slipping in my own blood, bound hands clawing uselessly at the ground.

Then I heard the soft cracking. Not darkness forming. Something older. Like ice on a pond as the sun touched it. I tried to focus, to blink the pain from my vision as I saw a golden vein of metal beneath me, running through the dark earth.

A seal.

I was lying on a seal. The golden metal forged by the Kysillian Kings, magic to ensure such darkness never again broke free. I heard the crack. The drops of my blood as they touched that gold. Small cracks forming like spiderwebs. Dark tendrils of smoke seeping through the openings.

Awakening what slept beneath.

Run. That warning came again. Louder this time. I pulled brutally at my chains, weakness hindering me as I cried out.

'I wouldn't bother,' the creature mocked from the dark where it had been cast, words slurred and petulant after attack. 'Kysillians gave up their strength trying to break those chains long ago.'

There was a hissed scuttle to my right, and I turned to see a shape moving in the darkness. Low to the ground, humanoid with limbs that were too long for its body. The limbs bent unnaturally, covered in dark flesh that seemed to want to peel from its skeletal form. Its blind milky eyes were too large for its skull as it bared its sharp fangs, a hiss leaving its throat.

'You've met the galmoth before.' The creature in Fairfax hissed a laugh. 'It enjoyed you very much.'

Galmoth. A fear demon. The thing from the ruins, that madness that almost had me. Those fey Emrys had found, why their hearts had given out. It had driven them mad with fear.

I twisted against my restraints, desperate. A muted scream left my lips from the pain in my wrists, the weakness in my leg as the seal continued to crack. More dark smoke reached to be free around me, the horrid stinging cold of it searing right to my bones.

The necklace thrummed against my chest in alarm. Demonic laughter rumbled through the room, the galmoth growling as I panted through the torment. I willed myself to be stronger.

Then the wishing stone light went out.

The demonic laugher died. Silence consumed everything for a bare moment. A familiar sensation brushed against my skin, stilling me as the tension in the air mutated into something far more deadly.

An ominous growl rumbled through the dark, from the fiends hiding there. I turned, despite the pain it caused. Heart-stopping hope made my breath short, pain forgotten as the shadows stretched out from the darkness.

The ground trembled, dirt and stones bouncing across its surface. A solitary dark figure stood in that stream of light from above, dark smoke curling around his form, mixed with an ethereal volatile light wrapping around his hands and arms.

Emrys.

The fiends above scuttled and screeched ready for attack. Too many of them for either of us. There was a hesitancy to them at Emrys's mere presence. Spots danced in my vision and pain coursed through my blood.

'Don't make me waste her, Blackthorn,' the creature in Fairfax's body mocked as it staggered closer once more, one half of its face horridly peeled back to show bone, bloody flesh and teeth. 'You know the masters have been calling for too long. You know the rewards the Verr Princes will bestow upon us.'

'Your master is already before you,' Emrys replied, only it didn't sound like him. Too dark, too filled with rage as the ground continued to shake.

Then I saw why. His pulse pounded at his throat from the exertion of his spell casting, his bare chest covered in a webbing of dark veins.

Different than a dark spell, slate grey and soft, as if drawn with charcoal upon his flesh. Ancient marks from ancient worship. Darker and darker as they moved towards his heart. There sat a mark, in the shape of the crescent moon, the origin point from where his darkness began.

A symbol I'd seen in stories that had been forgotten by time.

The Moon of Serus. The mark of the first Verr Prince who survived a cursed blade to the heart in the first war, touching the purest magic that had created him, granting him the abilities of both worlds. An ancient magic. As ancient as Kysillian and just as forbidden. An enemy of my blood.

Emrys was Verr. A creation of the Old Gods.

The thing wearing Fairfax's flesh went still, as he finally understood who was standing before him the same moment I did. The blinding white of Emrys's magic and why he'd been reluctant to show it. *Demon fire.*

'That's not possible,' the creature sneered.

'Neither is this.' Emrys's voice was a rumble of deathly calm as a gleam of gold appeared in his hand. An echoing clang rang out as the object landed and tumbled across the seal next to me.

My father's hilt. It had allowed Emrys to manipulate it. It trusted him, just as foolishly as I did. Every dark creature in the pit shrieked together, sensing the ancient power of the weapon.

The darkness in Lord Fairfax turned and rushed for me with a feral screech.

I rolled as far as the chains would allow, slipping in my own blood, hands wrapping around the hilt, forcing myself upwards, ignoring the burn of the forsaken iron against my flesh as the blade appeared.

I turned just in time as Lord Fairfax screamed, metal nails extended for my throat, and slid the blade into the centre of his chest.

I thrust it upwards, feeling him droop as dark blood dribbled from his lips. I bared my teeth with the ferocity of my pain, giving the blade a sharp twist, listening to his gargled final breath. Those dark eyes took me in once more as the veins began to recede from his face. His body trembled, being consumed from within.

'*Brekver*,' I hissed.

To the never. A command he had no choice but to obey as I kicked his corpse off the blade as it continued to convulse, crumbling to ash next to me.

I turned weakly to swipe at the links of the forsaken iron chain still holding me to the earth, breaking them as if they were made of nothing more than glass. Shattered pieces clattering to the seal.

The creatures above began to drop to the damp earth of the chamber as I got my unsteady legs beneath me. My bloody leg wasn't working, every step sending the searing agony of that forsaken iron up my thigh.

The seal let out another loud crack, smoke pouring free, and at the exact same moment a strange, pained sound left Emrys as he crumpled to his knees. Darkness consumed his hands, curling up his forearms as he panted wildly for breath with the barest shake of his head as if something was talking to him.

'Emrys,' I called, voice strained with panic. Then there was another crack from the seal and a convulsion moved through his limbs. Somehow he was connected to it.

The dark calls all things back in the end.

'You think it wouldn't want you back?' a demonic voice mocked from the darkness. 'It's torn you open before for a taste, *Serus.*'

A roar peeled itself from Emrys' lips, his breathing laboured as his hands clutched his head, a tension rippling across his limbs. The brutality of those scars, catching the white demonic light.

Claws that had torn him open. Seeking something within. He had no chance in fighting it. All Verr belonged to the darkness beneath the earth.

Servitude to a master.

It was trying to take him back.

'Emrys!' I cried, trying to move towards him, but a shadow fiend landed in my path, jaws snapping like a rabid dog as it lurched forward. I brought my blade down in a swift arc, depriving it of its head, only for the momentum to send me to my knees. Weakness clawed at my limbs, my legs trembling with the pain of it. The skin of my wrists were raw and blistered, glistening with blood.

'See what waits for you on the other side, Serus,' came a mocking scream from the dark as chaos erupted. Dark fiends lunging for the kneeling form of Emrys, but he raised a hand, the bright white light shooting as straight as an arrow through the creature's chest, a crack of bones as they were rendered to dust.

Power to eradicate the dark. Power formed of the Old Gods that made them. Emrys's energy continued to tear through the chamber, flashes of light that illuminated the horror concealed here as he got back to his feet. Hundreds of fiends, hatching from the darkness.

It was coming for him. Just as he knew it would.

But he'd come anyway.

Come for me.

Fiends charged from behind him, a wall of dark, and before I allowed myself to think, my magic surged, protective and wild. A fire darting forward with a scream of its own, forcing the dark back. I commanded the fire to whip around the chamber, lashing out viciously, incinerating that foulness which clung to the walls. But it still wasn't enough.

The release of its potency doubled me over, hands slamming into the ground to stop my fall. I panted against the cursed earth. Not realising how much magic I'd already used, the pain of my injuries suddenly came sharply into focus. I wasn't as strong as I should be. I'd burned too brightly.

I heard Emrys call my name, felt him dragging himself closer, only for that storm of evil to cast us apart, dirt and ash on my tongue. Dark fiends dropped around me, hair whipped around my face. My magic was too slow. Dirt burned my eyes as pain made my limbs stiff and clumsy.

'Kat!' Emrys's warning tore through the chamber too late.

I was sent sideways, crashing into one of the stone walls, which cracked and crumbled around me. Breathless, I hit the dusty tile only to be pinned by the galmoth, its teeth gnashing dangerously close to my face. I pushed my forearm under its jaw to keep it back, its putrid breath washed over me.

With a scream I tried to summon my magic, but no flames would catch with the dampness in the air. The icy bite of fear stung my heart, my damp bloody grip on the galmoth slipped enough for those cursed fangs to bury themselves into my shoulder.

I bucked wildly as agony tore through me, screaming until my throat was raw with it.

Beg, the ghost of Daunton's voice hissed into my ear, sour drink so bitter on his breath I could taste it in my mouth. A razor-sharp blow came across my back, and a horrid animalistic scream filled my ears. It took me a moment to recognise it as my own.

The pressure left my chest, allowing me to move, to try and gain any distance between myself and the agony, but it followed me. My fingers clawed at the dusty earth. Another blow, just as sharp, sent me rolling, sent my screams into the seal.

Light flashed across my vision. Darkness faded until I was on Master Daunton's floor, Alma cold and immobile opposite me. Blood on her lips. I reached for her desperately, another blow stopping me. Another and another.

I cried out, batting wildly to get it away from me but my hand struck nothing but air. Another lash. Another. Cruel hands on my flesh, pinching and twisting. Laughter filled my ears, demonic and sinister like theirs had been. Another blow struck me, striking my head harshly until light danced across my vision.

I was back in the chamber. Streaks of Emrys's white light shot through the darkness, the roar of dark beasts and the golden glint of my father's sword caught my eye as it lay in the dirt.

Fight, Tauria. My father's command. Sharp and patient.

I reached out, dragging myself weakly until my fingertips brushed the hilt, but suddenly it wasn't the sword. I was

453

holding the cold hand of my mother, her unfocused dead eyes looking right at me. How sad they'd been in death. All the joy and laughter stolen too.

I wanted to recoil from the memory but it brought me something else. The last promise she made me make.

Live, Tauria.

I promise. My small broken voice answered even now as I watched her slip away. I'd promised her.

Kyvor Mor. The curse killer. The power of the old Kings. My father's magic, alive inside me. The power she'd wished to feel before she left me. His.

We protect what we love, Tauria. Even when it's far from our reach. My father's voice whispered so softly into my ear and I found myself looking to that white demonic light in the darkness as Emrys called my name. Only my name.

Another painful blow struck me, rolling me onto my back. The dark form of the galmoth hissed over me, one long sharp talon pressed over my heart as that dark storm roared around the cavernous space. My blood dripped from its fangs as the seal cracked beneath me. Ready for the final blow.

'Kat!' came Emrys's agonised scream, the room quaked with it. Debris fell, but everything faded into my nightmares once more.

In a blink it wasn't a demon before me, but the sneering face of Master Daunton. His hand fisted the small bodice of my dress, dragging me off the ground to hit me again.

Alma.

I turned to see her. Prone and bloody on the cold stone floor. How blood seeped from her mouth, bruises under her torn dress. Right before that saints' altar where he'd touched her.

I'll keep you safe. Always. My promise to her in the depths of the night. Trapped in that foul place.

Forgive me. My father's voice came next, whispered against my ear, the roughness of his beard, damp with tears.

Then that darkness abated so I could see him in my memory, kneeling before me on the sand, the ships sailing in the distance, and shouting for him to hurry before the storm came. How viciously the rain pelted my skin, filling my bones with a coldness I'd never lost.

Forgive me, Tauria. He had whispered into my hair, his hold tight. Making impressions in my very bones, making certain I wouldn't forget his love.

Not for leaving me. No. For teaching me this fear. Fear that had kept me safe, kept me hidden, but I would hide no longer. I was a being with a monstrous heart, and now I'd show them just how monstrous I could be.

I opened my eyes, seeing that creature once more, feeling its talons digging into the skin of my chest, the drip of dark sour rot from its fangs.

Live. My mother's command. I felt the chaotic fury of my magic rise in response to her words, along with vicious undeniable strength from my Kysillian blood. I thrust my hand up, catching the galmoth by the throat, twisting viciously until the bone protruded from its neck.

The dark smoke was unable to change in my hold as it tried to show me another nightmare, the demon peering down at me with fear in its deathly eyes.

It could show me nothing else. I had no fear left.

I screamed into its face; rage untethered. Just as I had into Master Daunton's as he tried to strike me one last time, tried to take more from me, tried to destroy me.

My power poured from my hands, engulfing me in an inferno. Everything around us was thrown backwards with the turbulent flames. Plumes of dead earth and dark fiends were cast back. The creature screeched, clawing at my flesh and snapping to try and get free. But I let the fire's intensity rise, shooting down its throat to melt its cursed flesh and bones. Hotter and wilder until it became nothing but ash in my grasp. Yet the magic kept going, kept building. My blood singing with the power of it. The beginnings of a storm that had brewed for too long surged around me.

My magic. Just as monstrous as me.

The cracking of the earth grew louder beneath me with every drop of blood that ran from my fingertips, from the bite at my shoulder, as molten fire consumed my veins, feeling the warmth of the magic that slept within them. The same fire that had formed the First Queen, Kysillia. The seal beneath my feet held that same warmth, dirt obscuring the ancient marks.

Reimor.

Kysillians had never been cowed by the darkness. That's why the dark fiends and the mortals that worshipped it hunted us so desperately. Kysillians had sealed this earth before, sealed it even in a place as dark as this, and so I could again.

Tauria. Chaos of the Heavens. Why my father chose that name for me.

I screamed as that agony raced through my body, the metal shattering like delicate glass beneath my bare bloody feet. That dark smoke seeped through, forming claws that grabbed my ankles, pulling me down and clawing at my flesh. Refusing to let me go. Starved of its vengeance.

Then it began to crawl across the earth wildly towards Emrys. To take him too. To feast.

'Kat!' Emrys called, but I could only see a blurred image of him. Darkness crept into my vision, bright white light flaring before me the only evidence of his presence.

Control and devotion to something greater than yourself. I remembered those words as my father pressed my hand onto the stone statue of Kysillia, at the temples of old. As I promised never to fear myself, or the blood in my veins.

I was a liar, but I'd be a liar no more.

Kysillia might have given us her name, but she gave us something else, too: a power only her blood could wield. The power to destroy magic.

I heard the screeching roar of the fiends, saw them scurrying and running for that hole in the ceiling. To the outside. Then came the memory of pain, of those fey above, overwhelming me with the agony of it.

The carefree grin of William, the lack of fear in Alma's eyes. Safe. Finally.

Only for me to remember those boys in the village foolishly hunting mort berries. The desperation of Mr Thrombi trying to save his village. The sad ghostly face of that girl in the wood. Trapped. The phantom press of a blade against my throat, the horror and agony of her death. Of all their deaths.

Then I knew, I couldn't let this darkness out. Couldn't let it touch this world. I felt the demonic wind whip around me, the thunderous roar of Emrys's magic. Undeniably his, and dark beyond measure.

Verr couldn't lie.

The most beautifully chaotic thing I've ever seen. He hadn't lied about any of it. He couldn't.

Tears ran down my cheeks as I felt myself reaching the depths of that abyss of chaos inside of me, knew there was no surviving this. Not for me. Just like my father. To be consumed by the fire we protected.

I understood my curse then. No matter how I loved something, it would never be enough to keep it with me. I wasn't made for living. Yet I looked to Emrys's demonic light one more time, arching through that darkness, trying to find a way through despite the fiends and my flame.

I won't leave you alone to that darkness, Kat.

He hadn't. I wasn't alone.

'*Kyslor.*' The word fell easily from my lips. Raw magic rose and flooded my palms. Bright blue and purple flames, wilder than before, drenching the dark dismal place with chaos.

The fiends recoiled, screeching and scattering for what little shadow was left. The wind they formed as a weapon became my own, catching the flames and building momentum. Melting the forsaken iron cuffs that remained at my wrists. My flames entwined as tightly as metal chain, a cyclone of fire that whipped about the chamber, reaching for the endless darkness above.

The room trembled under the roar, and I stood at the heart of it, allowing it to build in me. A storm of my own making fuelled that fire. A vast barrier between me and the dark.

The seal began to glow bright beneath me as fire poured from me, dragging every last ounce of strength from my bones as my knees began to buckle. The force of it pushed down on me, my control slipping with every moment that passed.

My hands trembled, weakness poisoning my limbs as doubt crept in, breaths harsh and shallow between my teeth.

The heat intensified, a scream pealed from my lips from the pain of my exertion. Tears fell from my eyes only to dry instantly on my cheeks. Skin so painfully tight I feared a mere breath would reduce me to ash. Yet it was waiting for something; the madness wanted a command. It sought order as I watched the metal bleed back together beneath me and I gathered the last of my courage to give it one.

'*Caevus.*' *Seal.* I commanded over the ferocity of my magic.

The firestorm crashed down on top of me to hit the seal at my command. The energy encompassed me, pressing the air out of my lungs as it roared in my ears and filled the chamber. The screeching intensified, the creatures leaving their fight to scramble for the seal as if their determination to stop me would be enough.

The minute they crawled towards the flames, they were incinerated, sealed to the molten earth beneath my feet, their screeches horrific and wild as they tried to pull themselves free, slowly becoming the metal they wished to break. The ones that clawed at the dark earth were sucked into the fiery wind, dragged to their destruction upon my command.

The intensity pressed me down, harder and harder, until my knees gave out like those of a weak foal, hands pressed against the metal. My arms trembling as the last of my will was extinguished.

Torment coursed through my blood. Shapes moved before me, a mixture of black smoke and sharp white magic with flashes of pale flesh beyond the wall of flames that continued to whirl.

I collapsed forward, cheek pressed against that heat, arms numb at my sides, breaths too tight. I tried to focus on anything but the roaring in my ears. A space just beneath the mess, showing me the darkness of the room beyond. A dark veined hand reaching out towards me, that small crescent moon at the knuckle.

Emrys. Pressed flat against the bloody ashen earth, his arm reaching for me as his mouth moved, desperate and pleading. Roaring something over the firestorm.

I couldn't hear him. There was nothing but the blistering pain of it all. My body was no longer my own, drained and fuelling something beyond me.

'Tauria!' he commanded, the name striking me like a blow, raising a will inside of me I thought the fire had incinerated.

Live, Tauria. My mother's words came back to me, fierce and real. She knew this was my fate and she commanded me not to die. To not let this world have me too. Not yet.

Live.

Live.

Live.

I wouldn't betray her, not now. My arm moved automatically, sliding across the hot ash to reach him, as I panted for breath. Every inch I managed his voice became clearer, his eyes wet. A mixture of fear and desperation.

Then the coolness of his fingers interlocked with my own and with one sharp tug, he pulled me out from under it. We tumbled and rolled until a pressure was on top of me, my arms curled weakly around the damp muscular expanse of his back, face hidden in the crook of his neck.

All I could smell was the strange woody scent of his skin, the bitterness of old spells and the chaotic smoke from my magic, tangling together between us as the ground shook, a roar filling my ears as he made a cage of his body around me just as the ceiling came down. Dirt and rubble threatened to bury us, but I held on to him. Tried to gulp down cool air as Emrys's trembling hands ran over my burning face. Words of encouragement were soft in the silence as I looked up at him, concern marring his features.

'I'll burn you,' I whispered weakly through dry lips, cautious of the intensity of the heat, but he only held me tighter, bringing me to his chest. I relished the chill of his exposed throat against my flushed skin.

A coldness seeped into my limbs, eyes too heavy, my thoughts too distant. Sunlight streamed from above, right over his shoulders, bathing him in that golden light. But still the darkness crept closer.

'No,' he commanded, shaking me gently, pulling my limp body further into his arms. 'Stay awake, Kat.'

There was the sharp tear of fabric before something pressed harshly against the side of my throat. The pain of it made me recoil but he wouldn't let me go. A wetness on my skin I didn't understand, couldn't open my eyes to see.

I didn't want to go. My hands curled around his wrist, trying to hold on to the chaotic thrum of his magic. To find my way back to him. Trying to press his strength into my skin, trying to stop myself slipping away.

'Fight, Kat.' A stubbornness in his tone as my hand found his where it applied pressure to my throat as I dragged in unsteady breaths, feeling them weakening despite how hard I tried. Too tight and too slow.

Everything had left me. My magic. The strength in my blood. But not him.

I opened my eyes, seeing the dark smoke-like veins that covered his pale flesh. Signs of his true form when using his blood magic, like a pattern drawn by an ancient artisan, and I was captivated in my delirium to see him as he was meant to be. Bathed in that golden light.

My weak fingertips traced his jaw, leaving a smear of blood on his skin, following the lines over uneven flesh before he captured my hand in his own, pressing my filthy palm against his lips. Skin damp with his tears.

'Stay with me, Kat.' He bowed his head, breath brushing against my lips.

The darkness of his eyes, of the power that rested in his soul. So much the opposite to mine and yet it unmanned me all the same. None of it mattered, just that he was holding me, and I wasn't alone.

461

'*Amartis*,' I breathed, tasting blood on my lips. My mother's last promise. Now mine.

I didn't have the breath left to tell him what lingered in my soul, the intensity in his gaze telling me he could sense it.

'Kat,' he begged, his forehead resting against mine as his hand came to cradle the side of my jaw, our breaths mingling. 'Please.'

It was too late. Blackness seeped into the corners of my vision with a horrid coldness, but before I could let it take me, he shook me again, his hold tighter, the pressure on my throat firmer.

'Kat. Stay and fight with me.' An order, his breath brushing upon my lips. He kissed my skin, but it stayed cold. 'Stay and forgive me. Please.'

I already had. I'd forgive him anything.

'Y-you came,' were the only broken words that could escape my lips. How easing it felt not to be alone as that dark came for me.

'I'll always come for you.' His thumb brushed my cheek. That promise he'd given me. The one he'd kept. Even till the end. The thing I held closest to my heart, that soothed everything else.

I wasn't alone as that darkness crept closer. Numbness flooded too swiftly through my body.

Serus. Something whispered distantly in my mind, desperately trying to hold on. Dark enough to come from his lips, but I lost it as I tumbled into the nothingness of my death.

Acknowledgements

I wrote Tales of a Monstrous Heart after a lot of failure and at a strange crossroads in my life. As a twenty-seven-year-old who didn't have anything figured out and feared she never would – I still don't haha but the journey is less daunting now – Tales was a book that helped me find myself and healed me in so many ways and as Tales makes its way into the world, I hope it finds the people who need it.

So perhaps I'd like to thank Kat first, for popping into my brain. For being brave and broken but still fearless in the pursuit of her dreams. For making me braver and relentless in my pursuit to chase the dream of getting this book published.

I owe a massive thank you to my agent Nina Leon, my first yes after a forever of nos. Who took a chance on a shy and sad girl, believed in the bones of a story, and let her be who she wanted to be. For walking this new path with me, for the laughter, the tears, and the relentless passion for my books. Thank you for choosing me and helping make my dreams come true. Who knew our love of Chicken Run would lead us here? You're the best.

None of this would have been possible without the wonderful team at Gollancz. Especially Jenna and Lucy. Two beautiful human beings that I'm lucky to have on my side.

Most importantly, I will forever be thankful to my amazing editor Áine Feeney. The editor I could only have dreamed of. Who from my first call – as we fangirled over The Hunchback of Notre Dame – I knew how lucky I was to have your passion, humour and unwavering support. This story, and I, would be nothing without you. Thank you for meeting an anxious girl in Euston station and making me feel as if I could do anything. For constantly reminding me I deserve to be here, that my characters mattered and so does my voice. I'll forever wonder how I got so lucky as to have you in my life. You're extraordinary.

None of this would have ever begun without my mum and dad. Thank you for all you've done for me. For your sacrifices, hard work and endless love. For growing up with me and giving me two amazing friends as well as parents. To my mum for being playful and supporting every dream no matter how foolish or small, and to my dad for giving me my love for fantasy. For showing me Lord of the Rings and possibly changing the course of my life.

To Hanna, my big sister. For being my best friend growing up and my arch nemesis all at once. For your love of Buffy and books - for making me want to be just like you. To my younger siblings – Christa, for teaching me the true meaning of unconditional love. To Tyler, Casey and Trudy for making sure I didn't grow up too quickly. For the chaotic laughter and the endless love.

To Trish and Gary, for listening to all of my dreams and making me feel special. I love you both. To my beautiful cousin Delaney. For finding me again.

To my Nanny Margaret and Granddad Paddy – who never got to see any of this dream but who I wish to tell more than anyone. Alma's first form in this book is a little tabby cat with one ginger leg and she was inspired by my own beautiful little tabby, Cora. Who was such a special little character and I miss her but I'm so happy she can live on in this small way.

To my bestie Suzanne, for being my friend and confidant. For never complaining when I read for hours straight or work endlessly on my stories when we're on our adventures.

To my boys Cal and Paris for their unwavering support – from university workshop to my first ever author event. Paris for being enthusiastic about my writing and any of my ideas- even when I was close to giving up. My beautiful friend Criss for your endless excitement and love even after all these years. The formidable Jade Lyons, for helping me heal and making me feel as if I could do anything when I felt powerless. To Jade Lloyd for listening to my ideas and when I text asking what would happen if someone wrote a fantasy retelling of Jane Eyre, and she text back – 'write it'.

To my Fundle girls for your excitement and to Tash for always being there. To Laura and Ashleigh for showing up for me and supporting me in this dream. To Donna, for listening to all my publishing woes, even when the dream of being published seem so far away. To Carys and Kate for seeing me through the madness of balancing work and trying to be an author. Especially to Kate for coming into my life and helping me in ways nobody had before. Thank you for never making me feel like a burden.

To Sarah Hawley for being an amazing friend, a listening ear, and a much-needed companion in all this madness. For sitting in a pub with me and making me suddenly feel a little less alone. To Lucy Rose, for the voice notes and the relentless support. I met you for five minutes in a packed room and if only I'd known how beautifully you'd change my life and this debut journey. Esmie Jikiemi-Pearson for welcoming me with open arms, for the gift of your kindness and your time.

Scarlett St Clair for meeting me in a cupboard in Liverpool Waterstone's and being the kindest human being. You're amazing and I'm so glad I got to meet you and make you laugh.

To my sampler fiends! All you beautiful people who shared and spoke about the first two chapters of this book. Your excitement and love for books made so many things possible and you'll never understand how grateful I am to all of you. To my first ever reviewers Erin, Camilla, Alex, Imogen and Sophie. Thank you for your bookish love and your kind words about this story will live in my heart forever.

Lastly, to a girl who felt lost in the world. Who didn't understand why she couldn't do things the same as everyone else. Who tried and tried but got nowhere. Who had a small dream and wouldn't let it go. To the younger me, who would never believe we ended up here. So, I want to thank myself, for never giving up – even when it was the most painful thing to keep going. We made it.

Credits

Jennifer Delaney and Gollancz would like to thank everyone at Orion who worked on the publication of *Tales of a Monstrous Heart* in the UK.

Editor
Áine Feeney

Audio
Paul Stark

Contracts
Dan Herron

Design
Nick Shah
Rachael Lancaster
Joanna Ridley

Editorial Management
Charlie Panayiotou
Jane Hughes

Finance
Nick Gibson
Jasdip Nandra
Sue Baker

Marketing
Lucy Cameron

Production
Paul Hussey

Publicity
Jenna Petts

Sales
Jennifer Wilson
Esther Waters
Victoria Laws

Rachael Hum
Anna Egelstaff
Sinead White
Georgina Cutler

Operations
Jo Jacobs
Sharon Willis

BRINGING NEWS FROM OUR WORLDS TO YOURS . . .

Want hot-off-the-press info about the latest and greatest SFF releases?

Look no further than the Gollancz newsletter! Your one-stop shop for news, updates, discounts and exclusive giveaways.

Sign up now:

@gollancz